# About

**Chloe Blake** can be found dreaming up stories while she is travelling the world, or just sitting on her couch in Brooklyn, NY. When she is not writing sexy novels, she is at the newest wine bar, taking random online classes, binge watching Netflix or searching for her next adventure. Chloe has published two erotic novels under the pseudonym Chloe Blaque. Readers can find out more about Chloe and her books from her website at chloeblakebooks.com

**Joss Wood** loves books, coffee and travelling – especially to the wild places of Southern Africa and, well, anywhere. She's a wife and a mum to two young adults. She's also a servant to two cats and a dog the size of a small cow. After a career in local economic development and business, Joss writes full-time from her home in KwaZulu-Natal, South Africa.

**Rebecca Winters** lives in Salt Lake City, Utah. With canyons and high alpine meadows full of wildflowers, she never runs out of places to explore. They, plus her favourite holiday spots in Europe, often end up as backgrounds for her romance novels because writing is her passion, along with her family and church. Rebecca loves to hear from readers.

# Sugar & Spice

# Sugar & Spice:
# Glass Half-Full

CHLOE BLAKE

JOSS WOOD

REBECCA WINTERS

MILLS & BOON

First Published in Great Britain 2024
by Mills & Boon, an imprint of HarperCollins*Publishers* Ltd,
1 London Bridge Street, London, SE1 9GF

www.harpercollins.co.uk

HarperCollins*Publishers*
Macken House, 39/40 Mayor Street Upper,
Dublin 1, D01 C9W8, Ireland

Sugar & Spice: Glass Half-Full © 2024 Harlequin Enterprises ULC.

*A Taste of Pleasure* © 2018 Tamara Lynch
*It Was Only a Kiss* © 2013 Joss Wood
*Falling for Her French Tycoon* © 2020 Rebecca Winters

ISBN: 978-0-263-31982-8

This book contains FSC™ certified paper and other controlled sources to ensure responsible forest management.

For more information visit: www.harpercollins.co.uk/green

Printed and Bound in the UK using 100% Renewable Electricity
at CPI Group (UK) Ltd, Croydon, CR0 4YY

# A TASTE OF PLEASURE

## CHLOE BLAKE

To Amy, who found a happily-ever-after of her own.

My heartfelt thanks to my agent, Christine Witthohn, and to the team at Mills & Boon. My love and appreciation goes to my friends, who are my chosen family. And last, my biggest thanks to the readers who chose this book. Your support inspires me to keep writing.

# Chapter 1

Chef Danica Nilsson spread her knives on the long table and plucked the twelve-inch slicer from its pocket. With the bride and groom's cake cutting ritual finished, it was time to serve the flowered and jeweled creation she had baked to the three hundred wedding guests that flew to Brazil to see her best friend Nicole get married.

"He's looking at you again." Liz, a longtime friend to her and the bride, leaned on the tabletop and crossed her arms.

Dani didn't look up as she worked. "Maybe he's crazy."

"Crazy doesn't look *that* good. That man is handsome."

Dani half listened as she urged herself to hurry. The seven-layer masterpiece had been chilled to withstand the Brazilian heat, but even sitting under the shade of the tent, which had been spread across the entire vineyard, the icing was beginning to sheen.

"Maybe he wants some cake."

"Oh, he definitely wants some *cake*." Liz raised her brows and stared at Dani's ass. Dani shook her head at her friend, thinking that she had enough "cake" to feed all of Brazil.

"Wasn't he married to a model or something? He's not trying for—" Dani looked down at her size-sixteen figure "—all of this."

"You never know. Sometimes people go for the complete opposite of what they've had before." Dani heard Liz take her therapy tone, something the good doctor did unconsciously when she was trying to make a point.

"I'm not trying to find a man here, Liz."

"I just want you to have a little fun…and to forget about Andre."

With just the sound of his name, Dani felt her guard go up. She'd *been* trying to forget, but the more she tried, the more she thought about him. Andre had refused to attend the wedding with her and had made it clear he didn't harbor the same feelings for her that she had for him.

Andre loved running the New York restaurant together— translation: he loved that she did all the work running the kitchen, but anything more than sex was out of the question.

Dani picked up her knife and squeezed.

"Look, you go for him. I'm gonna cut this cake."

The guests drank and danced as Dani took apart the layers and began plating slices of each. At first each cut made her feel more single, but as she worked she began to feel better.

The cake was her gift to the couple, a chef's gift, and each layer was infused with different ingredients that told the story of their love—the bold New Yorker and the brooding Frenchman finding each other on a vineyard in Brazil.

A Brazilian chocolate sponge foundation, Nicole's favorite, with a second layer of lavender French vanilla, Destin's favorite. A third layer of traditional Brazilian fruitcake and a fourth layer of New York cheesecake. The last three layers she was most proud of, a Cab Franc–infused red velvet. All topped with wine-infused icing and candy jewels.

"*Dio mio*…is that wine? *Brava!* You're an artist," said a deep accented voice. Dani pulled her focus from slicing the cake to find Antonio Dante Lorenzetti, Destin's best man, licking his finger.

"Did you just stick your finger in my cake?" The grip on her knife tightened.

Toni licked his lips and flashed a boyish smile. Sweat darkened his honey-colored hair around the temples, and his shirt was open to reveal a slightly damp chest. She briefly craned her neck to take in all six feet and three inches of him.

Liz was right, he *was* handsome. He was the type of guy that could have any girl he wanted. She wondered which one he'd choose to take back to his room.

*Shit!* Her cut faltered, breaking one of the perfectly two-inch cake slices in half.

"Sorry." Toni shrugged an apology and slipped his hands in his pockets. His sleeves were rolled and a glint was in his eye, making him look undeniably masculine.

Dani set the knife down and rose to her full five-foot-eight-inch height. She quickly dabbed at the sweat on her brow with a towel. And if Toni hadn't been standing there, she would have dabbed at her cleavage, as well. The bridesmaid dress her friend chose hugged her full frame nicely, but the open neckline showed a bit too much cleavage for Dani's taste.

"Nice ink." His gaze ran over the colorful swirls of flowers and symbols on the tan skin of her left forearm. Dani studied his expression; some people had a thing against tattoos, but Dani saw no signs of aversion. Still, she was certain that a woman like her was definitely not what he was used to.

Dani pulled her shoulder-length hair into a bun on her head, the shaved undercut of her hairstyle letting in more cool air. Screw decorum, she wiped at her cleavage, then tossed the towel on the table. She lifted a brow when she caught his gaze rising from her breasts. *Men.*

"What can I do for you, Toni?"

"You looked like you needed help."

"A finger in my food is not help."

He smirked. "I mean, where is the champagne for the dessert?" She looked around. Good question.

"I thought Anton was rounding it up with the catering staff."

Toni frowned and leaned closer, swiping his pointer finger through the icing of the broken cake by Dani's side.

"You're lucky I don't cut that finger off."

"*Bella*, you won't serve that piece." His lips attacked said finger. "The icing is subtle, to complement the sweetness of the cake I assume? Lovely. You need the Clos d'Ambonnay for this."

"No, I asked for the Lambrusco."

"Absolutely not. That will be too sweet."

Dani fought the urge to stab him.

His Italian arrogance aside, she remembered Destin introducing Toni to her as a fine wine merchant, and currently working to distribute Deschamps, Destin and Nicole's award-winning wines. His family had been restaurateurs in Italy for generations. Apparently, he knew wine and food.

But so did Dani. She'd been cooking with one of Milan's premier chef's since she was a teenager, but she wasn't going to throw her experience, her schooling in France or her current two-star Michelin restaurant in New York in his face.

What she was going to do was try to respect the groom by not killing his friend.

"Look, Toni, we've already had our tastings and this is the wine Nicole prefers with the cake. You know how sensitive her palate is. So thank you for the suggestion but I've got it under control. And I don't think we ordered any Clos so—"

"I brought some with me. Just in case you ran out. Six cases of Lambrusco seemed low to me, but then again Italians are prone to excess."

Dani's hands flew to her hips.

"And how would you know how much I ordered?"

Toni rocked on his heels. "You ordered it from me."

Dani blinked. "We ordered from a Brazilian warehouse."

"My warehouse."

Dani looked him up and down. No wonder he was so arrogant; he didn't work for the distributor, he owned it.

He smiled. "Don't worry, I gave them a discount."

Yep. Money was no object. She should have known by that close-cut beard, which was perfectly trimmed to look like five o'clock shadow.

The catering staff appeared with wine bottles and began filling the idle flutes with bubbly—some red, the Lambrusco, and some mysterious white, which Dani assumed was the Clos. Dani slid her gaze to Toni, who was averting his eyes toward the guests.

"Well, looks like someone found your Clos."

Toni's apologetic smile was the perfect match of sheepish and wicked.

The staff took the plated desserts to the tables and left fresh dishes for her use. Dani bit her tongue and took up her knife again, unwilling to tell him that having red and white bubbly for the dessert was a good idea.

Ignoring him, she grabbed another layer of cake and prepped it for cutting.

"What restaurant did you say you worked in again?"

"Via L'Italy," she said over her shoulder, surprised he was still standing there. Her knife made quick work of the cake.

"The one on Bond street? Isn't that Andre Pierre's restaurant?"

Dani's knife faulted again and a fruit-filled slice crumbled.

Biting her cheek, she slowly lowered the knife to the table and faced him.

"It's *my* kitchen."

He frowned. "So are you a sous-chef?"

"I'm *head* chef."

His frown got deeper. "Alongside Andre?"

Yeah, it sounded ridiculous. Dani took a deep breath, unable to bring herself to say the term *ghost chef*. But that's what she was. She was the blood sweat and tears behind Andre, the famous chef who conceptualized the restaurant. A YouTube phenomenon turned celebrity chef, Andre opened several restaurants in the world under his name, but never stepped one foot inside the kitchens.

She had taken the job years ago thinking she would be working directly with a master. She found out quickly that he was limited in his skills. Proper editing and a ghost chef equaled smoke and mirrors. Many times she'd thought of leaving, but once the restaurant began earning Michelin stars, Andre made it worth her while to stay.

They had even begun sleeping together.

The kitchen was hers, the menu was hers and the Michelin stars…they were because of her.

But to the outside world, it was all Andre.

Dani let her gaze fall, unable to meet his bright blue questioning look. She arranged the broken slice on a small plate with a fork and handed it to him.

"Yes, Andre and I collaborate quite well."

Toni took a bite and uttered a low groan of pleasure. She hated that his reaction made her proud…and a little aroused.

They'd been at the same table for dinner. He ate like a bear, dipping into everything, taking his time with the dishes he liked, eating seconds and sometimes thirds. She'd always liked a healthy appetite in a man.

Not that she was watching, or wondering if he made love the same way.

He slid the fork from his lips.

"That cake is art. Maybe you'll cook for me one day?"

Her eyes snapped to his clear gaze. Was he flirting?

"I mean, I could come to your restaurant."

Of course, he wasn't attracted to her. He liked super-thin arm candy that ate salads and wore tons of makeup. She pressed her lips together. Her lipstick had melted off hours ago.

"Sure. Stop by next time you're in New York," she said politely.

"Erm…you have—" He stepped closer and reached for her.

"What?" She looked down her body.

He swiped a finger across her upper breast and a jolt tore through her. Shocked, she followed his hand, which pulled away with a small dollop of icing on his finger.

She grabbed a towel and handed it to him, but he shook his head and placed the tip of his finger in his mouth.

"So good. I get another piece at the table, yes?"

She nodded absently as he walked away, blinking against the tingly sensations that lingered on her skin and swirled through her body.

Toni stood at the edge of the crowd and watched the throng of women in evening wear get ready to fight over the bouquet. The bride teased the group with a wave of her flowers, then turned her back.

Toni sighed and smoothed a hand over his brow.

*I can't do this anymore, Toni. I don't want this life.*

He downed the rest of his champagne and turned to go. He couldn't watch anymore.

A large hand landed on his shoulder. "She's hot for you, man. She's been staring at you all night."

Toni forced himself back around and smirked along with his fellow groomsman. Reluctantly he slid his gaze to the thin blonde in the red dress and sure enough, she was staring right at him.

She smiled. He forced a grin back in an effort to be polite, but he quickly looked away.

Virgin Mary help him.

She was beautiful…and way too reminiscent of his ex-wife. Being just out of a divorce, weddings were not high on his attendance list, but he couldn't let Destin down. Nor did he want to bring his baggage to the happy day.

Toni turned his head to where the groom was staring lovingly at his bride. Toni supposed he'd done the same at his wedding.

*This isn't want I signed up for.*

He tried to shake the angry voice of his ex-wife from his head. He lifted his glass to his lips. Empty. When the show was over he'd head to the bar, and then everything would be all right.

Fortified by his new plan he looked up and prayed the spectacle would soon be over. There was a shot of whiskey with his name on it. Toni focused on the bride, who had stopped midthrow and was waving at someone. His thoughts were wiped from his brain.

Danica let her curling hair fall around her shoulders and made her way from the cake station into the crowd of single ladies. He licked his lips, as if trying to taste the icing that had landed on her cleavage again. And what a stunning bosom it was. She was tall and hourglass shaped with full hips that he couldn't take his eyes from as she walked in her heels.

"That's too much woman for you, bro."

Toni chuckled.

"There is no such thing as too much woman, Leo."

Leo laughed in agreement and slapped him on the back.

"You can't have all of 'em. Save some for the rest of us."

"Don't worry, brother. I only want one." He was half kidding, thinking that a good night's sleep didn't sound so bad. But as Dani stood close to the back and slightly away from the women jostling for position, he couldn't help but imagine her naked in his sheets.

The bride tossed the bouquet and he compared the scene before him to the game-winning goal in the World Cup. The girls moved as one toward the airborne flowers. The blonde in the red dress dove. Dani put her arms up for the block. The blonde grazed the bouquet and tipped it into Dani's hands.

The crowd oohed.

But Dani swatted it into the hands of a young flower girl while the blonde lost her footing and hit the ground.

The crowd ahhed.

The blonde looked pissed. Dani sauntered away. And Toni headed for the bar.

Dani put the top layer of the wedding cake in the refrigerator for the newlyweds, closed the door and officially ended her maid of honor duties. Although the DJ was still playing, the party had thinned out once the bride and groom conspicuously disappeared. And it took Dani a minute to realize that her friend Liz had also left with one of the groomsmen, which meant the Dani would have to enjoy one last drink alone.

She found a seat at the bar, ordered a shot of whiskey, and paid no attention to the tall, broad-shouldered man with his back to her. Her thoughts drifted back to her encounter with the best man. Who did he think he was arguing with her over the wine? He looked damn good in a suit though. And those eyes, they glittered like a rainbow after a storm.

Dani cursed her weakness for tall, handsome and cocky.

As for Andre, when she got back to New York, she'd put an end to their sexual relationship.

If she could just find a sweet, humble, not shorter than herself man, then life would be perfect. Okay, maybe he could be a little shorter than her, but he'd have to have muscles to complement her figure.

And he'd have to be cool with her work schedule. Running a kitchen was a 24/7 job, which is why she had a penchant for sleeping with her coworkers. She sighed. This cycle had to stop.

Dani's gaze darted back and forth, and then she pulled out her phone and opened up her dating app. Swipe left, swipe left, swipe left. Someone brushed by her back and she pulled her phone close. No one needed to know how pathetic she had gotten to be swiping at a wedding. When the coast was clear she made one more swipe.

"He's cute," said a deep accented voice behind her.

Mortified, Dani sat up and pulled her phone to her chest, ignoring the goose bumps his voice sent down her bare arms. Slipping her phone back in her purse, she slowly turned and met Toni's amused steady gaze.

His hair was spiked like he'd been running his hand through it, but he still looked gorgeous.

"Stop sneaking up on me."

"Sorry, I didn't mean to interrupt," he said with a smirk. "Aren't there enough eligible men here for you?"

They both turned when one of the more inebriated guests fell off his chair.

She chuckled and turned back to him, her gaze caught in the ripples of his chest as he too laughed.

"Um, No. And I'm not really looking for a guy, I was just having a drink before I went to bed."

"What a coincidence. Me too." He downed his whiskey and held up two fingers. "Bartender, two more."

Dani held up her hands, then gestured toward the empty stool. "No, no, I'm not trying to be that guy." But before she could slip away he leaned in so she could feel his warm breath on her cheek.

"Then how about we find more of that icing, and you can tell me which body parts you want me to lick it off of."

Shock had her turning her head slowly, unsure if she had heard him correctly. His heavy-lidded gaze held hers and an explosion of sexual heat shot to the tips of her breasts, which were now diamond points, down to the V between her thighs, which felt on fire, and down her legs to the tips of her toes.

Time slowed and her heart pounded.

"It's just one night," he whispered, sensing her hesitation. "I'm going back to Milan tomorrow."

"Milan? I didn't know you were from Milan."

"It doesn't matter."

Without breaking eye contact, he brought the back of her hand to his lips and kissed the warm skin, making every cell in her body shiver with unnamed desire. Suddenly nothing mattered but him.

"Let's go," she exhaled, hoping she had enough icing to cover him, as well.

# Chapter 2

They left the reception separately with a plan. Dani would grab the icing and meet Toni in his room, which sat ocean side on the ground floor of the resort.

Unfortunately Dani was out of icing, but they still had a case of Clos left and what better way to enjoy a $1700 bottle of champagne then before, during and after sex.

Dani was inside the walk-in pantry when two strong arms appeared by her temples.

"I got impatient."

Toni was at her back, reaching over her to help keep the wine locker open and simultaneously kissing his way down the back of her neck.

"There is no more icing. I'm improvising."

She pulled two bottles from the slats, and then backed into him to shut the door.

"I like how you think. Mmm, you smell like vanilla," he said low against her nape. He was a solid wall of muscle and she shamelessly rubbed her body against him. His hands found their way over her hips and ran up her front to cup her breasts.

She struggled to keep hold of the bottles, feeling exposed to his roaming hands, and tightened her grip. Never would she waste such a beautiful bottle of wine, and never could she walk away from the pleasure this man was offering.

The briefest thought of Andre came and went, replaced by a sense of entitlement. She deserved to feel wanted and she was going to take what Toni was offering.

Toni spun her around and captured her mouth in a kiss so deep, so powerful, that Dani was instantly lost. She almost whimpered when he pulled back and took the bottles of champagne from her grip.

Her chest heaved as she leaned against the wine locker and watched him open one of the bottles with a loud pop. He held the bottle to his lips and exposed the strong column of his throat, and then he brought his mouth to hers.

The sweet wine trickled into her mouth as he nipped at her lips, biting softly at the sensitive flesh. He paused again, holding the opening to her lips. She closed her eyes and drank deeply, swallowing the fizzy elixir, thinking in some way she was taking him inside her.

When she opened her eyes, he was standing over her, his gaze fixed on the front of her dress. She arched her back in a sexy tease, and he groaned.

"*Potrei guardarti tutto il giorno.* You look beautiful in that dress, but it needs to come off."

The pulsing between her legs got stronger at his words. His fingers traced the plunging U-shaped neckline of her dress, softly trailing the quivering flesh of her cleavage. He watched her face as he cupped her breast and ran a thumb over the small dots made by her straining nipples.

She ran a hand over his shoulder to cup the back of his head.

"We aren't going to make it out of here, are we?"

He looked down at the front of his pants. Her mouth went dry at the straining outline of his erection. "I'm not sure I can walk."

"Then do what you want to me, and the dress."

His eyes flashed. Before she knew it, the bottles were discarded and he hiked her skirt up around her waist. Her breath left her body when Toni's fingers ran up the back of her thighs to the naked flesh of her ass. He kneaded her backside with bold strokes, fingering her lacy panties, then pulled one of her legs up, pushing past the wisp of fabric.

Dani arched into his hand, grinding, wordlessly begging. The mound of his palm and his gentle kisses drove her into an insatiable frenzy.

Dani had always been conscious of her body when making love, but the way he was touching her, gazing at her, made her want to tear at her clothing until she was offered up to him naked and raw.

And she wanted him naked too.

She grabbed at his shirt and tore it open, soliciting a wicked smirk from him. Her fingers trailed over the crest-like tattoo on his left pectoral and found their way down his hard torso to cup the huge, hard shaft that was pressing against his tuxedo pants—she swallowed hard.

With her other hand, she forced his face to hers and plunged her tongue into his mouth. A collective moan came from beneath their kiss. He lifted his mouth from hers. "I want to see you," he said in a low voice.

Dani turned around and felt Toni's mouth on her nape as he slowly tugged down her zipper. He then took the opportunity to run his lips up and down her spine, causing her to lose her mind with need.

She slowly turned back around and let the dress slump down her shoulders and catch on the edge of her strapless bra. One small movement and the dress would hit the floor. He reached for the bunched up fabric, but she playfully slapped his hand away. He whimpered and she laughed. She liked teasing him. Liked being in control.

She reached for his open shirt and yanked it off his shoulders.

"I want to taste you," she said, and then her lips and tongue found the strong pulse of his neck. He massaged her back, sending shock waves over her skin. In seconds, her strapless bra was on the floor, and his sure fingers wrenched at her dress, pulling it down over her hips in a flame-hot caress that ended with her lifted into his arms and her legs wrapped around him.

Wine bottles rattled as her back hit the wine locker. Toni widened his legs and wedged their bodies against the glass door. Dani reached for his belt as he brought his mouth to her breasts, licking and sucking at the sides of the soft, plump flesh.

Dani moaned, her hands full of Toni's thick, sandy-colored hair, her head thrown back, her back arched. She pushed herself against him, unapologetic in her pursuit of pleasure, begging for the sweet agony of his onslaught.

"Patience," he teased, taking her ample breasts into his hands. Reverently, he ran his thumbs lightly over the tight buds, then back again.

"*Sei bella.* You're beautiful," he said softly. His mouth found every square inch of her breasts, rising up from her rib cage to the sensitive tips of her nipples.

"Please," she whimpered, her sounds of pleasure mingled with the jingle of the bottles. In answer, he carefully lowered her feet to the ground, and then he kissed his way down her body, taking her panties down her thighs and untangling them from her ankles.

He crumped the lace in his hand, looked into her eyes and brought the fabric to his nose.

"Vanilla and spice," he groaned.

Suddenly, Toni's head was between her legs, his hands on the back of her thighs and his tongue between her folds. "Yes," she gasped, throwing her head back as pleasure so deep and raw sang through her body. She instinctively opened her legs up wider and pressed her hips up into his mouth. He held her firmly, laving her with long, slow strokes. She tangled her fingers into the hair on the top of his head and moved her hips in rhythm with his tongue.

Never had she been so hot for a man. Not even Andre

had made her wild like this. She cupped her breasts and toyed with her nipples, enhancing what he was doing to her, unconcerned if someone discovered them.

"You taste better than the icing," he said before he reached for her and brought her mouth to his. She tasted herself on his lips and felt her insides go liquid.

"Please, Toni," she begged, her legs parting wider, her body searching for his. He ran his hands over her thighs and leaned just inches from her lips.

"Say it again."

"Please."

He licked his lips and shook his head. "No, my name."

"Ton—" He took command of her lips before she finished. They were out of breath and trembling when he pulled back. "We're going to finish this in my room. I want you in my bed. You have five minutes, or I come find you." Dani blinked as he stepped back. Was he serious? His gaze roamed over her as he calmed his breath and righted himself, a hand forcefully adjusting the erection in his pants.

He swallowed hard. "Suite 102." He took her panties from the floor and put them in his pocket. "I'll be waiting," he said, looking into her eyes.

The door closed behind him. She felt cold suddenly, and quickly put on her bra and her dress, zipping it up just enough to keep it on. Her heart still pounded as she slipped her shoes on, and when she walked out the door, a bottle of champagne in hand, she could feel the naked heat he'd left between her legs.

She stepped back into the kitchen and made her way past the bar where a few people still lingered. Her heels struck the walkway from the winery to the resort accommodations. She fingered the palm leaves that grew out into the pathway.

It wasn't like her to sleep with someone she'd known

for such a short time. She could go back to her room and avoid the morning after, she thought. But what fun would that be? She could still taste the whiskey that lingered on his kiss, and her nipples still ached against the satin of her dress. He'd started a fire within her, and she wanted him to put it out.

Room 102 marked a white door in gold letters. She raised her fist to lightly knock. Shirtless and eager, Toni ripped open the door and pulled her into his dimly lit room. She kept a tight grip on the bottle as he picked her up, to her delight, and plopped her on the bed.

Light music played and she caught a clean musky scent in the air. The room was similar to hers; king-size bed, large bay windows overlooking the ocean, and glass sliding doors.

He kissed her as he peeled her out of her dress and unsnapped her bra, his gaze flaring when her breasts tumbled out. In seconds she was naked and staring up at the angular planes of his handsome face.

Toni kissed her again, and then pulled back. "Now tell me what you want."

She didn't even have to think. Dani positioned her legs on either side of him. "I want you inside me."

He thrust against her in answer. "I think I can handle that."

Toni whipped his belt to the floor; at the same time Dani tore at his pant buttons. She ripped his pants down and she came out of her skin at the sight of him hard and throbbing in boxer briefs.

"Touch me," he commanded low.

She cupped him, but it wasn't enough. She reached inside the waistband and grasped him firmly, feeling how warm and ready he was to give her what she was almost begging for.

His head rolled back as she slowly stroked. "That's good," he breathed, his body a pillar of lean rigid muscle. Before he was too far gone, Toni gently cradled her face and pulled her up to meet his body. He nudged her knees apart and gazed down at her with heavy-lidded blue eyes. His fingertips ran down her slick folds, rubbing and sliding over her, making her moan and quiver.

"You are so beautiful. So sexy," he breathed. Dani shuddered, her body ready for release.

"Now, Toni," she panted. "Please."

Toni reached past her and pulled a gold-foiled condom from atop the nightstand, quickly rolling the latex in place. Then all thoughts vanished when he palmed her thigh and slid deep inside her in one swift motion, thick, heavy and hard. Dani clawed at his shoulders as he pulled back slowly and drove home again, and again and again. She moaned as he continuously filled her, overwhelmed by his size and strength, but eager to take everything he was giving.

Dani undulated under him, coaxing rough grunts from him, nipping at his mouth with each thrust. Tremors wracked her, her legs falling open farther as he caged her with his body and slid in deeper. Dani felt her muscles clench around him and her heart started pounding out of her chest. She thrust up and held on to him as she came, vaguely aware of his lips on hers, and the sound of his rough cries against her mouth.

# Chapter 3

*One year later*

"**S**ervice!" Dani screamed from behind the chef's counter where she was meticulously preparing Andre's special plate—veal shank with saffron infused risotto. The wait-staff within earshot paused at her shrill voice, then quickened their pace to grab the two entrées sitting idle under the heat lamp. She understood the confusion; technically she was "off," allowing Michele, her sous-chef, a crucial step in his training—running a Friday night dinner service.

"Feel the rhythm of the kitchen, Michele. You're behind, which makes them—" she pointed to the servers "—behind. Step it up." The young man gave Dani a solemn nod and a "yes, Chef," then barked his own orders.

Chef Andre Pierre may be the owner and famous face attached to the restaurant, but Dani had built the kitchen of Via L'Italy into a two-star Michelin rated powerhouse of culinary masterpieces, and wasn't going to stop until she got a third star.

Of course, if she and Andre landed the TV show they pitched to the Food Network, she'd no longer be worrying about that star. The world would see her cooking beside Andre, instead of behind him. Ghost chef... Dani could barely stand the term. Andre was the great and powerful Oz of the culinary world, while she was the little guy behind the curtain making it all happen.

She had tried to leave and pursue her own restaurant

once, but Andre increased her salary and made it worth her while to stay. When they got their first Michelin star, she got paid even more. On paper, she was successful. In real life, she felt like she was achieving none of her goals.

Dani no longer wanted to be a ghost chef in Andre's kitchen, or in his bed. They'd become more public with their relationship, meaning some of the staff knew, but she still got the feeling Andre was fighting boyfriend status. Her schedule was more grueling than his and they never saw each other much outside of the restaurant. But they made sense together. Slowly but surely, Dani knew that Andre would one day see that they made a good team.

"Is that for Andre?" Michele said, his voice always turning a bit acid when he mentioned Andre's name.

"Yes, I'm going to the office to cheer him up. He's been sulking since he got back from the network. I'm nervous he got bad news."

Dani slipped off her apron and ventured toward the dining room, skirting whizzing servers and bussers. All greeted her with a respectful "Chef." Andre's back office was empty. She passed by the storage alcove where the coats were lined and found a few had fallen from the rack. A muffled sound came from the closed storage door.

She moved forward, her hand on the knob when an audible moan was heard. He heart hammered, afraid to see what she knew was coming. Quietly she turned the knob. Andre was inside with Bette, their hostess. His back was to the door, pumping hard as she lay on the cluttered desk with her dress raised and her legs spread.

"You're going to be a star, baby girl," Andre gritted out in between thrusts.

The young hostess's eyes were closed, and then they fluttered open and found Dani. The girl yelled in horror, which didn't stop Andre's furious thrusts until she hit at him and pushed away.

He was breathing heavily when he snapped his head around to gaze at Dani. The hostess shoved her dress down and scurried past Dani into the hallway. Andre's shoulders slumped and he zipped up his pants. But what she saw in his eyes was not an apology. It was resignation. "I'm sorry you saw that. But what did you expect?"

Dani's eyes narrowed. "I expected loyalty."

"We never see each other. I can't even remember when we kissed last."

"We kissed this morning in bed."

"That goodbye kiss you gave me at 4 a.m. when you went to the fish market?"

Dani took in a deep breath. "Your customers are loving the fish."

"All you care about is the kitchen. Anywhere we go, anything we do, you end up at the kitchen."

"This is a 24/7 job as you well know. And it's not my kitchen, Andre, it's your kitchen. I am doing this for us!"

"No, you're not. Your focus, your drive…it's for you, Dani. You have no insecurities in the kitchen."

Insecurities? Dani's hands perched on her full hips. "What the hell does that mean?"

"It means all you think about is the kitchen. It's where you have control."

Dani rolled her eyes. She didn't need to listen to psychobabble from a cheater and a liar. What she did need was to find out what happened at the network.

"And what about the show, Andre? Does that get thrown away along with our relationship too?"

"They want to do it—" he paused "—but they want someone else to cohost. Someone with a millennial appeal." He had the decency to look apologetic.

"I'm thirty-three, Andre. I *am* a millennial."

"They want someone…like…a model or something."

"Ohhh, now I get it. I'm too fat to be on your show."

He slowly shook his head. "It's not my decision, Dani."

She cut him off. "And who is going to cook for you? The model that… Wait a minute, is Bette going to be on the show?" If anyone wanted to be a star, it was that woman that ran out of the room with her skirt up.

Andre's eyes hit the floor in answer.

"How long have you been screwing her?"

"Does it matter? We weren't exclusive."

She didn't think her heart could sink any lower. She refused to cry, replacing the emotion with pure anger.

Andre's voice turned to syrup. "Look, let's be adults about this. The show still needs you. *I* still need you. She'll be the face, but it will be your food. You'll get paid more than her, I'll see to that."

Her gaze went hazy. He wanted her to be a ghost chef for his new girlfriend?

"Fuck you, Andre." She threw the plate of food at his feet.

He jumped as it crashed and spilled, his gaze holding a challenge she wasn't interested in meeting.

He was predictable. She mused that she had been waiting for this moment, and now that it had happened, she had a kitchen to run. She turned and let the door close behind her, muffling whatever rant he was shouting at her back. She no longer cared. Actually she felt relieved. Wondering when he would screw up was a drain.

Her mother had always told her she played the game of love wrong, that she loved the men more than they loved her. She had fallen in love with Andre, she thought.

Michele was waiting for her when she walked back into the kitchen. His eyes fixed on her face. Did he know? A quick glance around the room caught raised eyebrows and concerned gazes. Did everyone know?

"Everything all right, Chef?"

She nodded with a neutral expression, alluding to nothing. Images of Andre and the hostess flashed in her mind. The other woman stood at her post smiling, welcoming a couple and ushering them to their table. Her dress was in place and her makeup was flawless. The man checked out her size four frame as she walked.

Dani cringed, fighting the urge to pull Bette's weave out in the dining room.

She decided to leave instead. Her presence was undermining Michele's practice. This was his night, his initiation into the wonderful world of chefdom. Should she tell him he'll never have a life? That his partner will get mad and leave him? Because running a kitchen was like being the head of a family, and you don't abandon your family, not even for love.

Dani made busywork of tasting the sauces. She turned to find the pasta and almost walked straight into Andre.

*Get out of my kitchen!* She cleared her throat. "Yes?"

"Since my dinner is on the floor, I'd love a plate of... whatever."

"Of course." Dani loaded a plate with penne, then drizzled the garlic and oil. "I suggest a white wine with this."

Andre looked at her for a long moment, and then scanned the room of staff that were working and simultaneously watching under their lids.

"Thank you." He nodded, then jammed a fork into the pasta and into his mouth. "Mmm" came from his throat. Then his face scrunched. "That's too much garlic."

A tidal wave of anger hit her.

"How dare you come into my kitchen and insult this food! Do you have any idea what I have done for you? Do you think you could have made two stars with that bull you were serving three years ago? You would have been closed had it not been for me!" Her voice cracked. The staff stilled. She grabbed the plate from his hands and tossed it on the counter. "I hope she was worth it," Dani spit.

Dani turned on her heel and found her bag under the counter. Then she stomped to the wall and grabbed her coat. She hugged Michele and held him at arm's length. "Michele, you're ready." Dani had to look away when his face drained of all color. He'd be fine. They all would. She trained them well.

She stepped toward the door but stopped when she saw movement in the dining room. It was Bette, opening a bottle of wine, laughing with a young couple. Dani found herself next to the hostess, startling the girl midpour.

"Your pour should be just less than half the glass." Dani grabbed the stem of the glass and tossed the ruby liquid in the girl's face. Her squeal mingled with the collective gasp of the room. Rivulets of red dripped from her chin. "See, too much." Dani set the glass down in front of the gawking couple and executed a perfect pour, then held it up. "Now, this is a glass of wine." Dani splashed the second glass in Bette's face, this time hitting the dinner guests.

"You fat bitch!" The girl's tears were pink.

Dani shivered with rage at the word. "I'd rather be fat and smart, than skinny and stupid."

Andre appeared, wrenching the wineglass from Dani's hand and apologizing over and over to the couple.

"He's all yours," Dani said to the girl.

Dani felt the eyes of the room as she marched toward the front door. Skirting waiting couples, she pushed through the door and hailed a cab downtown, watching the city smear by.

She walked into her apartment like seeing it for the first

time. It was a mess, like her life. She picked up her phone and dialed Nicole, but got no answer. Then Liz, again no answer, but a text came through saying she was on a date and would call later. Her father, a fashion photographer turned tattoo artist, was backpacking through Asia. She scrolled through her phone and stopped at Mom. Her thumb hesitated. It was almost ten at night in LA. She was sure her mother would be getting ready for bed, if not in bed already. The woman had a regimen stricter than a marine. Dani dialed, sure her mother wouldn't pick up.

She's not going to answer, Dani thought, debating if she should hang up. Maybe it was a sign, emotional conversations with her mother didn't usually make her feel better. She'd thrown that tidbit in her mother's face once during an argument, to which her mother had calmly replied, *I'm not like other mothers.*

The second her mother answered, the tears she was holding back slid down her face in hot streaks. "Mom," she choked out.

"Danica, you know I'm about to go to bed. I need twelve hours or…" She paused. "What on earth—" A half sigh. "Are you crying?"

It was the exasperated sigh that pulled Dani from her fetal position on the couch. She dabbed at her eyes and wiped her nose with a tissue, then took a calming breath. Her mother never stood for such theatrics, even though she was still the most dramatic woman Dani had ever known.

"Yes." Dani swallowed. "It's been a rough night." Dani heard rustling in the background and imagined her mother in a face mask and silk head wrap resting in her king-size bed.

Although her mother was still considered a supermodel, at fifty-five years old—sixty-five if you paid attention to birth certificates—Francesca Watts was rarely offered work anymore, but she still treated every night like she was waking for a photo shoot the next day.

"Well, do I have to guess what happened or are you going to tell me?"

"I quit the restaurant."

"Good, now you can start your own. I'm sure Daddy would give you the money." Dani noted that her mother didn't offer. She also wasn't sure either of them had that type of cash just lying around anymore.

Dani sniffed. "That's not all." Dani made it through the abbreviated story of her breakup with Andre without another wave of tears.

"He wasn't strong enough for you, dear, I told you that. Not many men can handle women like us."

It was the same thing she said to Dani after her father had left and moved back to Sweden. Dani began to think the call was a mistake.

"Mother, just once I'd appreciate a little sympathy. I just want a virtual hug and for you to tell me it's going to be okay."

"Well, if you had moved to California with me instead of choosing to be nearer to your father, then I'd be able to hug you in person and do *all* of that."

"That is *not* the reason I stayed, Mother. I chose my career over the *both* of you—it just happened to be in New York."

"And now you're crying."

"There is no correlation." Dani quelled her rising voice and shook her head. "God, why can't we have a conversation like normal people?"

"Normal people?" her mother sneered. "We are *not* normal. Normal people aren't Michelin-starred chefs, Danica. I made love to David Bowie, for God's sake."

Dani chuckled as she cringed, feeling a little better.

Her mother actually sounded proud of her. "Please, I can't handle that story now."

"Yes. Yes. Now stop this crying. Did you get the dress I sent you?"

"It's too small."

"Well, did you gain more weight?"

And that lovely feeling came crashing down. "I don't know, Mother, I don't weigh myself on a daily basis like you do."

"Well, that designer runs a bit bigger, I thought it would fit."

"I'm fat, Mother, get over it."

"You're not fat, you're full figured. Lots of women would kill for your hourglass shape. Women are paying thousands of dollars to achieve your natural breast size, my dear. But now that you're done with that backbreaking job you can go back to Pilates."

Her mother's personal trainer had almost killed her one summer. She'd only lost a pound.

"No, thanks." Dani sipped a glass of wine, trying to ignore the fact that her mother still thought of her as someone who just needed to work out a little more and *poof*, she'd be a size four. "*She* called me fat."

"Who did?"

"The hostess Andre is cheating with."

"And did you tell that hood rat that she was just a sex toy?"

Dani laughed then. She knew her mother had issues about her weight, but she never allowed another person to say so.

"I'm glad you're laughing. Now, pull yourself up and take one step forward. You'll figure out what to do. I have to go."

Dani frowned. "Early breakfast with that old Persian billionaire?"

"No, darling, that ended months ago. I'm on my way to Milan tomorrow."

At the mention of Milan, Toni's firm lips and lean body popped into her mind. She ran a hand over her hair and shook the vision away. "Oh. Why?"

"I'm in a campaign for Chanel. Ageless, timeless, something or other. It was a cat fight between Naomi and me, God forbid they have two African American models in the campaign, but they chose me." She waited a beat. "I was the first black model to walk in Paris, you know."

Dani knew. She'd heard all of her mother's groundbreaking stories. Had seen all of the pictures of her slim, satin-skinned mother gracing magazine covers.

Her mother's success had been a series of highs and lows, with more and more lows as the gracefully aging beauty got older.

"That's great, Mom. Why didn't you mention anything?"

"You know how this goes. I'll get there and they may not even use me."

"So it's like a test thing?"

"Mmm...something like that."

Dani couldn't imagine the blow to her mother's ego. It was a go-see. An audition.

"They'll be idiots not to use you."

"Yes. They would." Her mother seemed to hesitate. "Would you like to come? It's been a while since we were in Milan together. I can get us a suite at the Baglioni."

"You want me to come with you?"

"Well...yes. Why not? You're not working." Dani blinked, intrigued, but unsure if that was a good idea. The last time Dani had been invited to one of her mother's shows had been during Milan Fashion Week when she was eight. The nanny canceled and the hotel staff couldn't watch her, so her mother had to take her along.

*You do not make noise or speak,* Francesca had insisted in the limo to the photo shoot. *I'm going to put you in my dressing area. And if anyone asks you who you are, you do not say a word. You run and hide. They might think you're a homeless Italian child and just leave you alone.*

*But I want to see the cameras.*

*No.* Francesca had sent her a look that could melt steel. *Why?*

*Because your mother needs to protect her image.* Dani hadn't known what that meant, she'd just known Mom meant business.

As the pair ran unnoticed into the dressing room, Dani thought of the whole thing as a game. But when Dani had laughed a little too loud, she had seen that look on her mother's face and shut it down. Dani didn't know how long she had been in the dressing room by herself, but the thought of the cameras was too enticing. She'd tiptoed behind some tall equipment in her little Keds and ran into a king's spread of food. Sandwiches, cheeses, grapes and…cookies!

Dani was stretched over the lip of the table when her mother's makeup artist had found her with her fingers curled around a macaroon.

Bella? *Dov'è tua madre?* Dani had turned to run but she knocked over a microphone stand. *Francesca, do you know this child? I asked her where is her mother, but I think she's mute.*

Heads swiveled between Dani and her mother. The little girl flinched when Francesca's eyes sparked with split-second rage. Her mother turned to her makeup artist.

*Robbie, do I look like I've had a child?*

Roberto waved his brushes in the air. *Of course not. I doubt your baby would be so...robust.*

The room laughed.

*That is just baby weight*, her mother had quipped, *but... I'm sure she must be with one of the production managers or something.* She'd narrowed her eyes at Dani. *Would you like an autograph, sweetie? How about you sit* quietly *in my chair over there and I'll give you one when I'm done. Okay?*

Roberto had left Dani by the table. *You are so charitable, Francesca.*

*I try to give back whenever I can, Robbie.*

Never would Dani forget that day, or ask to go to work with her mother again. But she wasn't a kid anymore, maybe this time it would be fun.

"You'll be able to see Marcello," Francesca sighed. Dani heard the jealous sound of her mother's voice. Not long after Dani's first and last time going to a photo shoot, her mother again couldn't find a sitter, and dropped Dani off in the hotel restaurant.

Chef Marcello Farina, her old mentor and owner of three-Michelin-star rated Via Carciofo where she trained, had found her in the corner, put her in a white coat and gave her odd jobs around the kitchen. She had loved it. Marcello was like a second father, and probably the reason she was a chef.

"Just say yes already. I have to sleep," Dani's mother said at the tail end of a yawn.

Maybe talking to Marcello would give her some perspective, Dani thought. What could it hurt? "Okay, I'll go."

# Chapter 4

*New York*

Toni sank into the back seat of the car service and watched out the window as they sped up the West Side Highway. The call he'd gotten from Louis, the manager of his Upper West Side warehouse, had been frantic, making it necessary for him to interrupt his trip to JFK Airport. He checked his Omega timepiece and estimated that he had a little over an hour to fly standby on the next flight.

Street vendors doled out coffee to groggy workers while children were dragged by the hand into prestigious-looking school buildings. It was a sharp contrast to the slick glittering nightlife where the drinks were just as cool as the people. He sighed, disappointed that he had to cut his trip short.

He'd called his daughter yesterday to wish her a good night and found that his ex-wife had left Sophia home alone again. Yes, at thirteen years old his daughter could take care of herself, but it was the way she was taking care of herself that worried him. A boy had answered Sophia's phone when he'd called.

Since he'd moved out over a year ago, she stayed with him every other week, which gave him limited glimpses into her life. The weeks she was with him she was an angel—if teenagers could ever be angels. She was safe and out of trouble at least. But the weeks with her mother, like this week, had become increasingly problematic. He blamed it on Ava's new boyfriend and her penchant for going out more than staying home.

The second the call picked up he'd heard a chorus of

"shhhs" followed by the lowering of music. She had been having a party. Girlfriends doing makeup and watching movies, he presumed. Then a deep voice said her name. He recalled the conversation like it was happening all over again.

"Papà?" Her voice was apprehensive.

"Why is a boy answering your phone?"

"He was just being stupid, Papà. It's not what you think."

"It better not be what I think, Sophia. Where's your mother?"

"Um—" giggles in the background "—upstairs in the bath?"

"Go get her."

"She'll be mad if I interrupt."

"Stop lying to me. I'm calling her right now."

"No, don't! Okay, she's not here. She's out with Bruno. But she'll be back later. I'm fine."

"Who is there watching you?"

"I don't need a chaperone, Papà. It's just a few friends, we're watching a scary movie."

"You hate scary movies."

"Not anymore." He bet that boy just loved scary movies.

"I want everyone out of that house and I'm sending Nonna to check on you," he said over her whining protests. "I'm coming home tomorrow and we are going to discuss this with your mother when I get back."

After a quick call to his mother, she agreed to drive the twenty minutes from her country home into the city. He sent a scathing text to Ava and received no response. Yeah, the three of them were going to have a serious sit-down when he got home. Toni sighed his frustration just as the car pulled into the shipping lot behind the warehouse. He jumped out and quickly crossed to the large building.

Toni heard the echo of the argument the minute he

walked through the freight entrance. Skirting trucks and small forklifts, he propped his bags on a tall stack of wine crates and shouted hello to the operations manager, who stopped his crate packing and jerked his head in the direction of the commotion. Toni quickened his pace to the front of the store.

Andrea Gomez of Star restaurant group had shown up expectantly without an appointment and, by the way her voice was rising, seemingly irate. Toni stopped just at the threshold to button his suit jacket, then realized with a sigh that he wasn't wearing it, opting for only a navy T-shirt and trousers for his trip back to Milan.

He debated running back to the town car sitting idle in the shipping lot, then thought against it. There was no time. He needed to catch that earlier flight, needed to get home to his daughter. A shrill female voice pulled him over the threshold into their show and tasting room.

"Do you hear what I'm saying? I'll pay retail if I have to, just get me something that won't embarrass me!" Andrea's hair was wild and she had both of her hands on the counter as if she was going to jump over it. The wineglasses lined up on the tasting bar trembled, as did Louis, who had taken a step back and was clutching the bottle in his hand like a life raft.

"Andrea," Toni said, his arms wide and voice jubilant, making sure to pronounce her name with extra Italian flair. "On-drea-uh," a sexier spin on the American "Ann-dree-uh." He kissed her on both cheeks.

"Antonio! Oh, I had no idea you were in town." Andrea immediately straightened and jammed her fingers through her hair.

Louis visibly relaxed.

"When I heard you were here, I had to come. You look ravishing." Andrea's lids fluttered and she shifted ner-

vously in her big coat, sweatpants and Uggs. It was almost
10 a.m. and Toni could only assume Andrea was not having a good morning.

Toni took her shaky hand in his, steadying her erratic
behavior and demonstrating that the drunken kiss she'd laid
on him several months ago at a wine conference in Verona
did nothing to harm their business relationship. Not that he
would have minded a night with her, but he never mixed
business with pleasure. "I was only here a few days. I'm
on a flight back this morning. Now, *bella,* what has happened that has you in such a state?" He was laying it on
thick, but if he was going to get this done in ten minutes,
he needed her attention.

"I'm hosting a wedding tonight for the mayor's daughter at John-Duc and those Figgertons sent me cases of
spoiled wines. They are like vinegar! This is the mayor's
daughter—it could ruin me!" Andrea's face reddened with
every word.

Toni knew the Figgertons well. A distributor of self-
proclaimed "elegant" wines from smaller less known vineyards. Which appealed to a hipster sensibility of indie
winemaking, but Toni knew it really meant the wines were
less traceable, amateur at best and definitely not worth the
price he knew Andrea had paid.

"You know I would have come to you, Toni, but she's
a vegan hippie and insisted on small vineyards, as if this
woman knows anything about wine, and—"

Toni stopped her and urged her to take a deep breath.
His specialty was in fine wines from more established vineyards, vintners he knew personally. All had a reputation for
the highest quality grapes, rich terroir, flawless production
and generations of knowledge. It was a combination you
could actually taste.

And as their distributor, he made sure they got the price they deserved. Discounts were for the Figgertons.

She was looking at him with doe eyes, as if she wanted to apologize for going somewhere else. It didn't bother him that she didn't come to him first. In fact, he was elated that he found an opportunity to kill two birds with one stone. Toni was personally representing his friend's rebuilt winery in Brazil. Getting it in front of the mayor could be excellent for business.

"Louis, bring the Deschamps."

"But, sir—"

"I know, Louis. Let's have a taste." Louis darted to the back and Toni watched Andrea's gaze travel down his front. He inwardly urged Louis to hurry.

"So." Andrea stepped forward, letting her coat fall open to reveal a white low-cut T-shirt, with a tiny coffee stain on the front. "How have you been?"

Louis had a new glass on the bar and a bottle of Deschamps Cab Franc open and poured in seconds. Andrea looked at the bottle, then at Antonio.

"This is a Deschamps. I can't do a fine wine, the bride will never go for it."

"This one is from the smaller biodynamic vineyard in Brazil."

Andrea gasped. "Didn't they have a fire?"

"Yes, but they have risen out of the ashes like a phoenix. Taste it." Toni leaned in as she lifted the glass to her lips. "There is a story in that wine any hippie would love."

Andrea swallowed and tried to hide her satisfaction, a tactic he knew she used for negotiation, but Toni had seen the pleasure in her eyes. She signaled for one more taste, which Toni approved by a slight nod.

"Hmm," was all she said as she stared at the bottle. The

forest green label etched in gold writing with trademarks and family seals meant...*cha-ching*.

Andrea was still trying to play it cool, but her Uggs were shifting. "Is this all you have to show me?"

"Of course not, but I think it's what you need to make your bride happy."

"How much is in the back?"

"Enough for a wedding of, say, four hundred." Louis began to fidget, wide-eyed.

"Price?"

Toni stepped forward, his smile on full wattage. "*Bella*, for you? I'll make you a deal."

Minutes later Toni was in the back grabbing his bags. The pit stop ran later than expected, but he still might be able to just make his flight. He breezed by his operations manager. "Marco that entire palate goes to Jean-Duc on Park Avenue right now." Marco and his staff stopped packing the crate and frowned.

Louis skidded to a halt. "But we are shipping this to Bagatelle Miami tonight! And we have none left in the other warehouses."

"I'll call Destin, Louis. We'll ship straight from his cellar in Brazil. I'll call you later."

Toni climbed into the car and shut the door, nodding at Louis's anxious wave. He'd just sold more than expected of his friend's wines and made a fortune on the up-charge he slid by Andrea. He should be happy, but all he could think about was getting home.

With literally minutes to spare, Toni stepped onto the boarding dock and heard the doors close behind him. Someone upstairs was looking after him today. He found his seat in first class and then placed his laptop bag on the floor, along with the several gifts he bought for Sophia.

"Coffee?" He took the cup and thanked the stewardess,

then settled into the leather seat. He was about to put in his earbuds when a gray sweatshirt landed in the empty seat and he heard a soft thank-you to his right. A woman was standing by the seat, her arms extended as she rummaged in the overhead compartment. Her generous breasts quivered under her V-neck T-shirt which was tucked into a pair of high-waisted jeans.

Toni unfolded himself carefully from his seat, about to offer his help, when the woman slammed the compartment shut. He dragged his gaze from the curve of her hips in anticipation of seeing her face. He was met with large black sunglasses and a waterfall of dark hair that fell into her face and past her shoulders.

He folded himself back into his seat, still on alert if she needed anything. He decided to mind his own business, when a light pleasant fragrance teased his nose. From the corner of his eye he could see her twisting her hair into a ponytail, lifting her torso and chest up and out, and he found himself captivated. What was it about the way a woman moved?

Feeling like a pervert, he grabbed his coffee, only to glance back when he noticed her looking his way. She smiled. He smiled back, and then the pilot began to speak and the cabin readied for takeoff. The woman was lovely, but his thoughts had traveled to mocha-colored skin and floral tattoos. An occurrence that happened randomly and more frequently as the months went by. He assumed it was because his personal life had become a source of frustration. Dating wasn't going as well as he'd hoped. He mused that he was no longer just looking for love; he was looking for a life partner. Stability. One who could also love his daughter and deal with his ex. It raised the stakes, and kind of killed the romance of it all.

When had love gotten so complicated? And when had

he become so jaded? The old him would be flirting with his flight companion, instead he was avoiding her eyes.

The small cries of Dani's orgasm rang in his ear and he downed another sip of his coffee He wished he could have seen her during this trip to New York City. He'd gotten in three days of work and a few visits to his favorite haunts, but today had been the day he looking forward to the most. He'd made his reservation at Via L'Italy months ago. Yes, it was one of the best restaurants in the city, but he was more interested in seeing Danica again and that was where she worked. He smiled as his thoughts drifted to their delicious night of champagne and sex almost a year ago. Waking up alone the next morning had been a jolt to his ego, but he wouldn't change a thing about that night.

There'd been no rhyme or reason for his planned visit. He understood that she could be seeing someone, hell, he'd been dating quite a bit, but his intentions were not to have another one-night stand. He just wanted to see her.

Unfortunately he had to skip that reservation.

Toni began to feel very tired then. He didn't know what he was going to say to Ava when he got home, not that she'd listen, but he had hours to figure it out.

Toni fished his phone from his pocket to turn it off and found three messages from his mother. Each was an up-date on their new restaurant project Via Olivia, a farm-to-table dining experience just outside of Milan, along with a list of things he needed to accomplish when he got back.

For generations, his family has been in the wine and res-taurant business. There were no titles or job descriptions, just his mother, the matriarch of their large family, telling everyone what to do. If you were in the family, you worked for the family. Strangely enough it was successful. Lorenzetti restaurant group owned several restaurants throughout Italy, including a three-Michelin-starred restaurant in the center of Milan run by his uncle.

Although Toni had his wine business, he was also an active partner in the restaurant group. While he had a small stake in all of the restaurants, this new venture had been his idea. Five years of landscaping, gardening, designing the perfect villa, he had invested a lot of time and money into making it a success. And with his uncle overseeing the menu, Toni knew it would be *fantastico*. Just a week or two now and they would be open.

He quickly texted his mother back, then balked at the last text that came through.

Ava still hadn't arrived home.

Toni turned off his phone and pinched his nose, praying the plane could make warp speed.

# Chapter 5

*Milan*

Dani arrived at the Baglioni Hotel Carlton in the early morning but her mother had already left for work. A little jet-lagged, she ordered up a sizable pot of coffee and some pastries to the two-bedroom suite, then unpacked her toiletries and an outfit for the day. After some digging in her bursting bag, she hung up a dress in the closet for later, then decided that unpacking the rest of her bag could wait.

The rainfall shower in the black marble spa bathroom made her seven-hour red-eye worth it. She began to feel like a human again as the water slid over her skin. *Milan.* She hadn't been back in years, not because she didn't want to, but because running a kitchen in New York had proven as consuming as Chef Marcello had promised. Knowing Marcello was working, she planned to surprise him later that night and maybe get some life advice too.

Dani toweled off and let the high-thread-count towels caress her skin, lingering over her sensitive breasts as images of Toni Lorenzetti naked and thrusting into her took over her thoughts. Even as she and Andre had committed to each other—she'd thought—flashbacks of Toni were a spontaneous occurrence that she couldn't help. Someone would smile and she'd see Toni. A tall man would walk through the door at the restaurant, she'd see Toni. She'd hear an accent, any accent. Toni. She chalked it up to the great sex because what other explanation could there possibly be?

He was here in Milan, she thought. She exited the bathroom and sat on the bed, running complimentary lotion over her legs. The soft duvet reminded her of the duvet they'd had no use for in Brazil. She'd woken up groggy from the champagne, her body aching from the high-octane sex, and warm from the humidity of the air and the heat of his body. She had slid from underneath his heavy arm, almost tripped over the pile of sheets on the floor, found her clothes and tiptoed out the door, and back to reality.

You could call it a walk of shame, but she hadn't been ashamed. It had been a perfect night and she didn't want the memories ruined by an awkward morning after. So she had left without saying goodbye to Toni Lorenzetti.

Which was why now, even in his gorgeous city, she wouldn't be saying hello.

Dani put on her robe and strolled out onto the terrace overlooking Via della Spiga, one of the best shopping streets in the city. Designer logos on the buildings glittered and beckoned while severely fashionable men and women were already on the streets. A woman in camel-colored leather pants strolled by. Dani felt envy prickle her chest; they probably didn't even make those in her size.

She hugged her robe closer, remembering that everyone in Milan looked and dressed like a supermodel. She recalled the suits hanging in Toni's room—Cavalli, Brioni, Armani, all custom. She shook her head at the obsessive thoughts of a man she hadn't seen in almost a year. She could see him with the girl wearing the leather pants, not with her. She was not fashionable, nor was she a supermodel. She was just a chef.

Or at least she used to be.

After a light lunch in the lobby, Dani strolled the marble streets, visited the La Scala theater, awed at the sidewalks filled with busy café seating and strolled by the cathedral—which always took her breath away.

Dani texted her mother to join her at Via Carciofo, but

her mother was already on her way to dinner with Chanel's people. That was a good sign. So Dani put on her black lace dress and her heels and ordered a car to the restaurant.

It had been almost eight years since Dani had worked as a sous-chef at Via Carciofo. It was still the most beautiful restaurant she had ever seen. Tucked away in a secluded courtyard of one of Milan's oldest hotels, vine-covered stone columns hid the small stairs that led to the mezzanine patio where twenty tables were perfectly staged with tea lights, white roses and fine china.

Back there time didn't exist, hence the ambiguous hours of operation—open at dusk. The lack of time limits only enhanced the romance. Reservations were recommended and hard to come by. Once you booked a table, it was yours for the night, no matter what time you got there. And the kicker? There was no menu.

Upon securing a reservation the hostess noted any allergies or preferences. Once recorded, Chef designed a seven-course prix fixe menu of his choosing paired perfectly with two to three wine recommendations. She had never seen one dish come back to the kitchen. In this space, eating was purely for pleasure.

Dani's heels clicked up the stone steps and she breathed in the fragrant pastel-colored lilies that lined the entrance. Easter was in a couple weeks and she made a mental joke that what she gave up for lent was her job. She slowed, wondering what to say to Marcello. How do you tell your mentor that you've given up on life?

The hostess was gracious when Dani told her she was just visiting Marcello and turned down her offer to be announced. Dani wanted her visit to be a surprise. She walked past the tables, glancing around to see if she recognized any of the servers. She didn't. Then she looked for Wendall, the maître d'hôtel of almost forty years, but he was nowhere to be found. Strange. He never left the dining floor.

Reaching the bar, she ordered a drink and asked the bartender to tell Marcello someone had a complaint. Game for a prank, the bartender went to the back. She smiled, anticipating Marcello's blustering red face. She heard a muffled crash of pots and pans and envisioned Marcello yelling at his staff. She smirked. She'd felt that rage and had given it to her own staff many times.

She turned to the packed tables to see if anyone else had heard. She saw only smiles and laughter while a bar back went table-to-table lighting the tea candles.

An audible shout came from behind the bar. Dani put down her drink and leaned over the bar. She spied someone sprint past the windows in the double doors. Something was wrong.

Dani pushed through the double doors. The wall of heat that assaulted her was forgotten when she saw the kitchen staff gathered around Marcello, who was laying supine on the floor in the bartender's arms. His right hand held his left arm close to him and his face was scrunched with pain.

Wendall stood to the side with a phone to his ear speaking in urgent Italian. Dani's Italian was rusty but she recognized the word for *hospital*.

"Signora, please. You cannot be in here." One of the staff came forward. Dani ignored him, trying to get her head around the fact that the man that had once been like a father to her was having a heart attack.

Amid quizzical looks, she dropped her clutch and dropped to her knees, taking Marcello's free hand.

"Marcello. It's Dani," she whispered through budding tears. He'd aged the superficial way men do. His hair was thinner and had turned white, but his face held few wrinkles.

Marcello pried his eyes open and they widened in recognition. His mouth hung slack with breaths and grunts. Dani could see him straining to speak, but he couldn't form the words. Medics burst through the back door.

Dani backed away as they huddled around Marcello armed with medical supplies. In seconds his black chef's coat was ripped open and monitors were attached to his chest. Dani feared the worst and wrung her hands as she prayed a silent prayer.

Servers came through the kitchen doors and stalled. No one moved as Marcello was strapped to a gurney and hooked to an oxygen tank. His eyes drifting open then closed. Dani watched the deep movement of his chest as they began to wheel him away.

As they passed by her, his arm shot out and swung at the air between them. She stepped forward, grasping his hand. His other pulled at the face mask.

"*Per favore*, I think he wants to say something," Dani shouted.

"Cuh…Cuh…" Marcello stuttered.

"Chef, stay calm. I'm coming to the hospital."

"Nuh." Marcello shook his head. "Kit-en."

Dani frowned. Kittens? "Marcello, put your mask back on. We can talk later at the hospital."

Marcello rapidly shook his head and a medic stepped forward.

"Step back, signora. We must get him to the hospital."

She did as she was told, watching the pointed look in Marcello's eyes. The medics were quick to restrain him and the mask was placed back on his face, but not before she heard him speak one last time.

"Kitchen."

The man was staring death in the face and he was concerned about the kitchen?

Wendall did a double take as he followed the gurney out

the back door. "Danica? Oh, Dani! My God, it's so good to see you." He ran over and gave her a quick hug. When he pulled back, tears sprang to his eyes. "They are taking him to Milan General. I must go with him. Please, find Gianni, the sous-chef. Please!"

"Go. I'll find him."

Just as quickly as they arrived, the medics and Wendall departed, leaving Dani and the staff bereft in their wake.

No one moved. The hostess cried. The line cooks blinked. The waitstaff were gaping from inside the double doors.

A burnt smell filled the room. Dani looked around and saw filets burning. Pots boiled over. A steak was sitting idle on a plate under the heat lamps. Vegetables lay midchop.

*Kitchen.*

Dani looked around the room for the sous-chef, who would be attired in black just as Marcello was, but she only saw white coats.

"Which one of you is the sous-chef?"

Heads swiveled, but no one came forward. She asked again, this time in her choppy Italian. "And get those fillets off the burners. Now." A line cook jumped.

The hostess came out of her stupor and raised her voice.

"Start shutting down. There will be no more service tonight. I'll inform our guests that we will be closed for the unforeseeable future and—"

"You will do no such thing," Dani interrupted.

"Signora, it seems you are a friend of the chef, but—"

"But nothing. Chef wants this kitchen open. And it will stay open. You have a room full of people out there expecting a Marcello Farina dining experience. Chef put his blood, sweat and tears into this restaurant. I'm not going to let you ruin that. I practically grew up in this kitchen, and I'm happy to stay and help. Now, where is your sous-chef?"

"Yes, where is Gianni?" the hostess asked the room.

"He's on break in the cellar," someone shouted.

"I'll get him," the hostess said, turning to leave. Dani stopped her.

"No, I'll get him. I know where it is." Dani had taken many breaks herself in the basement pantry. "You go out there and keep our guests happy."

The hostess gave Dani a wary look, then walked through the double doors.

"Start two new fillets and put a steak on the fly. I'll be right back."

Dani marched down the short hallway to the fridge, her mind racing with how to explain who she was and what happened to Marcello. She hoped the sous-chef could handle taking over the kitchen for a night. Or several nights if needed.

The cool air of the cellar was like a balm on her skin and she surveyed the frigid cuts of meat as she found her way around the shelving to the back.

"Ciao? Hello?" she called out. "Gianni? Oh, *scusa*," she apologized; startled when she found him bent over a rack. At first she thought he was gathering food, and then she saw the thin white line spread on the shelf and noticed the same powder dusted on his black coat.

He pinched his nose and looked at her quizzically. "*Scusami.* Are you lost?"

Dani blinked, trying to keep a lid on her emotions. If this were her kitchen, he'd be fired. And she doubted Marcello knew about this man's habits or he wouldn't be wearing that coke-dusted jacket.

But she didn't have time for morals and ethics. What she needed was a chef. Quickly she explained who she was and what happened, with Gianni seeming genuinely concerned.

Yet he balked when she asked him to run the kitchen, but then reluctantly agreed.

Gianni sweat bullets as he looked at the backup of orders. An erratic waitress burst into the kitchen needing her meals, her table was becoming belligerent. Then the hostess followed, with more problems.

"The key to the wine cellar is missing. I think Wendall had it." Dani knew that was where they kept the most expensive wines. What a disaster.

*"Scusami,"* Gianni said with a sniff. The room watched Gianni put down the orders and walk out of the back door.

Dani looked around. "Did he just leave?"

The hostess's face drained of all blood.

Useless, Dani thought. She looked down at her cocktail dress, then grabbed an apron off the wall. Entrées began to fill her mind and she cursed the irony. Yesterday she quit this life, now she was thrust back in it. Taking a deep breath, she addressed the staff.

"Okay, first, my Italian is rusty. I need a volunteer to translate for those that do not speak English. *Grazie.* Consider yourself sous-chef," she said to the young man who raised his hand. "Second, someone needs to gather the orders that have come in so we can start at the top. Third, Marcello created something special here. We won't let him down tonight. My name is Dani, but tonight you can call me 'Chef.'"

Dani kicked off her heels and slid her feet into a pair of spare Crocs by the wall. She yelled out the first three orders to which she received a resounding *"Sì,* Chef."

Dani turned to the hostess. "What are we going to do about the wine locker?"

"I just called the owner. He should be here soon."

Immersed in her preparation of the dishes, a song played in her head as she chopped, sautéed, skewered and assembled each dish to an artful perfection. Her heart was pounding; she was sweating the edges out of her blowout and getting oil stains all over her dress.

But she also just pumped out three of the best entrées she'd ever created on the fly. Linguine con scampi, osso buco and risotto alla Milanese were prepared and served at lightning speed. She'd forgotten what it was like to cook like this.

Marcello had warned her about working for Andre. That he'd do none of the work and take all the credit. Those Michelin stars were hers and that poser knew it. But no one else did.

When the *mazzancolle* was ready she was bent over the plate, trying to ignore the crick that was building up on her neck. On a slow inhale she picked out the herbs and spices in the air. Saffron, cardamom, cumin, paprika, basil…a whiff of burned butter caught her nose.

"Who is watching the octopus?" she shouted.

"*Capito*, Chef!" came from behind.

The line cooks were pumping out dishes like crazy and servers were pouring complimentary champagne from the few bottles left in the fridge.

"Coming in!" A frantic server announced in an English accent as he burst through the kitchen door. He stopped just inside. "I've got a table asking for Lafite '82. Please tell me the cellar is open!" Dani sighed. It was a two-thousand-dollar bottle of wine and if that locker didn't open soon she had a feeling that all hell would break loose.

"Someone is coming," one of the line cooks shouted.

"Well, where are they?" the server repeated, running a hand through his perfectly gelled hair. He began to mutter softly, then grabbed his apron and chucked it to the floor. "I quit! I quit!"

Dani understood his tantrum. In this business your reputation was everything and losing a customer for whatever reason was bad for business.

"Coming in!" said a deep male voice. The door opened behind the irate server and Dani shot upright. Lean frame. Impeccable suit. Electric-blue eyes.

"Pick up your apron, Liam. I need to open the cellar and— Danica? Is it really you?" His eyes traveled over her, then a wide smile burst onto his face. "What is it with us and kitchens?"

# Chapter 6

Dani picked her mouth up from the floor and froze. She couldn't believe that Toni was standing in front of her, and that his first image of her since the wedding was like this—frazzled and sweating.

"*Buona sera*, Chef. It's good to see you."

His voice washed over her and for a second she'd forgotten that they weren't the only two people in the room, until one of the line cooks jolted her out of her head.

"Chef? The *mazzancolle*?" The young man slid a plate in front of her and scurried away. She looked down at the bright orange prawns, then back to Toni.

"What... How... What are you doing here?"

"I could ask you the same."

Liam clapped his hands and steepled them as if in prayer. "But we have no time for reunions. Sir, please, my table."

Toni's curt nod was followed by a look Dani interpreted, as "we're not done." And by the aggressive way her blood was pumping through her veins, they weren't done. Not by a long shot.

Dani turned back to her dish, but her mind was on the man that was opening the wine locker. How did he have keys to Marcello's wine locker? More images of the two of them in Brazil had her sending out the dish with the server, then calling it back when she forgot the sprig of parsley. She needed to get it together. On a deep inhale she focused on the spices in the air again. Oregano, red pepper, sultry musk...huh?

Dani whipped around and there was Toni leaning against the stainless steel counter, his arms and ankles lightly crossed, smiling. He looked gorgeous, maybe a little leaner than she saw him last, but his facial hair was perfectly trimmed, his navy suit over the white T-shirt was impeccable and his sandy-blond hair was just the right kind of messy.

Liam was shouting a thank-you to the heavens and waving around bottles of Lafite.

She wanted to go to the bathroom and freshen up. She wanted to kiss that smile right off his face.

"How is this possible?" he said, his gaze roaming down her front, then behind her to the entrées at her back.

"You tell me. How do you have keys to Marcello's locker?"

"We own this restaurant. How are you standing here cooking for my guests?"

"I came to visit Marcello. What do you mean *we* own? This is Marcello's."

"And his family's. I am his nephew. How do you know him?"

"I used to be his sous-chef."

Toni jumped up. "Here? When?"

"It's been eight years now."

"I was in London at school then." Toni's eyes narrowed. "How did this never come up at the wedding?"

Dani's eyes darted around the room before she spoke.

"We didn't do much talking."

His wicked smile took Dani's breath away. "No, I guess we didn't." He shook his head. "I can't believe you are the one saving our asses."

"I can't, either," she said, grabbing the floral displayed artichoke she cut by hand.

"I don't know how to thank you." His tone turned serious. "He would have wanted—"

She shot upright, tears rushing to her eyes. "Oh God. Don't tell me—"

He grabbed her shoulders. "No, no, no...he's stable. My mother is with him." Dani sighed in relief. "I was saying he'd want to thank you himself. I'll be happy to take you to the hospital later."

People buzzed all around them, heat rose from the ovens and pots clattered on granite tops, but she felt the tension ease from her body and realized he was lightly rubbing his thumbs over her shoulders. It should have been awkward, but it felt grounding.

"Ahem!" They both stepped away from each other and turned their heads. A tense Liam stood on the other side of the kitchen counter.

"This reunion is lovely, really, but are any of these dishes mine?" Ignoring Toni, she bent over and worked quickly, handing Liam two plates and a "get the hell out of here" look. Liam studied the steaming plates, then gave her a once-over before loading them both on his arm.

Toni chuckled behind her. "Liam is our best server. His Instagram is full of our regular customers. They all ask for his table."

"He's intense." Dani stood and turned around, catching his gaze sliding back up to her face. She blushed and adjusted her dress, realizing that the skirt was probably riding up as she bent over.

"I've been thinking about you. It's good to see you," he said, the emphasis on *see*. Dani shivered, hoping she wasn't giving him "fuck me" eyes, because it was all she was thinking about.

"Coming in!" Another server burst through the doors, giving her a welcomed jolt.

She had to pull herself together. She had a kitchen to run. "Yeah, it's good to see you too. Look, I need to get back to work."

Toni clapped his hands. "How can I help?"

Her brows rose. In her experience, many restaurant owners did nothing but cash their checks. Kind of like Andre.

"I don't know, Toni, what can you do?"

"Where is Wendall?"

"He went with Marcello."

"Then it looks like I'm the new maître d'."

Toni straightened to his full height, buttoned his jacket, then tossed a white towel over his arm. He crossed the room in long easy strides and picked up a bottle of champagne. With the swift flick of his wrist, he popped the cork. It shouldn't have been sexy, but it was. Toni caught her gaze and winked before disappearing through the kitchen doors. Dani couldn't help it. She left her plates and peered out the small window to the dining room.

There was Toni, smiling, engaging customers, pouring champagne. The hostess was running a hand through her hair and righting her dress, watching him seductively. She walked back to her plates thinking that scene was way too familiar.

Movement in the corner caught her attention. Dani got closer and found a young slim girl with waves of dark hair fixated on the screen of her phone. Dani scrounged up some Italian.

*"Scusami? Sei qui con qualcuno?"*

Her head came up and electric-blue eyes appeared out of the dark curtain. "I'm waiting for my papà."

"Oh, where is he?"

She pointed to the dining room and Dani assumed he was a server. Quick flashes of memories assaulted her. Marcello standing over her with his hands on his hips, shaking his head when her mother begged him to watch her while she was at work. She mopped, she chopped, she was dead on her feet when her mother came back to the hotel. But Dani had loved it and volunteered to do it daily.

"Well, I don't allow loiterers in my kitchen. If you want to be here, you've got to help out."

Dani prepared for attitude. Instead the young girl turned off her phone and shrugged. *"Va bene."*

The hours went by quickly, with Toni being a gracious host and the kitchen pumping out seven courses of delight. His knowledge of wine was impressive, and unyielding, arguing with Dani over her recommendations for each dish. Finally she gave up, but she noticed he took one of her suggestions, conceding only with a slight nod. It reminded her of their first meeting and she schooled herself to concentrate.

It was two in the morning when the last customer left and Dani and her crew were scouring the grills, mopping the floors and wiping down the burners, all with the hope that Marcello would be all right and the kitchen would see another day.

Toni came through the doors carrying soiled linens and instructing the waitstaff to close up the dining room. He stopped when he saw her, threw the linens on the floor and pulled her into a bear hug. She kept her soapy hands in the air, but the rest of her body reveled in the feel of him. He pulled back slowly and looked into her eyes.

"Thank you."

"You're welcome."

He then turned to the whole staff and praised them, making everyone join in a round of applause. His gaze ran over the staff and paused.

"Sophia, are my eyes deceiving me? You are cleaning?"

The teen stood with a mop in her hand.

"You know her?" Dani asked.

"Come," Toni said to the girl, arm outstretched. Mop in tow, Sophia fit her slim frame against Toni's. "Dani, this is my daughter, Sophia. Sophia, this is Danica, a friend of mine and Marcello's."

Dani looked at Toni in wonder. He'd never mentioned a daughter, but she supposed she'd never asked. Suddenly the resemblance was uncanny. Sophia was tall for her age and those eyes were definitely his. She was going to be stunning, Dani thought.

"Nice to meet you, Sophia," Dani said as they politely shook hands. "Thanks for helping out."

"Now, I see you missed a spot over there," Toni teased Sophia, giving her a kiss on the head as the girl resumed mopping across the room. "How did you get her to clean?"

Dani shrugged. "I asked her."

"Humph," Toni said. Sophia always balked at chores.

"She's beautiful."

His smile was pride itself. "Yes, thank you."

"Do you have any more?"

"No." His head whipped around. "Do you?"

Dani shook her head, remembering that Andre didn't want kids, so she assumed she wouldn't have any. Now that things had changed, could kids be in her future? Her stomach made an embarrassing sound. Suddenly she was starving, since her plan to have dinner had turned into cooking dinner for fifty people.

"I'm starving. Have you eaten?"

Toni placed a hand over his stomach. "Not since lunch." He eyes darkened and he smirked. "Are you going to cook for me?"

Dani half smiled. He'd said the same thing at the wedding, but at the time her answer had been a resounding no. "I'm going to heat some things up for you. I think you've earned it."

"You honor me, Chef."

Fifteen minutes later, Dani heated up a simple pasta

marinara. Most of the staff had finished cleaning and gone, leaving Dani, Toni and Sophia to their late-night dinner. Toni's sounds of pleasure as he enjoyed her pasta assaulted her senses in a myriad of ways. She was pleased, a little too pleased, that he loved her cooking, but the sounds he was making were reminiscent of their night together. She was glad Sophia was there as a buffer.

"You can cook, Dani."

"Well, thank you, Toni. It's just marinara."

"I really like it too," Sophia chimed in, sitting on the island swinging her legs.

"Yes, but what's in it?"

"Well, I could tell you, but then I'd have to kill you."

Toni's eyes widened. "*Top Gun.* You just Top Gunned me."

Dani laughed. "I did. Sorry, Goose."

"Goose?" Toni's head jerked back. "Did you see me out there tonight? I was Maverick."

"I'm Maverick, obviously."

"That's ridiculous."

"What's a 'Maverick'?" Sophia asked, forking more into her mouth.

Toni swallowed. "It's an '80s film about fighter pilots."

"Oh! Yeah, I think I saw it with Mamma."

Dani noticed Toni's eyes darken a bit and she was reminded that he was divorced. A silence descended as the trio finished their meals. Dani stretched out her hand for their empty plates, but Toni took hers instead.

"The cook doesn't clean," he murmured, staring at her lips. She felt that look between her legs.

He and Sophia shared the sink and left their clean plates to dry in the rack. Then Toni tossed a towel on the counter and turned to both girls.

"I'm going to stop by the hospital. Who's game?"

"I am," Sophia shouted. All Dani saw were long legs and hair as Sophia gathered her things then disappeared into the bathroom.

"How is she not tired? She's lucky it's the weekend," Dani said to Toni with a smile.

Her smile faulted when she looked into Toni's eyes, something dark behind them. He glanced at the closed bathroom door, then came for Dani. In three strides he was in front of her, cupping her face, capturing her lips with his, his tongue commanding her own. The kiss was fire and burn, filled with months of pent-up longing, at least it was for her, but by the way he was eating at her mouth and pressing her body into his, she'd say if his daughter wasn't there, he'd have her back down and legs spread on the kitchen island.

He pulled his lips just inches from hers. "Are you seeing someone?"

"No," she whispered.

"Good."

They heard the door click and, just as quickly as the kiss started, it ended in a rush of breath and blinking eyelids. Toni pulled his body away from hers and walked calmly toward the door. Dani slowly turned around, acting like she was gathering towels when she was really trying to calm her breathing.

Sophia stood by the bathroom, her eyes darting between them. *"Pronto?"*

"Ready," Dani said under her breath.

# *Chapter* 7

When Toni explained to the hospital staff that they were family, a kind nurse took pity and let them in Marcello's room. They were quiet, feeling better being by his side. But the stress of the day finally got to all of them, and one by one they all dozed in their chairs.

Dani woke and raised her head from the hospital wall. She blinked against the grogginess of jet lag and pure exhaustion from the night before. The room was dim, but a sliver of daylight shone through the closed curtains. Steps away, Marcello lay in a deep sleep hooked up to beeping monitors, and her mind ran through the events from the night before.

Marcello had almost died.

She relived seeing him lying on the floor and wheezing out the word *kitchen*. Was that what he cared about most? Dani thought back to what Andre had said to her, that all she thought about was the kitchen. That wasn't true...was it? Would she be dying on the floor one day using her last breath to say "kitchen"? Nothing about that thought was appealing.

Then there was Toni. *That kiss*. She turned her head and found him at the other end of the room slouched in his chair, his eyes closed and head resting on the wall. He was too tall and broad for the small metal frame and she suspected he'd be feeling pains in his back later. Sophia was curled up in the chair next to him, her body leaning into his. A protective arm was slung around her.

Long deep breaths came through his slightly parted lips, emphasizing his sensual mouth. He had a beautiful easy smile that had charmed even the hardest customer in the restaurant. By the end of the night everyone knew his name, and loved him.

Kind of like Andre, she winced. Charming the ladies right out of their pants.

But she hadn't expected Toni to be so competent and collected. Men like him wanted attention, nothing more. And yet he'd served more dishes and poured more wine than the staff. Eight hours on his feet without complaint. Andre never worked that hard a day in his life.

*Are you seeing someone?*

Grabbing her little bag she quietly found the bathroom and recoiled from her reflection. Her flawless night-out makeup had melted down her face, settling into creases around her eyes that didn't need to be emphasized. Baby hairs frizzed around her face. And her lips were drained of color.

And she smelled. She had worked too hard and long for there not to be a tinge of BO, but her beautiful dress had also absorbed every splatter and aroma from the kitchen. She pulled the soft band from her hair and shook out the waves over her shoulders. Yeah, her hair got it too.

Dani ran the hot water and prepared for a thorough whore's bath in the sink. She placed her hands under the water and pulled back at the sharp sting. Burns, she'd forgotten them. Tiny fresh marks from oil splashes and hot plates. They were a chef's badges of honor and she'd gotten used to them appearing in all sorts of places on her body, but she had no ointment to rub on them. Maybe she could trouble a nurse for some.

She pumped the little hospital soap dispenser and in only a few minutes she was fresh faced with her damp hair up and smelling like medical grade hospital soap rather than a garbage dump. Digging in her little clutch, she pulled out a nude lipstick and felt like a woman again with each glide over her lips.

Satisfied that she no longer looked like a zombie chef, she tiptoed back into the room intending to go into the hallway and call her mother. Instead she walked straight into Toni's solid chest.

He was gripping his phone and although it was still dark she could see the concern in his bright eyes. "Are you all right?" he whispered. Sophia and Marcello both still slept.

She nodded and held up her phone in silent communication. He nodded back and they both softly shuffled into the lit hallway.

"I need to call my mother," Dani said when the door shut behind them.

While she was working, her mother had sent several texts, the last one a sarcastic plea: You better be with a man.

She didn't know whether it was good or bad that after long absences her mother had never assumed she was dead or dying. Dani had "run away" when she was ten. It was Paris Fashion Week and in protest of being left again with the hotel housekeeper, Dani had run down to the parking garage and hid behind a cluster of bins. Where she fell asleep for hours.

Knowing she was in trouble, little Dani ran back to her hotel room and walked through the door to find the hotel manager, a policeman and the maid who was watching her—all sighs and relief to see her safe. The maid had actually dropped to her knees in tears.

Her mother? On the couch in her pink silk lingerie set and heeled slippers, reading the evening paper. Francesca had half lowered the paper and peered at Dani over a bent corner.

*See, she's fine. Just out exploring. Thank you all so much for coming, but I must get some sleep.* Dumbstruck, the group had filed out, but not before the maid kissed Dani on the head. Dani had bet she would make a good mother one day.

Alone in the room, neither moving from their prospective positions, Dani had crossed her arms. *You don't care about me!*

*Of course I do, don't be ridiculous. And is that grease on your shirt? You better get in the shower before you come tracking all that stuff in here.*

*I could have been killed!*

*But you weren't.*

*Someone could have taken me!*

Francesca had rolled her eyes. *This is Paris, not New York. There is no better place to get lost.*

*You weren't even worried!*

Her mother had stomped across the room in her heels and stood her five-foot-eight-inch frame in front of Dani. Dani had dropped her arms and prepared to run. *Did you see all of those people I called? Yes, I was worried, but stress lines on this face won't do, young lady. You are going to stop this nonsense. And that maid is going to be fired for letting you out of her sight.* Dani had gasped and run to her room.

"Hey, where'd you go just now?" Toni was standing close, his voice low and a frown on his handsome face.

"Sorry, I'm just tired."

"I bet. You were incredible last night. I don't know what we would have done had you not been there. Fate, no?"

She shook her head and shrugged. *Fate?* She'd just call it coincidence. "I'm just glad I could help."

"I was in New York recently. I had made reservations at Via L'Italy." His hands went into his pockets. "I wanted to say hello, but my plans got cut short." He frowned, trying to make sense of it. "And here you are, saving my family. I say fate. You must be some sort of angel."

She paused, glad he hadn't come to L'Italy, preferring he not know that she was a ghost chef. Or that she and Andre had been lovers.

"I'm no angel, Toni. I think you know that. I'm just a chef—who needs to call her mother." She lifted her hand and waved her phone. His hands flew from his pockets and grabbed her hand.

"Angel, what is this?"

"What? Oh, it's just a burn." She winced when he touched it. Then his hands ran up her forearm and over the colors of the tattoo, frowning at the bumpy texture of her skin there. The burn had been so bad that the skin had scarred, so her father created some artwork for her and covered it up.

Toni's gaze scanned the hall and then focused. He shouted at someone and in a blur of activity several nurses arrived and ushered her into a florescent room. Several coats of ointment and one bandage later, Dani's burns no longer stung.

"Let me see," he said when she emerged, slowly inspecting their work as if he would make them do it over if he wasn't pleased. He nodded his approval. Toni walked to the other end of the hall and made a call. Dani did the same. Her mother picked up on the third ring.

"You know how I feel about worry lines, Danica."

"I'm sorry, Mother." She explained the events of the night.

"Well, I know how you feel about Marcello. Is he going to be all right?"

"I'm not sure, he hasn't woken up yet. But he's stable."

"And who is this man who helped you?"

"Toni, Marcello's nephew. He's part owner."

"And?"

"And what?"

"Is he cute?"

From the corner of her eye Dani watched Toni slide his phone in his pocket and walk back down the hall toward Marcello's room. He looked pale and his broad shoulders slumped with fatigue. He fought a yawn and rubbed at his jawline, disturbing his perfectly lined beard.

His long legs carried him gracefully and his muscular thighs stretched at the fabric as he walked back and disappeared through the hospital room door. She recalled that he had to have his suits customized to fit his length. He'd need a custom bed, she thought, briefly recalling his naked form tangled in white sheets.

"Are you still there?"

"Sorry, yes."

"Well? Is he?"

Suddenly the door to the room opened and Toni jerked his head toward the inside. His wide smile touched the light in his eyes. *He's beautiful*, she thought. Maybe too beautiful for a woman like her.

"Umm…he's okay. Look I have to go, I think Marcello is awake. I'll see you later."

"I hope so, but I'm leaving for hair and makeup after lunch. The Chanel show is at 7 p.m., Danica. Wear something fabulous. If I don't see you before then I'll leave your pass on the table."

"Okay. I love—" She heard the click and sighed, then walked back to Marcello's room.

Marcello's eyes were slits under bushy white brows and his voice was more gravelly than usual, but the grip the old man had on Toni's hand was strong. He'll be okay, Toni thought-wished.

"Do you remember what happened?" Toni half whispered, careful not to wake Sophia.

Marcello nodded, gesturing for water, which Toni poured quickly and handed to him. "The restaurant," Marcello said after a few sips from his paper cup. "What happened?"

"We took care of it, but I don't think you should worry about this now."

"Who cooked?" Marcello barked, color coming back to his cheeks.

"Gianni walked out, so your old friend Danica stepped in."

Marcello smiled like a proud father. "How was she?"

"She's a remarkable chef. A bit stubborn. Too precise when it comes to plating. Obviously the dishes had an American twist to them, but overall it was successful."

"Wow, I feel like I just got graded by a substitute teacher," Dani said behind him, flashing Toni a dark look. "Marcello," Dani whispered with tears in her eyes. "I'm so glad you're awake."

Toni stepped back as Dani and Marcello embraced and Toni caught a tear in Marcello's eye, as well. Because he had no children of his own, Marcello had spoiled Toni rotten. He had the feeling he'd done the same to Dani too.

"Let me see your hands," Marcello asked Dani. Marcello always said burns were his badges. A real chef had scars. Marcello inspected the marks on her hands, then pulled her fingers to his lips for a fatherly kiss. "Now, tell me, what did you make last night?"

Letting them catch up, Toni sat down and put a hand on his sleeping daughter. He looked forward to the day they could talk like Marcello and Dani were, instead of this constant push-pull of rules and values.

"Toni thought the Nebbiolo was the best choice for the dish," Toni overheard Dani say, "but I thought the Sangiovese was a better choice."

"The Nebbiolo was a 2010 from Asti, Marcello. Perfectly balanced. They loved the wine."

Dani whipped around as if she was surprised he was listening. "Sure, it was a nice wine, but it was so rich it overpowered the shiitake mushrooms."

"It was perfect with the spiced lamb, Danica."

"I wouldn't call it perfect. It was too full-bodied."

"Since when is a full body a bad thing?"

Her head whipped around again and he suppressed a teasing smile. He shouldn't have said that but it just came out.

Dani's gaze was steady on his, probably debating if he meant what she knew he meant. Her lids narrowed slightly as she mentally debated a response. She wore her temper on her face. It was adorable, Toni thought. He held his breath at her reaction, but the mood was undercut by a rumbling that turned into loud laughter.

"You two," Marcello sighed. "I can only imagine what it looked like in that kitchen." The old man slapped his thigh and Dani pursed her lips at Toni before giving him her back. "You both have a point, but I would have gone with the Dolcetto. Big enough for the lamb, but light enough to allow the mushrooms their flavor."

Both Dani and Toni opened their mouths then closed them. He smirked at the side-eye she gave him over her shoulder.

He'd meant what he'd said about their meeting feeling like fate. And each time he felt drawn to her; an unfamiliar feeling since his divorce. He shook his head as he recalled the phone conversation he'd had with Ava that morning. On and on about her night out, not one inquiry into Sophia or Marcello until he brought it up.

He couldn't understand how he had fallen so hard for a woman who was clearly selfish and narcissistic. The only explanation was that he had been selfish and narcissistic too. Once Sophia was born, he'd changed, but he still wasn't sure he could trust himself and his feelings when it came to women.

Which made it even more difficult to achieve his ultimate goal of having a stable family for Sophia. Marry a woman who was a good role model for Sophia. Love could be learned, right? It didn't always have to be the tractor pull of desire. That had proven to be a trap.

Dani's full laugh broke his train of thought. She was still wearing her dress from last night, which sparkled in places under the bright lights. He wondered how she managed to still look beautiful after a night on her feet and a few hours of sleep in a hospital room.

"You're staring at her." Sophia uncurled from an awkward fetal position and piled her hair on top of her head.

"I am not," Toni said back, pulling her in for a kiss on her head. Maybe he was.

A nurse and doctor entered the room and shooed them out while they performed an examination.

"He seems good," Dani said to Toni.

"Let's hope the doctor thinks so. I need to get Sophia home. I just want to talk to the doctor first. I can drop you off at your hotel too."

"Thank you." Dani nodded.

"First we need some coffee."

Toni arrived with espresso and pastries just as the doctor came out of the room. The doctor took her glasses off and pulled Toni to the side.

"Your uncle suffered a mild heart attack. We found some calcified arteries around the heart and one of his valves gave out because of it."

"What does that mean?"

"His heart is working overtime. This was a warning."

Toni frowned at the doctor's serious tone. "I understand your uncle is a chef and spends hours on his feet. If he doesn't have surgery to unblock those arteries, he won't be able to continue without the threat of something far worse."

Toni tried to wrap his head around the fact that Marcello may not be able to run the kitchen any longer, or possibly die.

This wasn't good.

"Okay, so what happens now?"

"He needs rest. We are keeping him for a few weeks for observation and depending on how he wants to proceed with treatment, maybe longer. If you need to discuss anything with me please call during my office hours." The doctor turned and entered another room.

Toni's gaze shifted to Dani and Sophia, who both were staring pointedly at him.

"He's okay. But he needs to stay here awhile."

"What about the restaurant?" Sophia asked.

"Nonna can take care of it."

"I mean the other one." Toni looked gravely at Sophia.

Dani turned and looked between the two of them. "What other one?"

They filed back into Marcello's room and Toni grabbed Marcello's hand. "We can postpone the opening. You need to get healthy. With Mamma running Via Carciofo we have no one in the kitchen and—"

"No, I am getting out of this bed. I feel fine."

"That's not the doctor's orders."

"I don't take orders, young man, I give them." Marcello rolled up to sit, then clutched his chest as pain showed on his face.

Dani flew to his side. "Lie back, that's an order. Now. What's going on?"

"We are opening a new farm-to-table experience next week a few miles outside of Milan on our family villa," Toni said.

"It's taken over ten years to build," Marcello continued. "The garden is fully grown and the vineyard is now producing enough for wine making."

"A vineyard?" Dani asked.

"Toni has been growing wine grapes and selling them to wineries for years. We finally got him to start producing wine. They are excellent."

"Let me guess. No menus."

"No menu. And only produce from the farm. The rest is sourced locally."

"Wow. You've been talking about a country restaurant since I've known you."

"That's why I am getting out of this bed."

"Uncle, you could die." The room stilled at Toni's truth.

Dani took Marcello's hand when the old man's bottom lip quivered. "Postpone it. It took ten years, what's a few more weeks?"

"Yes, we'll contact—" Toni started, but Marcello cut him off.

"No! Invitations have been sent. Ryan White sent me a personal email and said he was coming. Ryan White!"

Dani sighed, the food critic for *The Taste* had a blog that could make or break a restaurant.

"Dani can run it," Marcello said into her eyes.

"What? No, I can't…"

"You handled it last night. Toni said you were amazing."

Dani glanced at Toni, whose gaze hit the floor.

"I'm not going to be here that long."

"You have an open-ended ticket."

"Because my mother doesn't know where she is going

after this. I'm not you..." Dani took a deep breath and said it aloud. "I'm a ghost chef."

"You are more than that."

"No, I'm not."

"I agree with Dani. She shouldn't do this," Toni said behind her.

Dani's mouth dropped. What the hell? Shouldn't he be begging her to do this?

"We invited a ton of press," Toni said to Marcello, avoiding Dani's eyes. "I'm not sure having her there would attract the type of press we want."

"Antonio Lorenzetti you are out of line!"

"Please, sir. I mean no disrespect, but we have sunk too much time and money to have negative press attached to this project from the start."

Dani rose from Marcello's side. "Excuse me? But what the hell are you talking about? I ran a two-Michelin-star kitchen!"

Toni's mouth was a thin line. He pulled out his phone and held up a familiar blog. When the Chef Can't Cut It splashed across the page of *The Taste*. She began to shake before she grabbed his phone and scrolled.

Sous-chef Danica Nilsson had a meltdown...
Rumored lovers...
Andre taught her everything he knows. She was talented but missed the nuances of certain dishes. It didn't phase Andre, who delivered a fantastic chef's special of veal shank.

That was *her* chef's special!

Hate for Andre and hurt from Toni made her legs weak. She handed the phone back to him and fell into a seat. "He's right. You can't have me there," she said quietly, handing the phone to Marcello.

"I don't have my glasses," he said, waving the phone away.

"It's not good, Marcello," Toni said.

"You be quiet," he barked at Toni. Sophia chuckled, then was silenced by a look from her father.

"Dani. I don't care what that blog says. I need your help." His eyes slid to Toni. "We need your help."

Toni shook his head, his gaze locking with Dani's.

# *Chapter 8*

It was a little after ten in the morning when Dani arrived at her hotel. She tossed her purse on the table, announced her presence for which she got no response, then stripped off her clothes, wishing she could erase the night.

Toni had said she would be bad press. It took everything she had not to lash out or, God forbid, cry. Instead, she declined Marcello's offer, kissed her mentor and Sophia, then walked out and hailed a taxi to the hotel, trying to forget the way Toni looked at her.

Because he was right. That blog had shredded the little reputation she'd had and made Andre look like a saint for allowing her to work with him. No one deserved that type of press at a restaurant opening. She was embarrassed and took solace knowing she probably wouldn't see Toni again.

Her shower was heaven and the power nap she took made her feel refreshed enough to actually look forward to her mother's Chanel show later that night. Dani found her laminated event pass on the table, along with a note.

Danica, here is your pass. Show this at the door. The show starts at 7. I tried to get you something Chanel to wear but there was no time. I hope you brought something fabulous.

Dani rolled her eyes, deciding not to be annoyed by the Chanel comment. Chanel didn't have her size, as her mother well knew. But Dani did have something fabulous and she hurried to her suitcase and pulled out the black Zac Posen tea-length evening dress to air it out. It was beautiful. Black satin with long sleeves and a high neck. Dani fingered the sleek fabric as she adjusted it on a hanger. She had an idea to pull her hair back in a wet look like in those Robert Palmer videos, or like Trinity in *The Matrix*. She turned the dress around to inspect it and lost her breath. A large discoloration was splattered across the back.

"You have got to be kidding me." After a thorough inspection of the stain and her suitcase, she found an exploded bottle of benzoyl peroxide face cleanser laying waste to several of her clothes. She wanted to scream. Or die. Or both. The dress she wore to Marcello's restaurant lay in a plastic bag and smelled like food and body odor. The Posen was the only other dress she had brought...and it had been expensive.

She slumped on the couch. If this were *Pretty Woman* she could call downstairs and have someone find her a suitable dress, except she wasn't Julia Roberts, nor a size four. Her gaze landed on the clock. Her idea to relax and order room service before the show just got shot out of the water. She picked up the phone and dialed the concierge, who was not only appalled by her plight, but ready to drop his post at the hotel and go shopping with her. David, her new bestie, practically pulled her by the elbow to Via Montenapoleone. Dani hadn't done much designer shopping as a poor young sous-chef, but the Quadrilatero d'Oro or "rectangle of gold" was famous for its haute couture and Montenapoleone was one of its most famous streets.

They passed by Dior, Louis Vuitton and Prada before slowing in front of a posh-looking boutique. The glass exterior revealed well-dressed mannequins, racks of sparkling pieces along the back wall and a staircase to a second floor of shoes.

David embraced a tall man in an impeccable suit who

was smoking outside. He threw the lit bud to the concrete when he saw Dani.

"Miss Nilsson. Welcome. Welcome! David said you have an emergency. I'm Fredrick, at your service. *Sei davvero bravo!*" Fredrick yelled to David, who took off before Dani knew what was happening.

"Um, hello, I need—"

"A dress. I know. I have several already racked. Come, come."

"But…" How did she put this. "I kinda just wanted to walk around a bit and see if anything strikes me."

Fredrick looked her up and down. "Madonna, with all do respect. Many don't carry larger sizes. I, however, do. And these dresses are *magnifico*. You will look incredible, I can already tell."

Flattered, Dani followed Fredrick inside, then frowned when he locked the door behind them.

"You usually lock the door?"

"We aren't usually open during lunchtime, but I made an exception for David. Fashion emergencies are the best kind. Now—" Fredrick grabbed the sparkly dress rack and wheeled it her way. He held up a strapless gold lamé mermaid dress. "Let's get started."

An hour later she had gotten through only half the rack.

She stood in front of a full-length mirror in an eggplant-colored sleeveless cocktail dress with a plunging halter neckline and no back.

"Yes!" Fredrick shouted.

"No," Dani said back.

"Let your hair down," commanded the shopkeeper. She had put it up for the last dress, now it was coming down again. She remembered why she barely shopped, it was exhausting. Curling waves hit her shoulders. "Yes!"

"I'm naked, Fredrick."

"We'll put gold shimmer lotion on your skin…" He clapped his hands.

She shook her head and tugged on the neckline, which was showing too much side boob. "My breasts are out!"

"Of course. That's the style. They look fabulous! If I had a bosom like this I would show them to the world. The world must see this bosom."

Dani looked at herself. She could just see herself tripping and executing a Janet Jackson nip slip. Suddenly she envisioned Toni looking at her, his hand sliding inside the fabric to her naked breast. This was a "fuck me" dress, and after what happened that morning, that was never happening again. You know what else was never happening? Letting a man dictate her career. She needed to talk to Marcello again.

"I don't think so, Fredrick. Next dress. We have to hurry, I have one more stop to make."

Finally, she found a dress, received a much-needed pep talk from Marcello at the hospital, and got ready at the hotel, making it to the show just in time. The venue was buzzing with editors, photographers, bloggers and celebrities; all were talking one second and posing for a selfie the next. Dani flashed her pass and took her seat smack in the middle of the auditorium and only three rows from the stage. She ran a hand over her loose curling hair and adjusted her dress, a purple satin halter with a plunging neckline and gold heels. Fredrick had her so gassed she fell in love with the dress, but now, surrounded by the glitterati, she felt out of place.

The back of Anna Wintour's famous bob was down and to the left, while André Leon Talley's fur-clad shoulders were blocking everyone behind him to her right. For a second the lights dimmed and camera phone flashes burst through the dark like exploding stars. Then the stage exploded in music and a warm glow as young Amazon women began to prance down the runway like Thoroughbreds.

Dani couldn't get over how sleek the models were. No Photoshop or flattering camera angles. These women were slim goddesses. A woman in front of her held her camera in the air for video as a stunning blonde emerged in a gown. The crowd roared and chatter around her was peppered with "she looks great" and "she's still got it." Dani couldn't place the model, but in seconds it didn't matter. The music changed and her mother appeared on the stage.

Francesca's slower, stately walk created elegant movement in the gold taffeta and leather-corseted gown she wore. Her skin glistened with baby oil and she wore a pink wig piled high on her head. Marie Antoinette meets Grace Jones?

"Damn, I hope I look like that when I'm old," someone whispered.

"You wished you looked like that now," another said. "Is she really fifty?"

André Leon Talley threw a props snap in the air.

Her mother walked amid cheers and applause several times during the show, and by the end, Dani felt pride for her mother. They didn't always see eye to eye, and Francesca would never win a Mother of the Year award, but her mother never gave up on her dreams or her career, and for that she was inspiring. Dani had a dream of running her own kitchen and she'd made a decision earlier that day that would get her closer to that dream. Marcello had always told her that the best chefs pushed the limits. So that was what she was going to do.

Dani made her way backstage, weaving between tripods and news anchors praying the side of her face wasn't showing up in the background of interviews and photos.

Models were half-naked, changing anywhere they could find a spot and vloggers were talking into their phones. She found her mother still in the last outfit she walked in, surrounded by industry people.

Dani recognized an older and slimmer Roberto, her mother's make-up artist and dearest friend, buzzing silently around her mother with makeup brushes. A pat of powder here, a spritz there. Feeling like an eight-year-old again, Dani turned back toward the throng of people with the intention of texting her mother and heading back to their hotel.

"Daaanicaaa!" Roberto came toward her with his arms stretched wide. His hug was hot and sweaty, but welcome. It had been a long time. "Let me look at you!" He gave her a dramatic once-over. *"Belissima."*

Dani smiled a thank-you and tried to hide how uncomfortable she felt standing in the throng of size zeros.

"She did well tonight, Right?" Dani said.

"Oh! It was like 1985 all over again. She is fierce on that stage, like a panther." Roberto bared his teeth and clawed the air. Dani smothered a laugh.

"Well, she looks busy with press. Can you tell her I'm heading back to the hotel? And that I'm really proud of her?"

"No. No. No. Mommy dearest said you have to come to the after party." He handed her another pass. "Then you can tell her how proud you are yourself. *Addio, bella.*" He clapped his hands and kissed her cheek before disappearing through the crowd.

After party? The address on the card said the Armani Ristorante. There were three restaurants Dani loved to visit when she was in Milan and the Armani was one of them. She wondered if Martin still managed the place and felt her heart flutter. Martin had been a line cook and her first real boyfriend. She thought about their goodbye kiss years ago and then wondered if a taxi would be the quickest way there.

Where the hell was she? Toni prowled round the bar at the Armani Ritsorante and downed his second complimentary champagne. Sliding by a server, he switched out his empty flute with a full one and took another swig.

Ava's call took him by surprise. She wanted to talk... about what? And why here in this crowded space? He plucked a few crudités from the buffet table and blew out a frustrated breath. She had a way of manipulating him that he didn't see coming until after the fact, like tonight. He'd agreed only to talk, the next thing you knew he was arranging a babysitter for Sophia and going to the show. Watching her walk the show had brought back memories, good and bad. As did the Armani. Maybe that's why he was in a mood. The back couches were where they had gotten engaged.

A woman approached with a smile and an inviting gaze that ran down his body. He nodded politely, uninterested but conscious of offending the lady, and turned away. Dark eyes, generous hips and a floral tattoo had been haunting him all day. As did the look on her face when he protested her working at the restaurant. It wasn't his finest moment and all he could think of was begging her forgiveness, then making passionate love to her.

Toni chatted with the few people he knew by association, then sank into a couch in the back corner. He texted Sophia, who was at home with a babysitter, and smiled at the poo emoji she sent him. Because of the other night, he had vetoed her plans to go to the movies with her friends. They had yet to have their family talk, but the person he really needed to talk to was Ava. She needed a reminder that family was the most important thing in life. Not this charade, he thought, scanning the room of drunk fashionable people.

Speaking of which, he spied his ex-wife making her way through the crowd toward him. Her silver dress was as thin as tissue paper and hugged the slender contours of her body. Only a dead man would be able to look way, and yet the vision in front of him was blurred by years of painful baggage. He rose when she reached him and executed kisses on both of her cheeks. He was taken aback when her mouth slid to the corner of his on the last kiss.

Ava sat on the leather chair across from him and they exchanged pleasantries, with him congratulating her on the show, and her going into detail of the backstage antics. He sipped his champagne and nodded at the fluctuations of her voice. She hadn't mentioned leaving Sophia home alone, or the text he had sent, to which she had never replied. As usual, she hadn't inquired into his life, something he hadn't realized until after they'd married.

As she spoke, his gaze shifted as another barrage of people entered the bar and he glimpsed a shining cascade of black curly hair moving tentatively through the throng. Danica? She wore a purple satin dress that showed lots of skin and hugged her soft womanly curves. The tattoo on her arm looked like a wild accessory. He blinked as she wet her red lips and leaned over the bar to speak to the bartender.

"Are you listening to me?" Ava frowned.

Toni shifted his gaze back to his ex. He hadn't been, but answered with a confident, "Of course."

"Well, would you like to?"

Oh God, what was she saying? "I don't know…" *What you are talking about?*

"I think family dinners on Sunday would be nice for Sophia."

"Oh! I mean...you're right I think I can make it work."

He frowned as she stood and moved to sit next to him. "And then we can work on us too."

Suddenly the air in the space got thin. He took a gulp of champagne as she slid a hand on his thigh. He willed himself to relax. Ava could smell fear. And rejecting the mother of his daughter needed to be done with more finesse than a polite grin. He knew Ava, and as beautiful as she was, she was insecure. If she felt the tiniest bit rejected, she would try to hurt him by using Sophia.

He recalled how he went to court to stop her from taking Sophia to another country during their divorce. When he found out she still planned to leave, he promised her a generous monthly allowance if she stayed. He was still paying it.

Toni set down his glass and twisted toward her, taking her hand from his thigh and enclosing it in his.

"Ava, for Sophia's sake," he said as she leaned in and he dodged a kiss, "let's take this slow. We have to be sure this is what we want, no?" She tipped her face to his, her eyes glassy and unfocused. He inwardly sighed, suspecting she was on something.

"You want to be a family. So do I."

"We are a family. But you and I have history."

"History is good." Her other hand reached for his groin and he caught it and brought it to his lips.

"We need to know each other again. Let's start with the dinners," he pleaded.

"Don't you want me?" She pouted.

"You're very beautiful, Ava. Always." He was relieved at her smile. And he hoped this notion was a product of whatever drug she took, and that it would wear off along with the effects.

He let his guard down, satisfied that he had wriggled

out of a bad situation, when she grabbed the back of his head and crushed her lips against his. His first instinct was to struggle, but that wouldn't go over well. He leaned into the kiss, ran his hands over her arms and tangled his fingers in her hair, then gently cupped her jaw and pulled his lips from hers.

Ava gazed at him with a triumphant smile. He gazed back under lowered lids, hoping his eyes didn't reveal how annoyed he was. He pulled back farther and looked over Ava's head, right into Dani's eyes.

# Chapter 9

The severe beige, white and black decor of the Armani Ristorante was the perfect playground for Chanel's partygoers clad in sky-high heels, glossy hair and jewel-toned lips. Inquiring about Martin at the bar, Dani held her breath when she saw a man with dark hair and swarthy skin come out from a back room and make his way toward the bar. Dani caught Martin's attention with a small wave and his face lit up as he came around the bar to stand in front of her.

"Wow. It's been too long." He leaned over so his Spanish-Italian accent was thick in her ear, cutting through the music. "Nice dress." Martin was even more handsome than Dani remembered and the way his gaze dipped into her cleavage made her blush gratefully.

His flirty smile was infectious. She smiled back, feeling at ease suddenly. He hadn't changed, which was nice considering that she was still feeling out of place in the throng of the fashion obsessed. She wasn't used to showing this much skin, even though every dress that walked by was held together by a thin strap or a barely there chain. She shook her hair over her shoulders for a little cover, but Martin swiped one side away with his hand before suggesting they grab a lounge chair to catch up.

Dani and Martin dodged servers in pastel wigs, some stopping him for a quick issue. She remembered when they had both been poor, ambitious cooks taken under Marcello's wing. Now he was the manager of a Michelin-starred restaurant. And she was…she didn't want to think about it anymore.

Toni's look when he showed her the blog said it all. His

eyes had accused her of being a fake. Meanwhile, he'd kissed her in the kitchen like a man who'd been trapped in the desert. He hadn't been calling her fake then, had he? *That kiss.* Martin caught up to her and steered her toward the back of the room, his gaze running over her bare shoulders.

Martin was going to help her forget about that kiss.

Dani scanned the lounge area and did a double take when she saw Toni kissing a lithe blonde.

"Excuse us," she said, quickly turning away. Dani sighed. Would she ever get away from this man? "Let's have a seat over here, Martin." Martin followed closely behind, then stopped.

"Toni! And Ava! You two are back together?" Dani whipped around at Martin's declaration. Did Toni know everyone in this town?

Toni stood and grasped Martin's hand like an old friend. Dani noted that the blonde didn't turn around, taking the opportunity to apply more lipstick.

"You should come find me, Toni," Martin said. "I spoke to Anton, who spoke to Destin, who said I need to speak to you—" Martin poked Toni playfully "—about the Deschamps wine."

"I was coming to you, Martin. Of course we want Deschamps here." Toni slid his gaze to Dani and she responded by putting her hands on her hips. "But you are busy right now," Toni said, gesturing toward her with a flick of his chin, "so I'll find you tomorrow afternoon."

"I'm holding you to that." Martin turned to Dani. "Dani, come meet Toni."

Dani didn't move. "We've met. *Buona sera*, Toni."

"*Buona sera*, Chef. You look lovely," Toni said, sliding his hands in his pockets.

Dani raised a brow. Chef? Was that a barb?

Martins gaze darted between the two of them. "You know each other? How?"

"Marcello."

They said simultaneously.

"Ahh yes!" Martin continued. "Dani and I knew each other when she was his sous-chef. I heard he was in the hospital. How is he doing?"

"He's well. I saw him this morning…" Toni said.

"He's better. I saw him this afternoon…" Dani said.

They both started talking and then stopped, silently competing.

Toni cleared his throat and spoke to Dani. "This is my ex-wife, Ava." Ava finally twisted around to give Dani a once-over and a half smile that didn't reach her eyes. Dani looked away, doing her best not to feel self-conscious. She recognized Ava as one of the models that walked in the show and suddenly her designer dress felt like a potato sack. Of course Toni's ex was a model. It was par for the course, right? Hot guy, hot girl. The building blocks of every perfect match. Dani cringed inside.

"Would you like to join us?" Toni suggested, looking out the side of his eye at Dani.

"No!" Ava shouted. "I mean…they seem to have some catching up to do, as do we, darling."

Dani suppressed an eye roll. "We do have some catching up to do, but *grazie*. There is room over here, Martin. *Buona sera*, Toni. Ava."

Martin and Dani settled in the open seating and jumped right into old times. Martin was as funny and engaging as she had remembered, but Dani struggled to focus on the gorgeous man that was sitting in front of her. Instead her gaze drifted repeatedly to the couple about ten feet behind him.

Dani watched Ava lean toward Toni suggestively, then

saw Toni scoot back a little. If she didn't know better, she'd say he was dodging her advances.

"And then I met Vivian." Dani's gaze slid back to Martin.

"Who is Vivian?"

"My wife."

Dani's smile flickered. Martin wore no ring and she had allowed herself to hope that he might be single. But who was she kidding? Not everyone was as pathetic as she was when it came to relationships.

"That's great. Sounds like you have it all together."

"What about you? I heard you were no longer working with Andre?"

Dani balked. "How did you hear that?"

"We are a small community, Dani. You know that."

Oh God. He'd read the blog, of course he did. "Umm... I'm exploring my options right now."

Saying it aloud to Martin made her feel like a failure, not just in her career, but in life. She saw him frown and lean in to ask more questions but over his shoulder she glimpsed her mother taking selfies with fans. She abruptly stood. "I'm sorry to cut this short, but there is my mother. Come say hi. She'd love to see you."

Dani quickly quit the couch, staring straight ahead to avoid making eye contact with Toni. She made it to the bar when she felt a hand on her arm. Whipping around, her gaze dropped to the hand, then lifted to the serious look in Toni's eyes.

"We need to talk."

"No we don't." Dani tugged her arm back and he gently released her. Her eyes flashed and he found himself intrigued by how naturally beautiful she looked in just lipstick and mascara.

"I want to apologize. It wasn't personal."

"Saying I would bring negative press is personal." She angrily flipped the heavy tresses of her hair to one shoulder exposing the plunging neckline and an expanse of skin that looked like silk.

Toni sighed. "You have to understand how much my family and I have riding on this venture. Ten years of investment is a lot of money. We won't even begin to recoup some in the first few years."

Someone shifted at the bar, allowing Toni to slip in beside Dani. Holding up two fingers, he signaled the bartender and called out something by name.

"Noted, Toni. So whom have you secured to helm your investment until Marcello takes over?"

"We spoke on the phone a few hours ago. I've suggested a few people, but Marcello has been uncooperative."

"Meaning he didn't like your choices."

Toni smiled sheepishly. "No. He didn't." They paused when two glasses of red wine appeared on the bar. "But he assured me he knows someone who will do it. He just hasn't told me who."

Toni slid a glass toward Dani and with a light swish, brought it to her nose. Toni did the same.

"Maybe he's avoiding telling you because you'll object and call them negative."

"I never said *you* were negative."

Toni watched Dani take a sip, and took his own.

"Mmm. That's very nice. What is it?"

"It's the Dolcetto Marcello was talking about." He liked her chuckle and his gaze focused on her lips when she took another sip.

She nodded slowly. "He was right. I'll have to remember this wine when I head to the villa next week. I'm staying with your mother, I believe."

Her challenging gaze caught his over the rim of her

glass. Marcello had refused to tell him who his choice was and now he knew why. His reservations still stood, but he no longer had the urge to fight her. If anything, he admitted that he was happy to know he would see her again. Toni lowered his head as if thinking, then flicked his gaze to hers. "Does it feel good to thwart me?"

"Yes. It does." She smiled.

Toni couldn't help the slow smile that spread across his face. He held up his glass and motioned for her to do the same.

"A toast to our new chef."

"Temporary chef," Dani corrected.

"What are we toasting?" Ava appeared with her hands on her hips, staring daggers at Dani. Toni felt his stomach twist. Ava was unpredictable when it came to other women.

"Dani is going to be our new chef at the villa."

Ava cocked her hip and didn't smile. "Ohhh, you're the one that took over the other night? Sophia mentioned a 'Danny.' I thought you were a man."

"No, just me."

Ava raised an eyebrow and pursed her lips, giving Dani a deliberate once-over—intimidation tactics that Toni had seen before. He had to get Ava away before she insulted Dani outright.

"It must be hard to be around all of that food, no?" Ava said with deliberate disdain.

"Ava," Toni warned. Her insinuation was subtle, but direct. Dani straightened her back and glared at Ava, but refused to engage by taking a sip of her wine.

A commanding voice came from the side.

"Well, if you ate anything, Ava, you'd know that my daughter is one of the best chefs in New York. Speaking of, Ava, have you gained a little weight?" Toni watched in awe as Francesca Watts gracefully sidled next to Dani and kissed her on both cheeks.

Ava shrank. Dani suppressed a smile. And Toni couldn't stop blinking. Daughter? His gaze darted between the two. He saw it then. The eyes and the high cheekbones were the same.

"Mother, this is Toni. I told you about him."

"Oh my." Francesca leaned in. "So you're the young man who kidnapped my daughter last night." She held out her fingers, which Toni brought to his lips. When he looked up, he caught Dani's eye roll, and then her head turned to cover it up.

"Guilty, signora. Your daughter was our savior last night."

The foursome paused briefly when a server presented a plate of mushroom and cheese croquettes.

"Ladies first," Toni offered.

"We have a photo shoot tomorrow," Francesca said just as Ava reached for a bite. A silent look passed between the two models, before Ava lowered her outstretched hand. "And Danica doesn't eat after ten."

Dani's gaze touched his, then hit the floor.

Ava huffed away.

"I'll see you at the shoot tomorrow, darling," Dani's mother called after Ava, who briefly turned with a snarl.

"Are you coming?" Ava snapped at Toni.

*"In un minuto,"* Toni nodded, relieved when Ava sat with a group at a table.

"Odd girl," Francesca said.

"Mother," Dani warned. "That's Toni's ex-wife."

Toni almost chuckled at the questioning look on Francesca's face. It reminded him of how his own mother had looked the day he'd announced they were engaged.

"Well, I can't talk. You haven't lived your life if you haven't made a dozen mistakes."

"Oh my God, Mother."

Toni laughed. "It's all right. I find the frankness refreshing."

Francesca winked and touched Toni's arm in apology. "Forgive my American charm. And how is Marcello? The poor dear. I sent flowers to the hospital, the least I could do for taking care of Dani while I worked all those years. He was like a second father."

"Or a first father, since Dad had gone back to Sweden."

"Oh, Danica." Francesca frowned. "Your father is a creative soul." Then she turned to Toni "They're hard to pin down, which makes then so exciting I guess."

"You should visit Marcello," Danica admonished, giving him the impression they'd spoken of the subject before.

"And if I wrap early tomorrow I will. Case closed." She turned to Toni. "Now tell me about this restaurant that will be taking up my daughter's time."

"Speaking of time," Dani interrupted, "we should go. You need your rest."

"You go. Toni and I are going to have one more drink." Mother and daughter stared each other down for a moment before Dani's gaze shifted to Toni's.

After the loaded moment passed, Dani set her empty glass on the bar. "Good night, then." With a bland smile, Dani quickly moved through the bar and quit the hotel. Toni watched, fighting the urge to go after her.

When his attention came back to Francesca, she was staring at him with a half-cocked smile and an outstretched glass of whiskey. "Now, you and I have some business to discuss."

Toni froze as she pinned him with her heavily lashed gaze. *This can't be good.*

\* \* \*

"Who does that woman think she is?" Ava jammed the keys into the lock of her front door and stomped inside. It was after midnight, and Ava had griped about Dani's mother the entire ride home. Toni lifted his gaze to the dark second-story window of Sophia's bedroom, and then he crossed the threshold and softly closed the door behind him.

The neighbor's daughter appeared in the foyer with her things, waiting for her payment. Toni hesitated a second to see if Ava would reappear, then gave the poor girl a wad of bills. He found Ava barefoot in the kitchen with a bottle of wine in her hand banging through the cupboards.

"Shhh! Sophia's asleep." He frowned at her erratic behavior. "What are you looking for?"

"The opener."

"You're opening a bottle now? It's after midnight and you have a shoot tomorrow."

She twisted the corkscrew into the top, then tugged it out. "You sound like my mother. I just need one more drink to put me to sleep. And you, my love, are gonna have one with me."

He ignored the pet name. Toni didn't want another drink; he wanted to run screaming. Toni frowned as Ava poured them both a glass. "Did you check on Sophia?"

"No," she simply said.

Toni closed his eyes in frustration, then kicked off his shoes and quietly climbed the stairs. He softly opened his daughter's bedroom door and smiled at the chaos her sheets had gone through since she was a toddler. He headed back downstairs and found Ava lounging in the living room, her glass of wine to her lips.

"She's asleep," Toni said. Another glass was waiting on the coffee table. "I'm going to head out."

"Your drink!" she called after him.

"You drink it, Ava. I'm tired."

Toni barely opened the front door when Ava shoved herself against it, blocking his way out.

"What the hell are you doing?"

"Don't you ever think about us?" The sultry tone in her voice made alarm bells go off in his head.

"Not for a long time."

"Well, what if I told you I still loved you?"

"I'd say, what about your new boyfriend?"

"We broke up." He could have predicted that.

"I see."

She slid her body against his then and pursed her lips on his mouth. Startled, he gently closed his hands around her shoulders and peeled her body from his, and then he slowly pulled his head back and gazed into her eyes. Her cherry-red lips were soft and her small breasts teased his chest. There should have been a spark or a flutter of something he felt for her long ago. Nothing. He felt nothing. And by the darkening of her eyes, she suspected as much.

"Are you in love with that chef?"

Toni balked. "Why would you say that."

"Sophia can't stop talking about her and you couldn't leave her side all night!"

"That is ridiculous. I owe her a debt. I told you what she did for us."

"Then what is it? I heard you've been seeing that teacher at school. Is it true?"

"I saw her a few times," he said with a heavy sigh.

Ava jerked back. "Think about Sophia!" Toni didn't like rising to the anger in a woman's voice, but Ava's shrill tone always sent him over the edge.

"She is all I think about. Are you thinking about her when you are out all night with new boyfriends every six weeks?" he snapped, then regretted it instantly.

Ava burst into tears and Toni wanted to hit something.

"How did we get here?" she said in between sobs. Toni worried Sophia would come down and see her mother crying. He grabbed Ava and hugged her close.

"Please, let's talk about this when you aren't a little drunk. We are doing well raising our daughter, I don't want to ruin it."

"We could be a family again," she half whispered.

Could they? Would that be best for Sophia? Ava's glassy gaze pleaded with him, making him feel like a bad guy. He wasn't the one who was coming home drunk when Sophia was a baby. He wasn't the one who cheated.

The air between them got thinner. If she could finally change, could there be a chance?

# *Chapter 10*

The Naviglio Grande canal at night always took Dani's breath away. Romantically lit by dim streetlights, the oldest canal in Milan attracted its share of tourists, but late night boasted more locals enjoying live music and an array of food specialties. She ignored most of the soliciting from the restaurants and shopkeepers as she strolled along the canal.

Tables overlooking the water were full of family-style dishes, carafes of wine and rounds of group laughter. Charming boutiques sold an array of goods and live music filled the air.

She had her heart set on traditional Milanese cuisine. A little shellfish, maybe some veal. The perfect after 10 p.m. meal. Maybe she would snap a picture and send it to her mother. Dani rolled her eyes as she recalled the embarrassment of her mother's declaration. It had been years since Dani had followed that suggestion by her mother's dietitian.

Because it was a load of crap. Maybe it worked for nine-to-fivers, but Dani never ate while she was working—there was no time. Family meal for the restaurant she used to work in was at 4 p.m., which meant from 6 p.m. to 2 a.m., normal dinner service and clean-up hours, she was lucky to get a coffee in her system.

Those were the days that reinforced how disappointed her mother was to have a plus-size daughter. Her mother still hadn't gotten over it.

Would Francesca be asleep by now? Or would she have seduced Toni back to her hotel room? Dani thought her mother had grown out of that whole younger men phase and moved on to aging billionaires, but she could see her mother making an exception for Toni. Why else would she stay at the party?

His suit had been tailored to perfection, emphasizing his long legs and broad shoulders. She remembered his body: tall and lean, similar to a swimmer. Not overly muscular, but strong. She felt a quiver as she remembered when he lifted her off her feet. Call it a litmus test of sorts, but she liked to know that if she fell unconscious in a burning building that her man could carry her out. She chuckled to herself, imagining him carrying her limp naked body, and then she admonished herself for entertaining Toni as her man at all.

The guy didn't want her help, which was an insult to her and her cooking. That afternoon, when she had popped into the hospital to see Marcello, she agreed to do the job, but only if Toni was absent. Her mentor hadn't been happy about that contingency, but he promised her. No Toni. She didn't need the burden of sexual attraction.

And dear God, she thought looking at the moon, please don't let Toni end up being her stepfather.

"Beautiful Madonna, please!" called an older man from a narrow restaurant with tables outside. "You must try the risotto. You will think you are eating from God's own table." The man held his hands out in a dramatic plea, but she continued on the busy path with a smile and a small shake of her head.

After a few more minutes of walking, a small white-haired man with a tanned face stood proudly in front of Il Cantinori.

"*Bella*, if you are looking for the best meal in Milan you have come to the right place." She almost rolled her eyes at the boasting, but since she had been there before, she knew it was almost true. Il Cantinori was famous among locals.

No website, no phone number, just a family run place for generations.

Dani smiled and practiced her Italian. *"Quindi hai un tavolo per me?"*

*"Magnifico.* The best table in the house for the signora."

The old man turned toward the restaurant front with a shout, and a strong teen came flying out with a small bistro table. Dani was startled that the teen was working this late, but then reminded herself that while he was surely in school, working hard for the family was normal. He produced a white cloth from under his arm and draped it smoothly over the metal top. Then another boy set down a bottle of water and a small glass.

The old man stood behind a chair he placed facing the canal, helped her sit, then handed her a giant menu. To his surprise she placed the menu down and began to order.

"A carafe of the house red wine. The house wine is from a family vineyard if I remember correctly. And is your wife cooking tonight?"

"Signora has been here before." He winked and bowed. "I am Piero. And my wife is always cooking. I am not even allowed in the kitchen."

"Then I'll have the *pappardelle* pasta in wild mushroom sauce, the veal shanks, the scaloppine and prosciutto in the lemon and parsley sauce, the balsamic tomatoes, and the peppers with aged parmesan, all brought out together please."

He kissed the air. "The most excellent choices, signora."

When Piero stepped away, Dani slipped her feet from her heels and watched the cargo boats float by. One of the boys brought her carafe and she sipped the fruity wine from a small crystal tumbler that she decided to find and purchase before traveling home.

Home. Where the heart is? Not in her case.

Her phone buzzed. She expected to see a text from her mother, instead it was a call from Nicole, whom she hadn't spoken to in months. Dani answered.

"Girl, I need to talk to you so badly but my phone is about to die. Give me the two-minute Brazil scoop!"

"The only scoop here is that I'm still really, really pregnant, which is stupid because it's too hot to be pregnant."

Danica laughed, knowing that her friend was just being dramatic. Nicole loved being pregnant, and her husband took an enormous amount of pleasure caring for his pregnant wife. Nicole sighed as if she was relieved to sit down.

"How is Milan?"

"How did you know?"

"Destin and Toni are on the phone right now. He mentioned something about you no longer working at the restaurant."

"Wait, Destin is gossiping with Toni right now?"

"Well…they are talking about soccer or whatever. But it came up. Destin just told me. He's worried about you too." She paused. "Are you okay? Did something happen between you and Andre?"

As quickly as she could, Dani relayed what happened. "…but seriously this call may cut out my battery is red."

"Well, okay, I just wanted to know that you were okay. Nothing matters as long as you're enjoying yourself."

"I am. Remember that restaurant on the canal I met you at years ago when you were working in Milan?"

"Il Canti—"

"—nori. Yeah, I'm stuffing my face. Mother got under my skin tonight. That's a whole other phone call."

"Well, I want to hear about it. Call me when you can. I miss you."

"I miss you too."

Dani wasn't even sure Nicole heard her as her phone

went black. She tossed it on the table and smiled to herself at her friend's concern. It was nice to know you were loved especially when you were across the world. Minutes later, an expensive-looking car sped along the other side of the canal, then stopped on a side street.

Dani's mouth dropped when Toni unfolded from the driver's side and waved in her direction. What the hell? How did he know she was here? Destin! She watched him saunter over the bridge toward her. As he got closer, she noticed his shirt collar was open to the chest and his hair looked rumpled, like he'd just left a woman's bed.

"Umm…ciao," Dani said when Toni tossed his keys on the table and whistled at one of the boys for a chair. Rapidly one brought out a chair, while the other brought another wineglass. And of course, as if on cue, a procession of her meals arrived one after the other.

"You don't eat after ten, huh?"

"Do I look like a woman who doesn't eat after ten?"

He made a display of raising his brows and looking her over. A sly half smile spread across his face as he met her gaze. "I could say something but I'll embarrass both of us."

Dani narrowed her eyes. "I can take it."

"I think you look like a woman who enjoys life's pleasures. Actually, I *know* you are. And that is a good thing."

That was not what she expected. She prayed her heart would stop beating out of her chest.

"What are you doing here?" she asked lightly.

"Destin said you were here. I was watching *calcio* in the piazza in front of the Duomo with Destin on the phone."

*"Calcio?"*

"Erm, 'soccer.'"

"Oh, sounds manly."

"Very manly. *Dio*, this smells *fantastico*. May I?" he asked, gesturing to the spread.

"Sure." *Men*, she thought. *Watch, he is going to eat my whole dinner.*

Toni reached for a little plate and loaded it up with portions from each dish, taking care to select the best cuts, just as she would. Then he held it out for her to take.

"Oh…thank you."

His reach made his open shirt gape. She didn't mean to stare, but she spied the beginnings of his tattoo over his left pectoral. She licked her lips, remembering the champagne taste of that tattoo.

"Staring like that, angel, is dangerous." He fixed himself a plate and groaned at the first bite.

"Well, maybe you should close your shirt, your whole chest is out. And are you drunk?"

"I've been drinking. I'm not drunk." He took a few more bites and kissed his fingers.

"And your chest is out," he added. "You don't see me staring."

She laughed at that. He was rumpled and she reluctantly found it cute. But she couldn't help but get the feeling that something was wrong.

Toni sampled the wine and let out a pleased sound. As if full, he sat back against the chair, for which his body looked too big, and ran a hand through his hair. Dani dabbed at her lips, hoping her lipstick wasn't smeared.

"You're finished?"

"I don't want to eat all of your food."

"Then we'll order more."

"*Si?*"

At Dani's nod, Toni shouted out his order in Italian, to which the old man gave a thumbs-up. She smiled, what may be considered rude in America was almost charming here. Toni poured them both more wine, and an alarming thought came to her.

"Please tell me you didn't sleep with my mother."

Toni's head rose slowly and the look on his face registered pure disbelief. "Where did you get that idea?"

"You and she making eyes at each other? Having one more drink together? Huh?"

Toni laughed, making Dani red with humiliation.

Toni popped a cherry tomato into his mouth. "Do you think she's up for it?"

"Oh, so you want to sleep with my mother?"

"That's irrelevant, do you actually think your mother would seduce me?"

"She's done it in the past."

Toni's eyes popped out. "Do tell."

"You tell!"

"I did not sleep with your mother. In fact, she warned me off you. Told me that you'd had enough of men like me and to keep my hands to myself."

Dani's jaw hit the floor." You're joking."

"I'm not. It was sweet, actually." He paused, picking a bit more at the food. "I didn't tell her that you and I had already gotten to know each other, in the biblical sense."

Dani's mouth turned down at his phrasing. "I hope you aren't fishing for a thank-you."

"No fishing." He paused to top off their wine. "So, you and Andre."

"She told you?" Dani heard her voice crack.

"Not in so many words. But she did tell me that he was just the face of that kitchen, that you earned those Michelin stars."

Dani didn't want to feel pleasure at that statement, but she popped some scaloppine in her mouth and tried to imagine her mother giving Toni a hard time. More food came, and she commended his choices of aged parmesan risotto and fried zucchini. Again he made her a plate first, this time watched as she ate it, then fixed himself one when he was satisfied that she liked it.

"Speaking of work," Dani started. "I told Chef I'd take over the kitchen…as long as you weren't around."

Dani held her breath, waiting for a tantrum. Toni's attempt to spear a mushroom from the *pappardelle* was interrupted by his shocked look. "That's impossible. It's my restaurant."

"I thought it would be best since you had such objections."

"No," he said, leaning in to give her a pointed look. He jabbed the mushroom and sucked it from his fork.

Dani bit the side of her cheek. "Then maybe we should set some ground rules."

"All work and no plays make Dani a dull girl."

"First negative, and now you're calling me dull."

"I'd call you beautiful but you'd hold it against me somehow."

Wide-eyed, Dani stared at his gorgeous face. His gaze dropped to her lips and held. A memory of that mouth trailing down her torso and stopping between her thighs had her brain on stutter and stop. Suddenly an image of him kissing his ex-wife woke her like an ice bath. She blinked rapidly, trying to get a handle on her pulse.

"You're a compulsive flirt."

"I like your hair down."

"This isn't a date."

"No? Two single people?"

"You didn't look single earlier."

His look was pregnant with exasperation. She'd been right, his ex-wife's advances were unwanted. Ignoring her comment he continued.

"Good food. Good wine. You could do worse."

"I've definitely done worse." His half smile was too sexy.

"You're talking about Andre."

"Well, it's never smart to get involved with a colleague. I know better." *And I won't do it again.*

"So do I. I plan on not being *involved* for some time." She frowned, wondering what happened that he was so surly and disheveled.

"That bad?"

"That bad."

"Okay, good. First ground rule, no sex."

Toni paused.

Dani's right brow went up.

"No sex," Toni repeated.

"Second ground rule, what I say goes."

"No."

"I'm chef until Marcello comes back."

"You are responsible for the food. The rest is mine."

"The wines are part of the food."

"No." He didn't even look up from his plate.

"We'll see." She smiled when he looked at her under his lids. Toni shoveled more food on her plate while she continued. "The waitstaff is yours. They'll need training. I was thinking maybe Liam could come out and train them."

He pointed his fork at her as if he was about to say no. "That is a good idea."

She'd take that.

After dinner they walked a bit to digest their food, and were startled when the sun began to rise over the canal bridge.

Dani squinted at the pink-and-gold sky. "My God, what time is it?"

"Must be around five. Look. Over there."

Blues, yellows, purples rose over the canal. They were arrested by the beauty. Before they could turn to leave the bridge, a group of bicycles raced by and Toni held Dani close and out of the way.

It happened then. His hands spread over her back, his lips found hers and they were deep into a kiss. He sucked at her lower lip and she rose on her toes to jam her tongue fully into his mouth. She moaned and greedily clutched at his shoulders. His hands traveled down to her ass and squeezed, then roughly pulled her against him. They both withdrew, breathless. Staring at one another as if unsure that the kiss was real.

"I'm sorry," they said in unison.

"I don't... I can't," Dani started, unable to catch her breath.

"Me, neither," Toni said, his voice filled with sex.

"Good, so that's clear." Dani nodded, masking her desire to claw his clothes off.

"Yes," Toni sighed, gripping the bridge. "Clear."

# Chapter 11

They'd need markers to the restaurant, Toni mused as midafternoon traffic eased. He easily navigated the unmarked country roads that stretched a little more than twenty minutes outside the city limits of Milan toward the villa, but he'd been driving the area since he was a boy.

He tried to see the roads with fresh eyes. Maybe just a sign here and there to assure their guests they were headed in the right direction? He paused, wondering if part of the novelty of what he hoped would be the most sought after food experience in Italy could be actually finding it.

He tabled the thought for after the soft opening, for which the list of attendees was growing enormously. So was his anxiety.

In the seat next to him Dani dozed, her head lulling to the side after only ten minutes on the road. He smiled. Sophia watched a video on her phone in the back seat. Teenagers. What was he going to do when she was older and going on actual dates?

Dani stirred, her face rising briefly, only to drift slowly back to her shoulder. Her hair was in a severe ponytail, making him long for the soft waves he'd seen just a day ago. Sitting with her over red wine and good food had been one of the best dates he'd had in a very, very long time. Even if she was quick to point out it wasn't a date.

When Nicole had sent him to the canal to check on her, he'd taken the charge with no question. Dani had left the party abruptly and he felt he had some explaining to do, maybe even some apologizing, for his ex-wife's behavior. Yet he remembered Dani's cool countenance as Ava threw subtle barbs about her full figure, making him aware that Dani was clearly no stranger to the slights. He glanced at her sleeping form again, taking in her smooth skin and parted lips. He wanted to apologize. He wasn't sure why it mattered, it just did.

"Papà, how much longer?"

"Not long." Glancing in the rearview mirror, her head was bent over her phone. "Do you ever put that phone down?"

"Of course. But I'm doing homework now."

"Texting is not homework."

"I'm reading. But getting texts."

"We had a deal, Sophia. You pass your next test, then you can talk to him."

"It's not him, Papà." Her voice rose.

"It better not be."

"You have a boyfriend?" Dani stirred and twisted toward the back, her brows raising in teasing question.

Toni cringed at Sophia's blush. "No...he's just a friend."

"But you like him." Dani and Sophia smiled at each other like secret conspirators, making him uneasy, like he was seeing behind a pink curtain.

"Well...he's a year older."

"What does he look like?"

"He's tall. With black hair, like really black. And green eyes."

"Sounds handsome."

"He is." Sophia said with an unconscious hair flip.

"No, he isn't," Toni gritted out.

They both peeled into laughter.

"What's so funny?"

"Have you seen him?" Dani asked.

"Yes. He hides behind a tree when I pick Sophia up from school. He's skinny."

"Tall and skinny? Sounds familiar," Dani said with a wink to Sophia he wasn't supposed to see.

"I am not skinny. You can't compare the physique of a boy to that of a man. It's like apples and oranges."

"Oh really?" Dani said with a half smile.

"Really. That boy has no muscle tone. He needs to play a sport. Like *calcio*."

"Papà almost played professionally, so he thinks everyone should play." Sophia sighed.

"And you play beautifully, *cara mia*. I taught her everything she knows."

"Maybe you could teach her friend."

"Over my dead body," he whispered to Dani, who suppressed a smile before turning front.

"What did you say, Papà?"

"I said go back to your homework. We're almost there."

Bright green hills and measures of clear blue sky were peppered with huge stone houses and acres of wildflowers.

"This is stunning." Dani stared out of the window.

"It hasn't changed much in the years my family have lived here. The roads are better, but not by much."

"Tell me about your family. What does your father do?"

"He is in banking, but you won't meet him today. He's—"

"Grandpa is in Brazil with a whole other family," came from the back seat.

"*Cara mia*, read your phone." Toni said into the rearview. Then he turned to Dani's shocked expression.

"My parents are divorced. My father had an affair in Brazil where he traveled frequently for work. I have a half sister who is about six years younger than me."

"What! That's insane. I mean, that must have been really hard on you and your mother."

"It was, but my mother has always been supported by

her own family. She has five other brothers including Marcello. They helped us through."

"How old were you?"

"I was ten when he left."

"That must have been hard. A young boy losing his father."

He only nodded. He'd been devastated.

"I bet you are a better father for it though," she said low. "It makes sense why you are so protective."

Her insight surprised him. Being a good father was the most important thing to him in the world.

"All fathers are bears. Your father was protective, no?"

"No," Dani chuckled. "My parents were never married. And they both traveled so much that I only saw him for short stints at a time. Plus, my father is a Swedish hippie. He doesn't believe in discipline."

"I'm having a hard time seeing your glamorous mother with a Swedish hippie."

"He was a fashion photographer when they met. Now he owns a tattoo parlor in Manhattan." Dani held up her colorful left forearm. "It's an odd pairing, but they do seem to love each other in a strange 'I can't ever live with you' sort of way."

"Do you have siblings?"

"No. You?"

"Just Theresa in Brazil. We're actually quite close. She is a designer and sends gifts to Sophia all the time."

Theresa. The name sounded familiar to Dani. Nicole spoke of a blonde hottie who went out with Destin. "Wait, not the Theresa who dated Destin?"

"They didn't ever date, although she tried to get him into bed numerous times."

"The blonde hottie is your sister?"

Toni laughed. "Yes, and she was heartbroken when your friend Nicole came and stole Destin's heart."

"How does your mother feel about Theresa?"

"My mother tolerates my father but she loves Theresa. We are a strange family, but we've made it work."

"Amen to that," Dani said.

"And on that note. We're here."

Villa Lorenzetti rose centuries old and majestic above them with stone walls covered in vines and wildflowers. A large greenhouse stood off to the right while a newly finished barnlike structure took over acres to the left.

"You grew up here?" Dani stared in awe. Her gaze scanned the greenery and landed on the pond surrounded by ducks several yards away. "It's like a dream."

"I went to a boarding school in the city. When school was out, I was here."

"Luca!" Before Toni could switch off the engine Sophia jumped from the back and ran toward his mother's small beagle mutt, who was running toward the car at full speed. His mother appeared from the side of the house, sliding her feet from her gardening slippers into her heeled shoes. Toni felt a rush of affection for her.

"I should probably warn you now that my mother can be...commanding."

Sophia and his mother embraced, and then she waved Sophia and the dog toward the house. Toni suspected a full meal waited for them.

"Meaning she likes things her way," Dani said.

"Exactly. But she's gentle about it."

"I think I can handle that."

He recalled his meeting of Dani's mother and imagined she could handle it.

Unlike Ava, who met his mother's suggestions and invitations with flat-out refusals. Ava never participated in picking vegetables in the garden for a family meal. She didn't want to get dirty or for the wind to muss her hair.

She refused to pet the dog or even sit in the same room with him. She complained so hard that the Wi-Fi was spotty that he spent a ridiculous amount of money rewiring the house.

And his mother had tolerated all of it for him. She was his wife, after all, and the mother of her only grandchild. Yet his mother's patience, and maybe his own, had thinned the day his mother had thrown a family baby shower for Ava and she'd refused to eat the special meal his mother had prepared. It was too heavy, Ava had complained.

Just thinking about Ava's obsession with her weight during her pregnancy made him angry. She'd gained the minimum amount and Sophia was born premature with low birth weight. Seeing his baby on a feeding tube had been a nightmare. His mother had talked him through it.

Dani wasn't Ava, but what if there was something else? What if she hated the wind or needed to watch HBO? He refused to make his mother uncomfortable in her own home gain.

He sighed and slammed the car door, making Dani turn and search his face.

"Are you okay?"

He blinked. Ava had never been in tune with his moods.

"Yes. It slipped."

Dani opened the back door and reached for her coat and her smaller bag, which was nestled next to his and Sophia's belongings.

"I'll get that—"

She held their coats and slung both bags over her shoulder.

"You get the big ones," she said with a smile. Her ponytail swung and kissed her exposed neck. He tore his gaze from the supple skin at the open neckline of her Henley before it drifted farther down to the two undone buttons at her cleavage.

His body heated, recalling how soft she felt against him by the bridge.

"Antonio! Get her bags!" His mother's voice was like a splash of cold water.

"Mamma, she doesn't listen to me. Like you."

His mother came forward with a snort of laughter. Then she held out her arms to him, holding his face and kissing him on both cheeks. She turned to Dani with open arms.

"Welcome, Danica! Welcome. I am Grace Lorenzetti. We are so excited to have you here and I get to practice my English." Dani leaned in to the kisses with a smile and Toni relaxed, aware that his anxiety was popping through at random. He needed to calm down. It wasn't like he was introducing a new girlfriend. She would be working with them. And when Marcello was well, she'd be leaving.

He adjusted the roller bags in both hands and scowled.

"Food is getting cold. Come, come."

Toni watched Dani follow his mother into the house and once he'd gotten the rest of their belongings into the hall-way, he found the three of them in the kitchen.

Sophia noshed on a *pizzelle* and Dani held a full glass of wine. The kitchen island was filled with meats, cheeses, olives, herbs and fresh vegetables. Olive oil and bread acted as centerpieces beside a bouquet of wildflowers.

"It's lovely here. Marcello mentioned there was a vine-yard on the property."

"It's behind the restaurant. One of the special dining rooms has a gorgeous view." His mother opened the oven and removed two long pans of lasagna. "Sophia, stop eating all of the cookies and check the pasta."

"I'll do it." Dani found a fork and dipped it into the boiling pot. Expertly she rolled the spaghetti and flicked a string into her mouth. His mother caught his gaze and wig-gled her brows. He rolled his eyes back at her. It was an age-old test his mother performed on all the women he brought to the house. If they asked to help they got points. If they knew how to test the pasta, they were marriage material.

Ava had failed.

"One more minute. That lasagna smells divine."

Toni snatched a *pizzelle* from Sophia's hand and put it in his mouth. "Mamma, you cooked enough for ten people."

"You and Sophia polish off one lasagna by yourselves. Danica and I want to eat too."

Without asking, Dani reached for the strainer and tackled the pasta. "What else do you need? I see garlic. Do you need it chopped?"

"You will be doing enough cooking starting tomorrow. Sophia needs to learn how to dice properly."

"Nonna, I'm better. Dani showed me." Sophia popped up from the table and found a knife and a small garlic bulb. They all watched as she began to slice, slow at first, then with a little more fervor.

His mother let out a happy yelp and tears sprang to her eyes. She grabbed Sophia to her chest.

"Such a good girl."

"Ma, it's a little garlic."

"It's tradition. Now, Toni and Dani finish setting the table. Sophia and I will finish here."

Toni poured himself some wine.

"Follow me."

Toni stopped at the elaborate setting. The cherrywood table shined. His *nonna*'s good china and crystal goblets graced four place settings. A chilled decanter of Lambrusco sat at the head of the table. Silver utensils sat in a pile for placement.

What the hell? The last time his mother brought out the china he'd brought Ava to meet her. Alarm bells went off in his head.

He planted the wineglasses on the table and whipped around to Dani's confused look.

"I'll be right back."

"Sophia, go help Dani," he said, storming back into the kitchen. He waited till she left and lowered his voice to a whisper. "Mamma, why is the good china out?"

"Whaaat? I know it's not romantic having your mother and daughter at the table, but—"

"Romantic? What are you on about?"

"Marcello said you liked her."

"He what?"

"He said you couldn't stop talking about her when you visited last. I must say, she's not your usual type. She's a woman."

"Of course she's a woman—"

"I mean she's not a woman-child like Ava. This one has all the curves in the right places, huh? Like your mother." She winked and elbowed him, then turned back to cutting the lasagna.

Toni knew Dani's curves intimately, but he would never tell his mother that. Not because he was embarrassed. On the contrary, his mother was a modern woman, but he just wasn't sure Dani would feel comfortable and he was doing his best to keep his hands and his eyes to himself.

"I can't believe you just said that."

"I saw you looking at her body outside by the car. You like her."

They both turned when movement came from the doorway.

Dani put her palms up. "Um... I'm so sorry. Sophia spilled Toni's wine on the table. I'll just grab this cloth."

Dani avoided their gazes and quickly snagged the white cloth from the counter before leaving.

Toni sighed hard. "I can't believe this."

Toni stared at the doorway where Dani had appeared and disappeared.

"*Grazie*, Mamma."

"You're overreacting. She likes you too."

"Mamma, stop! Wait, why do you think that?"

His mother chuckled and picked up one of the lasagnas.

"A mother knows. Now bring the other plate. You need to eat something. You're too skinny."

Toni pinched the bridge of his nose and then dropped his hand when he heard a low snicker from the doorway. His mother was gone, but Dani stood laughing behind her fist.

"I've been sent to get you."

"How much did you hear?"

"If we are talking about the part where you were checking me out, then all of it."

"I wasn't—" he held up air quotes "—checking you out."

"I saw you, but it's okay. They are spectacular…"

"Oh, I remember how spectacular they are." Her blush urged him on. "But if making sure that you had a handle on the bags is checking you out, then fine. I did it."

"The bags weren't on my breasts, they were on my shoulder. You just did it again."

"Did what?"

"Looked at my breasts."

"Well, you're talking about them."

"Yes, we are talking." She circled her hand over her face. "And my eyes are up here. Ground rule number one…"

"Maybe you should take your own advice?"

"Excuse me?"

"You've been checking me out too."

"Don't be ridiculous."

"The other night. You couldn't keep your eyes out of my shirt."

"Um, maybe you should learn how to button it."

"Well, that shouldn't matter. My eyes—" he circled his face as she did "—are up here."

"You've lost it." Exasperated but smiling at the turn-about, she moved toward the lasagna.

Toni quickly picked it up and moved around her. He turned back when he reached the doorway.

"Uh, uh, uh, eyes up here." He smirked when her hands flew to her hips. She was looking. The thought made him smile.

Toni set the second lasagna on the table just as Dani entered, half smiling and shaking her head. They both took their seats.

"What, Mamma?" Toni said to his mother's cheerful expression. Her eyes darted between them.

"I'm going to get the champagne. Love is in the air!" Her arms rose toward the heavens.

"No!" Dani and Toni shouted.

"Mamma, no more wine for you."

"Mrs. Lorenzetti, I hate to be the bearer of bad news, but your son and I aren't in love. I'm only here to help Marcello and your family and then I'm going back home to… well… I'm not sure, but back to America. There's no love affair. Not even close."

His mother leaned in.

"It's because he's too thin isn't it?"

"Ma!"

"Toni, you lost weight during your divorce and never put it back on." His mother scooped the lasagna onto his plate. "Eat this right now."

"It's because of all the women he dates," Sophia said with a mouthful of lasagna.

Toni looked at his daughter. "Stay out of this. And get that phone off of the table."

"*Dio*, I hope you aren't doing that Timber, Toni."

Sophia tossed a prosciutto strip to the dog. "Tinder, Nonna."

Toni served Dani a large helping of lasagna and Caprese salad. "Ignore them. I do."

Dani laughed, then took a bite of her lasagna. The sound she made was one of pure pleasure. "Wow, this tastes even better than it smells." His mother beamed and served her another helping even though she was barely through the first.

Toni couldn't take his eyes off Dani as she closed her eyes and took another bite, slowly licking the fork clean. *"Magnifico."*

"Is there someone special in your life, Dani?"

Toni saw Dani tense. "No, not right now. But I'm not looking, either. I think it's time to reevaluate my priorities."

"Amen to that," Toni said under his breath.

"Maybe that's best, then love can overtake you when you least expect it." Her eyes darted between him and Dani.

His mother was as subtle as an elephant in a parade.

"I've always told Toni that what he likes is not what he needs. If he'd have listened, then you wouldn't have…well you know."

"Divorced," Sophia said with a mouth full of food.

Toni raised his eyebrows at the only good thing that came out of his marriage. "Enough."

His gaze shifted to Dani. She gave him a teasing smile and he was surprised at his body's urge to lean over and kiss her. He shoved his mouth full of food instead, grimacing when his mother continued giving *advice*.

"Danica, you need a man who can challenge you. It's more sexually exciting."

Toni and Sophia moaned in appalled horror. He glanced at Dani, nervous she was becoming offended by his mother's candid speech, recalling Ava's quick embarrassment every time his mother opened her mouth, but Dani laughed aloud, her brows lifted in wonderment.

"Mamma, please. Danica likes strong quiet types, like Martin, the manager at Armani Ristornante."

His mother blew a breath from her lips. "The man can do nothing without being told. You don't want that. Listen to an old woman."

"Can I try some wine?"

Three heads swiveled to Sophia. His mother, seeing it as a right of passage, poured her a little and guided her through the swish, smell and taste. It was a beautiful sight, but one Toni would rather put off for another ten years. His daughter was growing up. Boys, now wine. What was next? Tinder as his mother had brought up? At least the dating talk was over.

"Mamma, has Marcello decided on the surgery?" He needed a distraction from any more thoughts of who was and wasn't good for him. Because regardless of how much he teased his mother, he was beginning to wonder if what was good for him was sitting right next to him.

# *Chapter 12*

Dani quietly ate as conversation flowed around her. Marcello had opted out of surgery. She made a mental note to call him. Grace had taken over the kitchen at Via Carciofo, reducing their hours to three nights a week until Marcello was well. She'd decided to stay at Toni's apartment, leaving the two of them alone a few nights during the week.

She and Toni alone? Why did the idea make her nervous?

Grace passed Sophia the last of the Caprese salad.

"So, Dani, Toni tells me you two attended the same wedding last year." Dani choked on her wine and tried not to meet Toni's gaze.

"We did. But I didn't know of the connection to Marcello then. He never spoke of family."

"That's Marcello. Work is his life. Nothing else interferes. It's a blessing and a curse."

Toni pushed his plate away and rested his elbows on the table. "I've never known him to be unhappy with his life."

His mother began stacking dirty plates. "Marcello never slowed down. Never kept up his relationships with women. And now he's in the hospital with no children of his own."

Dani stabbed at her salad, the words hitting home harder than she'd like.

"Ma, stop." Toni pulled the dirty plates from his mother's hands. "Sophia and I will clean up."

"Okay, but we need room. I've made tiramisu."

The table groaned, too full to even think of another bite. His mother chuckled.

"Fine. You'll eat it later. Dani, I'm curious what you will

think of my tiramisu. My son couldn't stop talking about the wedding cake you made for Destin."

"Yeah, Papà even tried to make it once." Sophia scrunched her face and shook her head.

Really? This was news. Dani looked at him, but he was busy trying to get Sophia to hand over her phone. Dani recalled his intent to eat that icing off her body. She absently touched her chest, as if she could still feel his lips on her skin.

He'd just gotten a divorce then and she remembered Nicole saying that he'd been acting like a man out on parole. In other words, he wasn't looking for a relationship. But she couldn't help but feel that he seemed different. Less reckless and more guarded. She wondered just how nasty the divorce had been, and based on what she witnessed the other night, what was really going on between him and his ex.

Toni's mother finished off the last of the wine. "So, Dani, I hear you worked with Andre Pierre."

Dani tensed. "Yes, for a while."

"What's he like?"

Toni was silent and she wondered if he was thinking about their conversation at the canal. It was a fair question; Andre was famous, after all.

"He's…charismatic." Toni's lips pressed together. Dani wondered if he was thinking of the internet story. "He's definitely no Marcello. That's for sure."

"Well, few are. But I wonder why he would say that? Two Michelin stars is nothing to sneeze at."

Toni cleared his throat. "No, it isn't. You must be very proud, Dani."

Dani nodded half-heartedly, wondering why his compliment felt like a dig.

"And your parents must be so proud of you too. Tell me, what does your family do?"

Dani stopped to think for a moment. Was her mother proud? Toni saw her internal struggle and stepped in.

"Dani's mother is Francesca Watts."

Grace gasped with delight. Sophia yelled for her phone back so she could Google.

"*Incredibile*, you must have had such a wonderful childhood."

Sophia snatched her phone from her father and her thumbs flew over the screen.

"Wow. She's beautiful. Hey, there's Mamma. And—" Sophia's face changed and she put the phone down.

Toni straightened. "What's wrong?"

"Nothing."

"*Cara mia*, hand me the phone." Sophia did as she was told, then began to stammer. "She said she wasn't going to see him anymore. I thought you two were trying… I thought…" Sophia's gaze swept between Toni and Dani before she quit the table. Fast footsteps could be heard climbing a flight of stairs.

Dani stayed very still, unable to see the screen of the phone. After a few scrolls and a long pause Toni blew out a breath and went after Sophia. Grace took the phone and shook her head, then handed it to Dani.

"Oh, I don't think I should look."

"You're going to be a part of this family for a short while, you might as well know everything. In any case, your mother looks wonderful."

Dani touched the darkened screen and a picture of her mother lounging at Just Cavalli Club with Roberto popped up. Their glasses were held up in a sweet toast between old friends. A few more models sat next to her mother, including a svelte blonde on the end in a lip-lock with an older gentleman. Ava.

Dani's heart tightened, knowing what Sophia was feeling. How many times had Dani scoured the internet for her father, only to find him in pose after pose with girlfriend after girlfriend.

Dani let the phone go dark. "It's normal for her to want her parents to get back together."

Grace began to clear the table. "She's getting older, watching everything. I'm afraid that Ava's behavior is affecting her negatively."

Dani gathered the rest of the empty plates and followed Grace into the kitchen. Grace filled the sink with soapy water and let the lasagna pans soak. Grace patted the counter.

"Just sit them here, *cara*."

"I'm happy to wash them."

"No, we can do that in a little while. I want to walk you around the garden before it gets dark. Marcello hasn't finished the menu and I thought you'd want to see what ingredients we have for you to work with."

"I'd love that."

Grace led them through the mudroom and outside across the back patio toward one of the largest greenhouses Dani had ever seen. Several plotted gardens marked the way. Squash, eggplant, snap peas, to name a few. Toni's mother planted and cared for them all herself, only using the most organic resources to keep them healthy.

Sophia's raised, muffled voice came through the air.

Grace stopped, the look on her face one of anguish. "He tries so hard with her."

"He's a good father. Better than mine had been at his age."

Grace took a turn into some of the taller vegetation, caressing the leaves as she went.

"I hope I didn't embarrass you when I insinuated you and Toni should date."

"No. I understand. You're concerned about him."

"His relationship with Ava fell apart so fast. I knew they

were wrong for each other, but my Toni had always been in love with love. I don't think he ever truly saw Ava for who she really was. They were young and codependent for a long time, never leaving each other alone. Always going out. Always partying."

"Sounds like an addiction."

"Exactly. Love was a drug to them. Then Sophia came along." Grace's eyes gleamed. "The tiniest precious little being. And of course that's what opened his eyes."

"A baby sobered them up, so to speak?"

Grace nodded. "They were fine for a little while, but once Sophia was weaned things began to get strained. Ava was ready to go back to work, which was natural. But she also wanted to start partying again. Toni didn't."

"I'm surprised. Usually people slow down a bit."

"She hadn't changed. But Toni had. He hasn't once taken his role as a father lightly. She, on the other hand...oh look, buds have begun to sprout. Watch your step."

Dani stepped over the threshold into the greenhouse, her thoughts on Toni when towers of green vegetation rose in front of her.

"Wow. These are tomatoes?"

"And some herbs. All geothermal." Blooming pots lined the walls.

"How is that possible?"

"Marcello replicated techniques used in Iceland. They produce tomatoes year-round. Now so do we."

"Oh my God, they look amazing. I'd love to taste them."

"You just did. My tomato sauce comes from these tomatoes."

"Your family has built a masterpiece here."

Grace smiled. "And you are going to be a part of it."

Dani's heart almost stopped. *Just a ghost chef. Ten years in the making. A large investment for the family. The pres-*

*sure began to feel enormous. How did she get here?* She was supposed to be focusing on what she wanted from her life, not filling in for someone else's life. Been there, done that.

"Are you all right?" Dani felt Grace's hand on her shoulder. "You look pale."

"Maybe I had too much wine."

"I bet you're exhausted. Let's go inside."

Toni met them in the hallway. He had his hand on one of the bags when they walked in. Following his talk with Sophia, the smile he mustered was half-hearted.

"So, Dani, what did you think of our project?"

"It's amazing." Grace continued into another room and Dani touched Toni's shoulder. "Is she all right?"

"She'll be fine."

Grace appeared with a torn, handwritten book. "Marcello's menu, so to speak. You know he prefers to surprise his guests with a dish, but he always has a list of entrées prepared in case someone is uncomfortable with that concept. Oh, I just realized it's in Italian."

"That's fine. I should be able to stumble through it."

Grace turned to her son. "Toni, you can show her the kitchen tomorrow. How is Sophia?"

"Better, Mamma. Texting. Googling. Who knows."

"Ugh! Those phones. I'm going to clean up and make us all some tea."

"Let me help, Grace." Dani stepped forward but the spry woman stopped her.

"I won't have it. You'll be busy enough tomorrow. Toni will show you your room. Rest a little. You're still a bit pale."

Toni led Dani into a spacious room, propped her spinner against the wall, and plopped her carryall on the bed.

"Welcome to my old room."

Dani's gaze slid across the walls, which were riddled

with '90s-style posters of athletes, soccer plaques, medals and a few magazine tears of models.

"Wow. I feel like I'm in 1995."

He chuckled and pulled open the curtains, exposing a gorgeous view of the garden and the small patch of vineyard further beyond.

"My mother refuses to change it. Sophia stays here when we don't have company." He gestured toward the full-size floor mirror with stickers all around the edge. "The awards on the desk are hers. Up until a year ago, Sophia played *calcio*, er, soccer, for a top club."

Dani crossed to the corner desk and picked up one of five gold statues. Her name and 1st Place was etched on the plaque. Pictures of her in uniform from past to present were displayed on the wall. She leaned closer to an action shot that could have been taken by a professional.

"Why did she stop?"

Toni shrugged and his mouth became a flat line. "She said she no longer liked the game." He turned back to the window and stared at the purple and yellow streaked sky. "We used to play a lot together, but I guess she's growing up. Becoming a young woman."

"Women play sports."

He turned back to her and smirked at her belligerent tone. "Yes, they do. But she was no longer interested, so I let her quit. And her mother never approved of her playing, anyway."

"But she was good. Am I right?"

His smile was nostalgic. "She was good."

"Was she better than you?"

"Of course not."

Dani laughed at his matter-of-fact tone.

Toni slid his hands on his pockets and sat on the edge of a small desk. "Did you play sports?"

Dani chuffed. "Does this look like the body of an athlete."

"You're strong. I can see you playing, uh, baseball?"

"Baseball?" Dani laughed in shock.

"Yeah, like, um, who's the famous guy... Babe Ruth."

Dani rolled her eyes. Of course he picked the fat player.

"No. No sports. I traveled a lot with my mother, which took me out of school three to four times a year."

Thinking back on grade school always made her cringe. Tutors, summer school, her father even tried homeschooling her himself at one point. What a disaster. Her grades were always passable, but she was lucky all she'd ever wanted to do was cook, because she wasn't sure academia would have been an option.

"For the record, I didn't choose Babe Ruth because he was overweight."

Dani flicked her gaze to his and felt her heart beat a bit faster. *Overweight*. She hated the term, an assumption that there was one weight for everyone.

"It doesn't matter."

"It does if I offended you. I saw the look on your face."

Ugh, she had a way of showing her feelings on her face. "I think you could have said Derek Jeter or Alex Rodriquez, that's all."

"Who are they?"

"Yankees."

"Oh! Right. I've seen them play."

"You have?"

"I go to New York a lot."

"Hmm. I've never actually been to a game."

"I think they kick you out of New York for that."

She smiled. "Yeah, they do."

He ran his gaze over her face as if he was going to say something else. He clapped his hands together.

"Well, I'll let you get settled. The bathroom is down the

hall. My mother left you towels there." He pointed to a futon against the wall. "And anything else…just ask."

"Thank you."

He shifted his weight, then headed for the door. "Sophia is staying across the hall. Mother is at the very end. And I'm downstairs in the *seminterrato*."

She frowned, then realized he meant the basement. "Got it."

He walked out the door, but seconds later Dani looked up from unzipping her bag to see Toni standing still in the doorway with his hands in his pockets.

"Sandro Botticelli believed that flesh was a symbol of health, wealth and stability. Which is why he depicted the most desirable women to have fuller figures. Even the statues all around Rome are of women with round hips and bellies—signs of femininity and fertility."

"You're making this awkward."

"Have you seen his paintings?"

"Everyone knows *The Birth of Venus*."

"He's done so much more than that."

"What does this have to do with—"

"You're not fat, Dani. I saw your face when your mother shooed away the hors d'oeuvres at the party. I'm sure she's curbed your hand many times, the same way Ava does to Sophia."

Dani looked away, trying to find her voice. All that came out was a whisper. "She shouldn't do that to her. It will scar her for life." Dani felt the tears gather in her throat and she began to count backward, hoping they wouldn't spring a well in her eyes.

"I've always been a big girl. Even at Sophia's age. It doesn't matter if you don't think I'm fat, or even if I don't think I'm fat. Society says I'm fat. Do you know how hard it was to find a dress for that party?"

"You looked stunning."

She met his gaze and the look they exchanged was infused with a strange, thickened intimacy. She felt her heart rate increase. The deep, dark attraction sent luxurious waves of arousal through her body. He was so handsome. The classic bone structure and masculine jawline was the perfect backdrop for his infectious smile, but this, his declaration, the way he was looking at her, like he could really see her, had cracked open something inside of her.

She wanted him. Maybe it was the way he was with his daughter or the unapologetic way he spoke his mind. Maybe it was this, his inclination to call her out of her emotional shell. He can see her, wrapped in all of her insecurities, and as he stood there with his steady gaze on her, all she could think about was going to bed with him. To slide her hands over his shoulders and down his powerful chest. To press her lips to his skin. Then pin him to the bed and crawl up his tall, strong body.

She swallowed hard. "I'm a grown woman, Toni. I wasn't offended by your comment. I'm fine. Everything is fine." *Please leave!*

"I'd like to show you his work sometime. It's at the museum in Berra."

"Fine. Let's do that," she quipped, biting her lip against the odd mingling of emotions. She wanted him; she wanted to run. *Out. Out. Out!*

Toni's gaze stayed on her briefly before he nodded and left. Dani rushed forward and quietly shut the door, then threw her back against the door and let tears roll down her face. She wasn't quite sure why she was crying. And she wasn't interested in exploring it. She wiped her face and sniffed herself back to rights. She ran her hands over her breasts and down her belly as if she could coax the arousal back inside its dark cave. Her breathing evened and she slumped on the bed, Toni's bed. She imagined him sleeping in it, then mentally slapped the fantasy away.

Then her gaze landed on Marcello's recipe journal. She flipped through the pages, letting the recipes push away her insecurities. But suddenly new insecurities rolled in. What if she failed? She tossed the book on the bed and walked over to the mirror. She ran a finger through the shaved edges at her temple, air-conditioning for the kitchen heat. Her palm ran over her tattoos, feeling the burn scars they covered. She then studied her fingertips, full of marks from cuts. She ran her hands over her breasts, down her middle, then over her hips. The image in the mirror didn't look like a Botticelli painting.

# Chapter 13

Dani couldn't sleep. *You looked stunning.* She rolled to the side to shake off the conversation she'd had with Toni. His insight into the way she had been feeling was uncanny, and unsettling. Being vulnerable was bad enough, but vulnerable in front of Mister Confidence? No, thank you. And it wasn't like he could relate. He was tall and fit and always put together. She'd seen the way women looked at him. His mother was trying to make him fatter, not slimmer.

Venus in a half shell she was not. If only it was the 1400s.

The moon emerged from behind a cloud and shot a ray of light through the window to her nightstand where Marcello's book lay open. She sat up and let her eyes adjust to the writing on the pages. Tomorrow she'd begin testing the entrées, praying she could do them justice. Her eyes slid to her phone: 3 a.m. It was tomorrow.

Dani threw on sweatpants, zipped her hoodie over her tank top and padded barefoot down the stairs to the kitchen. She placed the book on the counter and as quietly as possible, began going through the cupboards. If Grace was anything like her brother, there would be huge jars of home-dried spices, sauces in the fridge, several cooking sherries, homemade pastas in the freezer and cuts of meat.

She found nothing. Other than the fresh herb pots lined along the wall, there wasn't a clue that the woman asleep upstairs even cooked. Dani walked back toward the mud-room and stopped when she saw a wide door to her right. It opened with a loud squeal, and Dani's jaw dropped. It was the walk-in closet of a chef's dream—a full steak locker, a full wine locker, jars of spices, pastas, canned sauces, barrels of ripe root vegetables and a giant refrigerator-freezer with every produce imaginable.

Dani turned on the burners and hit the ground running. Steak sizzled. Pasta boiled. The fish cuts luxuriated in butter. She tasted her first entrée and spit it out. Too much tarragon. Her second try was too spicy. Her third, meh. Fresh basil, truffles, a hint of dried persimmon. Gorgeous.

"Are you crazy? It's two in the morning." Dani whipped around to find Sophia in a big T-shirt and socks with her phone in hand.

"Yeah, maybe I'm a little crazy. I wanted to get a start on the menu. Did I wake you?"

"No. I just couldn't sleep. I thought I'd get some water." She shuffled to the counter and stuck her nose in the big pot. "What are you making?"

"It's a cream sauce."

"Can I have a little?"

"Of course! Take a seat."

Dani found a plate and served her a small helping.

"You're not going to eat?"

"I never eat when I'm cooking. Just tastings." Dani watched Sophia take a bite. The young girl closed her eyes and cocked her head dramatically. Then her eyes popped open.

"It's really good."

It was good to hear, but Dani wasn't yet satisfied and planned to make it again. She fetched the girl a glass of water and set it down when Sophia's phone went off. A text message from W came through saying, send me a pic. From the way the girl blushed and avoided her gaze Dani suspected it was from the boy.

"I used to code my boyfriend under bubbles. I don't know why I ever thought that was clever."

"Don't tell Papà."

"Okay. But maybe you should say good-night to W," Dani said before turning away. She did not want in the middle of that. Nor did she want to know what type of pics they were sending. She grabbed an onion and began dicing. When she looked up Sophia was next to her with a knife. Dani found her a cutting board and gave her several tomatoes. After a quick tutorial, Dani and her young sous-chef began to cook.

"Dani, have you ever sent a naked pic?"

Dani stopped dicing, she fixed her face and turned to Sophia.

"Um, I have. It was to a boyfriend whom I hadn't seen for several weeks."

"He says he misses me and wants a picture."

"Uhh, did he ask for a naked picture?"

"He wasn't specific, but..."

The girl's face said it all.

"He sent you one. Didn't he?"

"Yes."

"Sophia. You don't have to do anything you don't want to do and I advise against it. You don't know where that picture will end up. Send him a pic of the dog."

She giggled. "It's my fault. I asked him to send it."

Oh Lord. Dani's brows shot up, and then she pushed them back to neutral.

"It's none of my business."

"I didn't think he'd send it. We aren't having sex or anything."

"Whoa, I wasn't even thinking it."

"I'm not that type of girl." She frowned.

"I never thought you were."

"Papà thinks I am."

"He does not. He loves you so much. He's just trying to protect you from the big bad world."

Sophia's bottom lip trembled and Dani didn't know what to do, so she grabbed the tiramisu from the fridge and cut them both a piece. Dani coaxed Sophia to the table. They sat down and, after a loaded several seconds, Sophia shoved a piece in her mouth.

"I saw all of your trophies upstairs. Your father told me that you quit soccer. I mean *calcio*."

She shrugged. "I didn't want to play anymore."

"You don't miss it?"

Sophia shrugged with nothing else to say and Dani dropped the subject, happy that she was no longer on the verge of tears.

"Mamma and Papà fought about it a lot. I thought if I was a better daughter…"

Dani saw a tear plop into Sophia's dessert.

"You thought they wouldn't get divorced."

Another tear made it into the tiramisu and Dani grabbed her hand.

"Oh no, honey, it's not your fault. Trust me I know."

"How do you know?"

"My mother and father were never married, but we did all live together for a few years. I thought if I lost weight, then my mother wouldn't be so angry and my father would be able to tolerate her, so I starved myself for a month. No one noticed. But my mother kept complimenting me on how much weight I was losing, and then one day I passed out and woke up in the hospital."

Sophia gasped.

"My father moved out a week after I came home from the hospital and my mother blamed me and my 'stunt.'"

"That's crazy."

"My mother *is* crazy."

Sophia laughed. She finished her dessert and looked less on the verge of a breakdown.

"You should talk to your father."

Sophia grimaced. "He doesn't listen, just barks orders."

"You really like this boy, huh?"

Sophia blushed.

"You should get some sleep."

"I wanna help a little more. Cooking is fun."

Dani smiled. She thought so too.

Who the hell was up this late at night? Toni could no longer listen to the footfalls above him. He silently climbed the stairs and stopped in his tracks just beyond the entrance to the kitchen. Before him, Dani and Sophia had their heads together over small cuts of tiramisu. Not a bad idea, his mother's tiramisu was delicious. He took a step forward and stalled. Sophia wiped tears from her eyes.

A powerful need to rush forward gripped him, but he stayed when he saw Dani's hand settled over his daughter's. They exchanged soft words he couldn't hear and Sophia nodded sincerely, then smiled. After a few seconds, the two of them got up and began chopping vegetables at the kitchen counter.

Toni caught himself smiling at the pair they made. He contemplated going back to his room, content that Sophia was smiling again, unlike during their talk when she confessed that Ava had told their daughter they were getting back together.

He blamed himself, afraid that his promise to "think about it" had somehow led Ava to believe their reconciliation was actually happening. But he knew better than that. Ava was using their daughter as a pawn to trap him. It wasn't the first time. But, dammit, he needed to make sure it was the last.

Sophia's giggles broke into his thoughts. Dani wouldn't act like that. He shook his head, admonishing himself for the comparison. He wasn't on the market for another woman in his life, and yet he couldn't take his eyes from the scene in front of him. He'd be lying if he said his conversation with Dani hadn't been part of the reason why he couldn't sleep. The sadness in her eyes had made him want to hold her.

He motioned to slide his hands into his pockets, clenching his fists when he found he had none in his pajama pants. Something had shifted when they had been in that room together. She had looked at him with those sad, dark eyes, her body framed by his extra-large bed, and all he could think about was picking her up and pinning her underneath him. His lips at her throat and the swells of her breasts. His hands smoothing over her belly and down over her thighs.

"You can come out, Papà."

*Dio.* Now he looked like a Peeping Tom. A resigned smile on his face, he stepped out of the shadows and stopped just over the threshold of the kitchen.

"I was just seeing what all the noise was."

"You were lurking." Sophia popped something in her mouth.

"No, I was going back to bed."

Dani zipped up her sweatshirt before turning around. The action bothered him, like she was putting up another barrier over herself and her body. Dani gave him a weak smile.

"Sorry, Toni, this is my fault. Did we wake you?"

Toni mentally grimaced at her terry cloth armor that zipped to her neck. "No, I was awake, but I thought animals had broken in. What are you two doing?"

Sophia dipped her spoon in a pot and stirred. "We're cooking Uncle's entrées."

Dani flipped off a burner. "I couldn't sleep so I decided to practice a few dishes. Do you think your mother will be mad? I'm going to clean everything."

Toni held up a palm and came toward them, the smells making his stomach rumble. "She won't care. But you—" he pulled his daughter close for a kiss on the head "—bed. Now."

Vibrations came from the table and Toni turned to see Sophia's phone lighting up. Father and daughter lunged for the phone, but Sophia snatched it first and held it to her breast.

"Give it to me."

"No, please. I'll turn it off."

"You said that earlier and you haven't done it. Is that who I think it is?"

Sophia's gaze shifted to Dani, who quickly turned away and began stirring a large pot. "I won't answer him."

"The deal is off."

"No!" She quickly deleted the texts, turned off her phone and held it up for him to see. "It's off."

"Give it to me."

"No!"

"Now."

She slapped it into his hand and ran out of the room. He hung his head for a moment, then tossed the offending technology on the dinner table. He tugged at the collar of his T-shirt, wondering if his frustration was making his temperature rise or if it was the heat from the kitchen. Half turning, he stared into the hallway, unsure how to mend the volatile relationship he and his child were having lately. Dani continued to cook.

"She's having sex with that boy," he said to Dani's back.

"No, she's not." His head whipped up to see Dani handing him a small plate of *cavatelli* and a fork. He pulled out a chair and settled his plate in front of him.

"How do you know?" Without taking his eyes from her, he speared the pasta and popped it absently in his mouth.

His brain stopped, the garlic sauce was laced with saffron and basil, and left an aftertaste so subtle he couldn't put his finger on the spice. He forked more into his mouth and almost moaned.

"She told me just now. She's a good girl, Toni, she's just feeling a little off balance. And she's in puppy love, or whatever you want to call new love."

"She told you all of this just now?" His mood lifted dramatically. His baby wasn't having sex yet. He'd do cartwheels if he could. He'd— After another bite of Dani's heaven, Toni's mind ran toward the perfect wine pairing. He jumped up.

"Yes. She— Where are you going?"

Toni whipped open his mother's pantry and pulled out a black wine bottle, gathered two glasses and set them on the table.

"Taste this." He popped the bottle and poured with gusto.

"It's 4 a.m."

"Yeah, and you're cooking a seven-course meal. Taste it."

Her lips pursed but she acquiesced. Giving it a swish and sticking her nose in the glass before taking a sip. He smiled when her brows went up.

"Now try it with the *cavatelli*."

He watched her take careful bites and sips. She sat back and rolled her tongue over her teeth.

"I like it. Is it a Barbera?"

"No, a Montepulciano."

"Whose?"

"Mine."

She took another sip. "No, I mean, whose vineyard?"

"Mine. It's the family wine."

"Well... I hope it's showing up on the menu."

"Alongside Marcello's *cavatelli*," Toni said.

"Oh...this isn't on the menu. It's my recipe. I was just playing around."

Toni blinked. "I like how you play. It's going on the menu."

Dani looked stricken and shook her head. "I think Marcello has a better dish in his book, I'm just getting started really. I'm sure there won't be room for it."

Toni blinked, unable to figure out what had just happened. They'd been on the same page for a moment, and then it was as if someone had dumped cold water on them both.

"I should clean up." Dani grabbed her wine and crossed to the counter, scraping what was edible into bowls and tossing scraps into the garbage. Toni finished off the few bites of his plate, then began to run water into the sink. "I can do it."

"No, the cook doesn't clean."

Their gazes locked for a moment and Toni wondered at the sadness that seemed to have touched her eyes again. Dani broke their staring contest to hand him a plate and he noticed a small bit of sauce on her bosom.

"You have something here." She looked down at her sweatshirt and he swiped at the glob with his finger, pulling it back so she could see.

"I should have used an apron. Here."

She held out a towel, but he refused it, licking the sauce from his finger. Her dark eyes settled on his lips, then ran up to meet his eyes.

Toni stepped forward and slid his hand around the back of her neck. Before she had time to question what he was doing, his lowered his mouth and kissed her full on the lips. He wasn't prepared for the electric heat that burned through him. Her lips were soft and warm, his mouth moving over hers in a slow thorough exploration. He shifted and brought them closer, needing to feel her body against his.

Her hand moved from his neck to his cheek and he felt

the warmth of her palm as she cupped his face and kissed him back. Flashbacks of Brazil urged him on. He should have pulled away, but he could no longer hold himself back. Ground rules be damned.

He dragged her against him and plundered her mouth as if her kiss was an antidote he needed to survive. He was vaguely aware that his daughter and mother were upstairs, but his whole world came down to her mouth, the jagged rhythm of his heart and the slow, relentless pumping of his blood.

Toni continued to kiss Dani as he unzipped the offending sweatshirt and cupped her breasts through her tank top. Her moan was wild and needy, sending his brain into a fuzzy state of single-minded awareness. He needed to hear her moan again and his brain handled the logistics.

A flight of stairs to his bedroom or steps to the pantry?

# *Chapter 14*

Dani squealed when Toni snaked an arm around her and picked her up off her feet, spiriting them both into the dark closet full of food and wine. He kissed away her questions, pressed her against the shelving, found the waist of her sweatpants and slid two fingers inside of her panties.

"I remember how you wrapped your legs around me in the pantry at the wedding," he murmured against her ear. "How you spread them wide for me on my bed. How slick you were when I was inside of you."

He groaned when he found her wet and ready for him. He made gentle, torturous circles over her swollen flesh, then slipped his fingers inside her. He closed his eyes against the warmth, and the urge to flip her around and drive himself endlessly into her sweet body.

"I want to see you come again, Dani."

She gasped and clawed at his shoulders, her hips rocking into his hand in answer.

A muffled sound intruded into his sensual haze. He paused, his ear cocked toward the door. Their breaths mingled and their eyes searched each other's shadowed expressions. Seconds went by with no further suspicion. Then Dani's hand came up, closed around his wrist and set a dizzying rhythm of her own. "Don't stop," she whispered.

Their mouths met in a hard, feverish kiss. And Toni found himself further set on his goal to facilitate her pleasure.

"Toni? Are you in here?" Toni froze. His mother's voice boomed in the room next door.

While he was aware of the sensitive situation, his feelings were feverishly impenetrable. He'd felt the first tremors of the unequivocal passion that was ready to roll through Dani's body, and he wasn't interested in stopping. Toni felt rather than heard Dani's soft gasp of alarm and, checking that the door was closed, tightened his arm around her. His fingers quickened their pace and he bent his head next to her ear and breathed, "Come for me."

Dani closed her eyes as her body shook with internal thunder. She was white-hot and panting, her fingers digging into his back and her body opening further for him. He covered her mouth to taste her pleasure, taking her breath into his body along with her muffled cries.

Seconds later another call. "Toni, are you in there?"

"Oh my God," Dani whispered in the dark, the warmth of her body shifting away from him. No, he wasn't having it. After a deep steadying inhale, he answered in a calm, controlled voice, "I'll be right there, Mamma."

Dani was shaking, racked still by her orgasm, and rigid with the possibility of being caught.

Toni adjusted his pants, then gave her a measured look before he kissed her. "Don't move. This isn't over."

Toni slipped through the pantry door and found his mother in her robe drinking a glass of water.

"Are you cooking?" She frowned, automatically reaching for the soap and sponge.

"Sophia couldn't sleep so I made her a little something. I'll clean up. You should go back to bed." Toni grabbed the sponge from her hand and walked her to the foot of the stairs.

"*Va bene*, but don't be too loud or you'll wake Danica." Grace pulled herself onto the first step, then turned and put her palm against his cheek. "You need a strong woman, *figlio*."

"You may be right, Mamma." Toni took his mother's hand from his face and kissed her fingers. There was no question of whom she was talking about, but he wasn't in the mood for a pep talk. The subject of their silent understanding was waiting for his return, and he was eager to be received.

His mother's ascent of the stairs felt like an eternity and when he heard her bedroom door shut then lock, he flew across the room and slipped inside the pantry door. He closed the door behind him and tuned on the single overhead light. His heart dropped when he saw no sign of her, but he calmed when she peeked her head up from a crouched position behind the freezer.

Dani came out from her concealed space then, her clothes righted and zipped, her eyes wide with doubt.

"She's gone," he said, his feet moving toward her on autopilot.

"Oh my God. That was close. We shouldn't—" Toni took her face and kissed her, silencing her before she could voice her change of heart. He slid his tongue against her and brought all his skill into play, hoping her change of heart would melt away just as his intention to not get involved with a woman cracked every time he saw her.

Toni lifted his lips just above hers, pleased when she held her face tipped toward him. Her eyes blinked open and he palmed her cheek. "It's time for bed."

Her gaze dipped and she pulled back with a quick nod. They quietly made their way into the kitchen and down the hall toward the stairs. Toni stopped at the basement door and reached for Dani's arm as she continued to walk by toward the stairs.

"I meant *my* bed," he said low, gently pulling her toward him.

A breath went by as her gaze took in the descending wooden staircase. "I thought you meant separate beds."

He held her gaze. "I didn't."

"We had an agreement, remember? All work and no play. Maybe we should stop."

"We haven't started working yet. And I can't let you go tonight. If you won't come down here, then I'll come up there. But I'm making love to you."

"What if I said no?"

"Are you saying no?"

Her lips parted, but nothing came out.

He closed the basement door and moved toward the stairs.

"No, they'll hear," Dani said before he cleared the first step. She opened the door and disappeared into his bedroom. Excitement flared through his senses.

Dani was standing in the open doorway that led to the garden when he descended the stairs. She was bathed in the glow of a single floor lamp, gazing into the night. He turned off the light and the moonlit garden was suddenly visible. His spacious room with its king-size bed and tan leather couch was streaked with the moon's rays, and the sound of crickets were carried by a cool breeze.

"Etheral isn't it?" he said, touching his lips to the back of her neck. She nodded and turned, stepping into his arms. He could no longer hold back and brought his mouth down in an aggressive kiss. She leaned into him and wound her arms around his neck, pulling him closer. She matched his kiss and he tasted the delicious, savory flavor of her, the sweet lick of her fiery response, and the sultry erotic slide of her tongue. Lust jolted through him and she moaned into his mouth.

"Tomorrow we play by my rules."

"Tonight we play by mine." Without lifting his mouth from hers, he yanked her zipper down and shoved off her sweatshirt. Then he shoved his hands under her tank top and willed her arms up as he stripped the cotton fabric from over her head. His ears rang with her soft moan as he kissed and sucked her exposed neck, her shoulder and the creamy swells of her breasts. His palms played and teased, and he lifted the tip of her breast to his mouth. Her hands locked in his hair as her nipple hardened with the lap of his tongue.

She breathed his name when he transferred his mouth to her other breast. Her hands clutched his biceps to steady herself and her eyes were closed against the sensations. He couldn't remember when he had ever wanted anything or anyone as badly as he wanted her.

He eased her pants down over smooth legs and silken curves, feeling her tremble under the caress of his palm. His fingers skimmed the elastic of her panties, the last barrier to where he so badly wanted to be, and he whisked them down and off. She stood before him naked; a Botticelli come to life. Finally, she was here. His.

"You're beautiful." More words were threatening to tumble from his mouth. Words of want and desire. Words of longing and obsession. Words of love. He clamped his mouth shut.

Cupping her face in his hands, he found her mouth again and drank her in, deepening the connection until his body was screaming. He felt her hands tugging on his waistband and he pulled his mouth away to help her. His T-shirt and pants were off in a heartbeat. He hauled her closer and she wound around him, her skin sliding against his, pressing against his rigid erection.

He walked her back to the bed and lowered her onto the soft duvet, covered her body with his, his arms sliding under her shoulders to protect her from his full weight. Her thighs cradled him and he was poised at her apex, feeling her soft nudges, beckoning him to fill her. She whimpered and he took the sound into his mouth, silencing her with a kiss.

"We have to be quiet." She nodded, her eyes dazed, her nails digging into his back.

"Okay," she murmured against his mouth. "Please, don't stop. I need you to—"

"I know, angel. I know." He slid his hand down between their bodies and found her silky-soft and dripping. He muffled his own groan in her neck. Then he eased his hand away and reached for the front pocket of his leather dopp kit which lay open on top of the nightstand.

Condom in place, her legs wrapped tighter around him and he entered her in slow, rhythmic thrusts, testing and filling her until he could no longer hold back. He covered her mouth with his and drove himself deep. He swallowed the desperate cry that bubbled from her throat. He stilled, overwhelmed by the feel of her. Warm and tight; honey and wine. Waves of acute pleasure engulfed him.

"Toni?" He came up from the sensory overload at her whisper. Her hand was on his face, tracing his lips and jaw. Her hips urged him on and he pulled back and surged into her again, driving the breath from both of their bodies. He rocked deeper inside of her and her eyes fluttered closed until he softly ordered, *"Guardami."* "Look at me." His hand slid under her bottom, and he lifted her to meet his full, hard length.

"Oh…" she gasped, and then she slammed a hand over her mouth and stilled. They looked at each other wide-eyed and both peeled into a silent chuckle.

"I feel like I'm fifteen," Toni said, nudging her hand away from her mouth with his lips for a kiss. "But sex was never this good then."

He rotated his hips slightly to touch all of her lushness and drove home again, watching her back arch and loving the way her hands fisted in his hair. The words began to fall from his lips then. Staccato sayings in Italian, he wasn't sure she understood, but that he felt deeply. How good she felt. How much he loved being inside her. How he dreamed of her for almost a year. That she was his and he'd kill anyone who hurt her. That he loved her. He stopped himself then, thinking that maybe he was getting carried away.

Her eyes were glassy and unfocused, her breathing was ragged, ending on whispered sobs. Her body trembled and undulated, searching for release. With eyes locked and mouths locked, and bodies in perfect accord, Toni kept up his driving rhythm. Dani's hands traveled from his shoulders and torso to the base of his spine, and he felt her nails dig into his sides. She was close. He lifted her lower body again to meet his long strokes, sending her closer to the edge.

In a rush of breath, she shook under him and he felt her body clench around his shaft. He gave up control and lost himself in her body. They kissed all the way through it, both bowled over by the power of their sex and by the fierce symmetry of their orgasms. He gave and she took. She gave, and he was lost.

Toni emerged from his blinding climax knowing two things: she was still the best sex of his life. And he was never going to be able to keep his hands off her like he had promised.

The clock read 7 a.m., but sleep was elusive. After silently leaving Toni's bed, Dani found her scattered clothes and tiptoed upstairs to the kitchen. She made herself an espresso, wondering why she felt the need to pack her bags and run.

Because this was how it had started with Andre. And Martin. And her boyfriend from culinary school. And they all ended with someone getting hurt, namely her.

She pulled in a deep breath and told herself this time

was different. Her time with Toni was limited and there was no time for feelings. They had four more days to get ready and a laundry list of things to prepare.

They'd had a lapse in judgment. But it didn't have to affect their working relationship. *Just stay focused*, she told herself, *and don't let your feelings get out of control*.

Feelings? She slumped against the counter and sipped her Italian roast, staring out the window over the green hills and into the purple horizon. *Do I have feelings for him?* she asked the sliver of sun peeking from behind the mountains.

Her gaze landed on the lush garden and meticulous rows of wine grapes. She couldn't run, but maybe a walk would do her good. She zipped up her hoodie and slipped her feet into a pair of wellies in the mudroom, then with coffee in hand stomped past the greenhouse and through the garden into the vineyard.

She couldn't help but finger the dew-covered leaves and grapes as she slowly strolled through the labyrinth. Wine had always been a complement to her dishes, but seeing the little grape that would eventually become the beverage of the gods was awe inspiring.

"Hey, little grape. You're going to make someone very happy one day."

She fingered the dew, the droplet somehow reminding her of Toni and how wonderful he was with his fingers. And his body. And his lips. He'd whispered Italian in her ear, making her go a little crazy for him. She didn't recognize all of it, too engrossed in how good he felt, but she thought she'd heard *Sono innamorato di te*. "I'm in love with you."

An inner voice told her to stop being ridiculous. If he did say that, it was in the moment. Andre would tell her that during sex all the time. It meant nothing, clearly. And Toni didn't love her. She was only there for a little while. They were just acting on impulse, and now that it was out of their systems, they could begin working together like adults. Adults who didn't have any more sex.

"Angel, it's freezing. What are you doing?"

She jerked, splashing lukewarm coffee on her hand. Toni approached in wellies and his pajamas. His bed hair stuck out at all angles, making him look sexier than anyone should so early in the morning. The events of their night rushed back to her. The feel of him, the weight of him, the length of him inside her. Heat rushed across her skin.

She bit her lip. Just one look at him. That's all it took. Her heart sped up as he got closer, then it jumped when he smiled. No, she couldn't have this reaction. Not if they were going to work together.

And not if she was going to leave Italy unscathed.

"Hey" was all she could muster. He reached for her, but she pretended to be checking herself for more spilled coffee and moved away, trying to get away from him and the electrically charged space that now swirled around them. Suddenly she wanted to touch him. And him to touch her. Just one kiss, she mused keeping her distance from him before mentally slapping herself.

From the corner of her eye, she saw him stop and put his hands on his hips.

"I don't like waking up alone."

"I was craving coffee."

He stared at her. "Trying to avoid me?"

His deep voice was thickened by sleep and sex.

"Of course not. I just needed a walk." She sipped her coffee, which had gone almost cold, and tried to find her voice.

"You're having regrets."

"No." It was true. She didn't regret it. But she was afraid he would.

"Then come back to bed." His voice was patient and his fingers grazed her elbow as if testing the waters. Then she was there in his arms and his lips were on hers. She held her coffee cup out to the side while he ate at her mouth and wrapped his arms around her waist. He didn't let go of her mouth as his palms smoothed over her bottom.

Had they been in his room, she might have given in, instead she gathered all the inner strength and wiggled from his arms.

She turned her back to him and caught her breath. Then she turned. His dark brows were scrunched and his chest rose and fell rapidly.

"What was that?"

"Your daughter and mother are around."

"They're in bed, where we should be."

"Toni, last night was great, but I think we should acknowledge last night for what it was."

"You mean this morning." His brows went up. "And what was it?"

"The last time. We have other priorities to focus on and sex would get in the way. We're expected to work together, not sleep together."

She was handing him an out on a silver platter. Later he would realize that he wasn't that interested in her. That she wasn't his type.

"We can do both."

"I can't."

"Try."

She chuckled at his insistence. "I don't want your mother to get the wrong impression."

"And what impression is that? That we like each other? That we made love several different ways hours ago? That would be the right impression."

"I don't want her to think that we are together or dating or whatever Italians do."

"They get married."

"Well, we're definitely not doing that."

His gaze didn't waver, and then he smiled a slow smile and held out his hand. "Come back inside."

"I won't be your lover and your chef, Andre." Dani's hand went to her mouth.

"Andre? I am not Andre." Toni closed the distance between them and cupped her cheek. "I'm *not* Andre."

"I know. I don't know why that came out like that."

"What are you afraid of?"

"Of being a cliché."

Toni cocked his head at the strange answer.

"How can I help you not become a cliché?"

"By pretending that last night didn't happen."

Toni's lips became a thin line.

"Fine. We can act like nothing happened." He pulled her face toward his and gave her a searing kiss. Then he looked into her eyes. "But we both know it did."

He dropped his hands and walked back to the house, leaving her feeling bereft and unsteady.

# Chapter 15

Grace and Sophia watched under frowns of confusion while Dani and Toni barely spoke to each other over breakfast. The silence got even louder when they walked out the door toward Via Olivia.

Dani's skin prickled with magnified awareness as Toni followed her down the cobblestone path from the villa to the restaurant. The path crested and before her she saw the sprawling one-story building made of glass and stone that sat majestically behind another garden of wildflowers, small ponds and a white statue of three dancing ladies.

"They are the Graces," Toni said, following her eye line.

"They look…graceful."

"You'll see more when we visit the museum."

Her stomach flip-flopped at the term *we*. He strode past her toward a large wooden door, but Dani stopped and let her gaze roam the property. She could see why this was ten years in the making. Gravel paths with benches were folded into the greenery and she could see the surrounding trees in the distance that shielded the estate from sight.

The veiled gem rivaled a king's country home. Dani traveled up the small steps to the main entrance where Toni stood. He was in jeans and a light sweater, and a light fragrance of pine lingered around him.

She'd smelled the same subtle fragrance on his skin when they had slept together and she fought the memories that flooded her thoughts.

"How are people going to find this place?"

"A map. There is a parking pavilion through those trees." His outstretched arm revealed a beautiful stone archway at the side of the building. "It's secluded, that's part of the appeal. And you should see it at night. There are lights in the walkways and hidden in the garden." He sent her a look. "It's romantic."

She bet. Her gaze landed on a glass room where wine bottles were artfully stacked.

"Is that a tasting room?"

"*Sì*. Come, Chef. You can taste anything you like." She ignored the comment, but she felt it in her panties. He held open the door and she slipped by him, feeling overly conscious of his presence.

"Nice bar," she said. The cherrywood gleamed. Toni smiled with pride and slapped a hand on the top.

"It's sturdy too." He looked at her under lowered lids. Suddenly her clothes felt too small.

"Good, then it can support a lot of drunk rich men."

"It can support more than that."

She looked him up and down.

"Are you trying to have sex with me on this bar?"

"*Sì*, Chef. I would love to have you spread out on this bar."

Dani fought her rising arousal. "That sounds unsanitary."

"But worth the health inspection, I bet."

"Toni. This is not what we discussed."

He straightened. "*Sì*, Chef."

"Show me…the kitchen."

His grin was mischievous. "*Sì*, Chef."

He acted as tour guide as they made their way through the complex.

"There are four dining rooms that face the back garden. All are connected." She stopped to study the elegant interior ripe with gilded wallpaper, perfectly set tables and crystal chandeliers. "A guest lounge." They passed a room with a fireplace and leather seating. "Guest washrooms are there and cell phone stations are there. We have separate areas for the staff."

Dani was impressed. Accommodations for staff were usually subpar.

"Who keeps this place together? It's immaculate." Someone had to be overseeing the space.

"Mamma, Marcello and I take turns. But if you're talking about staff, they are local people. We pay them well to be invisible, but only to the guests."

Toni made a turn toward the back of the room then out into a beautiful secluded patio where Dani counted fifteen staff members standing in a row, silent and still.

"Staff, I'd like you to meet Danica, our chef. Marcello would have no other here so please treat her with the respect that you would him."

They bowed in unison and one stepped forward. "*Benvenuto*, Chef."

"*Grazie*. It is an honor. You've outdone yourselves."

Toni went down the line and impressively introduced each of the members by name and background. When he was done and the staff dismissed themselves, Dani turned to Toni with a smile.

"You know them all."

"We are a sustainable restaurant. That means the people need to thrive here too."

Never had she felt so attracted to a man than at that moment.

His gaze lingered on her lips, and then he swallowed and continued. "This is the outside staff lounge. There is a den below these stairs with an inside lounge."

Dani followed Toni down the stairs and peeked her head through a wood door. Leather couches and a Persian rug graced the inviting space. Rows of unisex restrooms lined one wall and a cell phone station sat in the corner. Along with a laptop station.

"I can see myself taking a long break in here."

"I can see you naked on that couch."

Dani hitched her hands on her hips. "Is that all you think about? Sex?"

His brow went up. "When you're this close and no one is around? *Sì.*"

He leaned closer and she moved backward until her back was against the wall. He placed one hand on the wall by her head and half caged her with his body.

"You look delicious."

She made a dismissive noise. Knowing she wanted to test the kitchen, she'd thrown on a V-neck T-shirt and had put her hair in a ponytail. "I look like a farmhand."

His eyes dipped into the V of her shirt, making her breathing increase slightly. He hadn't even touched her, yet her body was screaming for him. His knowing gaze came up to hers.

"What would you do if I kissed you right now?"

"I'd leave."

He frowned. "Really? I don't think so."

"I thought we were going to cultivate our working relationship."

"We are." His lips moved closer and their breaths mingled.

"I thought we were going to forget what happened."

His fingertip ran down her arm. "Can you forget, angel? Because I'm having a hard time."

She shivered, not sure when the name went from an annoyance to an endearment she craved hearing.

They heard steps on the patio and Toni stepped back just in time for the doors to swing open. Two of the staff members she just met headed toward the restroom. Toni held her gaze as he opened the door.

"Come. Your kitchen awaits."

Just off the dining rooms and the rear gardens was a tall vented stand-alone building. They walked the wide path from the main building into swinging doors and Dani gasped at the silver and white beauty before her.

Marble countertops, prep islands, chopping stations, stainless steel appliances and heat lamps, copper cookware, ceiling fans, and hanging from shiny hooks were rows of white coats, with two black ones at the end.

She was home.

Her gaze scrolled over the burners, imagining bubbling sauces and sizzling meats and— She turned when she heard the door open.

"Where are you going?" Toni had one foot out the door.

"Letting you get acquainted. Your staff will be here in an hour. I'll be in the tasting room. Text if you need me."

He winked and left, leaving her a little speechless. How did he know she wanted to be alone with the kitchen? The memories of him driving himself inside her came from nowhere and she ran a hand over the cool marble as a distraction.

She thought she could forget, but her body was having none of that. She wanted him. Again. Would that set her free? One more time? Ten more times? She gritted her teeth and let her fingertips guide her to the ovens.

She spied a small alcove and delighted in all of the full freezers and jar storage. She smelled the dried herbs, inhaling long and hard to wipe away any thoughts of Toni.

She only had days to whip her kitchen into shape. She needed a way to get him out of her system.

An hour later the kitchen staff trickled in. Dani introduced herself to the handpicked selection of cooks who had worked with Marcello in the past and present. She recognized one or two from Via Carciofo, then outstretched her hand to Dao, a small Japanese man with a stern face. Marcello's other sous-chef, now hers.

"Chef." He bowed. Dani frowned at the thought of a Japanese chef in an Italian restaurant, but then, some had said she never belonged in an Italian restaurant, either. It made you work harder. She had a feeling they would get along well.

After introductions she put them to work, giving them a task of preparing five simple Milanese dishes of their choice. A test, so to speak. She watched silently and they worked efficiently, taking Dani's instruction where she saw fit to give it. Save one.

The French saucier looked at her tattoos and sneered.

"I came here to learn from a top chef, not a prep cook who slept with Andre Pierre."

Rage boiled under Dani's skin, but before she could act, Dao grabbed a French rolling pin, yelled in Japanese and cracked the long wood on the counter.

"Apologize!"

The room gaped and the saucier's eyes went wide. The Frenchman's gaze shifted back to Dani, and then he whispered, *"Désolé."*

Dao stepped forward. "Out!"

The saucier looked to the room for support, but none extended even a look. His spoons clattered as he shoved his pots away and tossed his coat on the floor.

The room stayed silent as he took his bag from the lockers by the door and swung wide the double doors.

"Chef, on behalf of the staff, our sincere apologies." Dao bowed again.

Dani made no movement, but inside she shook. The way he looked around for support meant things had been said. This staff thought she was a joke.

Dani grabbed the saucier's discarded pot and threw it

across the room. Tomato basil puree splattered the white brick as if remnants from a murder.

"Who else would like to leave?" Her raised voice echoed. "Go." She tossed another pot. "Go!"

No one moved. Her laser gaze hit everyone in the room.

"I don't care what you've heard or what you've read. You are here because you were handpicked by Marcello. And so was I! When you let me down, you let Marcello down. Now get back to work!"

All turned their backs quickly and focused on their stations. Head high, Dani slowly walked out the doors, took a deep breath, and then she felt the pull of tears rising from her throat.

She clutched her forearm and dug her nails into her skin, hoping to distract herself with pain. But her scarred and tatted arm was bulletproof, and she chuckled at her feeble attempt.

The tear subsided and as her fingers slid over the bumps in her arm she remembered that she'd paid her chef's dues over and over. They didn't just give out Michelin stars at Walmart. Unfortunately, her name wasn't attached to any of them.

It's her fault. Not Andre's, hers. She let him take the credit. She let herself be a ghost.

She didn't want to be a ghost anymore.

"We're ready, Chef." Dao's voice was low behind her.

"I'll be right in." She tossed over her shoulder. "And good work." She wanted to hug the man, but as second in command it was his job to keep the staff under control. If he hadn't have stepped in, *she* would have had to fire *him*.

Dani heard the door swing shut and she waited only a minute more on purpose, just to remind everyone that she could. Moving to go back in, her gaze swept the windowed dining area in appreciation, but she stopped midturn when she recognized Ava's blond hair and slender form in the guests lounge.

She was standing in a formfitting dress, looking every bit the hot girl, staring out over the garden when Toni walked into the room and handed her a glass of wine. They sat together on one of the leather couches and Dani tried not to let the fingers of jealousy tighten around her throat.

They could be talking about Sophia or taxes or…enemas. Whatever they were saying, they looked cozy. Dani felt a prickle of insecurity. Women loved Toni, just like Andre. *Hot girl, Hot guy.*

When Dani walked back into the kitchen, five dishes were lined up under the heat lamps, and the staff was standing against the wall. Dao handed her a fork and stood behind the first dish for Dani's inspection. They were seasoned cooks, but learning a new menu still took practice. She bent over each dish and graded for presentation, preparation, creativity and taste.

"The orecchiette is rolled perfectly." She popped one in her mouth. "Too much lemon juice in the pasta water. The broccolini is bit overdone and I'd want a bit more of a crust on the sausage. Could have been browned half a minute more." With each tip, Dao nodded his head. She speared a burst tomato. "Nice tomato. Overall, not bad."

She moved onto the next dish, a risotto in lemon and olive oil. She tasted it and then tossed the dish. "Overcooked." The third and fourth dishes received the same fate, but the fifth dish, a Swiss chard ravioli was almost perfect.

She stood and looked at Dao. "We have a lot of work to do. I want everyone here tomorrow afternoon."

Dao bowed.

It was 1 a.m. when Dani found her way to the restaurant kitchen, unable to get that saucier's sneer, nor the vision of Toni and Ava drinking wine together, out of her mind. She wasn't jealous, she told herself when she flipped on the burners and splashed some oil into the pan. Chopped garlic sizzled while Dani lay sweet peppers one by one into the pan, watching for them to blister just right. She just didn't want to be played like a fool, like she was with Andre.

The smell of the simple dish calmed her nerves and her thoughts wandered to the launch and dishes she and her team had yet to perfect, to the servers she had yet to meet, to the wines she had yet to taste…which led her right back to Toni. She turned the shining peppers as flashes of their night together broke through her thoughts.

The slide of his hands on her skin, the trail of his lips over her breasts, the fullness of him inside her. He was relentless in his exploration of her body and she burned for it again.

Her mouth went dry. She flipped off the burners and shaved parmesan over the steaming dish. It melted beautifully like a snow-topped mountain. With her fingers she brought a pepper to her mouth and let her shoulders fall at the comfort. She reached for another pepper and stopped, thinking a light wine would complement her dish.

She walked through the darkened halls to the tasting room, hoping to find the wine locker open or maybe a few random wine bottles under the bar. She crossed the threshold and was surprised to find a few of the overhead lights illuminating just the bar area and four empty wine-glasses on top.

"Hello?" Dani scanned the room and crept slowly toward the bar, wondering how the staff could have missed them. Could they have been Ava and Toni's glasses from earlier? *Looks like they had fun. Jealous much*, Dani chided herself. It was probably just— Dani jumped and let out a tiny yell when Toni appeared from around the corner.

"Toni?" Her heart hammered in her chest. "Oh my God, I thought you were a serial killer. What are you doing?"

"You mean lady-killer," he said with a smirk. "And I could ask you the same thing. But I won't." Dani lifted her brows at his flippant tone. His hair was messy and his pajamas were a little wrinkled, like he couldn't sleep. He eyed her for a second, letting his gaze travel unapologetically down her body. She was fully clothed in loose pajamas, but now she felt a little naked.

"Are you drunk?"

"Not yet." Toni popped a black bottle of wine and poured fizzing red liquid into the glass. His lips were a thin line.

"Are you okay?" She wondered if his behavior had anything to do with Ava.

"I will be when I drink this bottle. It's the Lambrusco made from our grapes. It arrived today."

"You're going to drink the whole bottle by yourself?"

He raised his glass to his lips and closed his eyes at the first sip. Nodding slowly as he savored the taste. His eyes popped open.

"No, you're going to join me. Taste." He pulled another glass from behind the bar and poured some for her. The fizz vibrated on her tongue. When she looked up he was watching her mouth.

"I'm up for one glass, but—"

"And then I'm going to make love to you."

"Wait…what?"

For all of her talk, you would think she would move when he stalked toward her. No, her body knew what it wanted and instead of weak protests, she threw her arms around his neck and kissed him like she was starving. She couldn't stop kissing him, couldn't stop feeling him. Their clothes came off in a frenzy, and then he lifted her and sat her on the counter. She wound her legs around him and he entered her in one hard thrust. She matched him kiss for kiss, thrust for thrust, their bodies moving in tandem, the erotic rhythm building until the first contractions of her body rippled against him. "*Ho un debole per te.* 'I'm weak for you.'" Toni's whispered words washed over her. They came together in a hot rush of entwined limbs and breathless moans.

## Chapter 16

The next morning Toni and Dani drove to Milan to drop Sophia off at school and visit the markets to schedule deliveries for the opening at the end of the week. Dani scheduled lunch with her mother, but before then Toni made good on his promise to show her the Botticelli exhibit at the Pinacoteca di Brera gallery.

Venus stood comfortable and seductive in her half shell making Dani wonder if someone posed for the painting or if she was a figment of Botticelli's imagination. The collection, on loan from the Uffizi Gallery in Florence, was curated to focus on the artist's more pagan ideologies as the walls were filled with paintings of Greek and Roman mythology. Gods were square and muscular while the goddesses were fleshy and curvaceous. *Sensual.* Toni had used the term to describe Venus.

Dani had never felt that sensual standing nude in front of a mirror but there had been exceptions, recently. The things Toni had whispered in her ear the night before had made her feel sensual, and she had definitely been naked.

"His muse was the love of his life. But she was married to another," Toni murmured behind her. His breath at her ear left tingles down her spine, as did the way he laced his fingers into hers.

It wasn't supposed to feel this way.

She wasn't supposed to yearn for his touch or get excited when he brushed her arm. They had rules, which they had broken more than once, but just as the dawn broke through the clouds that morning they had agreed to focus. The launch was in four days and they didn't feel ready.

They may have sealed that pact with a kiss or two, but the minute she crept half-naked back to her room and closed the door, Cinderella had turned back into the maid, er, the chef.

"Venus was a real woman?"

"Her name was Simonetta Vespucci and she was a figure in several of his other paintings, as well. She died at age twenty-two. And he asked to be buried at her feet when he died."

"Isn't that a little rude? She was another man's wife."

Amused, Toni's gaze ran over her face. "Some would say it's romantic."

"Some would say crazy."

"There is no sense in love."

Toni led her by the hand and held it as they stopped in front of another painting.

Dani recognized Venus-Simonetta instantly in her pagan gowns. Then her gaze settled on the three scantily dressed women dancing to Venus's right.

"The dancers look like the statue at the restaurant. What did you call them? Graces?"

"Very good. It was a way for an artist to show the female body three ways simultaneously. There are statues like this throughout Rome. Full hips, round bellies." He pulled her closer to him and looked into her eyes. "Beautiful."

Dani licked her lips and tried to get her lust under control.

"How do you know so much about this?"

"I studied art history."

"Oh, I thought you would have studied business."

"I learned business from my family. But wine, the arts, music. I studied in college, and life."

"Music? Do you play an instrument?"

"I play a guitar."

"Of course you do."

"What does that mean?"

"It means I can see young Toni luring women with his smile and acoustic melodies."

"Well, I didn't have a bow like Cupid. I improvised."

Dani felt the atmosphere thicken. She knew all too well how good he was at improvisation.

Dani turned to the painting. Cupid hovered above Venus, but his bow was raised toward the Graces and a nearby unsuspecting male god reaching for an orange in a tree above him.

"Looks like someone is about to get lucky."

"I think you're about to get lucky."

Dani turned just in time to catch Toni's lips, and then he pulled back and looked into her eyes.

"Oops. Did I break the rules?" he said with a wicked smile.

"Yes." Dani looked around and saw only a few morning patrons. "We said we'd behave."

"Why does the word *behave* make people *not* want to behave?"

"I think that's just you."

"*Va benne*, angel." He kissed her hand, then let it go by her side. It felt cold suddenly. "Have I told you how beautiful you look this morning?"

Dani cocked a brow. He did tell her right before they had gotten into the car. He'd pulled her into his bathroom, locked them in and kissed her senseless. There were broken rules all over the place.

Dani chose an off-the-shoulder top for lunch with her mother. Toni trailed a finger over her exposed shoulder. "I like this top."

She shivered. Who was she kidding? Things weren't going to go back to the way they were. They had achieved a new level of intimacy and the only way to keep things neutral was to keep having sex. Dani swallowed hard.

"I think it's time for me to go."

"Don't run from me."

"I'm not running from you, I'm going to brunch with my mother. After ten minutes there, I guarantee I'll be running back to you."

"I like the sound of that." His smile faded. "Do you regret our sleeping together?"

"No, but I think we need to be careful. I don't want to upset Sophia or get your mother's hopes up."

"You're so logical. How did I not know this about you?"

"I think it's because your focus is usually just on yourself."

He feigned offense and gazed at her under narrowed lids. "Now you owe me one last kiss."

Her blood pulsed a little harder. "If I must."

Toni put his hand behind her head and pulled her mouth to his. She hadn't expected the raw sexual heat of his kiss or her own passionate response. They were in the middle of a semicrowded museum, and all she could think about was getting him naked and putting her mouth on his chest tattoo.

"Toni?"

Dani heard the small voice, then felt Toni stiffen and pull back. He twisted around and unblocked her view. There stood Ava, a snarl on her face, her eyes darting back and forth between her and Toni.

"It's not what you think," Toni said to Ava.

What? Dani flicked her gaze to the side of his face, studying his reaction as if she didn't hear what she thought she heard. Ava's gaze traveled over Dani, making her want to hide behind one of the statues.

"I know you…you're Francesca's daughter. The chef. You've really gotten desperate haven't you, Toni? First that teacher and now…"

"Ava!" Toni snapped. "Whom I spend time with is none of your business." Ava cocked her head and looked at Dani.

"He didn't tell you we were back together, did he?"

Toni stepped toward Ava, but she turned and hurried away, but not before giving Dani a disgusted look.

"Wait!" Toni called after his ex-wife, then whipped his head around to Dani as if suddenly remembering she was there. He didn't touch her, just stared at her as if he'd never seen her before. "I have to take care of this. Text me when you are done, we'll drive back."

He was gone just like that. As were the feelings she had been experiencing all morning. Suddenly her heart thudded like a rock and her skin felt grimy. Stupid top. Stupid girl.

She felt invisible. Maybe she really was a ghost.

Toni wasn't sure why he was running after Ava. Habit? Sophia? All he knew was that he didn't like the vindictive look in his ex-wife's eyes. The last time he'd seen her like this, he received a call from his lawyer saying Ava had filed for full custody. And by the way she snarled at Dani, Toni wasn't the only one on her shit list.

After he handled this, he'd find Dani and explain. The hurt and confusion that had passed over her face tore at his soul. What was Ava playing at? He needed this charade with Ava to end. He wanted stability. He wanted...Dani.

Toni caught up with Ava and cut her off before she hit the exit. A sadistic smile spread across her face at the sight of him.

He took her roughly by the elbow and led her to a less crowded corner. Then gritted his teeth as he spoke with barely leashed anger.

"What the hell are you doing here?"

"It's a public museum, Toni. And I love Botticelli too. Remember?" Toni stared at her, hard. "Fine, Grace told me you'd be here."

"What do you want?"

"I wanted to see you."

"No, you didn't. That jilted lover scene was beautiful, Ava. You should have pursued acting instead."

"Did you see the look on her face? Nobody wants a guy with a crazy ex. But really, Toni, I did you a favor. She's not your usual style."

"And they don't get crazier than you, Ava. And I thank God she's not usual. It's refreshing to date someone who isn't a complete narcissist."

Her eyes narrowed. "Be careful, Toni. Our custody arrangement can always change. But that's not what I want. I want you."

Toni rolled his eyes dramatically. He wanted to say that she must overestimate her mothering skills to think a court would choose her over him. He took the high road instead. "What is this, Ava? Are you in debt? Because I am having a really hard time believing that you still love me when you have been recently photographed with another man."

"Ha! You're jealous."

"Jealous? Is that why you did it? To get to me?" He grimaced. "Sophia saw that picture and cried. Doesn't our daughter factor into any of your schemes?"

Ava's smile deflated into a hard line. "You're the one with the live-in girlfriend at the moment. After you promised we'd work on our marriage."

"We are divorced! And I never agreed to work on us. I said I'd think about it. I decided the answer is no. Meanwhile, you were perfectly happy signing those papers when your lover was around."

He could see that by the shocked look on her face that his barb hit home, but instead of rail at him, she broke down. Her shoulders trembled as she bit back tears.

"I don't understand how we got here, Ava. One day you're happy to be a mother to our daughter, the next you were out at all hours of the night with strange men. Was a family life with me and Sophia so bad?"

Ava clutched at her chest and a quick rush of tears sat in her eyes. She dabbed at them with a manicured nail, checking to make sure no one saw. Her tears had melted his heart many times, but this time he wasn't going to let this go. The look of hurt and mistrust in Dani's eyes had infuriated him. Whatever was going on had to be squashed. Now.

"What do you want, Ava? What do you really want?"

She gave him a long look under thick, perfectly glued on eyelashes and darkened brows. She was camera ready at all times, and yet Toni didn't recognize her, not anymore. When did she go from a fresh-faced cover model to this heavily made-up ice queen?

"My life hasn't been the same since we divorced. You were always the stable one, picking me up when I fell down. I want that back, I want us back. It will be better for Sophia..."

"Stop acting like you want this for Sophia."

"I do think of Sophia! Every day!" Her hands shook as she pulled out a tissue from her purse and dabbed more at her eyes. "My contract is up soon and they are not going to renew. My publicist and I tried to stage a few stunts to get my name out there again, see if we could force them into keeping me, or attract another avenue. Reality TV maybe?" She giggled uncomfortably. "They wanted me to do a sex tape—"

"For the love of God, Ava."

"I said no, Toni. But I had to do something. So I went out to the most prominent parties, got photographed with men. I'm not sleeping with any of them, I just needed the PR."

He crossed his arms over his chest. "Did it work?"

"No. Your new girlfriend's mother is all anyone is talking about right now."

"She's an icon."

"She's old! It's ridiculous."

"This has nothing to do with me, so why are you pretending you want me back?"

"I'm not pretending. I'm going to retire. I'm going to change. We were good together once. You remember, I know you do." She slid herself into his arms, then stiffened when she saw something over his shoulder.

He followed her gaze and saw two suit-clad men in the doorway, their gazes where locked onto her. Slowly, she stepped away from him and righted herself.

"Who are they?"

"Um, drivers. I have a shoot today." She placed her tissue back in her purse.

"Think about what I said."

"About what, Ava?"

"About us."

Dani flashed in his mind. "No. There is no us. We are co-parents and…we could be friends, but no more."

"I don't believe that. You're just caught up in love again. It will be over soon. You'll come back to me."

"This is over, Ava." He said it with pointed distinction.

"It will never be over, Toni." She began to walk toward her drivers, then turned. "Oh, and good luck with the restaurant. I'll see you Friday night."

Toni's eyes widened. He'd forgotten that she received an invitation.

He checked the time and hurried back to the Botticelli exhibit. He'd promised Dani that he would drive her to brunch. If they hurried she could still make it. He rushed to where he last saw her. The crowd had thickened with tourists and art lovers, but there was no sign of her.

# Chapter 17

Dani sat at the center table waiting for her mother and watched the ice melt in her water, reliving the way Toni ran after his ex-wife.

She hadn't been stupid enough to believe that the night before meant anything, so why was she so upset? A small gasp from the table beside her prompted her to look up.

Her mother wore large dark glasses and followed carefully behind the hostess in the tallest heels Dani had ever seen her in. The reverence on the hostess's face made Dani want to scream. She's a model for Christ's sake not the Pope.

"Nice shoes. I take it you won't be shopping today."

"That was yesterday. And you never know when you'll be photographed." Her mother's gaze shifted to the table behind Dani and she mouthed a gracious hello.

"Are we here to eat or boost your Instagram followers?"

Her mother's gaze locked with Dani's. "What's your problem?"

Dani was saved by their server, who read off the specials and nodded patiently while Francesca ordered something not on the menu, which only heightened Dani's annoyance.

"There is a menu, Mother, why don't you take a look at it?"

"Why should I when I know what I want? Chefs can cook anything, can't they?"

Francesca's tone rankled. The waiter diffused the tension by replying with an emphatic yes, taking Dani's order and quickly skirting the table.

Francesca cleared her throat and cocked her head. "You look very nice today. Is that lip gloss?"

"It's for your Instagram followers."

"What the hell has gotten into you?" she harshly whispered.

"Nothing. I just want Marcello to get better so I can go home."

"Back to your father?"

"No. Maybe I'll go somewhere else." Her mother narrowed her gaze.

"I've never seen you like this."

"Like what?"

"Sooo...indecisive. You've always known you wanted to cook. When you were a kid I'd come get you from the kitchen where Marcello was rolling pasta—" she chuffed "—but you would just cry when I showed up."

Dani managed a smile. "You told Marcello child slavery was illegal."

"Well, he wasn't paying you. And he said, 'she's not a slave, she's family.' Then he made you roll a few more tortellini."

Mother and daughter laughed, and then Francesca sobered. "You gonna tell me why you're in a mood?"

"I'm just tired."

"You slept with Toni, didn't you?"

"How the—" The food showed up; a small arugula salad with berries and two minuscule pieces of grilled chicken for her mother, and her risotto parmesan and Caprese salad.

Dani waited until all of the servers were out of earshot. "Why would you say that?"

"Your eyes are bloodshot like you didn't get any sleep and you're wearing a sexy top. I know all this skin isn't for me."

"So what if I did? It doesn't mean anything."

"Well, I'm happy to hear that, if it's true." Her mother's long look said she wasn't buying it. "Is it true?"

"Mmm-hmm."

"Oh Lord."

"What? I'm a grown woman."

"Who falls for every toxic man in a two-mile radius."

"Toxic? Is that why you warned him off?"

"Sharing secrets, huh? This is worse than I thought. Don't you see the similarities between him and Andre? Attractive, fast-talking, running around like a prince while you do all the work. Behind every good man *is* a good woman, because she allowed him to stand in front of her. You're just going from one disaster to the next."

"I'm really not sure I can take relationship advice from you, Mother. Regardless, you are taking this too far. I don't work for Toni, I'm just helping temporarily."

"Yeah, and every man loves temporary 'help.'"

"I can't believe you just said that to me."

"Let me tell you something, missy, you better hope Ava doesn't find out about you two. Talk about a bunny boiler. I'm convinced they modeled Glenn Close's character on her."

Dani closed her eyes. "She saw us kissing this morning."

"Oh Lord. What happened? Did she say something to you?"

"She ran off."

"Let me guess, he ran after her."

Dani closed her eyes and nodded. Just like Andre.

"You better end this."

"I will." Dani sipped her coffee, wishing she didn't care. "Tell me about your shoot." Her mother's phone rang and Dani prepared to be ditched when she saw it was Jessica, her mother's agent. But Francesca swiftly silenced the phone and went back to talking. The phone rang again.

"Mom, why are you avoiding your agent?"

"She's being insistent and I don't want to talk to her right now."

Dani's phone buzzed with an unknown number.

"I don't know who this is." Dani held up the phone.

"Let me see. The nerve of her!"

"Who is it?"

"It's Jessica. Don't answer it."

"What? How does she have my number?"

"I think you're my emergency contact."

"Oh. Well, maybe this is an emergency."

"It's not. Ignore it."

"Okaaay." Dani silenced the phone. But it rang again. "Mother, this is stupid. I'm going to answer it and tell her you're asleep or something."

"Just let it be—"

"Hello?"

"Danica!" Jessica squealed. "It's been so long, how have you been? Look, I need to talk to your mother, do you know where she is? *Vogue* won't wait any longer they need an answer. So, what did you think when she told you, were you nervous? Don't be nervous, it will just be one or two shots of you together but your mother will be on the cover, can you believe it? It's brilliant. I mean they are just piggybacking off of the Chanel campaign of course but to do a mother-daughter takes it a step further, don't you think? It would be you two, Cindy and her daughter, Claudia…"

The woman didn't take a breath and as Dani tried to piece together Jessica's rant, her mother began to look increasingly uncomfortable.

Dani frowned and briefly pulled the phone from her ear.

"Jess wants to know if we are doing the *Vogue* campaign."

"She's got nerve. Tell her no, we are not."

"She said you could get a cover."

"No."

Dani put the phone back to her ear and heard Jess still talking. "Hello? Danica?"

"I'm here. Umm, I'm not really sure—"

"No more unsure. Time is up, they need an answer today. You and your mother hash this out and call me back ASAP. I mean to be over fifty on the cover of *Vogue*. Huh! Are you kidding! Game changer! Okay, you two talk and call me back!"

Jessica hung up and Dani put the phone down.

"Sooo, Jessica wants to know if we are doing the *Vogue* shoot. She needs an answer today."

"She already has an answer. I told her no."

Her mother never turned down an editorial. Never. "Okaaay, but she mentioned a cover."

Francesca stopped chewing for a heartbeat, then stabbed another arugula leaf and shoved it in her mouth.

"It would extend my stay here by another week. I'm about ready to go home."

"Are you even going to tell me what it is? Maybe I'd like to do it?"

"You wouldn't like it."

"Try me."

Her mother shrugged. "It's a mother-daughter editorial. Just a few full page shots with a small interview attached."

"And the cover..."

"I suppose, but that's never a given. Beyoncé could break a heel on stage tomorrow and the whole thing could be replaced by an in-depth interview about how her wardrobe malfunction made her feel."

A film reel of all the times her mother shooed her away from her work played in her mind.

"Still hiding me, huh, Mother?"

"And what does that mean?"

"It means you still can't deal with having a fat daughter."

"Danica, You are not fat. You're—"

"Full figured. So, you've said. I'm surprised you haven't tried to take this plate away from me."

"Well, there is too much cheese, if you ask me."

Dani's shoulders slumped. "And of course you have jokes. Because a supermodel having a fat daughter is funny."

"My decision not to do the shoot has nothing to do with you! You're just upset because you got loved and left this morning. Don't take that out on me."

The sting of her barb turned into a burn. "Okay, then let's do the shoot."

Francesca blinked. "Don't you have to open that restaurant?"

"I'm sure I can make room."

"No. You just want to do the shoot because I don't want to. This is my career and I won't take jobs on a whim."

Dani jumped from her seat. "I can't win with you, can I. Or at anything else for that matter. Goodbye, Mother."

"Sit down. You're embarrassing me."

"Well, what's new? I've always embarrassed you, haven't I?"

Fuming, Dani left her mother in the restaurant and hailed a taxi. She'd been a fool, not once, not twice, but three times. First Andre, then Toni, and now her own mother. Dani stared out the window as they sped toward the hotel. To be fair, her mother hadn't changed; Dani just wasn't in the mood to placate her anymore. Or anyone, for that matter. She really *was* attracted to toxic, wasn't she? But then each one of these issues had a common denominator…her. She had to stop allowing toxic into her life.

Her phone vibrated with Toni's calls and texts, which she ignored, even the ones that said he was sorry. He'll be sorry when she doesn't come back to the restaurant, she thought. But in her heart she knew she would never go that route. One thing she wasn't was a quitter and she really did feel that restaurant could be great. She just had to get through a few more days with Toni, but for that she'd need some help.

Ignoring several more texts, Dani picked up a few personal items from the hotel then took a car to the hospital. Marcello's weak smile tugged at her heart. He looked gaunt and tired, the planes of his jovial face shadowed and sunken. The strength of his grip when she held his hand had waned and Dani did her best to keep her concern from her face. He didn't look good and she was afraid he would never make it out of that bed.

"Bella, you look worried. You must tell me everything." And aside from her concerns for his health, she did. She told him about the restaurant, how she felt about Toni and the issues with her mother. It felt like old times and as always, Marcello gave her guidance. "Dani, you are finished being a ghost, which you have been with both Andre and your mother. Step into your light and things will fall into place. That's all you have to do. Toni is waiting for you."

Dani blushed. "Toni has ex-wife drama."

"Toni thinks keeping Ava happy will keep his daughter happy." Marcello waved his hands in the air. "He wants everyone to be happy, but he never focuses on himself. But he is beginning to see himself with you, I saw it when you were here together."

Could she have misinterpreted Toni's need to run after his ex? Marcello broke into her thoughts.

"Your mother came to see me a few days ago. She thanked me, if you can believe it. She is proud of you, Dani."

Dani's head snapped up. "That woman is full of pride, but not for me."

"She said it herself," her mentor said with a gentle gaze. "She knows she wasn't the most nurturing parent, but you get your drive and determination from her, Dani. She is the reason why you are a survivor."

Marcello handed Dani a tissue as the tears began to fall. She squeezed her eyes shut and wiped her nose, and when she opened them, there stood Toni, his gaze full of remorse.

"It wasn't what it looked like," Toni said, stepping farther into the room.

"That's what you said to *her*." Dani hated the way her voice shook.

"I just don't want her to hurt you."

"I can handle her."

Toni gave her a lopsided smile. "I know. I'm sorry."

Dani stood and stepped into his arms. He hugged her tight, placing kisses in her hair, murmuring how stupid he was. He kissed her, sweetly at first, then more deeply, until a deliberate sound of someone clearing their throat interrupted. Dani pulled away and caught Toni shamelessly winking at his uncle. Dani's gaze followed Toni as he greeted his uncle with kisses. She caught herself smiling, then lost that smile as her phone vibrated with a text from her mother.

We are doing the photo shoot. Jessica will give us the details. I hope you are happy now.

I am. Thank you. I love you.

I love you too.

Marcello was right, it was time to step into her light.

# Chapter 18

Days later, Dani was standing in the restaurant kitchen, impressed. Marcello's pasta chef, a sixty-year-old woman with poor hearing, rolled a perfect sheet of dough and began slicing off precise strips of linguini by hand. *Perfetto*. Slowly Dani strolled past the staff, touching and tasting, praising and correcting.

They had been at it all week, perfecting a rhythm, getting to know the kitchen and each other. Now they had twenty-four hours until the soft launch and all were aware that Marcello was counting on them. Day and night they were in the kitchen working on versions of the dishes they plucked from Marcello's menu book. It kept her busy, too busy to think about Toni.

After the incident at the museum, they had come to a new understanding. They were dating for however long she was staying in Milan. No more rules or denying feelings. It would have been idyllic, except Toni had an emergency at one of his warehouses and stayed in Milan for a couple days.

There had been some sexting and a few filthy phone calls, but it wasn't enough to quench her need to touch him in the flesh. He'd arrived hours ago, hell-bent on making love to her, until he saw the dining room staff waiting for him.

Dani lifted her head to stare into the dining room. Toni was introducing the wines to the waitstaff. She couldn't hear him and watched as he poured tastings into each of their glasses and spoke animatedly with his hands.

She had to admit, the reprieve allowed her some much-needed kitchen time, and it showed. The staff was coming together nicely. Now all they needed to do was step into *their* light.

Standing off to the side, Liam caught her looking and gave her a cheeky wink. She returned his teasing with a frown and quickly turned, running headlong into her sous-chef carrying a rack full of lemon tarts. Her white coat looked like a Jackson Pollock painting.

"I'm sorry, Chef."

"No, Dao, it's my fault." She swiped some of the tart from her jacket. "That's pretty good."

"Is everything all right?"

Her heart thudded uncontrollably at Toni's voice. She only half turned.

"We're fine. Just a dessert mishap."

Toni moved closer, stuck his fingertip in one of the broken tarts and sucked the filling from his finger.

"That's divine." He picked up the tart. "May I?"

"Of course."

He took a bite. Dani tore her gaze from his lips and took the opportunity to skirt away. But he was right behind her, licking his fingers.

"Can I talk to you?"

He was wiping his hands on a towel when she turned and looked at him. He was casual in an old soccer jersey that hugged his biceps. His clear gaze was questioning.

She nodded and bit her cheek against her body's memory of how good he felt against her.

"Step into my office," he joked. He followed her into the meat locker, the only place in the kitchen with privacy.

"What's up?"

"How is Dao doing?"

"Great. He's very efficient. I see why Marcello chose him."

"Good."

There was a long pause before Toni moved toward her. "You're really close."

"It's cold. I'm conserving heat."

She stepped back and found herself against a leg of lamb. "Is there more to discuss?"

"My mother is coming back tonight. She is picking up Sophia and they are going to join us for dinner."

"A trial run? Okay, that's great."

"Is the kitchen ready?"

"Should I be insulted that you just asked me that?"

"You did just have an accident."

"We're getting used to the space. We're ready. I just wish Marcello could have blessed the menu."

"The menu looks perfect." Toni's chilled breath brushed her ear as he leaned closer. "What would you do if I kissed you right now?"

She was finding it hard to breathe. "I'd run screaming."

"Would you?" He chuckled, leaning in. "Did you think about me while I was gone?"

"No," Dani whispered, fighting the urge to touch him.

"Liar. Sophia passed her last test."

"Good for her."

"I told her to bring that boy to the launch. I want to meet him."

"Oh right. Now she is free to enjoy the opposite sex again."

"I was thinking of letting you enjoy me."

"Oh, just being considered is enjoyment enough."

"Dani, you can't avoid me forever," he said, his voice as thick as honey.

"I'm not avoiding you, I'm working. As you should be," she teased.

She pushed him aside, letting her fingers linger a little too long on his chest as she moved past him.

"Let me know when they get here," she tossed over her shoulder before exiting the freezer.

A few hours later Dani was finishing the garnish on a chocolate cake when she saw something whizz by the window to the garden.

Stretching her neck, she saw a blur of long dark hair and long legs stop a soccer ball, then execute a massive volley. Dani moved closer as Sophia fished a ball from the bushes, then threw it back out.

Dani inhaled when Toni ran into her view, expertly maneuvering the ball and kicking it back to his daughter. Despite the chilled afternoon, Toni had removed his shirt, giving Dani a reminder of just how hard his torso was.

Her lips had been all over that tattoo.

Sophia spotted Dani watching. She jumped up and waved at the window, prompting Toni to wave, as well. Dani blushed at his slow smile and laughed when Sophia kicked a ball right into his chest.

Hours later Dani kept a watchful eye from the kitchen as Grace and Sophia were served their meal. Liam and Toni coached the staff from a distance while six courses were served and cleared. Grace sliced her fork into the last course, a chocolate cake garnished in a Lambrusco sauce she made from their family wine. Another bite was tasted, then sent away. Dani wrung her hands and made mental notes of all the things the kitchen could do better.

Timing, for one, the third course was late. Prepping, for another. The only parmesan left had been aged three years, she would have preferred the five-year. She heard footsteps in the hall outside the kitchen. Dani checked that the buttons on her coat were still buttoned, ready to defend herself. They'd only had days to prepare. The new saucier was excellent, but still learning the menu.

The staff froze when Grace burst through the double

doors, Toni, Liam and Sophia trailing behind. The stern look on her face said it all. Dani opened her mouth to apologize, but instead was wrapped in a strong bear hug then held her at arm's length.

"I prayed to the Virgin last night that Marcello would get stronger and that our restaurant would be a success. I heard nothing. Today, I saw her face in that velvet artichoke soup. And when I tasted it, I knew." Grace clapped her hands and smiled.

Dani waited for more, hoping that Grace's beaming face was a good thing.

"Mamma, please, just say you liked it." Toni winked at Dani.

"Liked it? I loved it! *Brava. Brava!*"

"I did too! I want more cake," Sophia piped up from her father's side, and Dao fixed her another slice.

Dani felt relief wash over her. "Grace, I know it wasn't perfect. But it will be. I promise."

"I'm going to get the champagne. We are celebrating!" Grace kissed both of Dani's cheeks and thanked the staff. Her praises to the heavens could be heard fading down the hall.

Dao snapped his fingers and the staff began to clean. Liam waved a goodbye while Toni walked to stand right in front of her. He leaned in a little and spoke for her ears only.

"If we were alone I'd kiss you right now."

"Is that all?" She was feeling good, flirty. Happy. And she began to recognize that look in his eye, just as her body began to automatically respond to it.

His gaze flicked to the long marble tabletop littered with flour and freshly rolled tortellini. "No, we'd have to break in this island."

"Like we did the tasting bar?"

"Exactly."

"I was thinking you could be spread out this time. That Lambrusco sauce might taste good licked from your torso."

He blinked and licked his lips, a glaze appearing over his eyes. Toni was a take-charge type of guy, which was evident in his life, and his sex. She'd wondered how he'd respond if she was the assertive one, and she reveled in his primal reaction, making her feel a bit like Venus in her half shell.

Dani caught movement out of her eye. Sophia was watching them. She took a deep breath and stepped back. "Sophia is done with her dessert. And she's watching."

"I'd like dessert." She knew he wasn't talking about chocolate cake.

"Dao, could you cut Toni a piece of cake. Extra Lambrusco sauce."

"You're lucky you're surrounded by people," he whispered. "If we were alone, I'd already be inside you."

Dani's insides went liquid.

Toni stepped back and took his plate. "Thank you, Dao. Nice job, everyone. My family and I can't thank you enough."

Grace returned with champagne and raised her glass to the staff. *"Salute,"* said the room and in that moment it felt like everything was falling into place.

The day of the soft launch was a blur and Toni was doing his best to keep everything together. The deliveries were late, a light rain started and several RSVPs still hadn't been confirmed. By the afternoon, the dining room tables were covered in white, soft music lilted through the air, and the lighting inside and outside of the restaurant was romantically staged. Fresh flowers perfumed the hallways, the bar was filled and the wine locker was open. Their well-trained staff manned each room. Toni caught a glimpse of himself in the hallway.

His navy suit was impeccable and hid the fact that he was sweating, hard. Quick steps led him to the kitchen doors. He peered through the window and found Dani in her black coat and Crocs, vigorously stirring a pot and yelling out orders. He smiled when he saw Sophia in a white coat in the corner with the pasta chef.

"Don't stare, you'll make her nervous," his mother said behind him.

"How is she doing?"

"Wonderfully. I've sneaked in and tasted a few things. Brilliant. Just brilliant. This is going to be a defining moment. I can feel it."

Toni wished he could mimic his mother's optimism. The critic from *The Taste* had not RSVP'd. Maybe it didn't matter. The man moved in secret, so there was a possibility he could show up. But that wasn't his only problem. His ex-wife was definitely coming. He just prayed she didn't make a scene.

Dani caught Toni at the window and lifted her brows, a silent question. He just smiled and shook his head, then blew her a kiss. She blew one back, then got back to work. He nodded his head, a defining moment indeed.

Dani wiped her brow and took a slow steady breath. Basil, oregano, paprika, she began her calming ritual just as they were putting the finishing touches on the third course. So far everything was going smoothly and from her vantage point, Dani could see that the dining rooms were full. A few beautiful people lounged in the tasting room and she caught a few journalists trying to get a peek into the kitchen, but Grace was like a gentle bear, directing everyone back to the main house. Dani turned back to her food, trying to ignore the fact that her mother still hadn't shown up.

"Dani, are you going to stay now?"

Sophia carefully placed each pasta roll into the boiling water while Dani concentrated on getting just the right spices in her white sauce. "What do you mean, love?"

"I mean, are you still going back to New York?"

"Well, I'm not sure about New York, but once this is up and running and Marcello comes back, I'll have to figure something out."

"You could stay here, in Milan."

"I doubt it, sweetie, Milan doesn't need any more chefs," she chuckled, focusing on the food, unaware of Sophia's frown and the slump of her shoulders. Dani heard the double doors of the kitchen open and expected to see Grace.

She froze when Andre slowly walked farther into her kitchen, a smile on his face that didn't reach his eyes.

"What the hell are you doing here?" Her staff faltered at his presence, but Dani gave them all a look to keep working.

"I was invited," he said, his voice as smooth as dirty silk.

"No, you were not. Get out."

"Actually, I'm here with the editor of *Good Food*, she got the invite. You look well. The food is…it's fantastic."

"If you have something to say, say it, then please leave."

"I'm sorry. Bette and I are no longer together. The TV show fell through. Actually, it's all falling apart. We lost a Michelin star since you've left. I came to ask if you would consider coming back. The staff needs you."

Dani's mind raced, unsure if what she was hearing was real. Andre there apologizing. It was what she dreamed of, and yet she didn't care. She wasn't even going to dignify his question with an answer.

"If that's all, please go. We are busy."

His head hung, and then he nodded. "Maybe we can

talk later," he murmured before slipping through the doors. Grateful he didn't cause a scene, Dani turned toward Sophia, but the young girl was gone.

Just as the fourth course was being served, Dani ran downstairs to the staff restrooms. The next course of entrées was running through her mind when she ran headlong into a tall blonde in a fur coat. Ava. What the hell was she doing down there?

"You," she sneered. "I can understand him wanting something a little different, but you're not even on the spectrum, are you?"

"If you are talking about the spectrum where a smart woman can feed a man when he's hungry and has enough curves to satisfy a man when he needs it, then you and I aren't even on the same planet."

Ava's eyes glittered with hatred. "I'm going to get him back."

"No, you won't."

Dani grinned at Ava's wide eyes, and then she left the model there to stew while she used the ladies' room. She had a job to do and Ava wasn't going to get to her anymore.

Dani rushed back to the kitchen only to find Dao in a frenzy.

"A woman came in looking for Sophia, then told the staff they were doing a horrible job. I led her out."

Dani let out an exasperated breath. Ava. She should tell Toni, but there was no time. "That was Sophia's mother. You did the right thing, Dao. I don't think she'll be coming back. Let's get the fifth course ready."

"Chef!" Liam stood just inside the doors holding four plates of entrées. His eyes wide with horror. "They are sending them back."

Dani's heart seized. "What? Why!"

The server tossed the plates on the island. "Too spicy."

Dani grabbed a fork and jammed the food into her mouth. She spit it out. Then tried the other three. All the same. Cayenne pepper. But how? The spice was burning her mouth, just like she could feel her career and the restaurant burning up in flames. She slumped over the entrées ready to cry. She looked up from the island to see Toni just inside the doors, his face like stone.

# Chapter 19

Toni showed the last of their guests out of the door, found a single malt scotch under the bar and drank straight from the bottle. He took another swig as his gaze slid to the windows and locked on the lights of the kitchen. Ten years he'd been building this and it was already crumbling after one night.

He could see it now. The bad reviews would trickle in tomorrow, leaving a black mark on his family's reputation. He was avoiding the kitchen, unsure that he was ready to talk to Dani.

What the hell happened?

Everything had been going perfectly. The food editor of *The Evening Standard* had even pulled him aside and raved. But that was before the fourth course. He looked toward the window and saw bussers and servers taking plates back to the kitchen.

Few guests had stayed for the seventh course and those that did had left several dishes untouched. By the start of the dessert course, the dining room was near empty. Toni jerked off his tie and took another deep drink.

He wanted to scream at her and yet his body yearned to hold her. He knew she was just as distraught. This wouldn't bode well for her reputation either.

After another pull from the bottle, he looked up and caught a glimpse of Dani through the opened doors. Her hands were on her face and her fingers were wiping her eyes. Was she crying? His feet were in motion before he could think to stop himself. He was making quick work of the hallway when he spotted Sophia holding herself in the corner.

"*Cara mia*, you should be in bed."

"I want to go home, Papà."

"Nonna left the back door open. You can go—"

"No, I want to go home. I want to sleep in my own bed." Toni frowned. Her eyes were puffy as if she'd been crying and she wasn't meeting his eyes. He felt guilty suddenly that she was being affected by the family troubles.

He'd met her—dare he say it—boyfriend earlier in the evening and although he still had his misgivings, he seemed like a decent boy. Some chaperoned "dates" could be arranged, but that was it.

"Sophia, I don't want you worrying about this."

"But Mamma said the restaurant will fail now." Toni gritted his teeth at Ava's loose tongue.

Grace appeared and put her hands on her hips. "Nonsense. No one listens to those critics anymore. We will open next week as planned. I don't care what they write. It was a soft launch for a reason. Nothing is perfect on the first night."

Toni nodded his head at his mother's bolstering pep talk, but their exchanged glances over Sophia's head said otherwise. His gaze shifted over his mother's shoulder toward the kitchen.

"Mamma, what happened?" He asked low.

"My love, I don't know. I'm telling you, everything was perfect. She was fantastic. Go talk to her."

"I am, I just—" He shook his head. "I don't know what to say."

"Don't yell at her, Papà." Sophia wiped at her eyes and he again felt that she didn't need to be around the drama. Maybe it was best that he took her back to Milan.

"I'm not going to yell at her. Come, I'll take you home."

When Toni looked up, Ava was standing off to the side with a martini in her hand.

"I'll hitch a ride, too, if you don't mind." Toni didn't like that snide, satisfied look on her face. It gave him the feeling that she had something to do with the night's events. Grace gave Ava a once-over and left the hall.

"I thought you drove here," Toni said, wary of the little smile on her face.

"I took a car. I can't drive in these shoes." She did a little pose and pushed her stilettos forward. Then she held up her drink. "And I wanted to have a few of these."

He had wanted to speak to Dani first, but thought maybe a drive would cool his temper. They could talk when he got back.

"Fine. I'll get the car."

After a quick run to the main house, Toni parked in front of the restaurant. He left the car running as he got out and helped Ava down the stairs, her body swaying against his in what he felt were extra theatrics. After lowering her into the car, he made his way to the driver's side.

He had one foot in when the front door opened and Dani stood in her black coat and ponytail. The streaks on her cheeks almost pulled him from the car.

"You're leaving?" Her voice quivered.

"I'll be back."

They stared at each other for a moment, then he saw her gaze shift to the passenger side. He hated how it looked but had no choice. He told himself he'd explain later. He quickly ducked into the car, revved the engine and sped away.

The sun still hadn't risen when Dani woke in Grace's home. She groaned, that sunken feeling she'd had all night hadn't left her chest and her thoughts drifted to the sight of Toni driving away in the car.

He had been avoiding her. It was the only explanation for his not coming back to the kitchen. If only she could explain...what? That she had no clue how cayenne pepper made its way into her pasta sauce? It didn't matter how. She was responsible for the food. Ultimately it was her fault.

She had planned to wait for Toni at the restaurant, but after an hour she had decided to wait in her room. She figured he would find her there but he must have gone to his room. Dani tied her robe around her waist and went to look for him. She quietly opened the unlocked door and descended the stairs, her mind focused on what to say, but her explanation speech was forgotten when she saw that his bed was empty. And hadn't been slept in.

Ava. He was with Ava. She knew it in her bones. That image of him driving away in the car wasn't what bothered her, it was him driving away with his family. Ava was trying to get him back and what better way to do it?

Dani went back to her room and scrolled through her phone with hopes of a text from Toni. Nothing. There wasn't even one from her mother, who never showed. She swallowed back tears as she packed and zipped up her suitcase. Talk about getting kicked when you were down. If there was any other time when she felt like a ghost, this trumped them all.

Dani called a car service then left her bags at the foot of the stairs, intending to write Grace a note. There was so much to say. She had crumpled up three pages when Grace appeared in her robe. The older woman hugged Dani and tried to convince her not to leave.

"Please, stay. He'll come back and you can talk."

"He doesn't want to talk to me, Grace. I understand. The restaurant—"

"Bah! You think this is the first time our family has struggled? No. This will work out. But you and Toni, that's what I'm worried about."

Dani didn't know how to say it was just sex.

"We're not together, Grace."

Grace grabbed her shoulders.

"You're falling in love. Don't throw it away over this."

"No, we aren't. He's with Ava."

"He would never. I know my son."

Dani's phone chimed with a text that her car had arrived. Sure enough, a black car rolled slowly toward the house. Grace watched her with a pleading look in her eyes. Dani didn't want to disappoint Grace, but she needed to go. "Tell him I'm sorry."

Grace lowered her eyes then nodded. Dani grabbed her bags and shut herself away in the town car. During the ride she scanned the blogs for reviews, but none had posted yet. Doom was imminent, but for now she could ignore what was coming.

The closer the car got to her hotel, the more Dani thought about her mother's absence. And by the time she slipped her key card in the hotel room door, Dani was spoiling for a fight.

She found her mother in her infamous pink silk robe in front of the bathroom mirror peeling off a face mask. The surprise in her mother's eyes set Dani off.

"Too busy to come to your daughter's big night, huh?"

"Well good morning to you, too. What are you doing here so early?" Francesca asked Dani's reflection.

"That's what you have to say? You skipped my opening!" Francesca calmly put down her washcloth and turned around. Her mother's eyes held none of the concern she'd seen in Grace's eyes this morning, and it pissed her off. "Are you that ashamed of me?"

"Danica, I have never been ashamed of you."

The scathing laughter Dani let out came with a sneer. "Bull. You didn't come to the launch at Via L'Italy either? You've never once talked about me in your interviews. You prefer people not know that you have a daughter. I'm a black smirch on your perfectly manicured image. No one this fabulous could have a fat daughter who is a failing chef."

"Failing chef? What is this about? Did something happen last night?"

Dani blinked rapidly. "You're not listening to me."

Francesca stood from the vanity in the bathroom and walked past Dani to the breakfast table. She slid open a chair. "Sit down."

"No."

"Now!" Her mother's lips were a thin line.

Dani sat, biting her cheek, wondering why this woman still had so much power over her.

Her mother sat in a flurry of silk, angrily poured them both glasses of water, then took a deep breath and leaned in.

"Do you know what happens when I walk in a room full of press?"

"Mother—"

"Shut your mouth. Camera's pop out of nowhere, every one wants a quote, attention gets drawn away from the main event. My name gets splashed all over the press while yours gets buried. Your debut is important. I refuse to ruin that for my daughter."

Dani took a gulp of water, hoping she could drink the tears away. So many rebuttals and recollections of past hurts came to mind, but she shut her mouth and listened.

"I raised you to be a capable, independent woman. You don't need me there and I have a feeling you didn't even think about it until you were feeling unstable. You only look for me when something is wrong. So what's wrong?"

Oh God, she hated it when her mother was right. There was a moment when she had looked for her mother, but honestly her mother's presence was an afterthought. She felt like a bad daughter. Was this reverse psychology?

"No. No way, you are not going to do this to me. You didn't skip the opening for me. You were too busy. You are always too busy. Always working, where I am never allowed. Because you are ashamed that I'm not svelte and gorgeous like you."

Francesca frowned hard, her eyes filled with confusion. "Young lady, have you looked in the mirror lately?"

"Every day, Mother."

"And what do you see? Do you see what I see? What I know that Toni sees."

"Stop calling him *that* Toni—"

"You're beautiful, honey. Don't give me that look. You've always been beautiful."

"If you thought that you wouldn't have made me see your trainer."

"You were learning pastries that year and that's all you ate. It wasn't healthy!"

"See what I mean? You're always so critical of me. I know my weight is why you wouldn't let me come to your work."

Francesca sighed. "Not this again."

"So it's true."

"Danica, those people at my work are vultures. Yesterday I was told to only drink smoothies for a week. The samples don't fit me. I can't have my precious daughter with her grandmother's curvy figure anywhere near those fools. But I see it got to you anyway. It's my fault, I know. You see me starve myself and think I want you to look like this. But it couldn't be further from the truth. Never have I been ashamed of you."

"What about that time you told everyone I wasn't your kid?"

Francesca laughed. "You remember that? My agent told me to hide the fact that I had had a child. At the time the industry didn't want their cover girls being mothers. It promoted the wrong image, as if being a mother is wrong. But that's the way it was then. Christie had a baby and went from the cover of *Vogue* to the cover of *Ladies Home Journal*. Things are different now, hence our photo shoot together. Which is happening. So get ready. Once the cameras start they'll be telling you to suck it in, Photoshop this, stand this way so your wobbly bits look firm." The model rolled her eyes. "After all these years you'd think I'd be used to it. It's not what I want for you. That's why I didn't want to do the shoot."

Dani dabbed at her eyes. "Why have you never told me this?"

"You get defensive when I try to protect you."

Damn her mother's logic. "I love you, Mom."

"I love you too, baby. Now I'm going to order you some breakfast. Then you can tell me what's really bothering you."

Dani felt lighter as she ate and unloaded the event of the night. Her mother listened while sipping a fruit and kale smoothie.

"You were sabotaged. Sounds like Ava. I warned you."

Dani put down her fork. Could she have?

Her mother left the room to dress and Dani checked her phone. No calls or texts from Toni. Nothing. She was about to call him when her phone lit up with the Google alerts.

A Recipe for Disaster—The Daily Meal

Peppered with Brilliance—New York Magazine

Bittersweet to Taste—The Evening Standard

Dani read each review twice, her phone signaling more postings as she scrolled. The decor was praised while the food critiques were more specific about her failure. One thing was unanimous: they were delighted until the fourth course. Several of the articles skewed toward the idea that had Marcello been there, the disaster wouldn't have happened.

It was a silver lining for the restaurant. The critics had faith that once Marcello got back into the kitchen the restaurant would be spectacular. Dani chose one of the better reviews and texted it to Toni, disappointed when he didn't respond.

Danica Nilsson had failed, but the restaurant could survive. She put down the phone, feeling slightly better knowing that once she was no longer attached to the restaurant, Toni and his family would be okay.

But would she be okay?

# Chapter 20

"Dani?" Toni jerked awake, his head pounding and his gaze blurry. It took him a moment to realize he was on a couch. He scanned the room.

An open bottle of wine and two dirty glasses sat on the coffee table, his suit jacket was draped over a nearby chair, and his phone vibrated then fell onto the floor.

Unable to reach it, he groaned and let his head fall back to the pillow. He'd accidently fallen asleep at Ava's. He jerked back up and checked that he was still wearing pants. He was. Then he rubbed his eyes, trying to remember the events of the night before.

Sophia was abnormally upset but she wouldn't talk about it. And he'd gotten tired. His body had ached with tension and what was supposed to be a quick rest before driving back became a night on the couch.

He still hadn't spoken to Dani. He still didn't know what to say. He rolled half off the couch and grabbed his phone from the floor. His mother had called three times. Then left a text saying Dani had left and he needed to call her.

The second text was from Dani with nothing but the link to a review. He opened the review and groaned again. They would recover, he told himself. Marcello would get better and they could turn it around. But what did that mean for Dani?

He dialed her number, then cut off the call when Ava shuffled by in a long T-shirt.

"*Buongiorno*, Antonio." She gathered the wine bottle and empty glasses, bending over to reveal the tops of her thighs. She wasn't wearing panties.

Toni practically jumped from the couch and strode into the bathroom. Minutes later he emerged less rumpled and Ava was in the kitchen making breakfast.

"Thanks for letting me stay last night. I'm heading back. Tell Sophia I'll call her later."

"No breakfast?"

"No, thank you." He strode down the hall as she called after him.

"Good luck. I'm sorry it didn't go well last night. It was inevitable, really. I mean the kitchen looked a mess when I saw it. Honestly, where did you find her?"

Toni let his hand drop from the doorknob and he walked back into the kitchen.

"What do you mean when you saw it?"

"You know. I just peeked my head in and they were all just standing around."

"Why would you go into the kitchen?"

"Well..." Ava fiddled with her hair. "I was—"

Toni strode toward her slowly, alarm bells ringing in his head. "What did you do?"

"Nothing!"

"Ava, did you do something to the food to get back at me?"

"Toni, I would never. I just... I don't trust that chef. And I was right!"

"Ava, you are messing with the livelihood of us all!"

"I didn't do anything!"

"Ava!"

"It was me." The small voice was like a bullet breaking through glass. Toni and Ava stopped and stared at the young lady in her pajamas.

"What did you say?" Toni whispered.

"I put pepper in the food. It was my fault."

Toni couldn't find words. Sophia's face scrunched as tears fell to the floor. Toni ran to her and knelt by her side.

"*Cara mia*, why would you do that?"

"I thought we would have to open again and Dani would have to stay a little longer. And I know—" Her voice got caught and little huffs came out as she cried harder. "I know you like her, Papá."

Was he hearing this right? His baby sabotaged the restaurant so he and Dani could be together a little longer. His heart filled with joy and pride for his loving daughter. And for the knowledge that Dani wasn't to blame. He needed to tell her.

"I'm sorry, Papá."

"I know. We can fix it." He kissed her on the head. "We'll fix it." Toni looked at Ava, her arms crossed as she leaned against the counter. He assumed she was taking issue with the "I know you like her" comment. And he was tired of hiding it. He turned back to Sophia.

"When you see Dani, you have to apologize. Her reputation was hurt too." Sophia's eyes widened.

"She's gonna hate me."

Toni shook his head. "She won't. I'll make sure of it. I have to go."

Toni reached his car door when his phone vibrated again with his mother's call. He answered the phone intent on giving her an update, but she was in tears.

"Go to the hospital," she commanded. "Now."

"Pneumonia, the doctor said, which is why they were waiting to operate. He wasn't responding to the treatment. And now..." Grace burst into tears and Toni hugged her closer to his side. Ava held Sophia as the four of them stood in the empty room staring at Marcello's empty bed. He went peacefully that morning the doctor assured them.

Toni felt numb. Yesterday morning they had everything and in twenty-four hours his life had changed forever. His uncle was gone, the restaurant was a disaster and he was scared to death that he was losing Dani, as well. He had called her, but she didn't answer. And death wasn't the type of thing you left in a voice mail.

What was he going to do. What the hell was he going to do?

A soft gasp behind him broke his thoughts. Dani's hand was at her mouth, her eyes wide as she fixated on the empty bed. Her head began a slow shake. "No. Please no."

Toni rushed to her and she was in his arms. She clung on to him hard, her body shaking with uncontrollable tears. "How?" she choked out as she pulled back.

"Pneumonia. I called to tell you but you didn't answer."

"I was probably on the train. They called me because they had me down as family from the first night."

"You are family," Toni whispered. "We have to talk."

Dani's gaze shifted to Ava, then back to him. She wriggled from his arms. Her voice sounded cold. "Yes, we do."

They walked down the hall out of earshot. Toni moved closer, letting his hands run over her shoulders, but she stopped him, stepping out of his reach.

He frowned but let her move from him regardless of how awful it felt.

"Did you get my text?"

"I did. I read the review—"

"I think as long as you make a big splash about replacing me, you'll be fine. I don't know what happened, Toni, but as chef I was responsible. There isn't much more I can say—"

"It was Sophia."

"What was Sophia?"

"Sophia spiked the food. She thought you would stay longer if the restaurant didn't open."

Dani blinked with realization, and then her shoulders

slumped with relief. "I've been racking my brain, Toni. It feels good just to know what happened."

"I know what you mean."

Dani's face lit up, then it fell. "I almost said Marcello will understand." Her lip trembled. He wanted to kiss her tears away, but she had a determined look on her face to say more.

"I'm going home in two days. I have an editorial with my mother tomorrow. Then we are heading home."

"Back to New York?"

"I was thinking of trying California. LA needs chefs too."

"What if *I* need you?"

"You don't need me. You need a chef with a reputation for excellence. Not a ghost chef with a trail of disasters behind her."

"That's not what I'm talking about and you know it."

"I thought you slept with Ava last night." She put her hand up at his instant protests. "I know you didn't but I also know you aren't looking to get seriously involved and honestly neither am I. I don't know where I'm going to end up. I have to focus on me first and a temporary fling won't let me do that."

Toni held his tongue. He watched her face as she spoke. He wanted to touch the soft skin of her cheek and kiss her full lips. Even as she told him she was leaving. She was always leaving, he knew that and once again he let his heart run him into a wall.

Because of Ava, he had taken a break from dating, but that was before he realized he couldn't keep his hands from Dani. She had everything he wanted in a woman, save one. Stability. It was important to him, and her plans didn't feel stable at all.

"So you no longer want us to see each other."

"It sounds so formal when you say it like that. I'm saying my leaving might be for the best."

They blinked at each other for a moment, but Toni didn't get a chance to respond. Sophia tapped Dani on the shoulder and confessed. His little girl was so brave, he thought as Dani hugged her and told her everything was fine.

They watched Sophia run back into the room, then turned to each other, unable to ignore the pull between them any longer. Dani cried as their mouths fused in one long last kiss. They clutched each other hard, wishes on their lips and promises in the strokes of their tongues.

Dani pulled back first and looked at him long and hard. "Goodbye, Toni." And on that whisper, she was gone.

"What do you mean she's gone? Gone where?"

Grace glared at him the next day when Toni headed back to his mother's for a lunch. His mother was distraught for many reasons and he gritted his teeth against the anger she was directing toward him. Not that it wasn't warranted. He'd been struggling with the thought of her leaving. Her words made him feel like he'd lost his heart, leaving only a functional shell.

"Back to the States. She leaves tomorrow I think."

"Then she's still here. Go get her." His mother paced, her eyes flashing. "Why would you let her go?"

He was asking himself that too.

"She doesn't want to stay, Ma!"

"Did you tell her you love her?"

"Oh my God..." Toni looked at his mother like she was crazy, but her eyes only held anguish. He lowered his voice and hung his head. "No."

Grace cursed under her breath.

"I'm not sure she feels the same."

"How will you know unless you put it out there?" She

hugged him and kissed him on both cheeks. A knock on the front door sent Grace into the other room, while Toni stared out the window at the restaurant. All night he wished he could have redone their talk in the hospital. Over and over he asked himself if he had told her he loved her, would she have agreed to stay?

Antonio turned as footsteps came toward the kitchen and Grace entered, followed by an older gentleman in a suit. Grace introduced them.

"Antonio, this is Signore Russo, Marcello's lawyer. It seems he changed his will days before he passed away." The men shook hands and the three of them took a seat at the table. The lawyer was slow in his delivery, pulling out stacks of papers with Marcello's signature, explaining the reason he had come to his mother's home.

"It's fortunate I have you both here," he started, fumbling for his glasses. Toni's mother looked at him from out of the side of her eye when he started reading a bunch of legal mumbo jumbo, which he said in a monotone that had Toni almost asleep. "To my loving sister and executor of my estate, I leave my home and possessions to do with as you please and one-third of my restaurant Via Carciofo. To my loving nephew I leave my wine cellar and one-third of my restaurant Via Carciofo."

Toni and his mother gave each other a look as Signore Russo passed around papers to be signed. After gathering the documents, he put them back in his briefcase and shut the top.

*"Grazie,"* Signore Russo said as he stood and turned to leave.

"Wait," Toni said after he jumped from his seat. "Who has the last third?"

The old man fixed his glasses on his nose. "I am unable to give you that information."

Grace came forward. "But they will be our partner. How can you not tell us?"

"I must find them and tell them first. If I can find them." The latter he said under his breath as he labored toward the front door. Toni was following him close behind and stopped him one last time at the door.

"Signore, I may be able to help you find this man. Then you could go home and relax, huh?"

Russo narrowed his gaze and looked around to see who was listening. Then he leaned toward Toni. "It's a woman."

A thankful smile spread wide across Toni's face. "I know where she is."

# Chapter 21

"Look at this skin, it's perfect." Dani closed her eyes as Roberto pressed a spongy thing all over her face. If her skin was so perfect, why did she need so much foundation?

"Those are my genes, Roberto, make no mistake." Her mother was next to her, putting on her own false eyelashes in the mirror while three stylists buzzed behind them putting together the looks for the shoot.

"I know it. She's like your Mini-Me. Okay, Mini-Me, look up." Dani gritted her teeth as a mascara brush was dangerously close to her eyeball.

Walking through the offices of *Vogue* had been a bit of a dream come true, but sitting in a chair for hours in a small dingy dressing room? Not so much.

Roberto hummed RuPaul as he worked, instructing her to look up, then down, then purse her lips, then make an O. "This is so exciting. Mommy dearest is going to show you the ropes!"

Francesca's interrupted her blowout to turn her head. "Stop calling me that. I am not Joan Crawford." Her mother turned toward the mirror with a sultry look. "More like Dorothy Dandridge."

"Well, I heard she was crazy too," Roberto snickered. "Okay, all done. Open those eyes, Mini-Me."

Dani blinked at her reflection. She wasn't even sure it was her. If she saw a picture of this woman she'd think she was…gorgeous. Her gaze shifted to Roberto.

"You're a genius."

Roberto nodded. "I am. But you didn't need much help, Mini-Me. A little mascara here, some eyeliner there, and a BB cream to even out your skin tone. You're hot. Oh, to be young again. Right, Fannie?"

"You said it, Robbie." Francesca looked at her. "You look stunning, sweetheart."

*Stunning.* The word brought back heart-wrenching memories. She hadn't heard from him, which she supposed was normal when you said goodbye to someone, but in this case she was hoping he wouldn't listen.

She'd had fantasies of him barging into the hotel and declaring his love. Or at least a declarative phone call. She'd even accept a text.

"What's wrong, Danica?" Roberto put his hands on her shoulders and peered at her reflection.

"Nothing. I'm fine. Just nervous."

"She's having man trouble," her mother said, shaking out her roller-curled hair.

"Humph, aren't we all?" Roberto pursed his lips. "What'd he do? Cheat? Take your money? Is it drugs?"

"Robbie, who are you dating? Convicts?" said her mother.

He shrugged. "You know who I'm talking about."

"Oh jeez." Her mother rolled her eyes and Dani smiled at their easy friendship. Roberto turned to Dani and put a finger over his lips as he whispered.

"He's famous." Roberto giggled. "Dani, tell me everything."

"There isn't much to tell. He lives here and I don't. Plus he has family drama to work out. It's best that we ended our relationship."

Roberto stared at her with a sad face. "That sounds very mature. But why can't you find a job here and stay?"

"She doesn't want to. She wants to come to California with me," her mother said.

Roberto looked at her from the side of his eye. "You're

here all the time. You can visit her." He turned to Dani. "Are you in love with him?"

Dani blinked at her reflection, and then her eyes slid toward her mother's watchful gaze. She was relieved when the head stylists announced it was time for wardrobe.

They chose three looks for them both: denim, casual and glam. Dani posed with her mother for the first few shoots, feeling more comfortable by the time they got to the glam shoot.

Her red sleeveless bodycon dress had lace along her midriff and upper chest so only one solid covered her breasts. Paired with black heels, it was the epitome of sexy. And it fit perfectly.

She didn't "suck it in" nor was she instructed to pose a certain way to minimize her body. She had fun with her mother and at the end of her shoot, she felt beautiful. Like a Botticelli.

Would she ever stop thinking of him?

Then her mother posed alone for the cover shoot and things got intense. Dani overheard the photographer whispering about her loose skin, her sagging breasts, her small belly. There was the ugliness her mother had tried to keep from her.

Head high, Francesca walked off the photo shoot amid a round of applause, but when she got to the dressing room, she was depleted.

She magically took her strapless push-up bra off from under her dress and threw it on the counter.

"That was killing me."

"You looked amazing, Mother."

"I hate that photographer." Francesca then turned to Dani. "Are you sure you want to come to LA?"

"Yes," Dani shrugged. "I think I could find work there."

Francesca lowered her gaze, then turned back to her

mirror. "Roberto and I are going for dinner. Would you like to come? Oh, by the way. The dress and shoes you're wearing as well as the others are yours to keep."

"Nice perk."

"That doesn't always happen. But I wanted you to have them."

"Thank you, for the dresses. And for today." She felt closer to her mother in the last twenty-four hours than she ever had, but she still couldn't pull herself out of the dumps. Nor could she get Toni off of her mind. "I'm going to head back to the hotel."

Thirty minutes later Dani walked into her hotel lobby and turned her head at the concierge's soft gasp and nod of approval. Maybe she should have joined her mother and Roberto, she thought. Why let this make up and dress go to waste.

She was almost to the elevators when someone called out her name.

She slowly turned and scanned the lobby just as Toni stood from one of the lounge chairs.

Dani felt her heart flip-flop in her chest. Her first instinct was to run to him and throw her arms around his neck. Instead she gave him a neutral smile and strode toward him, frowning when an older man with a briefcase stood when she arrived.

"Hi, Toni."

"Dani." His gaze was fixed on her face, then traveled up and down her dress. His hands went in his pockets, and then he brought them back out. "Um, this is Signore Russo. He, um, he's handling Marcello's will. Why are you dressed like this?"

"I had a photo shoot with my mother. Did you say Marcello's will?"

"Oh, okay. And yes," he sighed, still staring at her with an intense gaze.

"You seem relieved."

"I am." His jaw clenched.

"What did you think I was doing in this dress?"

"Having dinner with someone other than me." Toni's gaze slid to the signore. "Russo needs to speak with you. Do you mind if I stay?"

"Are you going to frown the whole time?"

"Maybe." He gave her his seat and moved to an adjacent one, his gaze still on her.

"What can I do for you, Signore Russo?"

Toni didn't stop looking at her while the old lawyer found his glasses and shuffled through his papers. Toni looked like a lounging tiger ready to strike, his expression like a mask.

"Here we are. Miss Nilsson, you've been named as a beneficiary of one-third owner of Via Carciofo and one-third owner of Via Olivia. And it says here he has left you his knives. If you just sign here, the transactions will be complete."

It took Dani a moment to fully comprehend what Russo was telling her. It must have been all over her face, because Toni leaned over and grabbed her hand. "He left you his shares of the restaurants, Dani."

She squeezed Toni's hand. "And his knives." She was going to cry.

"*Sì*, signora." Once Dani signed her name, Russo handed her his card and left.

Toni took the empty seat in front of her. "Are you okay?"

"I think so. I just can't believe he's gone."

"I know."

"Did you know about the will?"

"I only found out today. He must have loved you very much."

"How do you feel about me having a part of your restaurants?"

"How do I feel?" The edges of his mouth flickered. "I know I said I didn't want to get involved but I haven't felt whole since you told me you were leaving. I don't want to run these restaurants without you. And I can't deny how strong my feelings are for you any longer."

"You have feelings for me?" She didn't dare believe it.

"Dani, you have no idea how much I want to poke out the eyes of every man that has seen you in this dress. You really have no idea how beautiful you are, do you?"

"Toni—"

"I can't stop thinking about you. Tell me you've been thinking about me too."

"I have. But—"

Toni unfolded from his chair, took Dani's hand and pulled her from her seat right into his arms. His mouth was warm and firm and he held her as if she was essential to his existence. Her hands ran over his arms, feeling the power of his body as he bent her back with the force of his need. It matched her own.

Toni eased her away from him when a group of tourists rapidly pressed the elevator button.

"Let's go to your room. This is too public," Toni whispered.

They didn't speak in the elevator, but Toni's hand secretly trailed up and down her back. When they walked down the hallway to Dani's room, Toni kept that hand solidly in the small of her back. Once inside the room, however, they crossed the suite to her bedroom and that hand spun her around and pressed her up against the inside of the door.

Their mouths fused, fierce and demanding. He pulled back slowly and his fingertips teased over the lace of the dress.

"Do you know how many men were looking at you in the lobby?" he said, shoving out of his jacket. His hand gripped then caressed her throat as he spoke, and then he turned her face to nip and suck at her neck. "Those men wanted to make love to you." He pulled back to look at her, his gaze burning with lust. "Just the thought of them touching you makes me crazy."

"Well, now you know how it feels. How is Ava doing?" His eyes flared.

"Ava is well aware of who I want." He jerked off his jacket and tossed it on the chair. Then she saw his gaze drop to her packed bags in the corner of the room. "How about I help you unpack those bags?"

"Why should I stay?" Dani remained against the wall, watching him prowl the room like a panther. His hands went from his pockets to run through his hair and back. She knew his cues now. Emotions were boiling she just needed them to spill over.

"You have a business to run now."

"Why shouldn't I just sell my shares to you and go home?" He ripped off his tie and threw it on the dresser.

"I'm not buying your shares."

"Someone will buy them." His eyes flashed.

"Don't you dare."

"I dare you to tell me why I should stay?"

He stopped then and stared at her. His mouth opened then closed. "We want to open the restaurant for good next week in Marcello's honor. He would want you to cook."

She slumped away from the wall and stalked toward him. She grabbed the back of his head.

"You chickenshit." Her lips crashed against his and Toni kissed her back with abandon.

He gently peeled her out of the dress, taking extra care with the lace fabric, kissing and sucking the newly exposed skin. Her bra and panties disappeared like smoke. "Leave the shoes," he instructed, ripping off his shirt and undoing his pants. "And get on the bed."

Dani lay back and reached for Toni. He stood over her, shirt gone, pants unbuckled. His gaze racked over her body.

"You're incredible," he murmured, pulling himself out of his pants and stroking the long length.

She was aching for him, getting hotter and wetter watching him run his hands over himself.

"Toni—" she breathed, his possessive attitude making her hotter and hotter.

"Spread your legs for me," he instructed, and her knees fell open at his command. "Mine," he murmured.

Her heart almost jumped out of her chest, desire pulsing through her at the thought of being solely his possession.

He lowered his mouth and nuzzled her breasts, his lips nipping and sucking her nipples until she was writhing uncontrollably.

"Turn over—get on your hands and knees for me." His voice was laced with raw need, making her shudder at the sound. She did as he asked and flipped her hair as she turned back to look at him.

She felt his palm smack then knead one bare cheek. The other hand smoothed over her shoulder and executed a light grip.

"You're not leaving," he breathed into her ear.

Then he thrust into her in one hard surge, burying his impressive length all at once. Dani moaned as the strength of his hips drove her face closer to the bed.

He groaned and stilled, bending to give her a small kiss on her back, and his hands settled on her hips in a strong grip.

He pounded into her, thick and strong, filling her fully with every relentless pump of his hips. One hand grabbed the heel of her black stiletto and bent her knee up, pushing her forward and opening her hips even more.

Dani clawed at the duvet as he drove deeper still, feeling like he was taking over her entire body.

He was wild and unapologetic inside her, and she loved every minute of it. Never had any man made her feel so desired.

She cried out as she came all around him, her swollen flesh gripping him, and pulled a throaty yelp from his throat.

Her body jolted and stars burst behind her eyes, yet he still surged hard and sure, gripped her body even more.

"You can't imagine how it feels," he said, his voice low in her ear as he leaned over her, "to have you come while I'm inside you."

Toni exploded in a rush of grunts as he thrust himself into her one final time, his hands digging into her skin as he rode out his orgasm deep within her.

They fell onto the bed into a heap of sweaty skin and heavy breathing, rolling over to lay next to each other. Toni moved onto his elbow and traced one of Dani's nipples with his fingertip. Dani let her eyes drift shut.

"I have to leave town for a couple days," he said, his voice throaty and full. "But I'll be back in time for the opening." His hand caressed her cheek, then gently turned her face toward his. "Unpack those bags. You're not leaving."

Dani opened her eyes and studied his handsome face. His voice sounded confident, but his eyes held a plea. "I'm staying," she said, looking into his eyes. Then added, "For now."

His brows slashed over his eyes at that comment, but he

stayed quiet. His eyes held a warning that made her smile a little. She wasn't going anywhere, but he didn't need to know that.

She part owned not one but two restaurants, she wasn't going to throw that away.

Dani put on a robe while Toni dressed leisurely, kissing and touching her without hesitation or persuasion, like she was his possession. His woman.

"I'll call you tomorrow from the airport to make sure you haven't changed your mind."

"Yes, sir."

"I like that."

"Don't get used to it."

She walked him to the door and she gave him a long thorough kiss in the threshold.

"Tell Sophia I said hi."

"Yes, Chef."

"I like that."

"Get used to it." He gave her one last quick kiss and turned into the hallway, running straight into Francesca and Roberto. Her mother's eyes were wide and Roberto's hand flew to his chest. Dani could only imagine what she looked like and clutched her robe closed further.

Toni kissed Francesca's hand and nodded a hello to Roberto, and then the three of them watched him walk down the hall. Dani broke the ice.

"So, it looks like I might be staying, after all."

# Chapter 22

Three days later Dani donned her black coat and took her place at the kitchen. Her kitchen. It was surreal and she planned on thanking Marcello by cooking the best meal Milan had ever seen.

But by the looks of the dining area, Milan wasn't ready to eat it. It was prime dining hour and several tables were empty.

"Coming in!" She recognized his voice before he entered. Charcoal suit and black tie, Toni looked dashing, and she immediately asked for his touch. It has been too long since the hotel room, but they had spoken every day and sometimes night on the phone. Something had shifted between them. He was more territorial with her well-being, more attentive than before. She had to admit that she liked it.

He greeted the staff, then sent her a wicked smile. She noticed a medium-size shopping bag in his hand. "Chef, may I see you in my office?" That meant the meat locker. She entered the cold storage room and was immediately pulled into a feverish kiss. Three days of pent-up desire rushed through them both. "Miss me?"

"Of course. How was business?"

His gaze roamed over her face. "I got what I needed." In their phone conversations he'd been cagey about what he was doing. Something about the warehouses blah, blah, blah. She got the sense it was something else too. He had hinted as much.

"And what was that?"

He presented the bag and she reached inside, delighted

to find a familiar rolled knife bag. Marcello's knives. "I had them sharpened."

Tears rose. "That's so thoughtful."

"There's something else in there."

She checked the bag and found a small velvet ring box. Her heart thumped as she met his steady gaze. He nodded. "Open it."

There were no words. A canary yellow diamond as big as her knuckle sat in a platinum setting of diamond baguettes.

"I love you, Danica Nilsson. And I want to spend the rest of my life with you. I would have told you the other night, but it didn't feel right without the ring. Regardless of what happens with the restaurants, I want you to know that I need you in my life."

She could no longer hold back the tears. She stared at the ring, her mind racing and her heart full for the man that stood in front of her. In her meat locker. She laughed.

"You're laughing."

"I'm not! This is just surreal."

"Say yes."

"Toni—"

"Look who's chickenshit now."

"Yes! You bully. Yes! I love you and I want to marry you."

Their kiss was freezing cold and wonderful. He took the ring and brought her hand up to receive it, but she pulled it back. "Toni, I can't cook with that on my finger. I love it, but I can't wear it right now."

He smiled and cocked his head. "I know, Chef, so I got you another one." He pulled another box from his pocket and opened it to reveal an angel hair–thin platinum band encrusted with the smallest diamonds she'd ever seen. It was perfect.

Opening night went without a hitch with Dani working endlessly to prepare her best meal. *Every night is opening night*, as Marcello used to say. She and the staff had begun cleaning when Toni and a wide-eyed server burst into the kitchen holding a table napkin.

"Dani, look at this." She took the outstretched napkin and saw handwriting in pen all over the surface.

"Who defaces a cloth napkin like this?" Dani squinted at the cursive letters.

Toni's eyes flashed. "Read it."

Miss Nilsson, I was devastated to hear of Marcello's passing and had come to this establishment to pay my respects. I know it was supposed to be his triumph. I must tell you that you have big shoes to fill, and from what I can tell, you are wearing them quite comfortably. Velvet artichoke soup? Never have I tasted anything so simple yet so rich. I must confess I was unaware of your contribution to the kitchen of L'Italy in New York until recently. Are you aware they have lost two stars? I will be retracting the scathing review I left. Although if you recall, I said the veal shank was excellent. My review will be posted tomorrow. Good luck, Chef Nilsson. I look forward to more from you.
—The Taste.

*One year later*

"It's time, Dani." Liz burst through the door of the kitchen, almost knocking over Dao and the tray of chocolates he was preparing. Dani frowned at her friend, who backed away with her hands up.

"Dao, put one of those little chocolates on each of the plates and a drizzle of Lambrusco sauce, please."

"I can't believe you. You have guests out there." Liz put her hands on her hips and raised her brows.

"Almost done." Dani swirled the icing over the seventh tier of the cake. "Dao, it's ready." She handed her sous-chef the knife and watched as her staff carried the cake away. Once she was satisfied that everything was set, she hurried toward the double doors.

"Woman, take that black coat off!"

"Oh!" Dani unbuttoned her chef's coat, revealing a floor-length strapless wedding dress with a mermaid hem and short train. She kicked off her Crocs and slipped her feet into her sparkly Jimmy Choos.

Liz tsked, then smiled at her friend. "You look gorgeous."

Dani walked with Liz back into the dining room, her eyes settling happily on their hundreds of guests, most of whom she had just met. But her heart filled to see Destin and Nicole, her mother, Grace and Sophia, and her father chatting animatedly with Toni.

She strode toward the two, her father looking stately in his suit, his neck tattoos peeking from the collar also making him look like an older David Beckham. "You look lovely, darling." Her father wound an arm around her shoulders and kissed her hair.

"Thank you, Daddy. You look nice too."

"Do you think your mother thinks so?"

Francesca was watching them from the side of her eye, and then she quickly turned away. She was ravishing in a blue sequined gown, and she knew it. Francesca was doing her best impression of ignoring her father, but it seemed a little more like foreplay. Gross. "Yeah, I think she does." Dani turned to her husband. "We have a cake to cut."

"Yes, Chef."

Dani spread Marcello's knives on the table and cut her husband a generous slice of marble cake with lots of red wine buttercream icing. His finger made it into the slice before she could serve him.

"You are asking for it."

"And I hope I get it," he said after sucking his finger. "Will you make this for me every night?"

She held his piece to his mouth and their eyes met in challenge. If she smashed the cake on him, he'd do it to her. She let him have his cake and when it came her turn, he was behaved, if not a little impish when he slid a fingertip into the icing and slipped a little more between her lips. He didn't know it yet, but she had made extra icing.

The crowd cheered and her staff rushed in to cut and serve.

"Where is the champagne?"

"I vetoed the champagne."

Her husband's head whipped around. "What? Why? I had the warehouse send the Clos." He looked over her head and whatever he was going to say died on his lips. The staff was pouring sparkling red for their guests.

"It's the Dolcetto. Marcello's Dolcetto. I asked them to bring it from our warehouse, but don't worry, as your supplier I made sure you got a discount."

His eyes were filled with love. "That's cute. Come here."

They kissed among yells and clinking glasses.

"Are you ready for your cake? It's the chef's special," Dani whispered, suggestively rubbing against him.

"You get the icing," Toni teased.

"And you get the Clos."

Toni's smile was wicked. "*Sì*, Chef. Whatever you want, Chef. Forever."

\* \* \* \* \*

# IT WAS ONLY A KISS

## JOSS WOOD

For my children, Rourke and Tess, who are
all things bright and beautiful.

# PROLOGUE

*Eight years ago...*

'SO, IN CONCLUSION, I think the marketing strategy your people presented to you is hackneyed, stupid and asinine, and pays absolutely no attention to your demographics, to the market research or to where your competitors are placing themselves. It's under-researched and knocked together, and if you follow it I guarantee that you will lose most of your market share in five years' time—if not your business.'

Luke Savage looked across his messy desk at the earnest young woman perched on the edge of her chair, her face animated with youthful zeal and a healthy dose of arrogance. What was her name again? He glanced down at the file in front of him. Jess Sherwood. She was twenty-two, he read, and was currently doing her MBA in Marketing. The file did state that she was over-blessed with brains—her school and university achievements were, to put it mildly, impressive—but it failed to mention that she was solidly gorgeous as well.

A true brown-eyed blonde.

She was quite a parcel and, boy, did she know it.

Luke kept his face impassive as she draped one long, slim leg over the other and lightly linked her hands around a bare knee, an index finger tapping away. She wore a short, flouncy dress, falling off one shoulder and showing a thin purple bra strap, and belted at slim hips by a broad leather belt. Falling to mid-thigh, it was too short, too casual, and too sexy an outfit for work—but she wore it with careless confidence.

Luke, who was seldom surprised at much, was taken aback by her self-importance and her balls-to-the-wall chutzpah. She'd been placed as an intern for the summer holidays, to gain work experience within St Sylve's marketing department—*his* marketing department, since he'd recently inherited the generations-old family vineyard. She'd ambushed him as he'd been about to leave, barged into his office and said that she felt 'morally obligated'—he curled his lip at the phrase—to tell him that his decisions sucked and his marketing plan was dreadful. And now she had the temerity to predict the failure of his business.

Her mobile rang and Luke hissed his annoyance as she dived for her bag and pulled out the phone, squinting at the display. She flashed him a wide smile that was charming but devoid of apology. 'Sorry—I have to take this.'

*Whatever—I'm just your boss. Why don't I just wait while you finish arranging your social life?*

He felt twenty years older than her, rather than six, and he probably was in experience. University was a dim and distant memory, clouded by the fourteen- to sixteen-hour days he'd been working for the past seven years.

Lately he'd felt perpetually exhausted, but if he'd had the energy he'd have got up and yanked her mobile from her ear and torn her a new one. Which he intended to do when she finished cooing into her mobile.

Her words rattled around his brain… *You will lose most of your market…*

Hell, he was losing St Sylve. It was failing… Not his fault or his failure, because failure wasn't what he did—well, it wasn't what he'd been allowed to do. Sport? He'd excelled at most. Academics? Scholarships and huge job offers had translated into his being able to set up his own company three years ago…one of the youngest venture capitalists in the country. Marriage? Okay, he'd dropped the ball on that one, but in a couple of weeks the divorce would be through and he'd be rid of the credit-card-digesting monster he'd married.

Now, if he could get this other creature out of his office without strangling her, he'd consider himself a saint.

Jess snapped her mobile closed, slipped it back into her bag and looked at him expectantly. Stuck-up, arrogant little witch.

Sexy, though….

Luke's boots dropped from the corner of his desk to the floor and he stood up slowly, knowing that his face displayed none of his anger. As a child, living with his volatile, demanding father—his mother had died when he was three—he'd learnt early that showing emotion of any sort could be used against him, so he'd perfected his stoic mask.

He watched her through half-closed lids. She looked relaxed, leaning back in the chair, a small smile edging the corners of her very sexy mouth upwards. Give her a couple of years and she'd be hell on wheels…if she could keep her cocky opinions to herself.

'Interesting perspective,' Luke said mildly. He saw her mouth open to speak and lifted a finger to silence her. 'If I cared.'

Mouth open but no words emerging…it was a start, Luke thought. Placing his hands on his desk, he leaned forward with a gesture that was meant to be intimidating and finally allowed her to see his fury. He felt marginally appeased when her eyes widened and she bit her bottom lip.

'You arrogant, snotty child!' He deliberately kept his voice even, knowing that harsh words delivered coldly had more of an effect than ranting and raving. 'How dare you walk into my company and my office and presume to tell me what to do with my business and how to do it? Who the *hell* do you think you are?' he suddenly roared, and Jess winced as his words bounced off the walls.

Jess lifted up her hands and he noticed that she didn't look particularly scared. Hell, she didn't look scared, period.

'You don't understand—'

'What I understand is that you are a bright young thing who has always been told that she's wonderful—clever and bright and talented. Pretty too. After so much unstinting admiration and affirmation, how could you think I wouldn't want to hear the pearls of wisdom that fall so effortlessly from your lips?'

Jess jumped to her feet. 'Luke, I—'

'It's Mr Savage to you! I'm your boss, not your friend! If you want to get anywhere you'd better bloody learn some humility and some respect! I have my own MBA, sunshine, and I've run a successful company for years. I have put in the sweat and tears and the work to earn the right to have an opinion. You haven't!'

'Stop yelling at me!'

Luke looked at her and shook his head. A part of him—okay, all his boy bits—thought she looked magnificent, with her heaving chest and wild eyes, fury staining her high cheekbones like the rasp of a lover's beard. She looked furious, but not intimidated, and a part of him had to admire her courage.

A very small part of him.

'It's not my fault your marketing plan sucks! I'm just telling you that the St Sylve vineyard will suffer if you do not adjust your strategy!'

'Because you say so?'

'Yes! Because I'm damn good at this. I just know it won't work!'

Luke rubbed a hand over his chin. 'So, now you have a crystal ball as well? Can you tell me if I'm going to get skinned in my divorce or whether the price of oil will drop?'

'Of course you will get skinned—that's what happens when you marry a gold-digger! And, no, the oil price is going to keep climbing. The markets are too unstable at the moment to allow a drop,' Jess replied.

Luke could not believe that she hadn't picked up his sarcasm. 'For someone who's only been here a couple of months, you seem to be firmly plugged in to vineyard gossip.'

Jess sent him a cheeky grin. 'Thank you.'

'It wasn't a compliment.'

'I know.'

He was going to kill her. Luke stalked around the desk and gripped her slim shoulders with his much bigger hands. 'I'm not sure whether to strangle you or smack you.'

Jess tossed her head of honey-coloured curls and looked up at him with bold and defiant brown eyes. A brown so deep it could almost be black.

'You're not the type to hit a woman.' Jess lifted one shoulder and sent him a look that was as powerful as it was ageless. 'And you're just annoyed because you know I'm right.'

'Annoyed? I'm way past annoyed and on my way to incandescently livid.'

Under his hands Jess lifted her shoulders. 'But why? I'm just telling the truth.'

He was exasperated at her cheek, but he was even more furious because she had his blood pressure spiking and his pants jumping.

'You are cheeky, conceited, smug and vain,' Luke muttered as his lips edged their way down to hers. He could see the challenge in those eyes that held his…and as well as not tolerating failure, he also never backed away from a challenge.

Jess tipped her chin up and he could feel her breath on his lips. She felt slight and feminine in his arms, and while he knew that he was playing with fire he couldn't let her go.

'Then why are you going to kiss me?'

'Because it's either that or put you over my knee,' Luke growled.

'But you don't like me,' Jess stated.

'God, how old are you? Attraction has nothing to do with liking someone.'

'It should.'

'You're naïve.'

'Kissing me would be a mistake,' Jess whispered even as her lips lifted to his.

'Too damn late.'

Electricity arced and thunder rolled as he yanked her slim frame into his solid chest, burrowing his hands into her hair to move her head so that he could deepen the angle of the kiss, could touch every corner of her sexy mouth with his tongue. His hand dropped to her lower back and he pulled her against him. His stomach swooped when he felt her hips against his, her small hands sneaking under his shirt to feel the skin of his back and shoulders.

He'd never been this hot this quickly for anyone. Luke closed his eyes as her quick tongue tasted his bottom lip, then tangled with his in a long, lazy slide. One hand held the back of her head and the other skimmed the side of her torso, its thumb sliding over the swell of her—

This had gone too far, Luke told himself. He had to stop this. Now.

Instead he ran the palms of his hands up the back of her silky-soft thighs and gripped her butt.

Holy hell, he thought as his hands encountered nothing but warm skin. Where were her panties…? Their kiss deepened and went from crazy to wild. He massaged her as he pulled her up against him and…oh, there it was. An ultra-thin strand of cotton. He traced his fingers upward and found the T of her thong, embellished with what seemed to be a fabric heart flat against her lower back. Luke hooked his thumb under the T and rubbed that gorgeous patch of skin. So soft, so smooth… He could snap the cord with a quick twist…

Luke wrenched himself away from her, sucked in a breath and hoped that she didn't notice him gripping the edge of the desk for balance. She looked glorious, with her flashing eyes, swollen mouth and mussed hair. He could take her right now, right here in the late-afternoon sun.

It shook him how much he wanted to see her naked, sprawled across his desk, her body exposed to his hot gaze, her creamy skin flushed with pleasure.

Luke summoned up the last reserves of his self-control and slowly felt his self-restraint returning. When he felt his big brain had the edge over his little one, he stood up straight and wordlessly pointed to the door.

Jess nodded as she straightened her shirt. 'Right—time for me to leave.' She rocked on her heels, then dug in her tote bag and pulled out a large envelope which she placed on his desk. 'A marketing strategy—an alternative to what you have now. Maybe we can discuss it another time?'

Un-frickin'-believable.

Had she heard anything he'd said before he'd kissed the hell out of her? Obviously not.

Luke shook his head. 'I don't think so.'

A tiny frown appeared between her arched brows. 'Why not?'

Luke walked around his desk and flopped into his chair. 'Because you're fired. Pack up your stuff and get off my property. Immediately.'

# CHAPTER ONE

*Jessica*
*I seem to be missing one of my Shun knives. A boning*
*and filleting knife. If you do not return it I'll be forced*
*to ask you to replace it as I bought it during our trip*
*to the States. They retail for around 200 US dollars.*
*Grant*

JESS SHERWOOD DROPPED her head as the e-mail on her screen winged its way to the deleted folder. Grant was smoking something very green and very strong if he thought that she had any intention of paying him another cent. Who had supported him and his extravagant lifestyle when he'd lost his job and while he'd struggled to get his fledgling catering business off the ground?

And, while she'd dished out the money and the sympathy, every day when she'd left for work he'd found something else to do. Or perhaps she should say *someone* else to do… the blonde living in the simplex opposite them.

*Jerk.*

The door to her office opened and Jess watched Ally enter, her iPad in her hand. Jess counted her blessings that her stunningly efficient office manager was also her best and most trusted friend.

'What's the matter?' Ally asked, dropping into the chair opposite Jess.

Jess waved at her computer. 'Grant. Again. Looking for something called a Shun knife. Um…what's a Shun knife?'

Ally, well acquainted with Jess's lack of culinary skills, smiled. 'It's a brand of expensive kitchen knives. Nice.'

'Well, if I find it in my kitchen it's yours,' Jess said glumly.

'What else is the matter?' Ally placed her iPad on the desk.

Jess waved at her computer. 'Grant's trying to yank my chain.'

Ally's bold red lips quirked. 'Judging by the scowl on your face, I'd say "mission accomplished".'

Jess wrinkled her nose. 'He's the larva that grows on the dung of…'

'Yeah, yeah—heard it all before. It was over months ago, so why are you still so PO-ed?'

Jess rested her elbows on her desk and shoved her fingers into her hair, considering Ally's question. It had been a year since Grant had lost his high-powered job as brand manager for a well-known clothing chain, and six months since she'd caught him in their bed with what's-her-name with the stupid Donald Duck tattoo on her butt…

Since she'd been on top when Jess had walked into the bedroom the image was indelibly printed on her mind.

Okay, so the incident had also catapulted her back to that dreadful period in her teens when— No, she wasn't going to think about that. It was enough to remember that she now knew the pain infidelity caused—first- and second-hand.

She was now wholly convinced that any woman who handed over emotional control to another person in the name of love had to be fiercely brave or terminally nuts.

She was neither.

'Well?' When Jess didn't speak, Ally shook her head. 'We've shared everything from pregnancy scares—yours—

to one-night stands—mine—and everything in between, so talk to me, Jessica Rabbit.'

Jess managed a smile at her old nickname. 'I'm angry, sure, but at myself as well as him. I'm livid that he managed to slip his affair under my radar—that I wasn't astute enough to realise that he was parking his shoes under someone else's bed.'

Ally stood up, walked over to the credenza and shoved two cups under the spout of Jess's beloved coffee machine. After doctoring them both, Ally handed Jess her cup, put her back to the window and perched her bottom on the sill.

'I spoke to Nick on my way to work.' Jess couldn't help the smile that drifted across her face. It was wonderfully good to have an open, relaxed relationship with her brother again, after years of him operating on the periphery of her life. 'He's so damn happy with Clem, and I know that they have something special. The last of my brothers—all of whom sowed enough wild oats to cover Africa—has settled down.'

'And you're wafting in the wind?' Ally placed her hands on the windowsill behind her. 'And that bothers you because it's something your brothers have got right and you haven't. Love is not a contest, Jess. Do you know what your problem is?' Ally continued.

'No, but I'm sure you're going to tell me,' Jess grumbled. She wasn't sure she wanted to hear what she had to say…Ally seldom pulled her punches.

'You raised the topic,' Ally pointed out. 'Do you want me to tell you what you want to hear or the truth?'

'That's a rhetorical question, right?' Jess took a deep breath. 'Okay, I'll take a brave-girl pill…hit me.'

'One sentence: you're so damned scared of being vulnerable that you try to control everything in a relationship.'

Hearing her earlier thought about control so eloquently explained floored Jess. Did her best friend know her or what?

'Being single suits you and not being in love suits you even better.'

'Can I change my mind and ask you to tell me what I want to hear?' Jess protested. She wasn't sure if she wanted to hear any more about her romantic failings.

'To you, being in love means losing control—and to a control freak that is the scariest thing in the world.'

'I am *not* a control freak!' Jess retorted, heat in her voice.

Ally's mouth dropped open. 'You big, fat liar! You are all about control. That's why you choose men you can control.'

'You are so full of it.' Jess sulked.

'You know I'm right,' Ally retorted.

This was the problem with good friends. They knew you better than you knew yourself, Jess grumbled silently. Deciding that Ally was looking far too smug, she decided to change the subject, vowing to give their conversation some more thought later.

Maybe.

If she felt like digging into her own psyche with a hand drill.

Right now they needed to work. She nodded to the iPad and listened and made notes as Ally updated her on the projects she wasn't personally involved with. Jess gave her input and instructions and ran through some office-related queries.

They were concentrating on interpreting some tricky data from a survey when Jess's PA put through a call from Joel Andersen, a much larger competitor whose company owned branches throughout Africa.

He was also one of the few people in the industry she liked and trusted.

Ally started to rise, but Jess shook her head and hit the speaker button. She would tell Ally about the call anyway, so she'd save herself the hassle. She and Joel traded greetings and Jess waited for him to get to the point. Joel, not one to beat around the bush, jumped right in.

'I was wondering...what did you think about Luke Savage's e-mail? I presume you're going to his briefing session for the new marketing strategy he wants to implement for his winery? I thought that if we catch the same flight to Cape Town we could share a car to St Sylve.'

Jess's heart did a quickstep as she tried to keep up with Joel. She sent a glance at her monitor; she most definitely had *not* received an e-mail from Luke Savage...

Not knowing what to think, she decided that the only thing she could do was to pump Joel for information. 'So, what do *you* think?'

'About St Sylve? He needs it... I heard that he commissioned market research with Lew Jones and is open to something new and hip. But with two hundred years of Savage wine-making history and tradition, that could backfire.'

She didn't think so... She hadn't eight years ago and she didn't now. It was about time he looked at updating his marketing, Jess grumbled silently. Over the years she'd kept an eye on the vineyard and was saddened by its obviously diminishing market share. The advertising was dry, the labels boring and its promotion stuffy.

And, since she was the only one who'd ever hear it, she sent Luke Savage a silent I-told-you-so.

Jess widened her eyes at Ally, who was frowning in confusion. 'My PA is just updating my iPad...what time was the briefing again?' she lied.

'Ten-thirty on Friday morning at the estate,' Joel replied.

Bless his heart—he didn't suspect a thing.

'So, shall I have my PA look at flights?'

'Uh...let me come back to you on that. I've been out for a day or two and haven't quite caught up. I have clients in Cape Town to see, so I might fly in earlier,' Jess fudged, and grimaced at Ally, who was now leaning forward, looking concerned.

'Well, let me know,' Joel told her before disconnecting.

Jess scrunched up her face. Damn Luke Savage and his injured pride. Her instinctive reaction was that the St Sylve campaign was hers—it had been hers eight years ago and it was still hers. There was no way she would allow another company to muck it up a second time...

Jess stood and placed her hands on her hips. 'What do you know about St Sylve wines?'

Ally's brown furrowed in thought. 'The vineyard has produced some award-winning wines, but it hasn't translated that into sales.'

It had taken a bit longer than Jess had thought, but her predictions about St Sylve had come true...and she felt sad. This was one of the few occasions when she would have been happy to be wrong...*wished* she was wrong. St Sylve was a Franschoek institution—one of the very few vineyards owned by the same family of French settlers who'd made their home in the valley in the early nineteenth century. She'd loved the three months she'd spent at the vineyard—had been entranced by the buildings, so typical of the architecture of the Cape Colony in the seventeenth and eighteenth centuries, with its whitewashed outer walls decorated with ornate gables and thatched roofs.

Apart from the main residence and guest house, the property still had its original cellar, a slave bell, stables and service buildings.

It also had Luke Savage, current owner, who'd fired her and kicked her off his property after kissing her senseless.

Jess quickly recounted her history with Luke to Ally, who was equally entertained and horrified. 'He *fired* you?'

'I deserved it. At twenty-two I thought I was God's gift to the world,' Jess replied.

Learning that she wasn't had been painful, but necessary. While she hadn't been wrong about the marketing of
St Sylve—as she'd suspected, the campaign had been a dis-
mal failure—she'd been arrogant, impulsive and rude, ap-
proaching him the way she had.

Jess paced the area in front of her desk. 'As much as I hate
to admit it, I owe Luke Savage a debt of gratitude for a major
life lesson. I needed my wings clipped and to learn that being
first in class, being able to regurgitate facts and figures from
a textbook, means diddly-squat in the business world.'

Jess put her hands on her waist and looked at the ceiling. Then she sent Ally a rueful look. 'We had this massive
shouting match and then he kissed me. He was a dynamite
kisser. A master of the art.' She blew air into her cheeks.
'The best ever.'

'*Ooh.*' Ally wiggled her bottom.

'I don't even know if I can call what happened between
us kissing…it was too over-the-top outrageous to be labelled
a simple kiss.'

But then Luke Savage had been anything *but* simple. Jess
sighed. He'd been one long, tall slurp of gorgeousness: bold,
deep green eyes, chocolate-cake-coloured hair, tanned skin.
The list went on… Broad shoulders, slim hips and long, long
legs…

'Jess? Hello?'

Jess snapped her head up. 'Sorry—mind wandering.'

'He sounds delicious, but the question is…what are you
going to do about St Sylve? Are you going to go to the briefing session?'

'Without an invitation?' Jess looked at the ceiling. 'I'm
tempted. I wish I could demand to implement a strategy for
him.' Images flashed through her head of possible advertisements. Her creative juices were flowing and she hadn't even

seen the brief yet. She *really* wanted to get stuck into dreaming up a new campaign for St Sylve.

But Luke was still the only man who'd ever short-circuited her brain when he kissed her…and if she was being sensible that was a really good reason *not* to work for him. She didn't think she'd be very effective, constantly drooling over her keyboard.

'Phone the guy and ask him!' Ally demanded, and Jess managed a smile.

'Not an option. We didn't get off on the right foot.' Jess held up her hand at Ally's protest.

Why did her stomach feel all fluttery, thinking about him? It had been so long ago…but the thought of seeing him again made her jittery and…*hot*.

She didn't want to get involved. She liked being single. She wanted to play on the edges of the circle and keep it all on the surface.

Why did even the *thought* of Luke feel like a threat to that?

Jess shook her head, utterly bewildered. Where on earth had *that* left-of-centre thought barrelled in from? Sometimes she worried herself, she really did…

Luke Savage sat on one of the shabby couches on the wide veranda of his home, propped his battered boots on an equally battered oak table and heaved a sigh. He lifted his beer bottle to his lips and let the icy liquid slide down his dusty throat.

He opened his eyes and watched as the sun dipped behind the imposing Simonsberg Mountain—one of a couple of peaks that loomed over the farm. As the sun dropped, so did the temperature, so he pulled on his leather-and-wool bomber jacket.

'I take it you saw the monthly financials for St Sylve?' Kendall said eventually.

'We're still not breaking even.' Luke sat up and placed his

forearms on his thighs, let his beer bottle dangle from his fingers. 'I can't keep ploughing money into this vineyard. At some stage it has got to become self-sustaining,' Luke added when his two closest friends said nothing.

Kendall de Villiers shook a head covered in tight black curls. His dark eyes flashed and his normally merry creme-caramel face tightened. 'We know that your father sucked every bit of operating capital out of this business before he died and left you with a massive overdraft and huge loans. You've paid off the lion's share of those loans—'

'With money I made on other deals—not from the vineyard bank accounts,' Luke countered. Kendall knew his businesses inside and out; he was not only his accountant and financial analyst, but a junior partner in his venture capitalist business.

'The wines we produce are good,' Owen Black said in his laid-back way.

Luke wasn't fooled by his dozy, drawling voice. Owen was one of the hardest-working men he'd ever come across. As farm manager, responsible for the vines and the olives, the orchards and the dairy, he got up early and went to bed late. Just as he did.

'You've won some top awards over the last few years, including Wine Maker of the Year,' Owen continued.

'It means nothing if we're not selling the bottles,' Luke retorted. 'Our wines aren't moving—not from the cellar here, and not from the wine shops.'

When both his friends didn't reply, Luke twisted his lips and said what they were obviously thinking. 'Because our marketing strategy sucks. It's boring and old-fashioned and aimed at anyone standing in God's waiting room.' Luke leaned back and popped a cushion behind his head. 'Why didn't I see it before?'

*Because a smart-mouthed girl once told me it was so and I was too full of offended pride to listen to her. And because*

*I had so much else on my plate. I figured I could let it slide for a while...* Stupid, stupid, stupid.

The Savage tradition of 'letting the wine speak for itself' was being drowned out by the splashy campaigns and eye-catching labels of their competitors. But Luke hadn't changed it because tradition was everything at St Sylve.

Hadn't his grandfather and father drummed that into him? Excellence and tradition—that was what Savage men strove for, what St Sylve stood for.

He got the reference to excellence, but tradition was killing him. He had to change something and quickly. Of course, he knew that both his father and his grandfather and every other type of forefather he had would do a collective roll in their graves...but if he didn't do something drastic to increase sales he'd either have to sell St Sylve or resign himself to using whatever profits he made on other deals to subsidise the estate. At some point he'd like to have a life, instead of working two full-time jobs.

Kendall had returned to the subject of the marketing strategy and Luke tuned in, idly remembering that somewhere he had a copy of the plan Miss Smarty Pants had tossed onto his desk so many years ago. He wondered what he'd done with it. It would be interesting to see what she had to say...

'Remind me—who is attending?' Luke asked Kendall.

His friend didn't need to consult his computer and quickly ran through the names.

'Not Jess Sherwood Concepts?' Luke asked.

'You specifically told me not to,' Kendall protested.

Luke raised his hand. 'Just checking.'

Kendall narrowed his eyes and shook his head. 'Why, I have no idea. Despite being a young company, Jess Sherwood has had some impressive campaigns over the last couple of years.'

'And you don't want her?' Owen asked Luke, puzzled.

'What's the problem? Why wouldn't you invite her to the briefing session?'

Jess Sherwood. He could still recall her big brown eyes and those honey-blonde curls, that gangly body and smooth, creamy skin. The way she'd tasted...strawberry lip gloss and spearmint gum. He could barely remember what his ex-wife looked like, yet he could remember that Jess had three freckles in a triangular cluster just below her right ear.

He would rather eat nails than approach Jess for a new marketing strategy—as good as she was reputed to be. Call him proud, call him stubborn, but she was a sharp thorn in his memory...the hottest and yet strangest sexual encounter of his life.

And, despite being so young, she'd seen the writing on the wall. With all his degrees and experience, his ability to look into the heart of a business and pinpoint the bottlenecks and constraints, he'd been unable to do it for his own vineyard.

Talk about not being able to see the wood for the trees. Or, in his case, the grapes for the vines.

Owen placed his bottle on the coffee table and frowned. 'What's your beef with Jess Sherwood?'

'Jess interned at St Sylve the summer I inherited this place. I was in the midst of getting divorced from Satan's sister and I didn't want to be here. I didn't want the responsibility of the vineyard, I was working all hours, and I was...'

'Miserable?' Kendall supplied when he hesitated. 'Depressed, angry, shirty, despondent?'

Hell, he'd been entitled to lick his wounds. He'd always wanted to be part of a family, and had thought that Mercia was what he needed to realise that dream. And she'd promised exactly what he'd wanted to hear...family, roots, stability... What was important to him had seemed to be what was important to her. She'd done an excellent job of camouflag-

ing her true agenda until they were hitched, and when he'd
woken up three months later he'd found himself legally bound
to a freedom-seeking, greedy, money-guzzling shrew. Over
the next two years he'd come to the dawning realisation that
he'd been well and truly screwed.

Again. And not in a good way. It still burned that he'd
been stupid enough to be so comprehensively manipulated.

As a result he'd made the decision never to get involved in
a serious relationship or to allow a woman to clean him out
financially and emotionally again. While he'd been grateful
to see the back of her, watching his lifelong dream of being
part of a family fade had stung. A lot.

Luke narrowed his eyes at Kendall. 'Do you want to hear
about Jess Sherwood or not?' he demanded. 'She was as gorgeous as all hell and she knew it. Entitled, privileged, unbe-
lievably annoying. I had barely been introduced to her and
had only seen her around a time or two. Then she just barged
into my office and proceeded to lecture me on my marketing
department. She called them a herd of dinosaurs and threw
all those marketing terms at my head. Told me what I was
doing wrong and how to fix it.'

'So you kicked her off the premises?' Kendall grinned at
Luke's nod.

Owen grinned too. 'She sounds like a pistol.'

'Jess Sherwood is such a madam that she'll gloat about
being right, rub my face in the fact that St Sylve needs her—I
need her. I just don't want to have to cope with her.'

*Especially if she's still as sexy as she was.* Luke didn't tell
them that he'd kissed her stupid and been kissed back.

'So I don't want to deal with her. Big personality clash.'

'It was a long time ago,' Owen pointed out. 'You should
at least have asked her to the briefing session to see what
she says.'

'No. I can't work with her. So what's the point of her quoting?' Luke stated, knowing that he said it because if she was still anywhere as hot as she'd been when she was younger he'd have a hard time keeping his tongue from hitting the floor every time she walked into the room. His attraction to her memory was still, crazily, *that* strong.

It wasn't like him. He had a calm, satisfying…arrangement with the owner of a wine store in the city. When either of them needed company, or sex, or a date to a function, the other was their 'go-to' person. No fuss, no expectation, no emotion—no imagining wild sex on his office desk in the afternoon sunlight…

Luke leaned forward and sent his friends a serious look. 'Look, this isn't about a business I've picked up and intend to flog. It's about St Sylve—about getting it back to where it was as the premier vineyard in the country. It's hard enough dealing with the situation my father left me, let alone her.'

Over the years he'd tried to distance himself emotionally from the estate and the winery, but he still couldn't manage to treat the multi-generational enterprise he'd inherited like any other arbitrary business.

It was his birthright—both his joy and his burden. His pleasure and his pain. A source of pride and an even bigger source of resentment. He loved and hated it with equal fervour.

'I think you're making a big mistake,' Kendall insisted. 'She's a professional…'

'End of discussion,' Luke said genially, but he made sure that his friends heard the finality in his voice. He valued their opinions, but the decision rested with him. Jess Sherwood was the type of woman who upset apple carts, turned things on their heads, inside out. While he reluctantly accepted that she was probably exactly what St Sylve the business needed, it would be detrimental to *him*, to his calm and ordered life.

Just this once he was putting himself first...surely at thirty-six he was entitled to do that once in a while?

# CHAPTER TWO

JESS, WITH ALLY at her side, walked into the tasting room adjoining the St Sylve cellars, looked at the chairs set up in two perfectly aligned rows and sighed in relief when she didn't see Luke Savage. Kendall De Villers, Luke's right-hand man, looked very surprised when she introduced herself, and she saw a momentary flash of panic flick over his face before he smiled slowly.

'Well, this is going to be interesting,' he told her, with a wicked glint in his fantastic brown-black eyes.

'Did he honestly think I wouldn't hear about this or doesn't he care?' Jess bluntly asked.

'Uh…'

Jess waved her question away. 'Anywhere I can hide where he won't see me? At least until he's finished the briefing?'

Kendall lifted his eyebrows. 'In that outfit? Not a chance in hell.'

Jess didn't bother to look down. She was wearing a black, body-hugging wraparound dress, black suede heels that made her calves look fabulous and a long string of fake pearls. With her bright blonde hair and bold lipstick, she was as inconspicuous as a house on fire.

'Where is he?' Jess asked, looking around the room.

'Probably doing something farmy…' Kendall pushed back

the sleeve on his immaculately tailored suit and glanced at his watch. 'Take a seat. We should be starting soon.'

'Rescue me if it looks like he's about to kill me?' she asked, only half joking.

Kendall grinned. 'I'm not that brave. Sorry, sister, but you're on your own.'

Jess took her seat next to the wall of the cellar, behind the broad shoulders of the creative director of Cooper & Co, and hoped Luke wouldn't recognise her.

She leaned her shoulder into Ally's and spoke in a low voice. 'Have I lost my marbles?'

'It's a question that keeps me awake at night,' Ally responded. 'Why?'

'We're across the country, in a briefing session we haven't been invited to, to listen to a briefing by a man who, I suspect, doesn't forgive and doesn't forget.'

*What was she thinking?*

'Mmm, if one of your staff did this you'd drop-kick them off a cliff.'

She loved Ally, but frequently wished she could be a little less honest, not quite so forthright.

'Why are we here, then?'

'Because this is still my campaign!' Jess hissed. It had been her campaign eight years ago and nobody else was going to get their grubby little hands on it.

She just had one little problem: convincing Luke to see it her way.

And there he was, striding in from a side door to the podium, tucking his cap into the back pocket of his jeans. Such an attractive man, she thought, in a hunter-green long-sleeved T-shirt that skimmed his broad shoulders and wide chest and fell untucked over the waist of over-laundered faded jeans. His dark brown hair brushed his collar and fell in shaggy waves over his ears; he desperately needed a haircut, and he could do with a shave… There was designer stubble and there was three-day-old beard.

And then there was that spectacular butt, hugged by the thin fabric of his jeans as he turned his back on his audience to talk to Kendall. Jess caught Kendall's wince at his lack of formal attire and thought that only Luke would walk into a room full of Italian suits and designer ties in his farm clothes and not give a damn. Jess leaned forward. Was that a greasy palm print on the pocket of his jeans? Then Luke crouched to tie the lace in his boot and his shirt rode up his back. She could see the line between his tanned back and his white hips above the soft leather belt. Jess swallowed the saliva that pooled in her mouth and wondered how warm that strip of skin would feel, how it would taste…

Ally let out a low whistle. 'Oh, my giddy aunt.'

'Gorgeous, isn't he?' Jess asked. This would be so much easier if he'd picked up a beer gut, lost his hair…

'Not him! Well, he is—but the redhead! I wouldn't mind it if he parked his shoes under my bed!' Ally muttered back, waving her hand in front of her face. 'Yum!'

He did have attractive friends, Jess admitted, but for her they were missing that X factor. The one that screamed power and control and sheer masculine presence. Some would say it was testosterone, some supreme self-confidence, but it was more than that. Whatever the mystery ingredient that made Luke more of a man, he'd been given an overdose of it at birth…

It was a good thing she was sitting down because seeing him, so tall and strong, cut her legs out from under her. He was all chemistry and potency and lust and pheromones and… Why was he still the only man she'd ever met who had the ability to vacuum every thought from her brain? Who was able to send her blood to pool in her womb, flush her face and body with pleasure, with nothing more than a look from those fabulous eyes?

Good grief, she thought as their eyes connected and held, if he kept looking at her like that—with barely concealed heat and open hostility—she would dissolve into a puddle on the floor.

Hot, hot, *hot*.

'He's clocked you,' Ally told her, very unnecessarily.

'Yeah, I noticed.'

'You're in trouble,' Ally sang, *sotto voce*. 'He looks like he wants to gobble you up in one big bite.'

Jess kicked her ankle to get her to shut up.

'If I'm really, really lucky,' Jess countered as those green eyes swept over her again, 'he'll just ignore me.'

She heard Ally's sarcastic snort. 'And maybe pigs will grow glittery fairy wings and fly.'

'You could, at the very least, have changed into a clean pair of pants!' Kendall muttered, looking exceptionally irritated.

'I intended to but I ran out of time,' Luke countered, jamming his hands into his pockets. On good days he never had time to spare, and even in July, the heart of winter in the Cape, there was work to be done. He and Owen were overseeing the pruning of the vines, and in the winery the wines needed to be analysed for pH, acidity, alcohol content and a handful of other tests that needed to be done.

'If you'd let me hand this marketing stuff over to you then you wouldn't have to nag me about my clothes. And you can nag for Africa, Ken.'

'Get stuffed,' Kendall retorted. 'And they want to see the Savage of St Sylve.'

'This isn't an estate in England! The Savage of St Sylve, my ass!' Luke grumbled.

'It's as close as it gets. Now, will you please get on with it?'

Kendall nodded to the podium and Luke sighed. The Savage of St Sylve? Today he would happily be anyone else, he thought as he turned to face his audience. His gaze skimmed over the self-satisfied suits to a slim, streaky-haired blonde sitting behind a wide-shouldered man in a grey suit.

*Déjà vu*... He'd felt this a couple of times over the years—the tilt of a head, a sway of hips and his heart would stumble. When he took a second look he was always disappointed that it wasn't her.

Out of the corner of his eye Luke caught the movement of a slim hand sliding into bright hair, and the moisture in his mouth suddenly disappeared. He remembered those slim fingers, and his heart bashed against his ribcage as his eyes flew back to her hair, that wide mouth, the long, slim body under a deceptively simple but figure-revealing black dress. God, she looked good. Slimmer, sophisticated, with a tousled shoulder-length hairstyle that was hugely sexy. It accentuated her high cheekbones, her round dark eyes, that amazing mouth.

Luke hoped his poker face was in place... She couldn't—mustn't—suspect that she'd sent his pulse rocketing, his mind into overdrive and his libido into orbit. Luke gripped the podium as he waited for his knees to lock. He couldn't stop his eyes from tracking back to hers, and when they connected, volcanoes erupted. Jess's eyes, if you looked carefully enough, were the windows to her soul. Beneath the heat of their glances he knew that she was rattled.

Good. It went some way to making up for the uncomfortable and unwelcome fact that he still wanted her...which was such a foolish description for what he wanted to do to her, *with* her.

Luke blew out a heavy sigh. He knew why she was here. He wasn't a fool. Word was out that he was looking for a marketing strategy and she'd heard…and, being Jess, she was probably annoyed that he hadn't asked her.

Jess, again being Jess, didn't make appointments or pick up the phone to discuss it like a normal person. No, she rocked up here looking hot and sexy and very, very determined.

He wasn't sure whether to admire her cheek or be annoyed at her pushiness.

Luke cleared his throat and thought that he'd better get on with the business at hand.

'Ladies and gentlemen, this is probably going to be the shortest briefing in the history of the world. I want some-thing new—something fresh that sells an enormous amount of wine. I want an overall marketing strategy, and then I want it broken down into website, social media, print and TV campaigns. All integrated. That's it. After your tour of the St Sylve cellars, Kendall de Villiers will take you through the market research report, and apparently there's a finger lunch and wine-tasting after that.'

Short and sweet. What else was there to say? He could have waffled on, but he was way more interested in having a very serious discussion with a certain brown-eyed blonde.

Jess slipped out of the tasting room after arranging for Ally to continue with the tour and get a lift back to the airport with Joel. She needed to slip away before she ran into Luke and was told that he wanted nothing to do with her. As she walked out she slipped on her knee-length black coat and pulled a thin silk scarf from its pocket. There was an icy wind blowing off the towering greeny-purple mountains that surrounded the estate. Jess walked down a path that snaked through the now denuded rose gardens, past the manor house and towards the long driveway where she'd parked her rental car.

Jess found a path between the manor house and the guest house. It led onto the driveway and Jess immediately saw

Luke, sitting on the top length of the pole fence that separated a winter-brown paddock from the driveway. Behind the paddock the vineyard started, and she could see his workers pruning the vines.

Jess stopped in the shadows of the house and just watched him.

He still fascinated her, Jess admitted. Oh, he was smoking hot, and he set her nerve-endings alight, but there was something beneath that attraction—something about him that engaged her internally as well. She knew he was smart, and she suspected that he could be ruthless, but it went deeper than simple pheromones and lust. Deep enough to have her mentally cocking her head.

One hundred percent alpha male and more than a match for her. The unwelcome thought popped into her head and settled. Jess stumbled, stopped and took a deep breath, and reminded herself that she was an alpha female and very able to deal with Luke Savage. She was an independent, successful, strong woman…

She was such a liar. Right now she felt as if she had all the inner strength of a marshmallow. She shouldn't be here at St Sylve, shouldn't be taking this project on. She really didn't need his business…

She especially didn't need the way he made her feel. Tingly, excited, a little unsure, a lot less confident.

Jess placed her hands on her waist and scowled at the ground. *Get a grip, Sherwood. You survived a childhood as the youngest girl with four older brothers, you run a successful business, you are independent, ambitious and in charge of this situation.*

*You will not let him get under your skin…*

Jess took a deep breath and stepped out of the shadows onto the driveway. Luke's head shot up. He jumped off the fence and pushed the sleeves of his T-shirt up his forearms as he scowled at her.

'Now, why aren't I surprised to see you here?' Luke asked in a very even tone.

Jess wasn't fooled. His green eyes were spitting spiders.

'Good to know you haven't lost any of your cheek.'

Sarcasm. He was still good at it.

Jess's rental car was parked closest to the fence and she dropped her laptop bag on the front seat, slammed the door shut and placed her bottom on the bonnet. She pushed her sunglasses into her hair and looked around.

As much as she wanted to, she would not get drawn into an argument right off the bat. Mostly because she wasn't sure she'd win it.

'I'd forgotten how beautiful this place is,' she commented idly, ignoring his opening volley. 'The air is so sweet, so pure. Cold, but sweet.'

Luke folded his arms as he loomed over her. 'What are you doing here, Jessica?'

Jess ignored his intimidation tactics and sent him a smile. 'I'm going to give you a marketing campaign that is going to blow your socks off, Luke.'

'Why? So you can say "I told you so"? To rub my face in the fact that I've failed? To push home the point that you, despite being so ridiculously young, were right?'

'No!' Jess put her hands on her hips and scowled at him. 'Why didn't you call me? Dammit, Luke. I know St Sylve. I know—'

Luke rubbed the back of his neck. He felt embarrassed and stupid and wished that she'd just leave him alone to try to fix the mess he'd made. Unfortunately his business brain also kept whispering that he'd be an idiot if he just sent her on her way without listening to her proposal.

There was a reason why she was reputed to be one of the best in the business…but why did she have to look even sexier than before?

The knowledge that he was still so attracted to her caused his temper to spike. 'You know *nothing*! You spent three months here eight years ago and you didn't know much then.'

'I want to help you…'

Luke shook his head. 'No, you don't. You want to make some money off me, do a deal, get the most sought-after contract around. You want to be proved right. You want to say "I told you so". You want to show me how clever you are.'

Jess shook her head. 'No, I— Come on, Luke, give me a break! I'm not the same cocky, over-zealous child I was eight years ago. I'm good at my job, and campaigns like yours are what I do best.'

Luke watched the heat of temper appear on her cheekbones, noticed the patches of red forming on her chest and neck. 'I don't need to watch you gloat. I have representatives of at least five other companies touring St Sylve right now, so they can—' Luke bent his fingers to emphasise the phrase '—"help" me.'

'I know that, but none of them are me. I've lived here, I've worked here, and I've always felt a connection to St Sylve. I can use that to create something special for you.'

She sounded sincere, Luke thought, but what did he know? He had vast experience of women—of people—turning sincerity on and off like a tap. Besides, he was tired and stressed and felt as if he'd been hit over the head by a two-by-four. 'Just go away, Jess.'

She lifted her chin and held his stare. 'No. Sorry, but, no. I *will* get the market research report and I *will* draw up a campaign for you. I don't care if you think I'm pushy or bossy or a pain in the butt—that is what is going to happen.'

Luke felt his temper bubble. 'Nothing has changed with you, has it? You're still over-confident and cocky—'

Jess hopped off the car, teetered on her heels and slapped her hand against his chest. Luke felt as if she'd branded him. He could see the pulse jumping at the base of her neck and noticed that her eyes had turned darker with...could that be embarrassment? Her obvious discomfort had his temper retreating.

'Can you be quiet for just a minute while I get this out?' Jess asked, her voice vibrating.

She seemed unaware that her hand was still on his chest, and although he lifted his hand to remove it, he didn't manage to complete the action. He rather liked her touching him...

Jess took a deep breath and raked tumbling hair back from her face with her other hand. 'I suck at apologising, so this might not come out right. But I'm really, really sorry for being so rude and revolting. I had no right to say the things I said to you, and you were right to fire me...in fact you did me a huge favour. I was intolerably cheeky and I'd really appreciate it if you accepted my apology.'

Huh? What? Luke frowned at her. That wasn't what he'd expected her to say...

'Are you apologising?' He just had to make sure. He'd had a tough couple of weeks. Maybe the stress was getting to him and he'd started imagining things.

Or maybe he just wanted to hear the words again.

Jess closed her eyes. 'Please don't make me say it again,' she begged. 'Once is embarrassing enough.'

Luke blew out his breath. 'What am I supposed to say to that?' he grumbled.

Jess made a sound that was a cross between a snort and a laugh.

'That you forgive me?' she suggested. 'That you'll let me design you a campaign that will sell an enormous amount of wine? That was an interesting briefing session, by the way. Short and—'

'Sweet?'

Jess's smile flashed. 'Just short. So? Can I?'

Luke, momentarily distracted by the tiny dimple that flashed in her cheek when she smiled, gathered his thoughts and told himself to be an adult. He couldn't just give her the campaign because she had a smile that made his belly clench, a body that begged to be touched and eyes he could drown in. Then again, it was *his* vineyard...

*Get a grip, Savage.*

'You can put in a tender for the job, along with everyone else.' Luke lifted up his hand when he saw Jess's face brighten. His next words were as much a warning to himself as they were to her. 'I'm not promising you a thing, Sherwood.'

Jess slowly nodded. 'Understood. Thank you. You won't regret this.'

Luke knew that on some level, at some time, he would.

Jess sent him a smile and a look that made his insides squirm with lust and, admittedly, fear.

'So, since I'm no longer trying to avoid you, and since I'm assuming that I'm not about to be tossed off the premises, I think I'll join the tour. Reacquaint myself with St Sylve.'

Luke, not keen to be inundated with questions from the rest of the suits but also not willing—*why?*—to leave Jess just yet, said, 'I'll walk you back to the cellar.'

'You don't have to,' Jess replied quickly. 'Besides, I was going to take the long route back—through the gardens and past the stables.'

Luke frowned. 'What on earth for?'

Jess lifted her shoulder. 'I have an idea for the campaign but I need to get a sense of St Sylve as it is now, not how I remember it.'

Luke lifted his eyebrows and looked at her sexy dress

and ridiculous heels. 'You want to walk in those shoes? That dress?'

Jess held out a foot and rotated it. 'What's wrong with my shoes? They're gorgeous.'

'But totally impractical for walking in—especially on farm roads. Take the path back, Jess.'

He could see her spine stiffening and her chin lifting. 'Thanks, but I'll take the circuitous route.'

Luke suppressed his smile at her stubbornness. Within twenty-five metres those spiky heels would be stuck in mud and her stockings would be flecked with dirt.

He gave Jess another up-and-down look and watched for her response. Her expression remained stoic while her eyes heated. He wondered what it would take to get her to lose the mask of sophistication she'd acquired.

He spoke casually. 'Do you ever think about what we did the last time we met?'

He didn't need to spell it out…she was a smart girl. Luke watched carefully and saw her composure slip for a fraction of a second, before her lips firmed and her eyes narrowed.

'No. Do you?'

'No,' Luke replied.

*My, my, my,* Luke thought as she walked away. *Look what good liars we've become.*

Jess, sitting on a hard seat at the airport, waiting for her flight to be called, looked at her shoes and grimaced. Once black, they were now streaked with reddish-brown mud and, she was certain, were beyond repair. Her stockings were splattered with runny sludge and dirty water. Her feet were aching from negotiating the uneven roads and paths at St Sylve in two-inch spikes and her toes had long since said goodbye to any feeling.

Damn Luke Savage for being right.

Jess felt her mobile vibrate in her hand and squinted down at the screen, where a message was displayed from the Sherwood family group.

*John: Just to let you bunch of losers know that I ran 5K today in 24:30. Eat my dust, girls.*

Jess had barely finished reading the message when a reply was posted.

*Patrick: For an old guy, that's pretty good. But I run sub 24 routinely.*

And they were off…

*Chris: Liar! Your last race time was 30 mins plus.*

*Patrick: I had a stomach bug.*

*Nick: Prove it, squirt. You run like a girl. Even the Shrimp can take you down!*

*Patrick: I was sick! And Jess couldn't catch me with wings strapped to her back…*

Jess, being the Shrimp and a girl, took offence at that. She was often faster than Patrick over five kilometres.

*Jess: Hey, brainless…name the time and place and be prepared to watch my butt the whole way!*

*John: What are the stakes?*

Jess wrinkled her nose. The last bet she'd lost to her brothers had ended up in her doing Chris's tax return. Maybe she hadn't thought this through.

*Nick: A weekend cleaning out the monkey enclosure at the rehab centre for the loser.*

*Chris: Good one!*

*Eeew,* thought Jess.

*John: Hand-washing our rugby kit after practice.*

Double *eeew.*

*Liza AKA Mom: Now, now, children...play nice. Mommy's listening. And the loser will replace all the washers on my leaky taps. And they will not pay anyone to do this!*

Jess twisted her lips. Unfortunately for her she knew how to wield a monkey wrench and thus would not be excused on account of gender. This was just another instance when she deeply regretted being a tomboy for most of her life.

And, really, when was she going to grow out of this absurd compulsion to prove that she was as big and as strong and as capable as her four older brothers? As a child she'd thought it deeply unfair that she'd been born a girl, and had decided early on that anything they could do she wanted to do better. So she'd studied hard and played harder in an effort to keep up with her siblings...and still always felt that she was on the outside of their 'brother circle' looking in. They were good-looking, charming, sporty and successful—a very annoying bunch of over-achievers… She thought that Luke would fit in very well with them.

The bet was madness, Jess thought, frowning at her feet and wondering how to get out of it. And as for her gorgeous shoes…they were history.

# CHAPTER THREE

JESS'S THIN HEELS made tiny square marks in the thick carpet of the passage outside the smallest conference room at the hotel where Luke had chosen to view the various campaign presentations. She was scheduled to present last, and was getting more and more nervous. Realising that her hands were slick with perspiration, she hustled off to the closest bathroom to wash her hands and check her face. *Again.*

She was being ludicrous, she decided, drying her hands for the third time in twenty minutes. Since her *contretemps* with Luke eight years ago she'd always been nervous before presentations, but no one besides Ally ever knew it. She appeared to be ice-cool and confident, unflappable, but underneath her façade her heart misfired and her brain spluttered.

Jess slicked on another layer of lipstick and smoothed down her scarlet mid-thigh-length jacket. The bottom of her short black pencil skirt just peeked out under the hem, and she wore a black silk polo-neck jersey underneath. With sheer black stockings and knee-high boots, the outfit was dramatic and eye-catching, and not what she'd usually wear to pitch for a job.

But if this was the last time she'd see Luke Savage then she'd damn well make sure that she made a lasting impression.

Ally stuck her head around the door to the Ladies'. 'Jess, it's time.'

Jess walked out of the Ladies' and was grateful for Ally's steadying hand on her back, unaware that she was biting the inside of her lip. 'Let's knock their socks off.'

'Okay…but maybe you should take a deep breath first…'

'Why?' Jess asked, picking up her laptop and boards.

'Your knees are knocking together.' Ally reached into her bag and pulled out a small bottle of Rescue Remedy. 'Open up.'

'Ally!' Jess muttered, but she obediently stuck out her tongue as Ally shook the foul-tasting drops into her mouth.

The door behind them opened and Jess's eyes slid over. She winced as Luke stepped out of the conference room.

'Hi—' He stopped suddenly and Jess yanked her tongue in. Could she feel any more stupid?

'What on earth are you doing?' Luke demanded, his hands in the pockets of his smart black pants. Jess noticed his button-down cream shirt with its discreet, expensive logo and sighed at how good he looked.

Mr Savage cleaned up very, very well indeed.

'Nothing,' Jess muttered.

'Rescue Remedy,' Ally said at the same time. 'Jess tends to get a bit nervous before presentations.'

'Alison!'

Luke smiled at Jess and her stomach flipped over. 'I would never have guessed. Jess doesn't seem to be the gets-nervous type.' Luke held out his hand to Alison. 'Luke Savage.'

'Ally Davies.' Ally shook his hand.

'How nervous?' Luke asked, and Jess willed Ally not to be her normal open, brutally honest self.

'Very. Her knees are knocking together and her hands are shaking.'

'Will you stop?' Jess demanded. 'Jeez, Alison! He's a client.'

'Relax, Jess, there's no need to torture such pretty knees.'

Luke sent her another of his slow, sexy smiles that were guaranteed to melt the panties off any female between eighteen and eighty. It was the smile she intended to use to launch his campaign. She was under no illusions. It was going to be tough to sell it to him...

'And I like the skirt you're almost wearing, Sherwood,' Luke added.

'Oh, shut up!' Jess told him before sailing into the room, her nose up in the air.

*Great start, Jess, telling your prospective client to put a cork in it. Not.*

Jess ended her presentation and caught herself biting the inside of her lip in the resultant heavily pregnant silence. She felt her heart thumping in her chest and wondered if the St Sylve contingency could hear it.

*Thump, thump, kadoosh. Thump, thump...* Oh, the *kadoosh* happened every time she looked at Luke; it was, Jess realised, her heart bouncing off the floor.

Well, okay, then. Good to know. Better if she knew how to make it *stop.*

Luke looked utterly inscrutable and non-committal—especially for somebody who, as she'd suggested, should be the new face of St Sylve wines. Did they love it? Hate it? Think that she'd not only crossed the line but redrawn it as well? Jess just wished they'd say something—*anything*!

About a million years later—okay, ten seconds, but it felt that long—Luke sat forward and rested his arms on the table. His eyes sliced through her.

'Let me get this straight... You want me to be the face of St Sylve?'

Jess nodded. 'Not just the face of St Sylve. I want the consumer to associate you and St Sylve with fun. Hip and cool, yet sophisticated. The plan isn't to sell your wine. It's to sell your life.'

Now Luke looked thoroughly puzzled. 'I don't have a life, Jessica! I work and that's about it!'

'The consumer doesn't know that, Luke. He sees you as this young, single, good-looking—' *smoking hot*, but she couldn't say that '—rich guy who has the world at his feet. He does hip and cool things…like parasailing, dancing, mountain-climbing. He plays touch rugby with his mates, has friends around for dinner, attends balls. And it's all done with, or followed by, a glass of wine. St Sylve wine.'

'I love it,' Kendall said. 'I think it's brilliant.'

Jess flashed him a grateful smile.

'I like the idea, but I don't like the idea of me doing it. Why can't you get a model to…model?' Luke demanded.

'It would have a bigger impact if the owner of the winery appeared in the adverts and, frankly—' Jess took a deep breath '—why would you want to spend a shedload of cash on a model when you are attractive enough to do it yourself?'

*And I managed to say that without blushing or drooling,* Jess thought.

'I'm really liking this,' Kendall stated.

'Actually, so am I,' Owen agreed, but Jess noticed that he wasn't looking at her but at Ally. Okay, so that was interesting. Jess swivelled her head. Ally was *so* looking back, the flirt!

Luke stood up abruptly. 'Thanks, everybody. It's been a long day. Let's sleep on it and meet on Monday to make a decision. Jess, if you'd wait, I'd like a moment of your time?'

Now *he wants a moment,* Jess thought. He's had three weeks. She looked at Luke, who was writing on her presentation booklet. Then again, it was probably about work.

She was acting like a lonely, lovelorn teenager. She was, it was embarrassing to admit, an utter drip.

* * *

Luke waited until the last person had left the room and the door had snicked closed behind them before walking around the table to the top of the room, where Jess was still standing by the projector screen, a laser pointer in her hand. He sat on the edge of the boardroom table and stretched out his legs. Jess seemed to get better-looking each time he saw her, he thought idly. She'd done something to her hair—there were now pale blonde streaks in the honey colour. It was also brutally straight today. He preferred it loose and curly...

Luke scratched his forehead, thinking that he was too far gone if he was wasting time noticing the details of a woman's hair. Which was chilling on a dozen different levels.

He was impressed with her presentation, her professionalism; no one would have guessed that this slick, cool businesswoman suffered from performance anxiety. He wouldn't have guessed it if he hadn't seen her sticking her tongue out for those drops. The entire episode made her seem not quite so aloof, a little warmer, a lot more human. Infinitely attractive.

'Um...what do you really think about my idea?' Jess asked, and he could hear a quiver underneath her professional tone of voice.

'I like it—apart from me being in the ads.'

'I should also tell you that I think you should start getting out, promoting the St Sylve name and its wine. I would strongly suggest that you go out more...social events, parties, balls...and that you host wine-tasting evenings and start networking.'

'Why don't you just take my internal organs? It would be easier.' Luke rubbed the back of his neck. 'Do you have an extra twenty-four hours in the day for me?'

'It's important, Luke.'

'I don't have the time, Jess. I'm working at St Sylve. I get home from the land and then I spend hours on business plans, financing… I'm running my other businesses at night. I don't have the time for advertising shoots, let alone for a social life.'

'Then I think you should be prepared to keep ploughing your own money into St Sylve or to lose it,' Jess told him bluntly. 'You need the wines to sell to get St Sylve sustainable, and to do that you need sales—for sales you need advertising.'

'Then why must I do the social stuff?'

'Because you need to be seen to be living the campaign or else the consumers won't believe in it.' Jess perched on the edge of the conference table and crossed her legs. 'Step out of your comfort zone, Luke.'

Comfort zone? He hadn't felt remotely comfortable since he'd set eyes on her again weeks ago.

Luke eyed her long legs in those sexy boots and felt his groin twitch. *Dammit!* He didn't like not being able to control his physical reaction to this woman, the fact that he thought about her far too often. And he especially didn't like the fact that she could talk so coolly about business when he was imagining her naked except for those boots, at the mercy of his touch…

'If I agree to hire you, and by doing so agree to any and all of your proposals,' he said in a voice that most of his staff and friends would recognise as non-negotiable, 'then I have a couple of conditions of my own.'

'Okay—what?'

'*You* work on the campaign. No passing it off to your flunkies.'

'Understood. I had no intention of doing that anyway.'

'And I want St Sylve to have your undivided attention. You move to St Sylve for however long it takes to get this wrapped up. Get out of *your* comfort zone.'

He saw the look of shock that flicked across her face. 'That's not practical, Luke. I have a business to run.'

'Skype, e-mail and phone. We live in the twenty-first century, Jess. Besides, Ally looks competent enough to take the reins.'

'She is, but—'

'And you also organise the networking. I don't have the time or the inclination and I have even less enthusiasm. And you accompany me to all these functions. If I have to do it, then so do you,' Luke told her.

'So, are you saying I've got the job?'

'Yep.'

Of course she had the job—was she mad? Hers was above and beyond the most exciting presentation of them all, and while the others wouldn't need his time, presence or input, they wouldn't have the effect Jess's would.

'Uh...good,' Jess said in a strangled voice. 'But I don't know if I'm going to manage living in Franschoek. I have a life, apart from my business, in Sandton.'

Luke shook his head. No, she didn't. She was as much a workaholic as him. 'Stop hedging. And you're not staying in Franschoek—you're staying at St Sylve.'

Jess thrust out her stubborn chin. 'I won't feel comfortable staying with you, in your house.'

'Why not?'

Jess rolled her eyes. 'Are you really going to be all coy and not acknowledge the...'

Luke lifted his eyebrows when she stuttered to a stop. 'Lust? Heat? Passion?' he suggested.

'Heat...stick to heat,' Jess suggested, her eyes everywhere but meeting his.

Luke grinned internally; it amazed him that she could be so businesslike about—well, *business*, but get so flustered when talking about their mutual attraction.

'Now who's being coy?' Luke muttered. 'Okay, you can stay in any one of the six bedrooms at the manor house.'

Luke stepped closer—so close he could almost feel her

breasts against his chest, smell the citrus in her hair. Those amazingly long lashes fluttered and lifted and he felt the zing of attraction arc between them. In that age-old subconscious display of attraction her mouth opened, and he nearly lost control when he saw the tip of her pink tongue flicker at the corner of her mouth. Stuff the marketing strategy and St Sylve. Stuff the world...Jess was here and he wanted her.

Her body, not her mind...

Luke jerked his head up and quietly cursed. And what was he doing? Acting on what was happening in his pants. *Catch a clue, Savage.* He wasn't fifteen any more, or even twenty, but he was still listening to his libido. He'd realised a while back that it was a very bad judge of character, time and situation, and it had the ability to lead him into deep trouble.

Luke stepped away from Jess, but couldn't resist tucking a long, straight strand of hair behind her ear. 'Don't disappoint me, Jess.'

'I don't intend to,' she replied in her husky, take-me-to-bed voice.

Jess finally looked him in the eye and he couldn't help himself; his thumb drifted across her bottom lip. 'You have the most kissable mouth I've ever seen.'

He saw sense and sensibility flow back into Jess's eyes—her mental retreat. A cool, polite mask dropped into place.

'Not a good idea, Luke. Any physical intimacy could blow up in our faces.'

'We should be smart enough to separate the two.'

Her shoulders came up and her spine stiffened at his challenge. 'Theoretically I'm smart enough—anybody is smart enough—to solve string theory, but that doesn't mean I can. Or will.'

'We have unfinished business, Jessica. You know it and I know it; we both want to finish what we started eight years ago.' Luke moved the backs of his fingers down her cheek.

Jess's eyes remained passionate even as she nudged his hand away. 'Luke, let me make it very clear that I don't do casual sex—especially not with colleagues, competitors or clients.'

He loved the snap he heard in her voice, the passion that slumbered in her eyes. The contradiction of the two had his heart in his throat and his groin twitching. This was going to be interesting, he thought, amused and still very turned on. She might be flustered but she wasn't intimidated, and she didn't back down.

He wondered who'd taught her that.

The day before Jess was due to arrive at St Sylve, Luke sat on the end of the antique double bed in the largest guest suite in the manor house and looked around the room. Angel, his part-time housekeeper, had worked her magic in the room he'd allocated Jess. The yellow wood headboard had been oiled, there was white linen on the bed and fresh flowers on the nightstand. Luke glanced through the large bay window opposite the bed which enabled the guest to wake to a stunning view of the mountains. Luke had never understood why this room, with its large *en-suite* bathroom, had never been used as the master bedroom instead of the smaller, pokier bedroom at the front of the house, overlooking the driveway.

Easier to see who was coming up the road, Luke decided. Friend, foe, tax collector... In his father's case, lover. There had been many, Luke knew. He remembered lots of women wafting around the house when he was a child... Some had paid far too much attention to him; others had paid him absolutely no attention at all.

They'd all left eventually. By the age of seven he'd learned to protect himself against getting emotionally attached to any of his father's girlfriends. That way he hadn't been affected when they'd dropped out of his life. Apart from the blip that had been his marriage, it was his standard operating procedure when it came to women.

Being a reasonably astute guy, he hadn't needed therapy to work out that he'd learnt to protect himself against emotional entanglements, and he'd honed his ability to keep his distance from people at a young age. Between his mother's death, his father's dictator tendencies and his girlfriends wafting in and then storming out, it had become easier not to care whether people left or not.

His ex-wife and his marriage had been the exception to that rule. While he now called her a crazoid, with the ability to incinerate money, he had to accept that his own issues had also contributed to the train wreck. He hadn't loved her, but he'd been monstrously in love with the *idea* of her: a wife, a family, normality. When he'd got it he hadn't known what to do with it...

Saying goodbye to his lifelong dream of being part of something bigger than himself had stung like a shark bite, and because Fate had thought that wasn't punishment enough, his father had died and he'd been yanked back to St Sylve.

He was still trying to come to terms with his legacy, and frequently wasn't sure how he felt about the estate. Some days he loved it. Then resentment got the better of him, and on other days, when the memories of his father bubbled close to the surface, he actively hated the place.

If only his mother had— Luke stomped over to the window and looked at the mountains in the near distance. There was no point in thinking about his mother, Jed and his childhood. Nothing he could do to change it.

Luke sighed and thought of Jess. He knew that she was right—that the intelligent decision would be to ignore this attraction bubbling away. He knew that when the lines between working and sleeping together were blurred, confusion and craziness generally followed.

But she was a modern, independent woman—one who didn't appear to need a man for emotional or financial support to make her life complete. She appeared to be controlled, thinking, cool—someone who could separate love from sex. A perfect candidate for a short-term affair.

She would understand that there would have to be rules. No sleep-overs, a strict division between work and play, no expectations of commitment or a relationship.

It was all in the communication, Luke decided. As long as they both understood the rules, no one would get hurt or could complain.

It was the adult, rational, sensible solution. And if she stuck to her guns and maintained that she couldn't, *wouldn't*, sleep with a client, then he'd do what any rational, determined man would do.

He'd seduce her into it. With the heat they generated, he didn't think it would be too difficult.

Thirteen hours in a car gave a girl lots of time to get her mind sorted, Jess thought as she turned down the long driveway leading to St Sylve. It was nearly ten at night and she was utterly exhausted. Her eyes were gritty, her body stiff, and she could murder a cup of tea.

She'd initially thought she'd take two days to do the trip, but when she'd reached halfway she'd thought she would push through. She now wished she'd stopped. She had a massive headache and, although she'd done nothing all day but steer, she felt dirty and sweaty. Her hair was unbrushed and her teeth felt as if they were dripping enamel from the energy drinks she'd chain-drunk earlier.

Jess saw lights blazing from the guest house, and when she saw Luke's Land Cruiser parked in the driveway she knew that he was home and not out on a date or—*eeew*—a sleep-over. Thank goodness.

Right. Before she saw him again, a quick recap on all she'd decided during the day. Living and working so closely with Luke was going to be a challenge. She got that. He was gorgeous, and she was crazy-mad attracted to him, but she couldn't act on it.

'No acting on the attraction.' She muttered her new mantra. 'No acting on the attraction.' She just needed to say it forty times a day—an hour?—and her brain would be reprogrammed. Maybe.

When she wasn't so tired she'd sit him down and lay out some simple ground rules. She was here to do a job, so kissing and touching and most especially sleeping together were out. She'd didn't sleep with her clients. It was unprofessional. And when trouble brewed it always mucked up the business relationship. Always.

Besides that, attraction spilt over into involvement, which tended to make her end up feeling as if she'd tossed her heart to a pack of rabid, starving wolves.

Luke would just have to understand that for the next few weeks he might own her time, but her body wasn't included in the deal. Her body, slutty thing that it was, wasn't very impressed with that decision. *Tough.* Someone had to be the adult...

In the light of her headlights she saw the front door of the guest house open and Luke's tall silhouette in the doorway. She parked her car next to his Cruiser and switched off her iPod, playing through the car speakers. Hard rock stopped mid-wail and there was blessed silence in the car. Why hadn't she done that earlier? Oh, right—the edgy album had kept her from falling asleep and drifting off the road.

Jess released the seat belt as Luke opened her door. She smiled wearily up at him, her eyes wide and blinking against the interior light. 'Hi.'

Luke rested his arm on the top of the car and stood in the doorway. Instead of giving her a smile and a warm greeting, she saw his face was hard in the dim light. 'When did you leave home?' he barked.

That wasn't a friendly woof. Jess frowned. No *hello*? No *good to see you*?

'Uh...this morning,' Jess replied. 'Is that a problem?'

'Damn right it is,' Luke whipped back. 'What do you think you are doing, driving thirteen hours straight? Without letting anyone know? If you'd had an accident how would I have known? You could be lying in a ditch somewhere and I'd still think you'd be arriving tomorrow!'

Jess blinked at his tirade. 'Uh–'

'Did you let *anyone* know?' Luke demanded, increasing his volume with every word.

'No, I—'

'It's stupid and irresponsible. Do you know what can happen to a woman driving on her own?'

'They arrive safely?' Jess asked, her temper starting to bubble.

'You could've hit a cow, broken down, had a puncture...'

Jess spoke in her coldest voice as she stepped out of the car. 'I'm a grown woman who doesn't need to check in like a child. I didn't break down, have a puncture or—good grief!— hit a cow! I am here safely. I want a cup of tea, a shower and a warm bed. Can I get any or all of those, or do you need to yell at me some more?'

'You would try the patience of a flipping saint.'

'And that saint wouldn't be you,' Jess snapped back. She opened the back door and yanked a large tote bag from the seat. Luke took the bag and Jess reached for it. 'I can carry my own bag!'

'Fine.' Luke dropped the bag to the ground and held up

his hands. This woman was going to drive him nuts, up the wall...

Jess picked up her bag, slung it over her shoulder and squinted at the dark manor house. 'No lights?'

'Obviously not. Since I was expecting you *tomorrow*!'

He'd planned on switching on the electrics and the geyser feeding her bathroom in the manor house in the morning, so he supposed he'd have to install her in his tiny guest bedroom/storeroom for the night.

Joy of joys. How was he supposed to sleep, imagining her in a bed not more than a thirty-second walk from his own?

'Can we possibly go inside?' Jess asked, her voice as cold as the wind that blew off the mountains.

Luke gestured to his house and followed her long legs in loose jeans. In low boots, with her stripy hair and belligerent expression, she looked like an angry owl. A *sexy* angry owl...

Luke shook his head as her shoulder dropped with the weight of the bag but resisted the urge to take it off her shoulder. Why was he was feeling so annoyed? Protectiveness? Could that be what it was?

Well, *damn*.

He'd always felt uneasy about her travelling across the country on her own, but since she'd planned to do the trip over two days, and would be driving during daylight hours, he'd told himself that she would be fine. When he'd seen her white face and blue-shadowed eyes in the light of her SUV he'd felt a rush of relief followed by a tidal wave of anger because she'd pushed herself so hard to get to St Sylve—driving those passes through the mountains while tired was simple stupidity. He was mad because protectiveness was a precursor to caring, and caring was a precursor to getting involved— which led to pain when someone left, and that wasn't something he was prepared to have happen again.

So... *Take a deep breath, Savage.* He had to find his self-control, get some distance between him and this fascinating woman.

And while he'd been a bit blasé about wanting her in his bed, now, with her arrival, he was rethinking that. Not that he didn't want her in his bed—he still wanted that as much as he wanted his heart to keep pumping—but he was thinking that if he saw her as someone he felt protective over instead of an independent, competent woman there could be massive complications down the road.

Was sleeping with her worth the complications? He really wished he knew.

Luke scowled at Jess's slow-moving figure. Apart from putting his libido on speed, she made his breath hitch and his heart stutter. He thought about her when she wasn't there and felt protective over her, though she was perfectly capable of looking after herself, and worst of all his world made much more sense now that she was here at St Sylve.

Luke blew out a frustrated breath; he was losing it, he decided. Years of working far too hard and playing far too little were catching up to him. Luke caught her low groan as she moved the tote bag from one arm to another. Frustrated at her independence, he stepped up and yanked the bag from her grasp.

Jess started to protest, but something on his face had the words dying on her lips.

Excellent. He was making progress.

For about ten seconds.

'I'm a modern, self-sufficient woman who doesn't need a man to carry stuff for her or lecture her on road safety!' Jess told him as he opened his front door and stood back to let her precede him.

Progress? One step forward, six back…

'Yeah, yeah—blah, blah. Just get inside the house, Sherwood, and stop being a pain in my ass,' Luke told her—and wondered if he had enough wine on the estate to take the edge off the frustration he felt when he was around this woman.

Probably not.

# CHAPTER FOUR

EARLY THE NEXT MORNING, Luke stood with Owen on the veranda of his house, two massive Rhodesian Ridgebacks lying at their feet. Both men held hot cups of coffee—a welcome relief after the freezing temperatures in the lands.

Owen lifted his mug at the magnificent Dutch-gabled manor house directly across from them. 'You've got to admit it's one hell of a building.'

Luke nodded. 'My ancestors were quite determined to make a statement that this was Savage land and that they mattered. Except for my father a seven-bedroom manor house wasn't spacious enough. So he ordered the building of my house as a smaller guest house.' Jed had also converted the carriage house into an office block, installed a gym, Jacuzzi and steam room, refurbished the tennis court, relandscaped the gardens...

'All on borrowed money,' Owen commented.

'Yep—money he didn't have and St Sylve couldn't generate.'

After his father's death Luke had immediately sold anything that wasn't nailed down—excluding the family silver and furniture—to pay off his father's debts. The money received had barely made a dent in the debt he'd inherited along with St Sylve.

Frankly, it would have been cheaper to buy his own wine

farm…oh, wait, he *had*. He'd bought and paid for his own inheritance. If he added up all the money he'd poured into the estate over the years, servicing the debt and the interest, he'd probably paid three times what it was worth.

'My father was intensely concerned about the image he portrayed. It didn't matter that he was on the verge of losing everything. As long as the illusion of perfection was maintained he was content.' Luke shrugged. 'Sometimes I feel like going beyond the grave and slapping him stupid.'

'Can I come too?' Owen asked.

'Who is going where?'

Both men turned quickly, and Luke's cup wobbled as he saw Jess standing in the doorway of his house, dressed in jeans and low boots, her face mostly free of make-up and her hair pulled into a messy knot.

Luke felt his stomach clench and release.

After he'd introduced her to Owen and they'd exchanged some small talk, Owen glanced at his watch and excused himself. Luke thought that he needed to get back to the lands too, but he felt reluctant to leave Jess. It wasn't good manners just to leave her on her own, he told himself…*lied* to himself.

'We need to get your stuff into the manor house. I switched the electrics on; you now have lights but it'll be a couple of hours until you get hot water.'

'Thanks.' Jess wrinkled her nose. 'I'll do that later. I want to explore St Sylve, if that's okay.'

'Sure.' Luke shrugged. 'I'll give you a tour. What do you want to see?'

Jess shrugged. 'Everything.'

'Everything?'

'I know the cellars and the buildings. I want to see the lands and the vineyard and the orchards.'

'Okay.'

Luke stepped into the house and deposited the coffee cups on the hall table. Yanking down a heavy jacket from the rack behind the door, he handed it to Jess, thinking of how icy it could get on the bike. He pulled on his own battered wool-lined leather jacket over his long-sleeved T-shirt and stuffed a beanie into one of the pockets. In the shadows of the mountains the temperature could drop rapidly.

'If you want to tag along, I need to check on how far along my staff are with the pruning, then I need to go across the farm to check on repairs to a fence.'

Luke gestured to his powerful dirt bike and led her towards it.

'My Land Cruiser has gone in for a service, and the farm truck has gone to town, so this is the only mode of transport I have at the moment.' Luke slung his leg over the bike. 'Hop on. Relax and don't fight me. Do you want a helmet?'

Jess sent him a cocky grin before sliding on behind him. 'No, I want my own bike.'

'You ride?' Luke asked, not able to imagine this city slicker in charge of a dirt bike.

'I have four older brothers. I ride, fish, surf, play one hell of a game of touch rugby, can start my own fire for a barbecue and change a tyre,' Jess said as she settled herself on the bike, her thighs warm against his hips, her breasts against his back.

Oh, hell, she sounded like the perfect woman. That was *not* good. Luke turned the key and the bike roared to life.

'Oh—and the faster the better!' Jess yelled in his ear. Luke grinned as he picked up speed. 'Yee-hah!'

Luke felt her hands, light on his hips, and smelt the occasional whiff of something sexy from her perfume. He knew that she was smiling, and when her body relaxed he realised that her tension had disappeared.

Luke felt the wind on his face, her warmth at his back

and felt...*content*? He let the thought roll around his head.../ contentment.

No, probably not. And even if it was, experience had taught him that it wouldn't last.

It was mid-afternoon before Luke turned the bike to head back to St Sylve, and Jess was past frozen. A cold front had rapidly moved in, with an icy wind that had blown in heavy clouds and was sneaking in under her clothes. Jess buried her face in between Luke's shoulderblades and gripped his hips with now frozen hands. She wished she felt comfortable enough to slide her hands up under his jacket to get her hands out of the freezing wind.

Jess pulled her head up as Luke braked and stopped the bike. He left it idling as he half turned to face her. He took her hands in his and rubbed them.

'I can feel you shivering. Sorry, I didn't mean to keep you out this long,' Luke said, blowing his hot breath onto her hands.

Jess quivered and not only because of the cold. Seeing that dark head bent over her hands and feeling his warm breath on her skin made the worms squirm in her stomach.

'How long until we're back?' Jess asked, her teeth chattering.

Luke winced. 'About forty minutes. This cold front came up really quickly.' He looked up and frowned at the black clouds gathering above. 'We might get wet.'

Jess shrugged. 'Well, then, we'd better get moving.'

Luke pulled a black-and-white beanie out of his pocket and pulled it over her ears, tucking away her hair. They were close enough to kiss, Jess thought. She could count each individual spiky eyelash, could see the gold highlights in his very green eyes, could make out the faint traces of a scar in his left eyebrow.

She really wanted to be kissed...

Luke's fingers were cool on her face as he tucked her hair under the cap and she wondered if she imagined his fingers lingering for a moment longer than necessary on her cheek-bone.

'At the risk of you taking this the wrong way, get as close as possible. Put your hands under my jacket—get them warm. The temperature is dropping fast,' Luke said as he turned back.

Luke waited while she wriggled herself as close to him as she could and until her hands were flat on his stomach—oh, the blessed warmth—before roaring off. Jess put her face back between his shoulderblades and felt so much more comfortable than she had just minutes before.

His stomach was hard and ridged with muscle and his back was broad, protecting her from the wind they were now riding into. She'd forgotten how much of a man he was, Jess thought as the first drops of icy rain fell. It wasn't only his impressive body—while he wasn't muscle bound, he was still ripped in all the right places, like the six-pack under her hands—but wherever he went on the estate he instantly commanded respect.

She'd watched and listened as he interacted with his staff. He gave orders easily, listened when he needed to and made swift decisions. His employees felt at ease around him—enough to crack jokes and initiate conversation.

She hadn't realised how extensive his property was or how much he was responsible for. He had a small dairy herd that provided milk to a processing dairy in town, orchards that exported plums and soft citrus, and olives that were sold to a factory in Franschoek that pressed and bottled olive oil.

'They all add to the St Sylve coffers,' Luke had said, a muscle jumping in his jaw. 'Thank God.'

'Are the St Sylve coffers empty?' she'd joked.

'You have no idea.'

Jess couldn't understand it...*why* did St Sylve have money troubles if he had all these other sources of income? Even if the wine wasn't selling that well, then the milk and olives, sheep and fruit should subsidise the winery.

It was a puzzle. Jess felt a big drop of rain hit her cheek and she shivered. Luke briefly placed his left hand over her hands, as if to reassure her, and Jess rubbed her cheek against his back and turned her thoughts back to St Sylve.

Luke and St Sylve were such a conundrum. According to the grapevine, Luke made money hand over fist from his venture capital business, so he was supposedly not hurting for cash. It was common knowledge that he had extensive business interests apart from St Sylve, and he was reputed to have the very fortunate ability to make money—a lot of which, she suspected, he poured into this estate. Although he was based in Franschoek she knew that he provided financial and management capital to high-potential, high-risk, high-growth startup companies for a stake in said company.

But the question remained: if he had all these other sources of income for the farm and he was still selling wine—not huge amounts, but enough—why would he imply that the farm was in the red? That it wasn't self-supporting?

It was very bewildering.

Jess silently cursed as the rain started to fall in earnest. Within a minute the drops had turned into icy bullets that soaked her jeans and ran down her neck into her jersey. Jess groaned. She'd look like a frozen drowned rat by the time she got back to St Sylve...

'Are you okay?' Luke yelled at her.

*I'm cold and I'm wet,* Jess thought, but Luke knew that already. What was the point in whining? 'I'm okay. Could murder a cup of coffee, though!'

'You and me both. Damn Cape weather!' Luke shouted, and Jess just caught his words before the wind whipped them away.

'There's ice in the rain,' Jess yelled in his ear. She knew this because she could feel ice in the drop that was rolling down her spine towards her panties. She resisted the urge to wiggle.

'I wasn't going to mention it,' Luke stated as he abruptly stopped the bike.

'Why are you stopping?' Jess demanded. 'I thought the point was to get home as quick as possible!'

'It is.' Luke looked at a small track leading off from the dirt road. 'How are you at cross-country?'

'I've done it.' Jess looked at him and pursed her lips. 'Will it get us home quicker?'

'It'll save us about twenty minutes. But it's tough. And muddy. And it'll mean going through a small stream.'

Jess shrugged. 'I'm soaked already. Let's do it.'

Luke squeezed her thigh. 'You're quite a package, Sherwood. And even more of a surprise.'

Jess wasn't sure if that was a compliment or not.

Luke had already polished off one cup of coffee and was on his second when Jess walked into the kitchen, dressed in another pair of jeans and a dark blue jersey.

'Coffee?' he asked, even as he poured her a cup.

'God, yes.' Jess took the cup, wrapped her hands around it and sipped. 'Oh, that's heavenly.' Jess took a seat at the wooden four-seater table in the centre of the room and sipped and sighed. When her eyes met his, she smiled. 'One hell of a tour, Savage.'

'I'm really sorry we got caught in the storm,' Luke said. It wasn't like him. He always paid attention. But his mind had been on Jess and his hyper-awareness of her. The way her body had felt against his, listening to her introduce herself to his staff and engage them in conversation, watching her as she suddenly stopped walking and just looked off into the distance, as if she were taking a mental snapshot.

She was a city girl, and her attitude today had impressed him and, if he were one hundred percent honest, thrown him off his stride. He'd expected her to whine and moan about being wet and cold, yet she'd sucked it up and said nothing, accepting that there was nothing he could do about the situation but get them home as quickly as possible. While he'd pushed the bike through mud and grass and that icy stream she'd said nothing to disturb his concentration, and he'd got them back in record time...wet and dirty but ultimately safely, and as quickly as he possibly could.

She hadn't griped or complained.

'My boots are covered in mud. At least I can clean these—unlike my suede heels that I had to toss.'

Luke's smile flashed. 'I told you so. You'll have to get a pair of gumboots.'

Jess shuddered. 'They are so incredibly ugly.'

Luke rolled his eyes. 'But made for mud and rain.'

Jess placed her cup on the table and looked past him to the window. 'It's really belting down.'

'Winter in the Cape,' Luke said. 'Want some more coffee?'

'Not just yet,' Jess replied. 'Thanks for the tour. I've already got some good ideas for the campaign...'

'Want to share them with me?' He took a seat at the table, propping his feet up on the seat of the nearest chair.

'Not yet. Still percolating.'

'So tell me why you wanted to work for me.' After what had happened between them he'd thought that she'd hold a grudge for ever. 'Why *did* you gatecrash my party, Jess?'

Jess rolled her cup between her palms. 'It's the most talked-about campaign around and I'm competitive enough to want to snag it. That was one reason. Another is that I have a reputation in the industry...I'm becoming very well known for tackling hard-to-rescue brands or campaigns. And I have a soft spot for St Sylve and this type of campaign is what I do best.'

'Even though I—?'

'Fought with me, kissed me and then fired me?' A small smile tipped the corners of Jess's mouth upward. 'I deserved everything you said to me. You were right to fire me, and the k— Well, it was all a long time ago.'

She'd been about to mention the kiss, Luke realised. He really wished he knew what she wanted to say about it. That it was fantastic? She wanted to do it again? They'd be amazing in bed? It *had* been fantastic, he *did* want to do it again and, yes, he wanted her in his bed.

Jess was staring at his mouth and he wondered if she was remembering that afternoon so long ago, how it had felt to be in his arms, her breasts mashed against his chest, his tongue in her warm, tasty mouth. Luke heaved in a deep breath and surreptitiously dropped his hand beneath the table to quickly rearrange his package. It seemed that Jess still had the same effect on him as she had all those years ago.

He was coming to realise that he really didn't want to be attracted to this woman. He felt that she could, if he wasn't very, very careful, be a threat to his emotional self-sufficiency, his resolve not to become emotionally entangled.

Sleeping with her wasn't worth the price that he would have to pay if he found himself emotionally trapped. And that was why she shouldn't be sitting in his kitchen on a rainy Sunday looking sweet and hot, relaxed and rosy. She looked far too enticing...

Luke shoved his chair back and abruptly stood up. 'Listen, I can't sit around and drink coffee all day. I need to get into my office.'

Jess lifted her eyebrows. 'No rest for the wicked? Even on a Sunday?'

'I'm still running another company...I have to take what time I can get.' Luke gestured to the fridge and raked his fingers through his hair. 'Help yourself to whatever you can find to eat if you're hungry. When the storm lets up I'll help you move into the manor house. There's a TV in the lounge, or...'

Jess shrugged. 'I'll grab my computer from the room and do some work myself.'

Luke shoved his hands into his pockets, desperately wishing he could just drag her upstairs to bed. 'Well, call me if you need anything.'

Jess nodded. 'I'll be fine, Luke. I always am.'

It was the first time in the history of the world that a film crew had been on time for anything, Jess thought as she roared up Luke's driveway to see the vehicles of the film company outside Luke's front door. Behind them she could see the portly figure of her favourite director, Sbu, the willow-thin stylist, Becca, and she recognised one of the two cameramen.

She hadn't planned to shoot the first ad only two nights after she'd arrived at St Sylve, but, as Owen had said, the pruning was nearly done and if she wanted to capture Luke working on vines that had some foliage on them she'd have to get moving. It was fortuitous that Sbu and his team were free today—well, they had planned on some editing, but she'd persuaded, bribed, threatened them into coming to St Sylve instead.

Jess sat in her car for a moment, knowing that the next couple of hours were going to be madness. She needed five minutes to gather her wits...

She was now officially installed in the manor house, in a beautiful bedroom with an attached study and large bathroom.

After the storm had abated Luke had helped her move her

mountains of luggage up to her room and then disappeared back into his office. Later she'd heard him leave on the dirt bike. She'd heard him come back around seven, and when he hadn't wandered over, she'd decided that she was too tired to deal with him anyway and tumbled into the enormous bed.

She hadn't seen him since, and thought the chances of her having to go yank him out of the lands were quite high.

Or not, Jess thought as she jumped out of her car. There he was, talking to Sbu, and—what was he wearing? A white button-down shirt and khaki pants...for pruning vines? Uh— *no*. Not going to work.

Jess grabbed her shopping bags—if she wasn't going to be sharing meals with Luke then a girl still had to eat—and strode over to Luke and Sbu. Luke greeted her and automatically reached out to take her bags, which she handed over gratefully. Ready meals, when bought in quantity, were quite heavy, and she was happy to sacrifice her feminine principles to get the feeling back in her hands.

'Hi, Luke.' Jess hugged Sbu, greeted the rest of the crew and then spoke. 'Good to see you, Sbu. Did you get my rough storyboard?'

'Mmm.' Sbu shoved his hands into trendy cargo pants. 'Not that it means anything, Jess. You always change stuff halfway through.'

'For the better,' Jess reminded him.

'Can't argue with that,' Sbu replied. 'Are you ready to get this show on the road?'

'Nearly. I need to put some stuff away, and Luke needs to change.'

Becca's exquisitely plucked eyebrows pulled together. 'What's wrong with his outfit?'

'Everything,' Jess replied. 'He looks like someone playing at farming, and that's not what I want. He's got to look the part and he doesn't in that outfit.'

'Thank God,' she heard Luke mutter.

'That's the most casual outfit I brought!' Becca protested.

Jess shrugged. 'Sorry, but it doesn't work. I'll be more specific in the future.' Jess looked at Luke. 'Let's dump these groceries and get you out of those clothes.'

Jess lifted her hand as Luke's mouth twitched in amusement.

'Don't even go there...' she muttered in a voice only he could hear.

'This wouldn't be happening if you'd used a model,' Luke grumbled as he followed her upstairs to his bedroom.

'I'm afraid it would. I'm obsessively detail-oriented. I'm an absolute pain in the ass to work for and a relentless perfectionist.'

'Control freak, are you?'

'Absolutely.'

'It would be fun to watch you lose control, Blondie.'

At his comment, Jess swung round and caught his eyes on her butt. He didn't make any effort to look contrite or apologetic and, damn it, she appreciated his...appreciation. Instead of feeling insulted she felt warm and feminine, and a little coy.

'Are you going to watch my butt the whole way up the stairs?' she asked.

'Absolutely...as it's in front of me it would be a crime not to,' Luke answered as they resumed climbing. 'So, are you just going to film me pruning the vines today?'

Jess explained that they were going to film him riding his dirt bike over the lands, pruning the vines and walking.

'Oh, joy,' Luke muttered sarcastically.

Jess sent him a sympathetic look over her shoulder. His eyes held a mixture of impatience and frustration and, more than either of those, a degree of insecurity that she hadn't suspected he felt. He was stepping out of his comfort zone and handing over control and he didn't like it. Jess empathised. If they'd asked her to prance around her business and smile for the camera she wouldn't be Miss Suzy Sunshine either.

She hated not being in control.

Jess stopped, put her hand on the railing and turned to look at him. For the first time since she'd met him she didn't have to tip her head to meet his eyes as she was two steps higher than him. 'Look,' she said, 'if you're uncomfortable with anything we do, just shout. Sbu and I need you to be as natural and relaxed as possible. If you're not then the camera will pick it up. So talk to me. I'll do anything I can to make this process as easy as possible for you.'

They reached the top of the stairs and Luke guided her into his bedroom. It was a good-sized room, Jess noted, with a king-sized bed. It desperately needed colour, Jess thought, being a study in neutrals. Beige curtains, cream linen on the hastily made bed... And then the painting on the wall caught her eye. It was of the vineyards of St Sylve in a swirling mist, with just the impression of buildings in the background. Jess just stared at the painting for a long time, caught up in the mystery, movement and the sheer magic of the art.

And she fell in love...with the painting and with St Sylve. It was inexplicable, but the painting smacked her in the emotional gut. She was an artist's daughter, but she'd never reacted to a piece of art as she had to this one. It was a massive canvas, nearly two metres square, but the scene was intimate and she felt as if she wanted to step into the frame.

'Jess?'

'Oh, I love that.' She eventually spoke, stepping forward to kneel on the bed and make out the signature in the bottom left corner. 'Who painted this? It's fantastic.'

'My mother.'

'You mother was an artist? My dad is an artist!' Jess told him. 'I wonder if they ever met.'

'Not likely.'

'You'd be surprised. I must ask him if he knew her.' Jess looked over her shoulder at him. He stood at the edge of his bed, his hands shoved in the pockets of his cargo pants, his eyes on the painting. 'She died when you were very young, right?'

'I was three,' Luke said in a flat voice.

Jess sat down on the edge of his big bed. 'Do you remember her at all?'

Luke took so long to answer that she thought he was ignoring her question. 'I have a vague impression of long dark hair.'

'Did you inherit any of her talent?'

'No. Did you?'

'My dad's love and appreciation for art, but not his skill.' Jess looked at the painting again. 'Do you have any more of her art? If you do, I'll buy one right now.'

'I only have this one and the one in the lounge downstairs.' Luke gestured to two closed doors on the opposite side of the room. 'My closet.'

Conversation over. Jess sighed. Damn it. He was as mysterious as his mother's painting, she thought as she crossed the room to his closet. Inscrutable and elusive and very, very compelling. Jess pulled open the doors and raised her eyebrows at the jumble.

And very messy.

There were shelves on both sides of the narrow passage that led to the *en-suite* bathroom, and the right side held a rail that was bulging with jackets and shirts. Jess itched to reorganise the jumble: there was a pile of T-shirts jammed into a space next to some files, jerseys on top of piles of paper, shoes and sports equipment in a heap on the floor.

Jess found some jeans and picked them up to find the pair he'd worn the other day—with the handprint on the seat. She turned her attention to his shirts. Flipping through them, she muttered as she pushed hangers to find what she was looking for...if he had it. His shirts were either too business-like or too smart-casual. She wanted something worn, but button-down—long-sleeved, but... And there it was, right at the back and half hanging off its hanger. A long-sleeved collared flannel shirt, missing a button and with its pocket half falling off, in a green-and-black check. Jess pulled it out and nodded. Perfect.

'Jess, that shirt is about twelve years old. I wore it when I spent a summer travelling Alaska. It's falling apart,' Luke complained when she waved it at him.

'It's exactly what I want,' Jess replied. 'Where's that hunter-green long-sleeved T-shirt and your leather belt?'

'Belt is in the bathroom. Green shirt? In a pile...' Luke grinned at her slight scowl. 'I suppose your closets are military tidy? Everything organised by type?'

And colour. But Jess didn't think she needed to tell him exactly how anal she was. 'Get changed. T-shirt underneath. This on top. Sleeves shoved up your arms. Your normal boots.'

'Yes, boss,' Luke grumbled, reaching past her to pull the T-shirt from a pile she hadn't looked in. Mostly because she'd thought it was full of rugby shirts.

God, this man needed a wife—if only to sort this mess out. Luke moved past her into the bathroom and Jess went back into his bedroom and walked over to a shelf where she could see a couple of photographs in silver frames. There was a photo of him and Kendall and Owen after a rugby match, looking much younger and splattered with mud. Another of two elderly people standing arm in arm in the doorway of the manor. Judging by their dress, Jess surmised that they were Luke's grandparents. The man had Luke's smile. The picture in the most ornate frame was very obviously of Luke's mother, holding and gazing adoringly at, even more obviously, Luke as a toddler.

Jess picked up the frame and looked into the feminine version of Luke's face. That was what his eyes would look like if he was happy, Jess realised. They'd dance in his face... His nose was longer than his mother's, his mouth a little thinner. But those eyes, the shape of her face and that luxurious hair...that was all Luke.

Jess replaced the photo and noticed that Luke's father wasn't in any of the remaining frames. Hearing him behind her, Jess turned around and smiled. Yep, that was the look she wanted—relaxed, casual...happy in his old clothes because, hell, he *was* the Savage of St Sylve. He didn't need to dress up and pretend to be something he wasn't...

Jess smiled. 'You'll do.'

'Good, because I'm not changing again.' Luke tugged at the shirt. 'I like this shirt. I'd forgotten about it.'

Jess thought about mentioning that if he cleared the cupboard out he'd be amazed at what he found. But it wasn't her house, he wasn't her boyfriend... She changed the subject. 'Why don't you have a photo of your father up with the rest of your family?'

'Because, while he might have been my father, he wasn't my family.' Luke snapped the words off.

*Whoa!* And didn't *that* tell her a whole lot about their father-son relationship?

'Can we get going? I still have real work to do today,' Luke said, gesturing to the door.

Jess nodded and walked out of the room. Her family might drive her utterly insane, but she couldn't imagine not having them in her life. If Luke had lost his mother when he was three, and if his father hadn't been much of a father, as his previous statement implied, then that meant Luke had grown up without any sort of parental support system...

Jess felt her heart clench. He might have grown up on this

beautiful estate, in a house full of very old furniture, but it sounded as if he'd grown up alone. Nobody, she decided, should grow up like that.

# CHAPTER FIVE

LUKE WATCHED from his lounge as Jess said goodbye to a strawberry blonde who had just deposited a massive art folder into the boot of her car. She hugged Jess before climbing into her car, and they spent another minute or two chatting before the car moved down the driveway. He saw Jess rub her arms as she turned around to head back to the manor house. Her blonde hair was tousled by the wind, and in her black jeans and short cream jacket she looked just as fresh as she had that morning—if he ignored the shadows under her eyes and the tension in her shoulders.

Luke saw her look at his front door, saw the indecision cross her face and caught the small shake of her head. She wouldn't invade his privacy, wouldn't step over the line between work and play by inviting herself in for a drink, a meal, a roll in the sack.

Luke half smiled. *Please feel free to invade my privacy,* he silently told Jess, *especially if you have more in mind.*

Jess walked over to the manor house. It was a lonely place, huge and oppressive, and he'd spent huge chunks of his life in it alone. On a cold winter's night it could be gloomy, and he didn't want Jess in the house on her own tonight.

Or maybe he didn't want to be on his own tonight, Luke thought. After a crazy day being trailed by cameras he also wanted something normal. A hot meal, a glass of wine, some company.

Before he could talk himself out of inviting Jess over, Luke walked into the hall, grabbed his jacket off the newel post and shrugged it on, and opened the front door. He grimaced at the icy wind and wondered if Jess was warm enough at night. The manor house had no central heating—his father had spent money like a Russian oil billionaire but refused to spend money to warm the house. There was a down duvet on her bed and a heater in her room, and the study had a fireplace—God, he'd forgotten to get some wood to her— but if she wanted to sit in one of the many lounges she'd need a ski-suit.

Luke hunched his shoulders up around his ears as he walked around the house and up the back stairs to the kitchen. Slipping into the room, he blew on his fingers and looked around the empty space. The kettle was on, and a teabag was in the mug next to it...

Luke stepped from the kitchen into the passageway and stood at the bottom of a second simple staircase. In the old days it had been the servants' staircase, and as a boy the only one he'd ever used.

'Hi.'

Luke looked up and saw Jess leaning on the short strip of banister on the first floor. 'Hey. I was wondering if you'd like to have supper with me.'

Jess grinned. 'What's on the menu?'

'Since you cook like a first-year uni student, you can't afford to be picky,' Luke told her. 'Get down here and come see.'

Jess's smile held enough energy to power a rainbow, Luke thought as she disappeared from view. Two seconds later she was at the top of the stairs and lifting her buttock onto the railing. 'Jess—no!'

Luke instinctively moved to the end of the railing and held

his breath as Jess flew down the railing and practically fell
into his arms. Luke banded his arms around her and bent his
knees to soften the impact of her slamming into him.

'Whoomph...' Jess muttered as they connected.

He held her as they swayed and regained their balance. Jess
recovered before he did, because she flung her head back and
her eyes sparkled with fun. Luke looked down at her and did
what any hot-blooded man would do in the same situation. He
kissed her. Hard and fast, with an already beating heart and
elevated pulse. He kissed her without thought, backing her
into the wall behind her, shoving his knee between her legs
to widen hers, rubbing the inside of her thigh with his knee.

Oh, God, she felt amazing. Soft and supple, slim yet strong.
Her perfect breasts were pressed against his chest, and he
wondered if she realised that she'd tilted her hips, bringing
her closer to him. Luke's hand dipped into the loose space
between her back and jeans—that special area above her butt.
Her skin was baby-smooth, warm, tantalising... He wondered if she still wore a thong and dipped his hand to find
out. Yep, there it was...a thin cord against achingly smooth
feminine skin.

Luke shifted so that he was even closer to her—so close
that he could feel the thump of her heart, catch those breathy
little moans as he tangled his tongue with hers. The scent of
her was clean and warm, the taste of her spicy-sweet—and
he decided that he'd never been this hot, this quickly.

What was it about this woman that sent him from nought to
three hundred miles in six seconds flat? She wasn't the most
beautiful woman he'd ever had his hands on, nor the most
built. But she made him spark and then burn. He needed to
have her, to taste her sweet mouth, see the brilliance of her
eyes, the warmth of her smile. He wanted to see her in his
bed, looking up at him, her body flushed with pleasure, legs
around his waist, her eyes closing with pleasure.

He felt Jess's sigh, her breath in his mouth, felt her hands flatten against his chest...

'I want you,' he muttered against her cheekbone, and heard the rough desire in his voice.

'I know,' she whispered back. 'But it's too soon. I can't...'

'Why not?' Luke demanded, snapping his head back. 'We're two single adults, mutually attracted. Nothing changes...'

Because he was hip to hip with her, nose to nose, he felt resistance invade her muscles. And heard the reluctance in her voice. 'I've never been good at one-night stands, Luke, and we have to work together in the morning. This campaign is too important to risk messing it up because we want to scratch an itch.'

'I'll risk it,' he growled, nipping her full bottom lip with his teeth.

Jess patted his chest. 'Back up.' When he pulled away, she shook her head. 'More. Seriously—I need room to breathe.'

So did he. Luke moved away reluctantly and slumped against the wall next to her. This woman was going to be the death of him. He'd be the first person ever to die of sexual frustration.

Jess was the first to break the silence. Her voice was forced-casual when she spoke. 'So, what did you think about my descent down the banister? Seven? Eight?'

'Five. Average.' Luke grinned reluctantly. 'Not too bad. Not good, but okay.'

Jess lifted her eyebrows. 'And I suppose you're better?'

'Miles.'

'Prove it.'

Was she challenging him? To slide down the banister like a child? Luke started to roll his eyes and then he saw the dare in hers, in that arrogantly cocked eyebrow.

'You are such a chicken,' Jess said, and made a clucking sound.

He shouldn't even be tempted. It was such a childish thing to do. Jess did her clucking sound again and he glared at her. 'I take it your brothers taught you to slide down banisters?'

'Who else? We have a long staircase at home. We used to put a mattress at the bottom of the stairs...shall I drag one down from the bedroom for you?'

'I am *not* sliding down the bloody banister,' Luke growled.

Jess hooted. 'You've thought about it a couple of times. Just do it. Go big or go home.'

Luke shook his head. 'You are such a brat.'

A man could only take so much when challenged by a woman, he thought. All his life he'd run up these stairs and slid down. The last time he'd done it had been a couple of weeks before his father's death.

He squinted down at Jess, who was still silently laughing at him. 'A chicken, huh?'

'Cluck, cluck, cluck.'

'Mmm. Well, if I meet your challenge then you have to meet mine.'

'And what would that be?' Jess asked, suddenly wary.

Luke grinned. He pushed her hair off her forehead and placed his hand on her cheekbone. 'I get to kiss you.'

Jess's eyes smoked over. 'You just did,' she pointed out with a hitch in her voice.

Luke shook his head. 'Again. No holds barred.'

'It's not a good idea, Luke.'

'Cluck, cluck, cluck.' See—he could make chicken noises too.

Jess scowled at him, but he felt her acquiescence before he heard her muttered agreement. It seemed that she couldn't resist a challenge either. Then he felt the sting of her hand on his rump.

'Let's see how the master does it.'

Luke grinned, stepped away from her and jogged up the

stairs. He placed one buttock on the banister and suddenly he was ten again and flying. He let out a huge whoop as he gained speed. He was flying off the end... Oh, *hell*. At the last moment he remembered to bend his knees, and he landed awkwardly but safely.

He placed his hands on his thighs and grinned up at Jess. 'I'm out of practice. That was less than elegant.'

Jess placed a hand on his back and patted him. 'I'd say. Now, what's for supper? I'm starving.'

Jess started to walk away, and his hand shot out and snagged the pocket of her jeans. She stopped mid-stride and swore softly.

'Are you welshing on our bet?' Luke demanded, wrapping his arms around her waist and burying his face in the crook of her neck.

Jess hauled in a breath. He smelt so good—that perfect combination of man and deodorant, sexiness and skin. He spun her around, placed his hands on either side of her slender waist and pulled her towards him. He captured her yelp of surprise in his mouth and, while her mouth was open, slid into the kiss. She could feel his fingers curling into her hips, the pads of his fingers branding her through her clothes as he re-explored her mouth. She'd been thinking about this kiss—and more—for the past three weeks. Hell, for the past eight years.

It didn't disappoint. *He* didn't disappoint.

Unable, unwilling to stop, Luke threaded both his hands into her hair, tipping her head to allow him deeper access, pushing his body closer to hers. He sighed when her arms encircled his waist, the palms of her hands flat against his back under his shirt to explore those ridges of muscle, that heated skin.

She wanted him...wanted to take this kiss further, she thought as he placed tiny kisses on her cheek, her jaw, pulled the neck of her jersey down to scrape his teeth against the tendon in her neck. He feathered his fingers against her ribcage and Jess succumbed to temptation and twisted into his hand.

Luke, hearing her soft whimper, bent his legs and, placing his hands under her thighs, lifted her up.

Jess instinctively gripped his waist with her thighs, vaguely aware that he had her against the wall. She felt the icy bricks against her back when he yanked her shirt up and over her head. His eyes heated as he stared down at her breasts, covered by a lacy lilac bra.

'You're exquisite.'

Jess couldn't find any moisture in her mouth to swallow. If she wiggled she'd go off like a cracker.

'Luke...'

'What?' Luke muttered, his mouth against hers. 'Rip my clothes off? Take me now?'

She wished she could say it. Wished she could surrender to him, lose herself in his arms. But that would require her handing over a smidgeon of control, and even that would be too much. Luke had the ability to overwhelm her, and she wasn't prepared to risk feeling vulnerable...*being* vulnerable.

It took everything to drop her legs and unhook her arms from his waist. She wiggled out from under him and left him facing the wall, his forearm above his head.

'Phew! Right, where were we?'

Luke scrubbed his face with his hands. 'I have no idea. Give me a minute to get blood to my brain and I'll tell you.'

'Dinner,' Jess said brightly, picking up her shirt and pulling it on. 'You were going to make me dinner!'

'I'd rather make love to you,' Luke grumbled, turning around and tipping his head back to rest it against the wall.

Jess looked at his strong, exposed throat, the muscles bunching as he folded his arms, the frustration in his deep green eyes.

He really wanted her. To have such a man feeling so frustrated over her made her feel powerful, giddy, intensely and completely feminine...

But, as with any other drug, the high was not worth the low that followed.

Jess sat at Luke's kitchen table while he made spaghetti Bolognese for supper. The aroma of fresh herbs and garlic and the satiny-smooth slide of the red wine Luke had pressed on her made her think she was in Tuscany again. She'd adored Tuscany—the food, the wine, the old buildings and the sleepy villages.

Of course in Tuscany she wouldn't have had her laptop open in front of her or her iPad next to her. She wouldn't be prefacing dinner with talk of work. But, knowing Luke's intensive schedule, she realised that if she didn't grab his attention now she might not have it later.

And, admittedly, she'd grabbed her computer to remind them both of why she was at St Sylve. She was here to work, not play. To work, not to race down banisters like children. Work, not exchange hot, melt-your-panties kisses against a two-hundred-year-old wall...

*Work, Jessica.* Tangling with that mouth, playing with that delicious body was not an option.

Jess looked at her screen. The letters were out of focus and jumbled. Not only did he make her hormones jump but she also wanted to delve beneath that inscrutable façade. She kept getting glimpses of his soul, tiny flashes of resentment, sadness and more emotion than she would have credited him with. Luke Savage had unplumbed depths...

And she shouldn't be thinking of plumbing those depths, Jess told herself. Nor should she be tempted by sleeping with him either. She knew the science behind attraction, Jess reminded herself. A girl thought she was just having a simple affair but the act of intercourse released the cuddle hormone—what was it called again? Oxytocin?—and while you intended to walk away you suddenly felt this man might be the one, your mate, your destiny, the father of your children.

Then months, years, decades later you'd find him in bed testing out someone else's cuddle hormone.

All because she'd scratched an itch.

Not going to happen...mostly because she suspected that if she ever started thinking of Luke in terms of *together for ever* and *one and only* she might as well yank out her heart and ask him to stomp on it. Hard. With Grant her head and her pride had been dinged. She knew that if she allowed herself to feel anything more than friendship for Luke it would be the emotional equivalent of being disembowelled with a teaspoon. And the fastest way to get to that point? Sleep with him.

So that wasn't going to happen. She hoped.

'I can smell the smoke from all those brain cells you're burning,' Luke said mildly, swiftly dicing onions with a wicked-looking knife. 'What are thinking about?'

Jess sent him a blank look. 'What?'

'You're miles away.' Luke tossed the onions into a pan with the sizzling garlic. He nodded at her laptop. 'And you brought work...not cool since I'm trying to seduce you with my culinary talents.'

Jess leaned back in her chair and lifted her wine glass. 'You should know that my ex cooked the most amazing meals and it still took him three months to talk me into bed.'

Luke raised his eyebrows. 'Cautious, aren't you?'

'Very.' Jess held his eyes for a long moment.

*It would be so easy for you to talk me into bed, but while you can easily walk away,* Jess silently told him, *I'm not so practised. Sex is intimate, it's binding, and I'd be handing*

*my body to you, and some of my soul, and that scares me.
I don't want to get hurt. I really don't want to feel anything
more for you than lust-coloured friendship.*

Luke saw something in her expression—possibly craziness—and turned away without saying anything.

Jess took that as a sign to change the subject and looked
down at her screen. 'And the reason I brought work over is
that I need to talk to you about the campaign.'

'Talk,' Luke said, sounding resigned.

Jess ran through the schedule for the next couple of weeks
and told him which society events she suggested he attend
during the next month. Some were in Cape Town, some in
Franschoek, and a couple were in the surrounding wine towns
of Stellenbosch and Paarl. All were high society, and it had
been easy securing an invitation for him. Actually, most he'd
already been invited to, but he'd binned the invitations without opening them.

'Guess I'd better get my penguin suit dry-cleaned,' Luke
muttered.

Jess powered down her laptop and sat back and looked
at him. He was leaning against the counter, ankles crossed,
the foot of his wine glass resting against his arm. His eyes
were warm and relaxed and Jess felt her throat tighten. It was
such a nice end to a busy day: a man cooking her supper and
looking as if he wanted to slurp her up. Casually romantic...

Jess gave herself a sharp mental slap. If she was going to
start having romantic fantasies about Luke then she shouldn't
be in his kitchen, in his personal space.

Jess's mobile rang and the glass in her hand wobbled. Putting the glass down, she saw the call was from her eldest
brother, Nick, and she smiled. For far too many years she
hadn't received any calls from Nick, and it still gave her a
kick to see his name on her caller display.

'Hey, you,' she crooned. 'It's so good to hear from you.'

As Nick started to speak she caught Luke's frown and asked Nick to hold on. Excusing herself, she walked out of the kitchen to the hall and into Nick's living room. Another painting dominated the room—a beach scene this time, of a deserted cottage and the wild and cold Atlantic ocean. It was atmospheric, but every brushstroke seemed saturated with loneliness. Luke's mother's work...

Jess shivered and went to stand by the fire. 'Sorry, run that by me again?'

Jess slapped her mobile against her hand as she walked back into the kitchen, her thoughts a million miles away. She missed the searching look Luke sent her as she picked up her glass and drained the contents.

'Hey!' Luke protested. 'That's fifteen years old. If you're going to throw it down your throat I'll give you something cheaper.'

Jess looked at her glass and grimaced. 'Sorry.'

'Problem?' Luke nodded at her mobile. 'Bad news?'

'Not bad news. Just trying to manage my family. That was Nick, my oldest brother, being bossy and trying to arrange my life for me.'

'You don't sound particularly upset.'

Jess half smiled. 'To be honest, he's the only one I accept it from. He was out of my life for so long that it's still a bit of a thrill to have him in it. I'm prepared to forgive his managing ways. Probably not for much longer, though.'

'And the problem is...?' Luke stirred the bolognaise mixture and dashed some olive oil into a pot of water, cranking the gas high to get it to boil.

'Next weekend is a long weekend—Friday is a national holiday.'

'Yes. So?'

'My family have traditionally always spent that weekend together. All the siblings, their kids, my parents, me... We usually go away somewhere for those couple of days. I told them I couldn't make this year because I'm swamped, and because…' Jess stopped and winced.

Luke sent her a look that insisted she finish her sentence. When she didn't speak, he crossed over to her, tipped her chin so that she had to look at him and lifted his eyebrows. 'And because…?'

'Because they keep dropping hints about my ex and me getting back together. He's good friends with three of my brothers. He often spent that weekend with us.'

'But you told your family it was over? Why are they pressuring you?' Luke asked, puzzled.

'Because Grant has said that he wouldn't mind us getting back together and I was iffy about why we broke up. My brothers think I'm being temperamental and picky and just need to see what I've lost. Grant is a good guy in their eyes.' Jess shoved her hand into her hair in frustration.

'He cheated on you,' Luke said with utter certainty.

Jess's mouth fell open. When she could find words, Jess spoke again. 'How did you know that?'

Luke tapped her nose before going back to the stove. 'I saw it in your eyes. Why didn't you tell your family?'

Jess dropped into a chair and rested her elbows on the table. 'Partly pride. He made a fool of me and, as I said, they are friends. Have been for years… That makes it worse. If they find out about him cheating, something awful might happen.'

Luke stopped stirring the sauce and looked at her, surprised. 'They'd beat him up?'

Jess pulled a face. 'They wouldn't mean to. But my brothers are very protective over me. Grant will say something stupid and a fist will fly…'

'Aren't you overreacting?'

Jess took a sip of wine and looked at Luke over the rim.

'When I was five I was bullied at school. My brothers hung the bully—a girl—on a hook. All four Sherwood boys, ranging from six to ten, ended up in the principal's office.'

'Huh?'

'I was thirteen, going to my first dance. My date was threatened by the quartet. He was so scared he pulled out and I went to the dance alone. Sixteen—another boy, another kiss… Nick sprayed the boy with a hosepipe. In winter. I could go on and on.'

'Lucky you.' Luke held out the spoon for her to taste the sauce.

Jess held his wrist, blew on the sauce and tasted. It was perfect—herby, garlicky, meaty.

'Yum. Lucky? Are you mad? They are the bane of my life. They're nosy and interfering and still think I'm a little girl in need of guidance and protection.'

'But it must be nice to know that you have four people standing in your corner, ready to wade into the fire for you,' Luke said soberly, and Jess knew he was right.

Yes, her brothers annoyed her, but she wouldn't trade them for the obvious loneliness of growing up an only child.

'Or to punch an ex for you.'

'I guess.'

'He cheated. He deserves it.' Luke shrugged. 'Are you sure he cheated or was it just a suspicion?'

'I caught them in my bed. She was on top.'

'Tacky,' Luke said, tossing pasta into the rapidly boiling water. 'You're not very upset about him cheating.'

Jess shrugged. 'I'm over it. Mostly.'

'Mostly?'

Jess looked at the ceiling. How did she explain that she felt stupid rather than hurt—embarrassed that she'd never suspected he was cheating? And his parting words still stung.

'He told me I was a ball-breaker, a control-freak-psycho.

It was messy and a big failure… I don't like mess and I don't like failing.'

She didn't like being out of control, and being a perfectionist was a pain in the ass sometimes. Jess repeated the thought to Luke and he grinned.

He reached for the bottle of wine and topped up her glass while Jess draped her arm over the back of the chair. 'Anyway, to come back to my conversation with Nick… My family are desperately trying to find a villa to rent in Cape Town, so they can be near me over that long weekend. So that we can spend some time together… And my father—sorry—wants to see St Sylve. My family are wine-oholics. They've asked me to keep my ears open for a place to rent that will fit the entire family. Including Grandma,' Jess continued.

'You won't find a place to rent at such late notice. They are usually booked quite far in advance,' Luke told her as he drained the pasta.

'I know.' Jess looked glum.

Luke stared at her for a long minute and Jess frowned. 'What?'

'Being with your family is important to you, isn't it?'

'Yes. Very. My brothers alternate Christmas with us and their wives' families, so we're never all together at Christmas. This weekend is one we've kept sacrosanct. We have to have a damn good excuse to miss it, and so far my mother is not buying mine.'

Jess saw the deep breath Luke pulled in.

'Invite them to St Sylve.'

'What?'

'The manor house will sleep twelve adults upstairs and another two downstairs.'

What a perfect solution. She could have her family close and work when she could, or after they all went to sleep.

'Eleven adults. Five kids under five. Is that a serious offer?'

'It's sitting empty,' Luke pointed out as he dished up their supper.

Jess stared at the plate he'd put in front of her, her brain whirling. 'I'll only suggest it to them if we pay to hire it.'

Luke considered her words as he grated Parmesan cheese on top of her food. 'I wish St Sylve was in a position to say no, but it's not. I'll do some research tomorrow and give you a daily rate.'

Jess bit her lip and wiggled in her chair in excitement. 'Oh, I could just kiss you.'

'Feel free,' Luke quickly replied, and Jess blushed.

She would, but she suspected that would lead to more kissing.

And then her food would get cold and sticky and she was starving.

'No?' Luke filled up their wine glasses. 'Damn. Well, then, let's eat.'

# CHAPTER SIX

THE NEXT DAY, Jess watched as Luke carelessly and confidently steered a hugely expensive superbike into the spot Sbu had designated and pulled off his helmet, sending a warm glance to the blonde giraffe sitting on the wall that separated the beach from the road. The sun was setting, the model had a bottle of St Sylve Merlot and two crystal glasses in her hand, and a sexy come-hither look on her very expensive face.

Jess ground her teeth. She knew she wasn't acting... nobody was *that* good. Luke strode over to the model, cupped her neck and tipped her chin up with his thumb. Their kiss was way longer than necessary, and Jess was sure she'd have no molars left by the end of this shoot. Sbu eventually cut the scene and Luke lifted his head. He really could look as if he was enjoying this a lot less, Jess thought, glaring at him as he grinned down at the giraffe.

Jess shivered and wished she had a cup of coffee in her hands. She was cold, tired, and she wanted a hot bath and to curl up in her favourite pajamas. She wanted a chick-flick and popcorn, a romance novel and chocolate... She did *not* want to accompany Luke to a wine-tasting hosted by one of the most well-respected food critics in the country.

Maybe the giraffe could go with him?

Luke was not amused when she put the suggestion to him five minutes later.

'I'd rather jump off Table Mountain than be forced to listen to her babydoll voice all night,' Luke retorted. He tipped his head to one side. 'What's your problem? You've been like a bear with a sore head all day.'

'I have not!'

'Please—your expression could curdle milk,' Luke said. 'You haven't been your normal bubbly self.'

*You didn't have to watch yourself kiss her,* Jess told him silently, and wrinkled her nose. So this was what true jealousy felt like. Jess twisted her lips. She didn't like it. It was so high school...

'Are you—?'

'I swear if you say it I'll swat you,' Jess warned him. 'I am *not* jealous!'

Luke grinned and his eyes danced. 'Really? Good to know. Except that wasn't what I was about to say.'

Jess desperately wanted to curl up into a little ball and whimper with embarrassment. 'What were you going to say?' she asked, forcing the words out between clenched teeth.

Luke's smile widened and Jess really wanted to slap it off his face.

'*Are you*...interested in a cup of coffee? I was going across the road to order some from that bakery over there.' Luke nodded to the bakery across the street.

Jess wanted to toss her head, blithely refuse, but she was chilled to the bone. 'Thank you.' She sent him a stiff smile.

Luke grinned, turned and walked across to the bakery. Jess wished there was a wall she could bang her head against. What was wrong with her? She didn't get jealous or snarky or grumpy...she wasn't the type. Why was she feeling possessive about Luke? They weren't dating or sleeping together, and a couple of sun-hot kisses didn't mean anything. Shouldn't mean anything...

Jealousy suggested an emotional connection which was

unacceptable on so many levels. She wasn't ready or willing to get involved again, and neither was he. They were both rational adults, in charge of their choices and their feelings. Theoretically.

Jess sighed. Maybe it was because she was spending too much time with him: familiarity breeding fondness.

Her mobile rang in her coat pocket and Jess pulled it out to see 'Mum' on the display. She greeted her mother and listened to the weekly family update. It was more rambling than usual and Jess, who knew her mother really well, wondered what her mother was up to.

When Liza finally ran out of trivia and didn't say goodbye Jess knew that she was about to be set up. Since her mother's and grandmother's choice of men was always dodgy, Jess rolled her eyes.

'He's a second cousin, spends his weekends in Franschoek. Lee. Darling, you have to remember him!' Liza pleaded after telling her that Lee was in set design in Cape Town. 'You spent a day on the beach together when you were about five!'

'Mum, I can barely remember the people I spent the day with on the beaches of Thailand, and that was last year! And, no, I'm not interested in dating.' Jess watched as Model Girl tottered across the road to help Luke carry the coffee and scowled at the warm smile he gave her. He might not like her voice, but he sure didn't mind sharing his sexy smile with her. 'Mum, just hold on.'

Jess thought for a moment. Maybe it would be a good idea to dilute Luke's overwhelming presence by spending some time with another man—give herself some distance, some perspective.

Jess could think of at least ten reasons why Luke shouldn't even blip on her radar: she was a city girl, he was a farmer. Being open and sunny herself—today, admittedly was the exception—she wasn't mad about brooding, private types.

While he occasionally mentioned his grandfather and great-grandfathers, he refused to discuss the immediate past history of St Sylve, or explain why he and his father had been at such odds. He refused to discuss his father at all.

But there was still something about him that called to her. Jess knew that she was intrigued and curious, which was more dangerous than the sexual heat she experienced around him. She could shrug off the heat but it wasn't so easy to ignore what was underneath the sexy package. His intellect, his dry humour, the well-hidden vulnerability in the tough, hard-nosed, reclusive man.

She wasn't going to be stupid enough to fall for him because, really, she wasn't a stupid girl.

The distraction of dating another man might give her some of that much-needed distance and perspective.

'Set it up, Mum.'

Jess had to grin at the shocked silence. It was the last reaction her mother had expected and it took her a minute to take it in. 'Are you pulling my leg?'

'Not this time,' Jess replied, taking the cup of coffee Luke held out. 'Give him my mobile number and get him to give me a call.'

Jess saw Luke's frown and ducked her head. *Impulsive behaviour again, Sherwood?* She didn't want to date anyone else. She wanted to date Luke. But in her mind he was undateable, and she *did* need distance.

Jess tucked her mobile back into her pocket and blew across the surface of the hot coffee. She stared out to sea, knowing that Luke was staring at her.

'You're going on a date?'

His voice was silky-smooth and she winced internally. He didn't sound happy…

Jess hedged. 'Not a *date* date. Dinner with a second cousin…it was my mother's idea.'

'You allow your mother to set you up with men?' Luke continued, in that cool, concise voice which hinted at the calm before a very big storm.

'No—yes! Look, it's just dinner with someone I used to play with!'

'Then why can't you look at me?' Luke asked, moving to stand in front of her.

He grasped her chin in his hand and forced her eyes upward. Jess's eyes slammed into his and she gasped at the emotion she saw churning within them. Need, power, annoyance...

'No.'

Jess wasn't sure whether her ears were working properly. She thought she'd heard him telling her what to do. *Nobody* told her what to do...

'Excuse me?'

'If you want to date anyone, it's going to be me. Because we both know where you and I are heading and I don't share. *Ever*. So, if you want to do the dinner-and-dating thing before we sleep together, I'm it.'

Jess, having lived with men bossing her around her entire life, didn't appreciate Luke going all Head Boy on her. 'You're delusional if you think you can tell me what I can or can't do.'

Luke's eyes were thin, very green slits. 'Try me. Don't test me on this, Jess.'

Jess tossed her head. 'And how do you think you can stop me?'

Luke grabbed the lapels on her coat with one hand and yanked her towards him. Jess held her ground and briefly wondered if she hadn't miscalculated by challenging him. She could see that he was grinding his teeth. His lips had thinned and his jaw was set.

Luke cursed and slanted his lips over hers in a kiss that was as powerful as it was sexy. She didn't go for the dominating, take-me-now type of embrace, but this was wild and crazy and more than hinted at the depths of Luke's passion. He wanted her, and he'd leave her and everybody else in the Southern Hemisphere in no doubt about that.

His arm slipped around her back and she felt the power in it as he pulled her closer up to him as his kiss deepened. Thoughts, feelings, emotions pummelled her as he took exactly what he wanted from her mouth, her kiss. Then Luke did something to her mouth that short-circuited her brain. Maybe it was the scrape of his teeth against her lip, the long slide of his tongue that had her womb melting.

Jess was thoroughly into the kiss when Luke dropped his hand and took a step back. She licked her top lip and blinked hard, trying to get her eyes to focus, felt Luke grasp her chin and eventually found the courage to meet his stormy eyes.

'Do not test me on this, Jessica,' Luke said again in a hard voice before dropping his hand and heading towards his vehicle parked on the opposite side of the road.

Jess closed her eyes and staggered over to the wall, ignoring the smirking looks of Sbu and the crew. They could think what they wanted...she just needed to get her breath back.

Breath, brain, composure... What the hell was that? She'd never been kissed like that before—an explosive mixture of furious and frustrated. Jess blew her breath into her cheeks and waited for her heart to stop galloping.

Thank goodness she was leaving for home on the red-eye flight tonight...some time away would be a good thing, she thought. That distance-and-perspective thing again.

Jess watched as Luke climbed into his car, his mobile at his ear, looking cool and collected and seemingly unaffected by their kiss. The man didn't stop working. She knew that filming took a lot of time away from St Sylve and his other business interests, but instead of whining or moaning he just made the best of the situation. He followed instructions, did what he needed to do, and in between shoots and set-ups, he jumped on his laptop or mobile to do what else needed to be done.

She knew that he was under enormous pressure, but nobody would suspect it. Luke just put one foot in front of the other and kept moving forward without fanfare and without drama. He did what he needed to do and she respected that—respected him.

D.I.S.T.A.N.C.E.

Pers...pec...tive.

She now had two mantras: *No acting on the attraction*—ha, ha! As if *that* was working—and *Keep your distance, find your perspective.*

She didn't think saying mantras was working. Stupid New Age thinking.

Three hours, a shower and a smart suit later and Luke was still annoyed. And his annoyance concealed a healthy layer of panic. Where had his caveman response to her dating someone else come from? It had been basic, automatic, primal... a reflex rather than a chosen thought...and he didn't like it. Hell, he hated it.

He'd never felt so jealous, so out of control, so plainly *ticked* as he had...did...at the thought of Jess with another man. He hadn't enjoyed the illogical reaction he'd had to the idea—hadn't appreciated the instinctive roaring in his head that had said this was *his* woman, *his* mate. Millions of years of evolution and he was still dragging his knuckles on the ground.

Maybe it was life jabbing him in the ribs? He'd been amused at the thought of Jess being a little green-eyed over the model—it had certainly stroked his ego. He hadn't once thought that he might be equally...okay, a thousand times more jealous.

Dammit to flipping hell and back.

But date someone else? He didn't think so.

Luke scowled and took a sip from his glass of '87 Merlot. Jess, dressed in a short, ruffled black dress and do-me shoes, was across the room, talking to Piers Hanson the food critic. *Flirting* with Piers Hanson the food critic… It was, Luke decided with a scowl, as natural to her as breathing.

And enough to make him go all caveman again.

There was no way he was going to watch her flirt with anyone else, he decided, even if the man was old enough to be her grandfather. Luke took a last sip of his wine, placed it on the table next to him and excused himself from the group of men around him—friends of his father who were recounting stories that he didn't want hear. *He was a great vintner, an excellent raconteur, the life and soul of the party…*

*Yeah, you didn't have to live with him, dude.*

Luke walked between the guests, exchanged comments but didn't get drawn into conversation. He approached Jess from behind and put a hand on her lower back, loving the feminine dip where her back met her buttocks. She knew his touch, Luke decided with satisfaction, because she instinctively stepped closer to him before remembering that they weren't talking to each other.

'Luke—Piers was just telling me that he'd love a tour of St Sylve,' Jess told him, and he saw the warning in her eyes. *Be nice, agree. He's important.*

Luke nodded. 'You're welcome at any time, of course, but it's winter and the vines are resting. St Sylve is beautiful in spring and summer.'

'I think it's stunning year-round,' Jess said fervently.

Luke heard the truth in her voice and felt warmth in his gut. He knew it had nothing to do with him. He'd often caught her looking at the buildings, touching the doorframes, staring at the mountains.

Piers tipped his bald head and his bright blue eyes were shrewd. 'You don't look like your father.'

*Here it comes,* Luke thought. *Another worshipper at the altar of Jed Savage.*

*Be polite,* Luke reminded himself.

'It's said that I look more like my mother.'

'You do. Your mother was a beautiful woman,' Piers replied and Luke felt his heart clench.

It took a lot to keep his face impassive. 'You knew my mother?'

'I did. I have two of her paintings,' Piers said. 'Such an amazing artist—and a lovely person. Threw herself away when she married your father.'

Luke's eyebrows rose at Piers's frank statement. He felt Jess's hand on his arm and was grateful for the contact. 'Uh—'

What was he supposed to say to that?

'Sorry, but unlike a lot of people in the industry I didn't like your father.' Piers shrugged thin shoulders in a dark grey suit.

Well, this was interesting. 'Why not?'

Piers looked around to check who was listening before continuing. 'I thought he was arrogant, condescending and generally a conceited ass.' He looked up at Luke and pulled a face. 'Sorry. I knew him for a long time.'

Luke's mouth kicked up. Finally, here was a man who saw Jed clearly. He wouldn't verbally agree with him—that would be disloyal—but inside he was cheering him on.

Piers sighed and shook his head. 'My late wife would be jamming her elbow into my side now, telling me to keep my mouth shut. God, I miss her.'

'How long were you married?' Jess asked, changing the subject.

'Forty-five years. Five kids.'

*Wow.* The mind boggled. That was what he'd wanted…one woman, one life, one marriage. Lots of kids. Now he knew that some dreams weren't supposed to come true. He didn't know how to do marriage and family—after all, he hadn't any experience of one and his father had been an anti role model.

Piers looked over Jess's shoulder and smiled. 'And here comes one of my favourite shopkeepers, purveyor of some very fine wines.'

And Luke's some-time, part-time lover.

*Oh, crap on a cracker.* Since Jess's arrival he hadn't given Kelly much thought—okay, any thought—and the notion that she might be at this wine-tasting hadn't even crossed his mind. They'd had an easygoing, no-hassle…*thing*…going for many months; Kelly was his go-to person when he needed a date, or sex—or even on occasion an ear. He'd meant to contact her and explain things, but with one thing and another—mainly Jess—he'd forgotten. And the thought of introducing a woman he'd recently slept with to a woman he *wanted* to sleep with made his skin prickle.

It was so Jed.

Luke, thinking that this day couldn't get any worse, quickly excused himself and stepped up to Kelly. Gripping her elbow, he steered her away from Jess.

'Kel, I—'

Kelly laid a hand on his arm and sent him a warm smile. 'Luke, sweetie, take a breath. It's all good.'

'You don't understand. I need to—'

'Call it quits?' Kelly's warm blue eyes crinkled up at him. 'Luke, when I heard via the grapevine that you had a blonde staying with you I kind of caught a clue. Honey, I'm ten years older than you. I've been expecting this for a long time. Besides, didn't we agree that we're just friends who occasionally sleep together?'

Luke shoved his hands into the pockets of his suit pants. 'Uh…okay, then. Well…'

Kelly laughed. 'You are looking very flustered. Tough day or tough girl?'

'Both. She drives me nuts.'

Kelly stepped forward and dropped a kiss on his jaw, holding her cheek against his to talk into his ear. 'Good. You deserve a girl who will drive you nuts. It makes for very interesting sex.'

*If we ever get anywhere near the bedroom,* Luke thought darkly as Kelly drifted back to Piers and Jess.

Piers took Kelly's hand and pulled it into the crook of his arm. 'It's so nice to see you, Kelly, and if these two lovely people don't mind, I'm going to steal you away to taste a rather nice Cab from Chile. Not as good as yours, dear boy, but palatable.'

When they'd left, Jess tipped her chin up to look at him and Luke felt like a bug under a microscope. She sipped her wine and just went on looking at him, her brown eyes wary.

'So, *that* was interesting.'

Jess's voice was so bland and so even that Luke knew she was seriously ticked. Joys of joys. Would this day never end?

He resisted the urge to tug at his collar. 'Uh…'

'How long have you been sleeping with her?'

Luke took a deep breath as he prepared to explain that he wasn't sleeping with her any more, that they were just friends, that he had no intention of resuming their arrangement.

Smart girls. Dammit, you just couldn't get anything past them.

Jess, with Ally asleep in the passenger seat, turned into the gates of St Sylve and steered her SUV down the long driveway. She'd deliberately not thought about Luke while she was away, and being insanely busy had helped. There'd been decisions to be made at work, projects to give input on, meetings to take. She'd had drinks with a potential client and dinner with another, and had returned to the office around ten to put in another couple of hours' work.

Luke and St Sylve had been put on the back burner, but now she was back and she had to deal with them. Luke had told her he wasn't sleeping with Snow White... The woman looked exactly like the popular children's character: black hair, white skin, blue eyes. Curvy. He had been, but he wasn't any more. That was all the explanation he'd given her and she admitted that it was all she was entitled to. But she wanted to know more. How long had they been together? How had they met? Had he ever loved her?

Why did she even care? It wasn't as if she had any claim on the man—she wasn't in love with him. She liked him—a lot—but she liked a lot of men... She just didn't want to have hot sex with any of them but Luke. She couldn't possibly be thinking about him as being something more, someone important...could she?

If she was, then she didn't have an IQ higher than a tree stump. She didn't want a relationship, and he certainly didn't want anything more. Did she have to draw herself a picture to explain the concept of going nowhere? Honestly...

Jess parked her car in the empty garage and switched the ignition off. Ally woke up, stretched and yawned. 'Are we here?'

'Mmm-hmm.' Jess tossed her sunglasses onto the flat surface of the dash and rubbed her eyes. 'Luke's not back yet. His car isn't here.'

Ally released her seat belt and opened the door, greeting Luke's two dogs as she hopped out. 'So where does Owen live?'

Jess rolled her eyes and pointed to the stable block. 'Luke

converted the stable block into a two-bedroom apartment for him.'

Ally squinted at the building and then back at the manor house.

Jess rolled her eyes before laughing at her friend. 'Yeah, the walk of shame won't be that long,' she teased.

Ally looked completely unabashed. She'd come to St Sylve to sleep with Owen, and the poor guy didn't stand a chance. Jess opened the back door and pulled out her suitcase and then Ally's. Ally had a very masculine way of looking at sex and men: bag 'em, tag 'em and toss them back.

Love and feelings didn't form part of the equation.

Jess still couldn't work out whether she found that sad or smart.

Jess hummed softly as she padded her way to the kitchen door. She was exhausted, and it felt as if every muscle in her body was protesting against Ally's idea of heading to a pub this evening and *'par-tay-ing'*. Jess draped her shoulder bag over the back of the chair and headed straight for the kettle, suddenly desperate for a cup of tea.

'Head up the stairs. Second room on the left. I've put you in the room next to mine,' Jess told Ally.

'How old did you say this place was?' Ally asked.

'Early eighteen hundreds.'

'Encountered any ghosts yet?'

Jess knew that Ally was pulling her leg about the fact that she believed in ghosts and wanted to see one. Like Luke, Ally was a firm non-believer.

She wrinkled her nose. 'Nothing. A house like this *should* have a ghost or two.'

'And it probably would, if ghosts existed,' Ally responded. 'Up and left?'

'Tea?' Jess asked.

'God, no,' Ally responded. 'Wine. Got any?'

'I'm currently living on a wine estate...' Jess looked around. 'Actually, I don't. Nor do I have any food. We might have to raid Luke's kitchen.'

Ally leaned against the doorframe. 'Do you do that often?'

'More than I should,' Jess admitted.

'Oh, baby girl, you have it bad,' Ally said before disappearing upstairs.

Jess poured water into a cup and poked at the teabag with her teaspoon, thinking of Luke and wondering how today's filming had gone.

She splashed a little milk into her tea and wrapped her hands around her cup, blew across the surface of the hot liquid. Hearing Luke's car pull into his spot outside the kitchen door, she put down her tea and walked to the door. Luke's smile widened as he saw her standing in the doorway and Jess felt her breath hitch.

It was frightening to realise how good it felt to be back.

Luke jumped down from his seat and, leaving the door open, took two strides to reach her. He cupped the back of her head in his large palm. His mouth covered hers in a long, slow, deep kiss that melted her organs from the inside out. Jess responded without thought, draping her arms around his neck and pressing up close to his body.

Hot, randy, slow, sexy, tender... How many ways could this man kiss? Jess held the back of his neck and thought that she could read his mood in his kisses almost as well as she could in his eyes. In this one she tasted fatigue...and a layer of stress. Happiness that she was back, relief that she was in his arms and, as always, the pulsing heat of desire. Kissing him in return, she rubbed her hand up and down his back, instinctively trying to ease the stress from his muscles, arching her own back to tell him silently that she wanted him as much as he seemed to want her, trying to tell him that she was thrilled to be back at St Sylve, with him, in the strong circle of his arms.

God, this was getting far too deep, too quickly. She should pull away, take a breath…

Luke read her mind and yanked his mouth off hers.

Jess licked her lips and tasted him there. 'What?'

Luke stepped away and put an inch of air between his thumb and index finger. 'I'm this close to yanking you into the back seat of my car and whipping your clothes off.'

Jess thought that she could go for that. It was crazy, it was wild, it was… Luke slammed the car door closed and she came back to her senses. Impossible.

She hauled in a breath and found her voice. 'Hi.'

'Hi, back. Good to see you.' Luke ran his thumb across her lips before placing his hand on her lower back and ushering her into the kitchen.

Jess wrinkled her nose when she heard her mobile ringing in her pocket. It was Lee, the five-hundredth cousin once removed, the man her mother had set her up with. They exchanged pleasantries and Jess was deeply conscious of the sardonic look in Luke's eyes. His eyes narrowed and his eyebrow lifted.

This was stupid, Jess decided. He knew and she knew that she wasn't interested in anyone else but him, so she quickly ended the conversation with Lee, declining his invitation to dinner as politely as she could. Trying to use him as a distraction was so high school and, frankly, beneath her.

She raised her brows at Luke. 'Satisfied?' she asked.

'Marginally. Take me to bed and I will be.'

Heat arced between them. She could so easily sleep with him and damn the consequences…

Owen rapped on the frame of the kitchen door and ambled inside. 'Hey, Jess, good to have you back.'

Jess returned his greeting and was amused when his eyes didn't connect with hers. He was too busy looking for Ally.

'Ally around?'

Jess grinned. 'Up the stairs and to your left.'

Owen didn't need to be told twice. His long legs took him across the kitchen in a couple of strides and then he was running up the stairs. They heard a feminine squeal, a large thump, the slam of a bedroom door...

Jess shook her head. 'You do realise that she's going to gobble him up and spit him out?'

'He won't have a problem with that.' Luke sent her a direct look. 'You ready to gobble *me* up and spit me out yet?'

He said it with such a mixture of humour and hope that Jess had to smile. 'Nope. Sorry.'

'Ah, well.'

Jess leaned back against the counter and cocked her head. 'So, how was filming today?'

'Long and tiring. I walked up and cycled down the mountain most of the morning,' Luke replied. Gloria, one of his dogs, whined at the door, and Luke looked from her to Jess. 'The dogs want their walk. Want to join us?'

Jess lifted one shoulder before nodding. 'Yes, let's do that.'

Luke lifted the heavy jacket of his she'd taken to wearing at St Sylve off the hook at the door and helped her into it. Opening the door for her, he waited for her to walk out before closing it behind them and whistling for the dogs. Two huge canine bodies shot down the driveway like bullets, tails thumping.

Luke jammed his hands into the pockets of his leather jacket, idly noticing that they had a day, maybe two more, of pruning.

Jess picked up his train of thought. 'Pruning's nearly over?'

'Yep. Time for the vines to rest and rejuvenate.'

Jess looked around her, smiled and pulled in a big breath. 'The air tastes different here.'

Luke squinted at her. 'What do you mean?'

Jess scratched her jaw. 'Back home you can taste the soot, the pollution in the air. Here I can taste fruit: the peaches and the plums, the grapes.' She turned around and walked backwards, looking at the houses in the setting sun. 'It's so beautiful, Luke. You are so lucky to own this place, to *be* this place.' When he didn't answer, Jess placed a hand on his arm and made him stop. 'You don't believe that, do you?'

Luke looked at St Sylve and then he looked away. 'No, not really.'

'Why not?'

He felt his shoulders lift towards his ears and made a conscious effort to drop them. 'I guess it's because I was never made to feel welcome here.'

Luke heard Jess's swift intake of breath and carried on walking, looking for the dogs, who'd disappeared down a bank. Jess's shoulder bumped his as she fell into step with him.

'I really hate it when you toss out statements like that and leave me hanging.'

Her grumpy tone made him smile.

'I'm a girl, and answers like that make me want to ask more questions.'

Of course they did. Luke sighed when he saw the determined glint in her eye and knew that he'd opened the door to a barrage of questions.

He'd expected a question about his father, so he was surprised by what she did ask.

'Do you love St Sylve?'

He remembered his thoughts the other day, standing in her bedroom. 'Love it, hate it, resent it... I suppose you want me to explain that too?' Luke took her hand, threaded his fingers through hers and tugged her along. 'Let's keep walking.'

Jess remained quiet, and when he'd thought about what he wanted to say he spoke. 'My father always told me that I wasn't worthy of St Sylve for a whole lot of reasons. I didn't want to be a winemaker. I couldn't wait to leave the farm—him—this valley. I didn't like my father very much and he liked me even less. But I was his only son so I inherited.'

'And?'

'And instead of inheriting an estate with normal death duties attached to it I inherited an operation that was so deeply, catastrophically in debt that I nearly lost my shirt, my skin and a couple of essential organs trying to save it.' He glanced down at her. 'Your warning eight years ago was slightly... ill-timed.'

'Now you're just being kind. I was a brat.'

'You *were* a brat.' Luke pulled her hair and wrapped his arm around her shoulder to give her a brief hug.

'So, when you say "in debt"...?'

'About-to-be-foreclosed in debt.' Luke's lips twisted. 'My father managed to rack up a debt that was three times bigger than what the estate was worth.'

Jess looked astonished. 'But...why? How...? The bank...? Why did they lend him so much money?'

Luke shrugged. 'The power of the family name—and do not underestimate the power of Jed's charm.'

'So what happened when he died?'

Luke removed his arm, stepped away from her and rammed his hands into the pockets of his jacket. 'It took every cent I'd ever made—every bit of credit I had access to—to keep the bank from taking it.' His eyes hardened. 'I don't have my father's charm. Since then, most of the money I've made on other deals has been poured into servicing the debt.'

'So there hasn't been the money to launch new marketing campaigns until now?'

'New marketing campaigns? I didn't have the money to employ a vintner. I had to learn to make wine—to do everything, really. We have a bit more breathing space now...so you don't need to worry about getting paid.'

Jess hunkered down into her coat and looked at him from beneath her long lashes. 'Can I ask you another question?' She didn't expect an answer because she carried on speaking before waiting for his reply. 'Why didn't you let it go?'

Luke looked at her, confused. 'Let what go?'

'St Sylve. When you inherited it, why didn't you just sell it and walk away? Why did you save it?'

He'd considered it. On more than one occasion he'd decided to do that...to say he wanted no part of St Sylve. But despite thinking that, feeling that, he'd never managed to take that final step to walk away from his responsibility, his heritage, his name. He couldn't allow the hard work of all his grandfathers and their grandfathers to be wasted, couldn't pass the land they'd loved into someone else's hands.

Jess remained quiet for a while after he'd explained that to her. Eventually she tucked her hand under his arm and rested her cheek against it. 'So, basically, you're telling me that a part of you loves it?'

'Sometimes,' Luke acknowledged with a faint smile.

'Well, I do. Love it,' Jess said fervently.

Luke whistled for the dogs. 'It's getting late. We should head back.'

Jess turned around with him. 'Ally is talking about getting some dinner, going to a pub later. Do you want to come with us?'

Luke thought a moment. 'Is Owen included in the invitation?'

'They'll have to come up for air and food some time.'

Jess smiled. 'So I presume so. If you don't come I'll just stay here, catch up on my own work. I don't feel like being a third wheel.'

Luke rubbed his jaw. 'Maybe we both need a break. We'll take my car. What if we leave at about half-seven?'

'That sounds good.'

'So, tell me about your trip...' Luke said as they headed back home.

# CHAPTER SEVEN

'GHOSTS DO EXIST!' Jess insisted, her glass of red wine wobbling dangerously.

Luke took the glass from her hand and put it back onto the small round table they were all sitting around in Rosie's Pub and Grill. It was his—and his friends'—favourite pub to hang out in: a relaxed atmosphere, pool tables and, on the weekends, a surprisingly good band that played all their favourites.

'You know, for a shockingly smart woman, your ability to believe in nonsense amazes me,' Ally said, picking up a chip from the basket between them.

Luke agreed with her, but was old enough and wise enough not to say so with quite so much emphasis.

'Just because you can't see it or measure it doesn't mean it's nonsense,' Jess replied.

'It just means that you have a vivid imagination and no respect for science,' Ally retorted, draping her arm around Owen's neck.

His friend had that goofy look on his face that suggested that he'd been expertly and thoroughly used…and he certainly wasn't complaining.

God willing, he'd have that same look on his face before long.

When the conversation drifted to the campaign, Luke thought that he'd moved from actively loathing the process of making the advertisements to tolerating the process. He enjoyed the physical stuff—riding the Ducati, surfing, even the mountain biking today had been fun. What *wasn't* fun about hurtling down a forest trail at speed?

It was the attention he loathed. The cameras and the people constantly watching him sent him straight back to his childhood. He couldn't shake the feeling that instead of having just his father waiting for him to mess up, now he had a posse of strangers waiting for him to fail. Jess helped him get through; she had a way of calming his churning thoughts with a quick smile. Hell, just her presence and constant chatter relaxed him...although he'd never admit that to her.

Luke sipped his beer and looked at Jess. He liked her, and it had been a long time since he'd just liked a woman. Along with the liking he also respected her; it took hard work and guts to build what she had, and he admired her dedication and work ethic. Jess, he realised, was not after a free ride from any man.

Luke looked across the room towards the pool tables. 'A table is finally empty. Who wants a game?'

Owen and Ally nodded and Jess shrugged. Luke pulled her to her feet. 'You and me against Owen and Ally. That'll make it a little more interesting.'

Jess frowned. 'Why?'

'Two strong and two weak players,' Luke explained.

Jess stopped in her tracks and looked at Ally, who grinned. 'And we're the weak players?'

Luke exchanged a look with Owen. They played most Friday nights and were pretty good at pool. Actually, they were excellent. 'Uh...yes.'

Jess sent him a look that made his hair curl. 'Well, let's make this *really* interesting. Ally and me against you and Owen.'

Luke shrugged and smiled at Owen across Jess's head. How could they lose? 'Sure. What are the stakes?'

'Dinner at the only Michelin-starred restaurant in the country—the one down the road. Losers pay.'

Again, how could he lose?

When Jess sank the winning shot, she rested her hands on top of her cue and shook her head at him. Her brown eyes sparkled in the low light of the bar.

'Make the reservation, Savage, and bring your credit card with the biggest limit.'

Luke shook his head at the empty table. 'How?'

'I keep telling you that I have four elder brothers. When are you going to learn?'

Luke placed his elbow on the table and looked at Jess, who was making patterns in the condensation of her glass. She looked tired, Luke thought, and glanced at his watch. It was close to midnight and the band had switched from dance music to blues. It was freezing out, but a fire roared at one end of the room and the mood in the bar was mellow.

Owen and Ally had made their way back to St Sylve, and he supposed he needed to get Jess home, but he was reluctant to end the evening.

'Crazy week ahead,' Jess said quietly.

'Like the last couple have been a walk in the park?' Luke responded with a wry smile.

'We're filming the family scene at St Sylve on Tuesday, and my own family is coming in on Thursday night.'

He hadn't forgotten. Luke licked his bottom lip and asked the question that he'd been longing to ask since he'd heard about her family. It was one he'd frequently asked of his friends growing up, trying to capture what it felt like to be part of a group, a clan...a family.

'Tell me about your family.'

'What do you want to know?'

Luke shrugged. 'I don't know…did you go on family holidays? Did your brothers tease you? What do you remember most about your teens?'

He sounded almost wistful, Jess thought as she put her elbows on the table and cupped her face in her hands. 'Um…I felt like I was playing catch-up most of my life with my brothers. They were always bigger, stronger and faster, and they gave me no handicap because I was a girl. It was keep up or go home. They teased me incessantly and I made a point of annoying them in retaliation. Family holidays…?'

Jess thought for a moment. 'We spent most holidays at my grandfather's cottage at the beach. It was tiny, and we were packed into the house like sardines in a can. We had the best fun: hot days, warm seas, ice cream, blistered noses, beach cricket, bonfires on the sand. My brother John would play the guitar and we'd sing along—rather badly. Those holidays stopped when I was about sixteen.'

'Why?'

Pain flickered in Jess's eyes. 'My grandfather walked out on my grandmother and he and his mistress hightailed it to that cottage.'

'And that rocked your world?' Luke commented. Why would the disintegration of her grandparents' marriage affect her so much? He wanted to know. Just for tonight he wanted to know everything about her. 'Why?'

'My gran thought they had an awesome marriage. She considered him her soul mate, her best friend. Hearing that he'd been having an affair for ten years side-winded her. She moved in with us for a while, and I watched a vibrant, intelligent woman shrink in on herself. It was as if someone had removed her spine.'

*Ouch,* Luke thought.

'And my mom took the strain because my grandfather still wanted a relationship with her, but he'd hurt her mother so badly… It was a nasty time, and because this was *my* family, highly volatile and voluble, nothing was kept from me. My brothers went to boarding school but I stayed at home, so I heard it all: the rants, the tears, the curses.'

Luke considered her words for a moment. 'So when you caught your boyfriend in bed with someone else it was a double whammy? A visit to the past wrapped up in the present?'

Jess half smiled. 'Along with dinged pride.' She dropped her hand so that it lay beside his and curled her pinky in his. 'Did your wife cheat on you?'

Luke waited for the fist in his sternum and frowned when he didn't feel the normal punch the subject generally instigated. 'I never caught her at it.'

'Why did you divorce her?' Jess asked, the side of his hand warm against hers.

Luke stared at a point past Jess's shoulder and wondered whether or not to answer her question. Because she had a crazy shopping habit? Sure. Because she was bat-crap insane? That was a really good reason. Because…because…

'Because I looked at her one day and realised that I really didn't want her to be the mother of my children.'

'Ah.'

'Not that she had any intention of being a mother. She told me that she'd pop a kid out for me but had no intention of raising it. Since I knew exactly what it was like, being raised by a parade of nannies and au-pairs, I knew that I wanted my kids to have a mother.'

She heard the thinly disguised pain in his voice and wished she could soothe it away.

'I realised a long time ago that I wasn't cut out for the picket fence and two-point-four kids.'

*Oh, Luke. You are so made to have a family.* Instead of the words she wanted to say, she asked, 'Why not?'

This was the trouble with smoky bars with low lighting and cool, vibey music. Confessions and confidences tended to flow.

'I think to have a successful family you have to be part of one.'

'I don't know that I agree with you,' Jess said, moving her hand across his. 'Do you think you'd feel differently if your mother hadn't passed away when you were so young?'

Luke wondered whether he should tell her or not...after all it wasn't a secret. It wasn't talked about, but it was not a secret. For the first time in his life he actively wanted to share this information with someone...wanted her to know a little piece of his soul. Normally that would terrify him, but in this warm bar, with soft music, a couple of drinks under his belt and a gorgeous woman looking at him with tender eyes, he couldn't keep the words from spilling out. Tomorrow he might regret it...

'No, I don't think anything would've been different. My mother—a fairly moody creature, from what I hear—bailed out on me when I was three and got herself killed in a car accident a couple of days later. And my father was fickle, selfish and changed women like he changed clothes. Kids raised in a dysfunctional home do not have functional adult relationships and families. Basic psychology.'

'That's such nonsense—but back up a moment.' Jess frowned. 'Your mother *left* you?'

'She had suitcases full of clothes and personal possessions in her car when she crashed. Nothing of mine.' Luke felt the muscle tick in his jaw and closed his eyes. It had happened over thirty years ago—why did it still sting? Why did he still wonder what she'd needed, wanted from her life that had made her step out of the marriage, away from *him*?

Freedom? Another man? And would he ever stop wondering what he'd done that had made his mother leave him instead of taking him with her?

He'd been three, for goodness' sake...even *he* couldn't have been that bad.

Jess shook her head and covered his hand with both of hers. She had a look on her face that Luke had come to recognise as stubbornness. 'Who told you that she'd left you behind? And when?'

'My father...all my life.' Luke shoved his hand into his hair. 'It was his standard way of ending a conversation—*No wonder your mother left you*... Fill in the blanks. Can't catch a ball, make the swim team, come first in class.'

Jess's mouth fell open in shock, and anger sparked in her eyes. 'That's...diabolical.'

'That was my father.'

Jess's eyes flashed. 'That's child abuse.'

Luke felt sparks jump in his stomach at her defence.

'How did you manage to become so successful, so together, so strong after having that constantly fed to you?'

Because he'd been too damn stubborn and too proud to let his father win.

'And, I'm sorry. I don't believe your mother left you. I saw that photo of you and her in your bedroom—the look on her face as she looked at you. Nope, I don't buy it,' Jess said, her voice saturated with conviction. 'She loved you...there has to be another explanation.'

Luke wished there was. But his mother was long dead and, as much as he appreciated Jess taking up the cudgels on his behalf, he knew that to think about his mother was useless and self-defeating. If he considered other scenarios he risked reopening old wounds.

He'd tried marriage. It had been a failure. Losing his dream of having a family of his own had hurt a lot more than losing his wife, but he'd come to terms with the idea that St Sylve would not be home to dirty kids running wild.

Knowing his mother's motives wouldn't change that. It was in the past and he couldn't change what had happened.

'What happened to your mom's things?' Jess leaned forward, her arms on the table.

'According to my father she'd moved quite a lot of stuff out. The rest he tossed.' Luke stifled a yawn. Suddenly he felt physically and mentally exhausted. 'I remember someone saying that she took all her paintings for an upcoming exhibition. They've never been found. Somewhere, if they haven't been burnt or tossed, there are about thirty Katelyn Kirby paintings floating around.'

'Where did you find those two paintings?'

He didn't speak but Jess read the answer on his face.

'You bought them? Oh, Luke.'

At an enormous price, from a canny dealer who'd known exactly what he had.

Jess seemed immediately to understand that he'd needed a connection to her—something of hers that held something of her soul. Luke drained his glass. 'Yep.'

Jess pursed her lips. 'Dead or not, I really don't like your father, Luke.'

He saw pity flash in her eyes and his spine stiffened. Of all the things he wanted from Jess, pity wasn't one of them. He glared at her. 'Don't pity me, Sherwood.'

Jess jumped to her feet and shook her head. 'I don't pity you. I think you are one of the strongest, most together people I've ever encountered. I think you're smart and resourceful and mentally tough.' She cocked her head and listened to the music. 'I love this song—dance with me?'

Luke blinked at the change of subject and looked at the empty dance floor. 'Now?'

Jess nodded and held out her hand. 'Yeah, now. What? Are you chicken?'

Luke grinned as he took her hand and led her to the dance floor. He placed his hands on her hips and rested his chin against her temple. Moody, romantic music brushed over them and Luke's voice was threaded with laughter when he spoke. 'You remember what happened the last time you called me chicken?'

'I ended up against a wall, halfway to naked,' Jess whispered back.

Luke's heart picked up an extra beat at her soft, promise-soaked voice. 'Willing to risk that happening again?' he asked, holding his breath.

'Cluck, cluck, cluck.'

Even he didn't need more of a clue.

Luke pulled her across the dance floor towards the door, stopping briefly to throw some money on the table to cover their bill and to pick up Jess's bag. As soon as they stepped out of the bar and into the frigid air he started to kiss her, and within a minute he had her up against the building, kissing her in the shadows of the doorway. His wonderful hands burrowed beneath her coat and slipped between her jeans and the skin of her back—touching, demanding, insisting that she match her passion to his.

She wanted this, Jess told herself. She *needed* this. If she was going to do this then she had to surrender to the moment, to stop thinking and enjoy this hard-bodied, hard-eyed man who had the ability to make her skin hum. For the first time in her adult life Jess switched off her brain and surrendered herself to the physical.

His hand, warm against her, made her feel intensely female. Sensation bombarded her. The rough spikes of his beard as he dropped kisses on her jawline. His tongue wet and warm

in the dent of her collarbone. The amazing contradiction between that heat of his mouth and the icy air on her skin.

Jess couldn't stop her hands from roaming up and under
his jersey and shirt. She explored the wedge of fine hair on his
chest. She traced the ridges of his stomach muscles, groaned
at that particular patch of skin just beneath his hipbone that
was so soft, so smooth, so male. Her thumb, sneaking beneath
the waistband of his jeans, swiped over the long muscles in
his hip, exploring the wonderfulness of him.

Luke groaned and lifted his head. He rested his arm against
the wall above her head and his forehead against hers. 'I love
the way you touch me.' He cursed. 'But we can't do this here.
I want you where I can see you, taste you, enjoy every inch
of you.'

'Well, then, maybe you should take me home.'

'That sounds like an excellent plan.'

# CHAPTER EIGHT

THE NEXT MORNING Jess pretended to be asleep when Luke silently slipped out of bed. Risking a peek, she saw the glorious back view of him as he headed for the *en-suite* bathroom.

So...no morning cuddle for her, obviously. Thank God.

Jess pushed herself up in the bed, pulled the sheets over her chest and leaned her head against the headboard. Damn, damn and—just for a change—damn again.

What the hell had she done?

Jess looked around the room and saw evidence of their crazy lust-filled night everywhere she looked. One of her leather boots was on top of the credenza. She couldn't see the other one. Her pink bra dangled off the lampshade. Her T-shirt was...Jess frowned and peered off the end of the bed... nowhere to be seen. Where had it gone? Jess rewound and remembered that Luke had pulled it off in the hallway, shortly after he'd started stripping her as soon as he'd pulled her through the front door. Her jeans were on the stairs—along with his shirt, shoes and jersey.

Panties? There was no point in worrying about them. They were history since Luke hadn't tried to take them off—he'd just ripped the thong apart and pulled it away.

Could anyone say 'awesome sex'?

Could anyone say 'big, huge, monstrous regret'?

Jess scrubbed her face with her hands. He'd been a fantastic lover: tender, demanding, controlled, sensual and generous in turn. He'd turned her to liquid fire, inside out and... And she couldn't do it again.

It was simply too much of an amazingly good thing. And she wasn't remotely in control of any of it. She couldn't control her reaction to Luke's touch. He just had to look at her with those eyes filled with passion and she was his for the taking—battling to control the situation, the way he made her feel...

And, damn it again, her cuddle hormone was beetling around her body, gleefully singing, 'It *could* be a stylish marriage; he *can* afford a carriage'.

And all because she'd been idiot enough to sleep with him. Okay, not much sleeping had happened, but she was splitting hairs. She'd allowed those feelings of attachment a little piece of fertile soil to take root. She'd have to dig up the bed before they took a firm hold and—what was with the gardening metaphors? She didn't even garden!

Jess dropped her head. Maybe this was more than sex, more than the scratching of a mutual itch... Because she now felt exposed, vulnerable, scared. So very out of control.

She couldn't allow it to happen again. Sleeping with Luke was *not* an option. If she felt this unhinged mentally and emotionally after one night, she'd be a train wreck after a week or so. And probably fathoms deep in love with him. And, not insignificantly, she had no intention of being that girl who was hopelessly devoted to a guy who did not feel the same way.

'You're awake and your mental wheels are spinning.'

Look at her—all mussed and grumpy, hair a mess and those fabulous eyebrows drawn together in an ominous scowl. Luke thought that he'd never seen her looking lovelier...and less accessible.

'Luke, I—'

Luke tucked in the end of the towel that rode low on his hips, walked over to the window and pulled apart the curtains. He didn't need to hear her words to know what it was that she wanted to say. It was written in neon ink all over her face. *Last night was a mistake...*

'We can't do this again.'

It didn't matter that he agreed with her. Her words still held all the sting of a powerful slap. Luke winced and placed his hands on the broad windowsill, looking out over his lands.

'Okay.'

'Is that all you're going to say?' Jess demanded, annoyance in every syllable.

Oh, *now* she wanted to discuss it? Why didn't she just put his pecker in a wringer and be done with it? 'You said we can't do it again. I agreed. Did you expect me to argue with you? Force you? Beg you?'

'No. I—I just thought that you might have an opinion...'

That it had been the best sex of his life? That he'd been mentally, emotionally blown away? That he could picture her in his bed when they were old and grey? That he knew that was impossible...?

Luke heard the rustle of bedclothes and looked over his shoulder to see Jess stalk—his mouth dried up—stark naked over to his cupboard and yank the doors open. She pulled a rugby jersey over her head and rolled the long sleeves up and over her hands. The hem of the garment skimmed her pretty knees and draped over her perfect breasts.

'Well, then, I suppose there's not much else to say,' Jess stated as she plucked her bra from the lampshade.

She bent down, briefly flashing the top of her thighs, and when she stood up a scrap of black lace fabric dangled from her finger. Her thong—which he'd destroyed with a quick twist.

'Except that you owe me a thong.'

* * *

Jess looked at Sbu and shook her head. 'I'm sorry, there's something missing.'

He was going to kill her, he really was, Luke thought as muted groans from the crew floated across the room. He caught a couple of eye-rolls from the other actors and knew exactly how they felt. They had a right to be frustrated, Luke thought. They'd been filming for the best part of the day: a mock Sunday lunch, drinking wine in front of the fire. She'd even had Luke playing chess with a father-like figure.

They were supposed to be showing him in a family/friends situation, but he knew that the entire day had been an absolute waste of everyone's time. His especially, since he was the only one in the room who wasn't being paid for his time.

'Take a break, everyone,' Jess said, and Luke walked out of the formal lounge of the manor house, where they'd been filming an after-dinner scene. Ducking into the empty study next door, he placed his hands on the back of a wingback chair and sucked in air. He knew that he was mostly responsible for the cock-up that was today. He hadn't managed to deliver the goods. He was stiff and uncomfortable and, as Sbu had pointed out, he would come across on film as being irritated and annoyed.

Mostly because he was.

They wanted to show off his home, his heritage, filled with laughing, happy people, and Luke looking relaxed and at home. Except that he wasn't. Luke walked up and down the Persian runner, its rich jewel tones perfectly complemented by the wooden floorboards. He wasn't relaxed and feeling at home because this wasn't his home. He might own it and be the last Savage, but he had no emotional connection to this house, the furniture, to the fact that his forefathers had walked these halls, to the long-ago Savage wife who had ordered this carpet.

He had the dysfunctional relationship with his father to thank for that.

It didn't help that he and Jess were barely talking. When they did, they were stiff and uptight, tiptoeing around each other. It made him feel uncomfortable and uptight and... dammit...so lonely.

*You're feeling sorry for yourself, Savage. Suck it up.* But acting out his childhood fantasy hurt like hell, and all that got him through was thinking of Jess and the night he'd spent in her arms. It had been a fantasy, perfection, emotionally and physically fulfilling. He'd found himself wanting to lose himself in her not only physically but mentally as well. He wanted to know her secret hopes, her biggest fears, her first memories.

Mercia, ex-wife and amateur psychologist, had once told him he had abandonment issues. Because his mother had left him and his father had never been available he wasn't able to commit emotionally, to let anyone in, to be intimate. Until the other night that had been true, and the knowledge terrified him.

He couldn't afford to feel emotionally connected to Jess... because if he did and she walked away he didn't think his heart would recover.

No, it was better this way...it *had* to be better this way.

'Luke?'

Luke lifted his head and saw Jess in the doorway, her eyebrows pulled together and her eyes radiating determination. She'd been a pain in the ass all day—demanding, precise, determined. Unbending and an utter control freak. 'We're ready for you. Sbu and I have rewritten the storyboard...'

He was done. There was no way he was going back in front of a camera and selling his perfect life. His father had done that all *his* life...acted affectionately towards him in company and treated him terribly when they were alone. He was done with it.

'Not happening, Sherwood,' Luke said in his most even tone—the one his friends recognised as deeply dangerous.

'Luke—Sbu is costing me a bomb. He charges by the hour so I'm burning money here. Can we get on with it?'

Her snotty tone had his hackles lifting. 'The cost of which will be passed to me, so don't pull that on me! I'm calling it a day, Jess, leave it at that.'

Sparks flashed in Jess's eyes. 'What is wrong with you? I have a room full of actors and equipment and crew who are all waiting on you. Let's just get it done.'

'What is wrong with *me*? What is wrong with *you*?' Luke's voice lifted. 'How could you do this to me, Jess? Is winning awards and making spectacular adverts more important to you than people's feelings?'

'What are you talking about?' Jess demanded.

She genuinely didn't know... Luke felt a knife embed itself in his chest. How could she, the woman he'd felt the closest emotional connection to ever, not realise how difficult this was for him? He walked past her and slammed the door closed.

'Luke!'

'This house! Playing happy families! It's my worst freaking nightmare. Pretending that I had one is killing me!' Luke roared. 'This was my father's office. Do you know how many times he took a belt to my backside in here?'

'I thought—'

'That corner where we were pretending to play chess? I caught him screwing my favourite au-pair there. She left the next day. I was seven and I thought that my world had come to an end.'

Jess covered her face with her hands. Luke stormed up to her and pulled them away. Tears brimmed in her eyes and they just made him angrier. He'd never told anybody this and he couldn't stop.

'The painting above the fireplace? Its frame is cracked at the corner. That's because he threw a glass at me when I was fifteen. It bounced off my cheek, cracked it, then hit the frame and cracked that. Do you want me to go on?'

'No! I'm sorry—I'm so sorry… I didn't think.'

Luke stormed away from her. 'I *knew* giving the contract to you was a mistake—I knew letting you back into my life was a mistake. I knew I was going to regret it.'

He heard Jess's sob and felt that knife slice his heart apart. He turned and looked at her, and cursed when he saw that she was shaking like a leaf. He resisted the urge to pull her into his embrace, to comfort her with his touch, to stroke away those feelings of hurt, replace the loneliness and confusion with passion…

Was that what he wanted to do to her or was it what he wanted from her?

The only thing he was certain of was that shooting was done for the day. Luke placed his hands behind his head and lowered his voice. 'Get rid of the crew, Jess, and leave me alone, okay?'

Jess nodded, turned and left. Luke, as he always had as a child, got out of his father's study as quickly as he could.

She was a horrible, horrible person, Jess thought as she pounded down the dirt road away from St Sylve. How could she have got so caught up in her job, in the campaign, and not realised the impact it would have on Luke? He'd told her a little of his father, that he didn't feel as if St Sylve was his home, but she'd been so bedazzled by the grandeur and beauty of the house and the furniture and the concept of St Sylve that she'd ignored and/or dismissed Luke's feelings.

She remembered thinking when she'd put the storyboard

together that if she got it right there would be another industry award in it for her. The setting was magical, the hero gorgeous, the story tugged at the heartstrings. At the very least
it would sell a shedload of wine...

She was embarrassed, humiliated...disgusted with herself. Awards were not worth hurting Luke for. She was such
a weasel.

Jess picked up her pace. She needed to run...run off this
churning emotion, outrun her self-anger, the confusion, his
words that were running on a never-ending loop in her head...

*'I knew letting you back into my life was a mistake...'*

Jess ran blindly, not sure where she was going, barely
aware that the light was fading, that black clouds were threatening a deluge and that she was in an unfamiliar part of St
Sylve. The road was becoming more rocky but she pushed on,
wanting the burn of her muscles, hoping for a rush of endor-
phins that would make her feel partly human and not a complete jerk. How could she fix this? She had to fix this... He
was too important to her and she cared about him too much
to brush this under the carpet.

She'd apologise, obviously, grovel if she needed to. She'd
ask him if they could try to be friends again, make him realise that while she was occasionally thoughtless she wasn't
by nature cruel.

She had to fix this...she *had to*.

Jess yelled as her foot brushed over a rock in the road
and she went sprawling. Putting her hands in front of her,
she cried out as her palms skidded along the stones and time
slowed down. She hit the deck and her knees connected with
the hard ground. Then her right shin caught the sharp edge
of a rock and she felt her skin split open and the warmth of
blood on her leg.

It was probably no less than she deserved, Jess thought as
she rolled onto her back, grabbed her burning leg and sobbed
liked a child.

* * *

Where was she? Luke looked at his watch again. It was past six, fully dark, raining, and Jess still wasn't home. He'd come back from the lands as she was leaving for a run and he'd watched her swift pace down the road. Still annoyed, he'd headed for his study and immediately immersed himself in work. When he'd surfaced, two hours later, he'd realised that the manor house was solidly dark—which meant that Jess still wasn't home.

Luke's stomach clenched as he yanked on his jacket. Which way had she gone? Where did he start looking? Grabbing a torch from a drawer and his car keys, Luke headed towards the kitchen door and jerked it open. As he stepped out he saw the shapes of his dogs running towards him, followed by a slow-moving Jess.

Pummelled by relief, he stood under the awning over the door and leaned into the doorframe. The rain was cold and hard and Jess looked like a bedraggled rat.

'Where on earth have you been?' he shouted over the whistling wind.

'Got lost. Fell down,' Jess replied, her words almost taken by the wind.

She was soaked through, Luke thought. Her sweatshirt and running shorts were dripping and her hair was pushed back from her face. As she came into the light he noticed that she had a smudge on her chin and that her shin was dark… *Was that blood?*

Luke, unconcerned that the rain was now belting down, walked over to her and crouched down in front of her. He winced as he noticed the rip in her shin, from which blood was rolling down her leg and soaking her socks and trainers. He cursed and knelt in front of her, lifted her leg. 'Sweetheart, what the hell have you done to yourself?'

He could feel the fine tremors rippling through her leg and

heard the quiet chatter of her teeth. He didn't need to look at her to know that her face was white and her lips purple.

'I tripped and fell over a rock.'

Luke cursed again as he scooped her up and headed for his house. He carried her easily and headed straight for the stairs. Thank God his floors were wood, he thought, glancing at the wound on her shin which was still pumping blood and dripping off the end of her now red trainer. Until he cleaned it up he wouldn't know if it needed stitches or not. He hoped not. The storm sounded as if it was building up for another, even bigger session, and he'd hate to have to haul Jess to the doctor in this weather. With luck, he had a couple of butterfly bandages that might do the trick.

Walking through his bedroom, he avoided the cream rug and walked her into the bathroom, placed her on the seat of the toilet.

She lifted her hands and gestured to her body. 'I'm so cold,' she whispered.

Luke smoothed her hair back from her face and dropped a kiss on her forehead. 'I'll get you something warm. Sit tight.'

Aware of the powerful storm raging outside, Luke flipped on the bathroom heater as he left the room. He pulled a thin cashmere jersey from a shelf in the cupboard and, tossing it onto the built-in dresser, reached for the first-aid box he kept at the top of the cupboard. The one in his car was better, but he wasn't risking the storm to get it.

Returning to the bathroom, he stripped off her wet clothes and dried her off. The pale green jersey did amazing things to her eyes, he thought as he tugged the garment over her soaked head, lifting her hair from under the jersey's rounded neck. Grabbing a gym towel from the basket, he wrapped her head in it and tossed the ends over the top of her head. Jess immediately pushed the jersey between her legs and tucked it under her thighs, shaping it over her legs until it hit mid-thigh and restored her dignity.

'Luke, I need to say something...'

Luke saw the misery in her eyes and knew that she was beating herself up for their earlier argument. God knew, he was. He'd totally lost it and he owed her an apology—but now wasn't the right time. He started to touch her chin and realised that the smudge of dirt on her chin was another graze. His heart lurched again.

'Let's park that conversation for later, sweetheart. Right now I need to patch you up.'

Jess pushed her wet hair off her forehead. 'I can do it. You don't need to...'

Luke brushed his thumb over her cheek. 'We both know that you are Superwoman, but let me do this for you, okay?'

'Okay.'

He heard her sigh of relief as the natural fabric and the heat of the bathroom eased muscles clenched from the cold. The faint hint of colour in her cheeks assured him that she was rapidly warming up, so the hot drink could wait until he'd sorted her injuries out. He had to stanch the blood, and her other leg had a graze that wasn't as serious but he imagined painful enough. Luke took her hands and opened her clenched fingers, wincing at the deep scrapes on the balls of each hand. Once the shock wore off she was going to be one sore lady.

Sitting on the cold tiles in front of her, he flipped the first-aid box open and lifted her foot onto his thigh. He patted her tense foot. 'Relax, Jess.'

'I'm not used to being looked after—especially by a man,' Jess confessed. 'My father was usually lost in his own world and he left my mother to mop up my tears, and my brothers generally told me to suck it up and stop whining.'

'And your exes? Didn't you ever get sick and need looking after?' Luke asked as he swiped away the blood with a damp washcloth.

'I never got sick and I was the one doing the looking after. I'm good at it,' Jess gabbled.

He could see shock settling into her eyes. Letting her ramble on was a good way to keep her mind off the injury.

'You're good at it too.'

'I am?'

'You do stuff for me—stuff that I don't ask you to. Even before we slept together you did things. You always made me coffee, you checked the tyre pressure on the wheels of my car. You reglued the heel on my shoe, worked out why my computer was slow.'

And it made her feel unhinged. It was interesting to realise that she wasn't used to being on the receiving end of generosity. If she was giving then she was in control...she was calling the shots.

'If you fall and hurt yourself I will mop you up,' he replied in a mild voice. 'I will check the tyres on your car if I think they are flat, because I don't want you stranded on the side of the road trying to change a tyre yourself. I reglued your shoe because the heel snapped in the kitchen and the glue was two feet away. If you have a problem, I will try to fix it. It is in my nature—hell, it's in every man's nature.' Luke flashed her a grin. 'Stop trying to control everything in the known universe, my little control freak.'

'I'm not a... Oh, hell—of course I am. Dammit, it's sore! Can I cry?'

'You can.' Luke ran his hand up her calf in a gesture that was as reassuring as it was tender. He rinsed the cloth and wiped her knees.

'Cotton wool would work better. You might not get the blood out of that cloth,' Jess said as she brushed tears off her face.

Luke looked at the cloth and shrugged. 'So? I don't have cotton wool.'

'I do. In the bathroom at the manor house.'

'I'm not going to go look for it in a storm when this is working,' Luke replied, and smothered his whistle when he saw the extent of her injury. He might just have to bandage it up and haul her to the doctor, storm or not. The cut was three inches long and deep. He could see something white and wasn't sure if it was bone or not. Blood still bubbled to the surface.

'Can I get some painkillers? Morphine? A general an-aesthetic?'

'Soon,' Luke replied, distracted. The cut needed to be dis-infected and closed, and the sooner the better. And sewn up...

'We have a hard choice to make, darling. This needs stitches—'

'No, it doesn't! Shove a Band-Aid on it and be done.'

'Jess, it needs stitches.' Luke drew circles on her calf with his thumbs. 'Now, I can either try to butterfly clip it closed, or we head to the doctor.'

They both looked towards the bathroom window and watched the rain hammer the pane. The wind had picked up speed and it whirled around the house.

'Butterfly clip it,' Jess told him, her jaw set.

Luke looked down and assessed the cut again. He could clip it closed. Then he'd haul her off to Dan in the morning, just to make sure. Mind made up, he patted her leg and reached for a bottle of peroxide. Past experience told him that this was the most painful part, and he decided that she might topple off the toilet when he disinfected the wound. Then he'd be sorting out head wounds and replacing a shower door. Maybe.

'Get off there and sit on the floor in front of me,' he or-dered. Jess looked as if she was going to refuse, so he placed his hands on the outside of her thighs, under the jersey, and rubbed her smooth skin. 'C'mon, Jess.'

'Why?'

He kept rubbing and felt her soften beneath his hands. 'Just trust me, okay?'

'Close your eyes,' she said.

He grinned. 'Bit late, since I've already seen you naked.'

'It's not the same,' she said tartly, sinking to the floor in a move that was as graceful as it was discreet and quick. 'Damn, these tiles are cold.'

Luke averted his eyes as she rearranged the jersey again, covering up and lifting her bottom so that she sat on the jersey and not directly on the tiles. When she'd settled down, he deliberately looked towards the window and cocked his head. Her interest caught, she followed his gaze—and he swiftly poured the peroxide into the cut and winced at her piercing, pain-saturated shriek.

He could hear curses in her screams and the occasional moan interspersing her sobs. Steeling himself, he tipped the bottle over the wound again and grabbed her hands when she attempted to wipe the peroxide away.

'You sneaky son of a—' she hissed when she found her breath, tears rolling freely down her face.

Taking a swab from the box, he doused it with peroxide and swiped it over the abrasion on her other leg. Grabbing the hand that flew out to hit him, he flipped it over and ran the swab over that graze. Her towel fell off her head and her toes curled in pain. Feeling like an absolute toad, he steeled himself against her weeping and asked her for her other hand, which she'd tucked behind her back. Jess used the top of her cleaned hand to wipe away tears and violently shook her head.

'Last one, darling, and we're done.'

Jess just sobbed.

'I know it's sore, but you need to give me your hand,' Luke

told her, sighing when she held out her hand and tipped her head back to look at the ceiling. Luke added more peroxide to the swab and cleaned the wound. 'And your chin.'

Jess lifted up her chin and he dabbed it with another swab. 'Done, sweetheart.' Luke blew on her chin, dropped the swab and cupped her face in both of his hands before dropping a kiss on her nose. 'Brave girl. You okay?'

'No,' Jess muttered through her snuffles.

Taking the towel that had fallen off her head, he used the corner to mop her tears up before dropping another kiss on her forehead.

Luke sat back and pulled her foot towards him. Starting in the middle, he pinched the skin together and started taping the wound together. Working swiftly, he spared a glance at Jess's white face and told her to hold on. He wrapped a bandage over the clips and, leaving the swabs and rubbish on the bathroom floor, stood up and helped Jess to her feet. Steadying her with a hand on her shoulder, he waited until he was sure her dizziness had passed and then asked her to put her weight on the injured leg.

'Can you feel the tapes pulling?'

Jess shook her head. 'It feels tight, but okay.'

Luke lifted her up and manoeuvred his way through the dressing-room passage and lowered her onto his bed. Scrabbling in the bedside drawer, he pulled out a bottle of painkillers, handed her two and nodded to the glass of water on top of the table.

Jess looked at the pills in her hand. 'I hate pills, but I'll make an exception tonight.' Jess tossed the pills into her mouth, taking the glass of water he held out.

Luke sat on the side of the bed next to her and brushed her hair away from her eyes. 'So, what do you think we should do for the rest of the evening? Watch TV? Play chess? Have wild monkey sex?'

Jess managed a small grin at his joke. Then she yawned. 'I'm feeling so tired.'

'The adrenalin is wearing off. Take a nap,' Luke suggested as he stood up. 'Call me if you need anything.'

'Thanks.' He was nearly at the door when he heard Jess's soft voice calling him back. He walked to the bed and looked down at her, soft and small and sad.

'I can't let you go without saying sorry. I was selfish and inconsiderate...I'm so sorry. It was so wrong of me.'

Luke shoved his hand into his hair. 'And I said a lot of things I shouldn't have. Around you, stuff seems to float to the surface.'

Jess dropped her eyes. 'Sorry. Again. I'm just really sad that you regret meeting me again. I never meant to turn your world upside down.'

Luke placed his hands on either side of her and caged her in. 'Yes, you did. It's what you do—who you are. And you know that was the one thing I didn't mean—the one statement that was totally untrue. I don't for one minute regret anything to do with you.'

Jess looked up at him with enormous eyes. 'So are we friends again?'

Luke placed a soft but determined kiss on her open mouth before lifting his head. 'Probably not, but we sure are something. Get some sleep, sweetheart.'

# CHAPTER NINE

JESS MANAGED TO SHOWER, get dressed and stagger downstairs.
Her family were due to arrive in a few hours and she had to
sort out the manor house. She wanted to air the rooms, put
flowers in them, and she needed to go to town to stock up
on food and drink. And morphine, and other Class A, B and
C drugs, because her hands and knees throbbed continually
and every step she took radiated pain into her cut.

Jess walked into the kitchen, walked around Luke, who
was stacking dishes into the dishwasher, and headed for the
coffee machine. He'd been wonderful last night—tender, protective, sweet. And when he'd climbed into his bed next to
her he'd been careful of her all night. She remembered him
forcing more painkillers down her some time during the early
hours of the morning, a warm hand patting her hip when she
briefly surfaced to protest against the pain.

Hearing her approach Luke turned away from the fridge
and sent her a smile. 'I was just going to bring you some
coffee.'

Jess pushed her hair off her face. 'Thank you for cleaning
me up last night.'

'No problem.' Luke handed her a cup of coffee. 'How are
you feeling?'

'Like I had a close encounter with a road.'

'That good, huh?' Luke jerked out a chair and sat down

at the kitchen table. He poured cereal into a bowl and added milk. He gestured to the box with his spoon. 'Help yourself. You're probably starving.'

Jess took the seat opposite him. She dashed muesli into her bowl. 'Not so much. But I need to eat so that I can take some more painkillers.'

'No more drugs until we get you to the doctor. You have an appointment in forty-five minutes.'

Jess waited for the familiar spurt of anger she always experienced when men told her what to do. It didn't come and she cocked her head. Strange. Maybe she was accepting his bossiness because he'd been so utterly wonderful last night.

Jess rubbed her forehead. 'Do you really think it's necessary?'

'Yes. If you don't get stitches it'll take that much longer to heal and it will scar horribly. Your legs are gorgeous, Blondie, let's try to keep them that way.'

Jess wrinkled her nose. 'It's just that my family are arriving later and I have so much to do.'

'Like what?'

'Shopping for food and wine—'

'Friends of mine own the deli on Main Street. You can phone an order in, they'll get it ready, and we'll pick it up after you see the doc. As for wine... Funny, I thought we had a cellar on the premises.'

'I can't expect you to fund my family's wine habit!' Jess protested.

'Knock the cost of the wine off my bill,' Luke suggested, and leaned back in his chair. 'Next?'

'I wanted to air the rooms in the manor, check that all the beds have linen on them, put flowers on the nightstands.'

Luke lifted his hips, pulled his mobile from his pocket, pushed buttons and held the mobile to his ear. After a quick conversation he disconnected and dropped the mobile onto the table.

'Who was that?' Jess asked.

'Greta. She used to be housekeeper at the manor. Her granddaughter Angel cleans for me to earn some spending money...she's at uni. Anyway, Greta's retired, but she'll grab Angel and get her to do what needs to be done next door. Next?'

Jess pushed her bowl away and reached for an apple. 'Want to come and work for me? I could use someone with your problem-solving abilities...'

Luke draped his arm over the back of his chair and sent her a long, slow, sexy smile. 'Why don't you come and work for *me*? I could use someone with your marketing skills on a permanent basis. Although we'd have to work on your independent, I-can-do-it, perfectionistic don't-help-me attitude.'

Jess rested her chin on her fist. 'Am I that bad?'

'Not bad. Just challenging.'

'Well, that was kind. My ex—exes—were a lot less complimentary.' Frustration crossed Jess's face. 'I was often told that I was too controlling and overbearing.'

'They sound like a bunch of—'

Jess saw Luke swallow down his rude epithet and look for a better word.

'Morons.'

'Initially they loved the fact that I was independent, then they hated it. They told me that they were into successful women, but moaned at the amount of time I needed to spend on my business. They loved me paying for stuff, but then told me that I flaunted my money in their faces.'

'And that made you start questioning yourself. Why?'

'When the romance wore off they didn't like the reality of living with me.'

'And, being a woman, you automatically think it's something you did wrong. They obviously weren't strong enough for you. And then there's male pride. None of them were as successful as you and they felt threatened by you. C'mon, Jess, that's basic psych. You know this.'

'But it doesn't matter who brings in more money. It's not important,' Jess protested.

'To you, maybe not, but to a man...? Yes, it's important! You're quite a package, Sherwood, and you need a man who is strong enough, secure enough, to allow you to fly.'

Jess wanted to ask him whether *he* was that man, whether he would hand her a pair of wings and watch her soar. Jess made herself meet his eyes and saw the regret in them.

'I'm not that man, Jess,' Luke stated quietly. 'Not because I don't think I could handle you, but because I don't want the complication of handling any woman.'

Jess forced herself to smile. 'That's okay, because didn't we decide that it was better to keep this—us—simple?'

'Yeah. But I still want to sleep with you.'

'And that is what makes it complicated.'

Luke's chair scraped across the wooden floor as he pushed it back. He walked around and put his hands on the table and her chair, to cage her in. He bent his head and his lips brushed against hers.

Jess lifted her hand to the side of his face. 'Thanks for looking after me last night.'

Luke kissed her again. 'You scared me stupid, coming back late and injured.' He pulled her up and into his arms, resting his chin on top of her head. 'Don't do it again, okay? I don't know if my heart can take it.'

Her family, in typical fashion, arrived earlier than expected, and Jess found herself opening the first of what promised to be many, many bottles of red wine at shortly after four that afternoon. Her extensive family was crowded into the main lounge of the manor house and was already settling in. Nick had made a fire, Chris was opening a packet of crisps and her two other brothers were sprawled out over the two leather couches. Anne and Heather, two of her sisters-in-law, had taken the kids for a walk, and her mother, grandmother, Clem and Kate were standing by the huge bay window, looking at the wonderful view of the mountains. Her father, bless him, was exploring the house and probably cataloguing the paintings.

'Good grief, how long before I get a glass of wine?' Grandma demanded, and Jess rolled her eyes.

'Well, if your lazy grandsons would get off their butts and help me it would be a lot quicker,' Jess grumbled.

John sat up. 'Hand over the bottle and the corkscrew, Shrimp.'

Jess wrinkled her nose at their old nickname for her and walked over to Nick, her favourite brother, who was standing next to the fire.

His grey eyes were sombre when he caught her eye. 'So, how bad was it?'

'How bad was what?'

'Your fall. You brushed it off with the folks, but you're limping and your eyes are slightly glassy.'

'I'm fine. Luke patched me up.'

'Who is Luke?' John asked as he handed her a glass of wine.

'The guy I'm doing the campaign for. He owns St Sylve.' Jess couldn't meet their eyes—especially Nick's. He was too damn perceptive and he knew her really well.

'Something cooking between you two?' he asked.

'What's cooking between whom?' Grandma demanded, and Jess groaned and glared at Nick.

'She's got ears like a bat,' John commented.

'I was just asking Jess what's going on between—' her

elbow in his ribs didn't stop Nick for one second '—her and Savage.'

'Nothing is going on!' Jess protested. Her brother and his big mouth.

'Is he why you wouldn't go on that date I set up for you?' asked her mum.

'No! I was just too busy!' Jess replied, and held up her hands. 'I want you guys to really listen to me. This is important.'

All the eyes in the room were suddenly focused on her and Jess knew that she had to choose her words carefully. 'If you get to meet Luke—and I'm not saying you will, because really we're just friends—I want you to go easy on him. He's not used to big families so I don't want you guys giving him a hard time...'

Her brothers looked at her, looked at each other, and burst out laughing. Talk about waving a red flag in front of a bull... Now Luke was firmly in their sights. She should have just played it cool. When was she going to learn?

'I wouldn't mind a friend like that.' Clem's comment floated over the masculine laughter.

Her female relatives had their noses pressed up against the glass of the window and they were not looking at the mountains. Jess prayed that the long-limbed figure walking past the window was Owen, but she knew she wouldn't be that lucky.

'Oh, my—smoking hot,' Kate said, her hand on her heart. She turned to Jess. 'Is that Luke?'

Jess nodded glumly.

'Nice ass,' Clem commented and Nick frowned.

'He's got swag...he's a real fly guy.'

Jess rolled her eyes. Her grandma had been watching MTV again.

But her mother was the absolute limit. Liza rapped on the glass and over her head Jess could see Luke turning, his eyebrows raised. Liza fumbled to open the window, and when she did introduced herself and practically browbeat Luke into coming for supper. Could she be more embarrassing?

Jess felt her face turning bright red and felt Nick's not-so-gentle elbow in her ribs.

'So, just a friend, huh? You sure about that?'

Jess heaved in some air and thought that it was going to be a very long weekend indeed.

He'd planned to keep his distance from Jess while her family were visiting, but that first evening he'd somehow found himself seated at the head of the two hundred-year-old dining table that had been brought out by one of the early Savage wives at the beginning of the nineteenth century. The Sherwood clan occupied the rest of the table...and, Lord, what a clan they were.

Loud, noisy, charming...loud, noisy. Well, all except for Nick, the oldest brother, who observed more than he partook in the conversation, a wry smile on his face. Of all of Jess's brothers this was the one he liked most...possibly because he didn't seem as if he was operating at warp speed.

He had to admit that Jess's brothers had spectacular taste in women...from Nick's fiancée, Clem—a stunning redhead and once-famous model, the ex-girlfriend of rocker Cai Clouston—to the other wives. Two brunettes and a blonde, they were all lookers. All educated and independent. One was an ex-teacher turned columnist, one a doctor and one a physiotherapist. The Sherwood brothers liked brains with their looks.

Just like he did.

Luke looked at Jess, deep in conversation with her father. Their brown eyes were identical. He'd have to be blind not to notice the speculative looks they'd sent his way, the not-so-subtle questions about their relationship. He'd ducked them all. He figured it was up to Jess to explain their relationship, and that she would be returning with him to his house tonight.

He just wished he could say, even if it was only to himself, that she would be sleeping in his bed with him again.

She was…beautiful, Luke thought, looking at her. Her hair was messy, her lipstick was long gone, and she had shadows under her eyes from pain—ten stitches, and she'd thought she didn't need to see a doctor!—but she glowed.

She loved her family, loved being around them, he realised. He'd watched their arrival from his lounge window and had heard her squeal when she'd seen the convoy of cars turning into St Sylve. The cars had barely stopped before she'd wrenched doors open and children and toddlers had clamoured for kisses and hugs from her. He'd gritted his teeth when one brother had swung her around—*stitches, dammit!*—before passing her like a pretty parcel to the next brother, who'd repeated the process.

Luke shook his head. Jess had never, not for one moment, doubted that she was loved…

This was the type of family he'd have sold his soul for as a child and teenager. If he could have ordered it this was what it would have looked like. Siblings, laughter, teasing, loud conversation.

'Quiet down, everyone…'

Luke turned his attention to Jess's dad as the conversation died down. David Sherwood lifted his wine glass. 'I'd like to thank Luke for opening up his house to our craziness, and fervently hope he doesn't regret it.' David narrowed his eyes and they bounced from one child to another. Jess, Luke noticed, wasn't left out. 'And that means no rough-housing amongst the furniture, no sliding down banisters, no flour bombs from the upstairs windows.'

Luke leaned towards Nick, who was sitting to his right. 'He's talking to the kids, right?'

Nick's grey eyes laughed. 'Unfortunately, no. My brothers and my sister can be quite wild on occasion.'

Luke grinned. 'And you're not?'

'I just don't get caught,' Nick replied with a chuckle.

'Anyway, thank you, Luke, for allowing us to be together this weekend.' David lifted his glass and when the cheers died down continued to speak. 'By the way, I knew your mother.'

Luke saw Jess's hand jerk her father's arm and he caught her eye. Sending her a reassuring glance and the slightest shake of his head, he silently told her that he wanted to hear about his mother. God, he knew nothing about her—of course he wanted to hear about her.

'Really? How did you know her?' Luke was quite impressed that his voice sounded vaguely normal.

'We went to art school together in Cape Town. I think I was half in love with Katelyn.'

'You were half in love with everyone at uni,' his wife said crisply. 'Katelyn...Katelyn Kirby? I remember her. Long hair, green, green eyes. *Your* eyes.' Liza leaned across Nick to touch his hand quickly with the tips of her fingers. 'I'm sorry you lost her so young, Luke.'

Such simple, sincere words. It almost made him want to tell her that he hadn't lost her, she'd already gone...

'I remember going to her older sister's cottage, near Lambert's Bay. The sister raised her—she was a professor of archaeology at UCT, often away on digs.'

David took a sip of wine and Luke swallowed. God, he had an aunt. How...? Why...? He'd never known he had an aunt.

Not that it mattered after so much time, he had no intention of tracking her down but...*wow*, he had an aunt.

'I loved her work. Adored her work,' David rambled on. 'She was destined for great things. Then there was Greg Prescott...'

'And Dad's off and running,' Nick muttered. 'Heaven help

us. He's going to give us a dissertation on every artist he ever knew.'

'Distract him—quick!' Luke heard another brother—John— hiss.

Patrick jumped in and spoke over his father. 'So, when are we going to settle our bet, Shrimp?'

Luke's head snapped up. Bet? What bet?

'We have time this weekend. We can find a five-kilometre route and settle this once and for all,' Patrick goaded Jess.

'Oh, goodie.' Liza clapped her hands. 'I'm sick of drip-ping taps.'

Luke saw Jess wince. What was going on?

When Jess didn't speak, Patrick leaned across the table and got in her face. 'Chicken, Jess? Are you being a girl?'

'I *am* a girl, frog-face.'

Luke saw stubbornness creep into her expression. He looked at Nick again. 'Want to explain what the bet is?'

'Who can run a quicker five-k.'

'Me,' Jess and Patrick chimed in unison.

Luke poured wine into his glass and took a sip before pin-ning Jess with a look. 'No.' He saw the protest start to form on her lips and knew that her instinctive reaction was to baulk. 'Not negotiable, sweetheart,' he added in his firmest voice.

Jess held his glare for a long minute before muttering mu-tinously, 'I'll be fine.'

'Ten.' Luke held up both his hands. He knew that she didn't want her family to know that she'd had stitches in her leg, that she didn't want them fussing over her—especially the two doctors—so he'd agreed to keep her secret. But not if she was thinking about racing her brother over five kilometres.

He saw Jess's lips move in a silent curse and hid his smile when she finally looked at Patrick. 'Not this weekend, slow-poke. I'm still a bit sore from my fall.'

Patrick seemed to accept that as a valid excuse, Luke

thought, feeling Nick's interested gaze on his face. He turned his head and lifted his eyebrows. 'What?'

'Well, that was interesting. Ten what?'

Luke ignored him, but Nick wasn't the only brother to have picked up on the tension between him and Jess. Patrick geared up to needle his sister again.

'So what's the deal between you and Savage, Jess? I think that's the first time in history that you've listened to a man without an argument.'

Jess leaned across the table and skewered him with a hot look. 'What's the deal between you and brains, Pat? As in... where are yours? And mind your own business.'

'You *are* my business. Our business.' Patrick spooned up his dessert and leaned back in his chair.

Nick rolled his eyes. 'Here we go.' He turned to Luke. 'Patrick and Jess have butted heads their entire lives. They are only nine months apart, and Pat loves to lord it over her. Not that we're not *all* interested in what's happening between you and our baby sister.'

'But you're just quieter about it?' Luke shot back, and read the warning in Nick's eyes. *Mess with her and you're a dead man.* Which annoyed him... After all, she hadn't caught *him* in bed with someone else.

And never would. He didn't cheat.

'I counted the bedrooms and there's just enough for all of us,' John commented. 'So, where are you sleeping, Jessica?'

Every single Sherwood, plus wives and partners, perked up. Her mother leaned forward in her chair. Her grandmother chuckled. Faces turned either speculative or protective and Jess threw Luke a desperate look.

Ah...this was the downside of a large family. The extreme lack of privacy. 'I offered Jess a place to sleep in my house for the duration of your stay. Since we do need to do some work this weekend, we thought that was the most practical solution.'

'So are you sleeping together, and if you aren't, why not?' Liza raised her eyebrows. Liza didn't give him a millisecond to respond. 'Are you involved? Married? Gay?'

'Mum!' Jess shoved her hands into her hair from frustration.

'What?' Liza sent her an innocent look. 'I just want you to be happy. And if you and Luke are just work colleagues then I have at least three young men who want your number.'

'Good grief,' Jess moaned. 'I told you—Luke and I are friends. Just friends.'

'Then maybe you and Grant can get back together?' Patrick suggested. 'I saw him last week. He was asking about you.'

A chorus of approval followed his suggestion and Luke felt his teeth grinding in the back of his jaw.

'He isn't seeing anyone else,' Chris commented. 'We took him out for a beer and he was crying into it, saying that you were the best thing that ever happened to him. Can't understand it myself, but there you are.'

'He's a nice guy, Jess,' John agreed.

Jess sent Luke a look of abject misery and mortification. He now knew what she'd meant when she'd said that her family didn't respect her privacy and that they had no concept of emotional boundaries.

Patrick waved his wine glass in the air. 'And he's a mean fly half. If he's prepared to forgive her for being so anal then she should consider giving him another chance.'

Clem shook her head at Kate. 'For a doctor, your husband can be extraordinarily thick on occasion.'

'Tell me about it,' Kate grumbled.

Jess pushed her chair back and stumbled to her feet. Luke saw the white ring of pain around her mouth and knew that she was at her limit—physically and probably mentally—and certainly not up to dealing with her family. When she swayed on her feet his protective streak flashed white-hot, and he was out of his chair to catch her as her knees buckled. He'd been wrong. She was way past her limit.

'Okay, that's enough,' he said in a hard voice.

Luke wound his arm around her waist and felt Jess's arms creep around him. He looked at each of her brothers in turn.

'God, you lot are a piece of work. Can't you see that she's not up to dealing with your crap? She's got ten stitches in her leg and she's battered and bruised.'

His glare had Patrick's retort dying on his lips.

'Jess and I—hell, I don't even know what's what between us. But—' he looked at Liza '—it is *between us*. And the next person who mentions her going back to that waste of oxygen she caught screwing another woman, in *her* bed, will get his ass kicked. By me.' Luke lifted his hand to cradle Jess's head against his chest. 'I am taking Jess home. She's had more than enough. She'll see you in the morning—if she's feeling up to it.'

Luke guided Jess out of the room and a silent Sherwood family watched them leave.

Nick broke the shocked silence that followed. 'Well, well, well. Jess has finally found a man who has a bigger set than she does. Good for her and it's about time. Pass that wine, Grandma, you're hogging it.'

For the second night in a row Jess slept in Luke's bed—in the proper sense of the word. There had been no euphemisms involved because shortly after carrying her up the stairs he'd handed her some painkillers and bustled her into bed. Her head had barely hit the pillow and she was asleep.

Sexy she was not.

Jess rolled over as she smelt coffee and swallowed saliva as Luke walked into the room, dressed in nothing more than a low-slung towel over his slim hips. Lord, he had a beautiful body...

He smiled down at her as he put the cup of coffee on the bedside table. Jess sat up and squinted at the clock. It was just past nine—an unusual time for Luke to be showering.

'When I came back from the lands your brothers were about to go for a run and invited me to join them,' Luke explained, sitting on the bed next to her. 'Obviously it was a test. Competitive bunch, aren't they?'

Jess groaned. 'Sorry. Did they go all he-man on you?'

'Well, they did try to outpace me.' Luke smiled into his coffee cup. 'I managed to keep up.'

Jess took her cup and winced when her injuries brushed the bedclothes. 'If you beat Patrick I'll kiss you senseless.'

'I beat Patrick. I ran twenty-three-ten.'

Jess's jaw dropped open. 'You beat them all?'

Luke looked like the cat who ate the cream. 'I *whipped* them all.'

'Woo-hoo!' Jess shouted with glee. 'You are the *man*!'

Jess settled back on the pillows and after a minute or so smiled at Luke. 'You know that you're going to have to marry me now, don't you?'

Luke spluttered tiny drops of coffee over his white towel. 'What?'

Jess patted his knee. 'By standing up for me last night, you—in my mother's eyes at least—practically declared your intentions. As I speak, she's probably planning our wedding.'

'God, families are complicated,' Luke complained. 'And yours is, I suspect, more complicated than most.'

'I'm the youngest child—a daughter with four older protective brothers.'

'Who threatened to cut off my balls if I hurt you,' Luke told her.

'Oh, grief, they didn't?' Jess blew air into her cheeks. 'Of course they did… Sorry. Did they thump their chests as well?'

Luke grinned. 'Yep. Then they spent the rest of the run

deciding what to do about your ex. Concrete shoes were mentioned.'

'Their anger will blow off and then they'll just ignore him. I hope.' Jess sipped her coffee. 'I'm sorry. I know that they are impossible and in-your-face. I'll understand if you want to keep your distance from them...'

Luke placed his hand on the other side of her stretched out legs and leaned on it. 'I haven't had much to do with large families, Jess—hell, with *any* families. I don't know how to act, what to do... Last night I was nervous as anything.'

'Seriously? You didn't look it.'

'Practice. My legs were bouncing under the table.'

Jess heard the insecurity in his voice and felt her heart jump into her throat. 'You just need to be who you are, do what you do. Don't worry about my mother and her machinations. If your little speech last night didn't get through to her, she knows that I can't and won't be forced into anything. So, what do you think about the fact that my dad knew your mom?'

Jess felt his mood shift from relaxed to wary.

'I guess the art world in the seventies was smaller than I supposed.'

'Are you going to try to track down your aunt?'

Luke lifted his head to look at her. 'Why should I?'

*Why should he?* Jess frowned. 'Luke, she could tell you about your mother.'

Luke's face hardened. 'I know all I need to about Katelyn. She was a really good artist who decided she didn't want me any more. Then she died.'

The lack of emotion in his voice whipped at Jess's soul. It spoke of hurt and betrayal buried deep. 'Your aunt could explain—'

'I'm thirty-six years old. She must've known about me.

She's had thirty-plus years to find me and explain,' Luke shot back. 'It's not like we went anywhere.'

His tone told her to leave the subject alone and Jess backed off. They'd just got back onto an even keel. She didn't want to argue with him and risk upsetting that.

Muscles rippled in Luke's torso as he leaned forward and gently touched her chin with the tips of his fingers. 'How are you feeling?'

Jess licked her lips at the passion slumbering in his eyes. 'Good. Much better.'

Luke moved forward and slipped his hand around her neck. 'Then did I hear you say something about kissing me senseless? Especially since I whipped your brothers?'

'I might have said that,' Jess whispered as his head dropped. She sighed when his lips met hers in a kiss that was as simple as it was devastating. She wanted more than just a kiss. She wanted him in every way.

Luke's tongue tangled with hers and she reached out her hand and patted his waist, finding the towel and tugging.

Luke pulled back and sent her a look full of regret and frustration. 'Sweetheart, we can't. Your leg.'

Jess tugged again. 'You'll be careful of me. I trust you,' she said against his mouth. 'I'm tired of just sleeping in your bed, Savage.'

Luke covered her as his towel fell open. 'Well, when you put it like that...'

# CHAPTER TEN

JESS STOOD at the kitchen sink in the manor house, washing dishes and watching Luke, Owen and Kendall taking her brothers on at touch rugby on the swathe of lawn just beyond the window. Luke looked happy, Jess thought. He was dirty and sweaty, but laughing at the creative insults her brothers traded on a regular basis.

Jess felt a feminine hand on her back and smiled at Clem. 'Hi.'

'Hi, back. Why are you hiding out in the kitchen?'

Jess lifted one shoulder. 'I needed a break.' She looked at Nick's partner and said a quiet thank-you to Nick for bringing such a wonderful woman into their family, her life. She adored her sisters-in-law but, despite not knowing Clem for very long, felt closest to the ex-model and socialite.

'Are you okay, Jess?'

Jess pushed her hair off her forehead with the back of her wrist and shrugged. 'Yes…no…confused.'

'Luke?'

'Who else?' Jess looked out of the window. 'He's got baggage, Clem…'

'Don't we all, sweetie? You have a frequently impossible family and a strong independent streak. I had no idea who I was or what I wanted before I met Nick. I was the ultimate spoilt princess.' Clem leaned her bottom against the counter next to Jess and crossed her long, slim legs. 'None of us is perfect, Jess-jess.'

'And he doesn't want a relationship. What did he say to me...? He doesn't want to have to "handle" any woman.'

'Ouch. And do you want a relationship with him?'

'Kind of.' Jess gave Clem a rueful smile. 'I've fallen in love with him. When Luke stood up for me to my brothers last night I knew that he was the man for me.'

'Yeah, I realised that too. He's strong enough, secure enough, smart enough—perfect for you.'

Clem just *got* it. Jess didn't need to explain that she felt Luke was the flipside of her coin. Strong enough to lean on, masculine enough for her to enjoy, even flaunt her femininity, with enough tenderness to balance out his machismo.

This was what love felt like, Jess realised. Like a multi-layered, delightful cake, each layer rewarding in its own right. Attraction that ignited a low hum in her womb whenever he looked at her, a touch that chased sexual shivers up her spine, a dry sense of humour and a sneaky intelligence that kept her off guard.

He was her perfect fit—except...

'Except he isn't interested. Not in permanence, commitment, marriage or any possible combination or permutation of the above.' Wasn't it just so typical that when she finally found someone she was prepared to fall in love with he was unavailable and uninterested?

Clem rubbed her shoulder with her hand in a gesture that was as sweet as it was comforting. Jess told Clem about the disastrous shoot earlier in the week and her part in it.

'I really wanted a family scene, but I can't—won't—put Luke through that again.'

Clem looked at her for a long minute, held up a finger and walked away. Within a couple of minutes she was back, a hand-held camcorder in her hand. Clem nodded to the window and handed Jess the camcorder. 'There's your family scene, Jess. Film it.'

Jess looked out and saw what Clem was getting at. There were the Sherwood wives—gorgeous and relaxed, wine glasses in hand, talking furiously—sitting on a patch of grass to the side of the mock rugby pitch. Jess lifted the camera and zoomed in, then tracked the outline of the manor house onto the veranda, where her father sat in an easy chair, a sketch-pad and John's three-year-old on his lap, directing his hand as he drew. Liza had a sleeping baby in her arms and was watching the rugby.

Jess panned the camera over the table between them: St Sylve wine bottles and half-filled glasses, an open book lying face-down, a baby's pacifier, a colouring book and crayons, a half-empty bowl of the apple crumble they'd had for pudding...

Jess went to Luke, hands on his thighs, his face turned away. He looked happy, she thought, relaxed—as she'd wanted to catch him the other day. Enjoying himself, having fun.

Jess carried on filming and her mouth curved into a delighted smile. 'You, Clem Campbell, are a genius.'

Clem looked at her nails and smiled. 'I know, but feel free to remind Nick.'

Luke followed the massive Sherwood clan to their hired cars and hung back as Jess kissed and hugged her family goodbye. The days had passed quickly, and Luke realised that he'd had more fun than he'd had in ages with her family. He hadn't had much time to himself or with Jess, and neither of them had got any work done, but he was okay with that. He felt as if he'd had a mini-holiday without leaving his house.

He'd taken them all over the farm, explained the winemaking process to her father and brothers, discussed the history of the property with Jess's mother and grandmother. He'd exercised with her brothers in the gym, been sketched by her father, taken the kids for rides on his dirt bike and tractor.

And now he was being thanked and hugged and kissed. Luke bent down so that Jess's tiny grandmother could kiss him goodbye, and then turned to shake her father's hand.

'Thank you for your hospitality, Luke,' David said. 'Look after my girl.'

'It's not like that...' Luke replied, feeling a cord tighten around his neck.

David's warm brown eyes laughed at him. 'Yeah, right.'

Liz elbowed her husband out of the way and tucked a piece of paper into Luke's shirt pocket and patted it. 'The name of your aunt and her address. I have an old university friend who had the details. Go talk to her.'

*Uh, no. Thank you anyway.*

'Take care of my baby.' Liza kissed him on one cheek and then the other.

The cord tightened. He had a break when the wives kissed and hugged him, and then there were the brothers, standing in one solid line, identical scowls on their faces. He looked around for Jess but she'd run back into the house to fetch a book her grandmother had left behind.

John pulled out a folded piece of paper from his back pocket and slowly opened it. 'As the oldest, it behooves me—'

'Behooves?' Patrick snorted.

'Shut up, squirt. It behooves me to establish whether you are worthy of Jess.'

Luke rolled his eyes. Really? Were they *really* going to pull this?

'Super 14 Rugby. Who do you support?'

'Really? This is what is important?' Luke felt insulted on Jess's behalf.

John ploughed on. 'Man United or Chelsea?'

'Liverpool,' Luke replied, just to be facetious.

'Do you drink and drive?'

No.

'Are you an aggressive drunk?'

No again.

'Do you cook?'

Yes, thank God, since Jess had the cooking skills of a tortoise.

'Do you understand the African tradition of lobola?'

Huh? What?

Luke frowned and Nick grinned. 'You know—paying the family for the honour of their daughter's hand in marriage?'

He looked across at David, who just smiled and shrugged. 'They negotiate for me.'

Luke folded his arms and kept quiet, scowling fiercely. Good God, what had he done so wrong in his life, or in a previous life, that warranted this?

'We want fifteen cases of that outstanding Merlot 2005, use of the manor house for family holidays, and Dad wants a breeding pair of silky bantam chickens,' John explained.

Luke threw up his hands. 'Chickens? You've got to be kidding me!'

'I wanted goats, but Liza put her foot down,' David replied.

'Good grief,' Luke said faintly, and rubbed the back of his neck. 'Listen, I hope this is your sick idea of a joke, because this is the most absurd conversation. I am not—*we* are not—talking or thinking about marriage. I don't want to get married!'

Chris grinned. 'None of us did, dude! But here we all are...'

Jess darted out of the house, book in hand, and immediately, Luke noticed, her brothers feigned innocence.

John gripped his hand and squeezed. Hard. 'You hurt her, you answer to us.'

Luke wished he could brush off his words as chest-thumping, but he knew they were deadly serious. If he messed Jess around he would be fish food. He shook Chris's and Patrick's hands, lost the feeling in his fingers again and resisted the impulse to nurse it before turning to Nick.

He scowled at Jess's favourite brother. 'Yeah, yeah...I get it. Don't mess with Jess.'

Nick shook his head and put his arm around Clem's waist. 'I was just going to wish you luck. You're going to need it, dealing with that brat.'

'Thank you,' Luke replied fervently. At least someone was on his side.

Nick slapped him on the shoulder before shaking—squeezing, *ow*, dammit!—his hand. 'But she sheds one tear over you and I'll stake you to an anthill.'

*Nice,* Luke thought.

He watched the cars disappear down the drive and looked at Jess, whose eyes were fixed on the backs of the vehicles. He caught the expression crossing her face as she jammed her hands into the front pockets of her jeans and watched them leave...a little sadness, a little relief. She was a strong, independent woman, but her family were her rock, he realised, her north star, the wind that helped her fly. While they occasionally irritated and frustrated her, she adored them, and she also missed them...

Being here, with him, at St Sylve, deprived her of them. It was just another reason in a long list of reasons why they could never be together long-term. She needed that family atmosphere and he couldn't—wouldn't—provide it for her.

Besides, even if they wanted to continue their...whatever it was, how would it work? Practically? Logistically? His life was here on St Sylve. Hers was across the country. She had a successful business based in another city—one that she'd sweated blood and tears to establish. He couldn't imagine giving up St Sylve, so he knew that to ask her to give up Jess Sherwood Concepts would be deeply unfair.

What was he going to do about her? He'd never intended to become involved with a woman again, but Jess, being Jess, had become more than a fling, more than a quick and casual affair. He couldn't allow himself to get any more attached to her than he already was. It would be easier to have open-heart surgery without anaesthetic than to risk loving someone and having them leave him.

Luke felt the sour taste of panic in the back of his throat and pulled at his shirt collar. He'd been living in a dream world these past few days and it was time to snap out of it. He'd been seduced—literally and metaphorically—by the woman in his bed and her family in the manor house.

It wasn't real and it sure wasn't permanent.

Nothing ever was.

'So, how is Luke?'

Jess sat at a small wooden table at a restaurant in Lambert's Bay, a cup of coffee in front of her, waiting to meet Luke's cousin. She was talking to Clem, all the way across the country at their safari operation, Two-B.

'Distant, irritable, moody and snappy.'

'Oh. Um…that's not what I expected to hear. I thought you would be burning up the sheets.'

'We are,' Jess replied. 'We're just not talking in between. We both know that I should be packing to leave but neither of us are mentioning it.'

When he was making love to her he was anything but broody and snappy. Passionate, loving, attentive, tender. His body worshipped hers…

'Have you asked him about it?'

'Mmm, a couple of times. Yesterday I asked why he was being so aloof, far-away…uncommunicative, and was told that he has a lot of his mind. That he's working on a couple of difficult deals and he's tired.'

Clem was silent for a moment. 'Is he back-pedalling?'

Jess rested her forehead on her fist and nodded, then realised that Clem couldn't see her.

'I think that's part of it. I also think he's thinking about his mum a lot. I think it's natural after being confronted with our family.'

She really believed that. When she'd caught Luke staring at the photograph of his mum this morning all the pieces had fallen into place. Spending so much time with her family, seeing how close they were, had to make him wonder about his own family—about the fact that he had an aunt. He would be wondering whether he had cousins, other family members he'd never met. So she'd raised the subject of Luke tracking down his aunt again and he'd brushed her off. She realised that his reaction was a combination of fear and bravado, and understood that he was anxious. Who wouldn't be? But he wasn't uninterested so that was why...

'I'm in Lambert's Bay, about to meet his cousin,' Jess said. She'd found the slip of paper her mum had given Luke, dialled the number of the cottage and spoken to Luke's cousin. Luke's aunt had died a couple of years ago, she'd explained, but she'd grown up with the tragic tale of Katelyn and would be happy to share the story with Jess—especially if she was living with Luke. Well, it wasn't a lie...she *was* living with Luke. She just hadn't felt the need to tell her that it was a temporary arrangement.

'Does he know?'

'No.'

'Do you think that's wise?'

'It's my gift to him, Clem. Knowledge about his past, his mother.'

It was her way to show him how much she loved him, that

she would love to make a family with him, to invite him to share hers. Like her brothers, she wanted to love and be loved, to create her own family within a bigger one.

'I want a man who loves me like Nick loves you—like Dad still loves my mum.'

'Oh, sweetie, I hear you. But I'm not sure if this is the right way to go about it,' Clem said. 'Changing the subject—how did the family advert turn out?'

'Sbu and I did the final edit on it this afternoon. It's wonderful—funny, warm and very accessible. Everything I wanted it to be. I just need to show it to Luke and get his approval to flight the ad and we're done, business-wise.'

'Meaning that you should be heading home?'

Jess felt her stomach sink. She didn't want to leave him—didn't want to go back to her empty life in Sandton. She wanted to stay at St Sylve... She had thought this through: if Luke asked her to stay she'd open another branch of Jess Sherwood Concepts in Cape Town, leaving Ally to run the Sandton branch.

She could have a remote office at St Sylve...what was the point of wonderful technology like video conferencing and e-mail if one didn't use it?

She'd miss her family, but being with Luke was non-negotiable.

'I don't know how I am going to leave him, Clem. If he doesn't ask me to stay it's going to break my heart...'

Jess looked up as the door to the coffee shop chimed and a tall woman her own age walked through the door. The first of Luke's family...she couldn't wait to meet the rest.

'I've got to go, Clemmie. Love you.'

'Love you too. Call me if you need me.'

*Good news, good news*—she couldn't wait to tell Luke. As she'd suspected, he had the very wrong end of the stick.

Jess flexed her hands on the wheel and eased up on the accelerator. As eager as she was to get home, she couldn't risk speeding along these windy roads, slick with incessant rain. The skies had opened up just as she'd left Lambert's Bay and the rain had followed her all the way to Paarl, and it obviously had no intention of stopping any time soon.

Jess drove her SUV through St Sylve's imposing gates and noticed that a dark green Mercedes Benz was parked outside Luke's front door. She wrinkled her nose. Luke had said that he'd be in meetings most of the day, and she hoped that his appointments hadn't run over and that he'd be finished at a reasonable time.

She had plans for him this evening...

Jess grabbed the envelope and CD that lay on the passenger seat, tucked them into the folds of the newspaper she'd bought earlier and, deciding that her bag and files could wait, ducked out of the car and sprinted as best she could in her high-heeled boots. The door opened as she grabbed the handle and she stumbled into Luke's hard chest.

'Jess!'

Jess dropped the newspaper and on a laugh flung her arms around his neck and planted her mouth on his. 'Oh, it's so good to see you. I've missed you so much.'

He grinned down at her. 'I saw you this morning, but that is nice to hear.'

Jess laughed into his bemused face, then caught a movement on the stairs. Her blood turned to ice as she saw Kelly drifting down the stairs, barefoot and wearing only Luke's favourite rugby jersey—*her* favourite rugby jersey. Jess dropped her hands and stepped back. Kelly's hair was tangled and her make-up was smudged. It didn't take a rocket scientist to work out that at some point in the afternoon Luke had removed Kelly's clothes. As for anything more than that—

she couldn't go there… Jess felt as if someone had shoved a red-hot poker in her stomach.

Luke followed her horrified stare and his muttered oath barely penetrated the roaring in her head. 'You've got to be kidding me!'

Then the red mist cleared from her mind and she shook her head. *This is Luke,* she told herself, *the man who says he doesn't cheat, ever.* He wouldn't do that to her. She trusted him.

Seeing Luke's thunderous glare, directed right at her, she knew she had to rescue the situation as quickly as she could. So she took a step forward and met Kelly at the bottom of the stairs.

'Hi—it's Kelly, isn't it? Did you get caught in the storm?'

Kelly, who'd been looking rather nervous, sent her a smile. 'I did. I was here to buy some wine. Luke, Owen and I were walking back from the cellar and we got caught in the rain.'

'Hey, Jess!'

Owen's voice drifted from the lounge and Jess briefly closed her eyes. Thank God she'd hadn't gone nuts and accused Luke of cheating…

'Luke lent me a pair of your running shorts. I hope you don't mind.' Kelly lifted up the edge of the rugby shirt and Jess saw her own shorts.

She told Kelly she didn't mind at all and watched as Kelly walked back into the lounge.

Jess started to follow her, but Luke's hand on her arm kept her in place. 'You thought that I slept with Kelly,' he hissed.

She thought about denying it but Luke would see right through her. She met his hard eyes and sighed. He was ticked…and he had a right to be. An apology was needed. Why did she keep putting herself in these positions?

She held up her hands. 'Habit reaction…' His expression didn't change and she sighed. 'Come on, Luke. I reacted, I realised I was wrong and then I tried to correct it. I'm sorry I doubted you but it really was for only a second.'

Luke narrowed his eyes at her. 'Don't do it again.'

Oh, well, this *wasn't* the way she'd thought this evening was going to go. Jess sent him an uncertain look before realising that she still had the envelope in her hands. 'Listen, I have news!'

Luke lifted his eyebrows. 'You look like you've had an interesting day.'

'I've had a great day,' Jess said as they walked into the lounge. 'I spent the day with Sbu. We finished the edit on the last advert.'

Luke frowned. 'What advert? I thought there wasn't anything you could use from the last shoot.'

'There wasn't, but I came up with something else.' Jess pulled the disc from inside the newspaper and waved it. 'Do you want to see it?'

Luke shrugged. 'Sure. What's in the envelope?'

Jess looked over at Owen and Kelly and thought that it wasn't something she wanted to discuss with an audience.

'I'll tell you later.' Jess walked over to the DVD player and inserted the disc. Flipping on the plasma screen, Jess walked back to stand next to Luke. 'I think you'll like this.'

He loved it.

He hated it.

He looked happy, he thought, jamming his hands into the pockets of his jeans, and he had been. It had been one of the nicest, most relaxed afternoons he could ever remember. The entire weekend had been a revelation; he'd laughed and kicked back, swallowed up by the warmth of the Sherwood clan. He wished that he could bank on the fact that there would be more of that type of family weekend, but that brought him back to the issue of permanence and commitment.

He'd noticed Jess and Clem filming that afternoon and into the evening, had thought it was just a video for the family archives. Jess had turned the footage into something special: gorgeous people in a gorgeous setting. It was an inspired move, Luke thought.

On film, Jess had captured all his hopes and dreams. There was John's son, Kelby, filthy dirty from digging up worms in an empty flowerbed, and Clem, lying back on her elbows, relaxed and gorgeous in the late-afternoon sun. Him and her brothers, sitting on the lawn, trading insults and getting to know each other.

Then the last frames of the film appeared on screen. Someone had picked up the video camera and filmed Jess walking towards him on the lawn, wrapping her arms around his neck and boosting herself up his body to laugh down into his face. Love and delight radiated from her. Everything she felt about him was written on her face. She was in love with him.

He didn't need her to tell him. It was there on the screen in front of him. Luke held his throat as he felt it tighten. He hadn't wanted this—hadn't asked for it. He didn't know what to do with this knowledge, her love, where to put it, how to act.

'So, what do you think?'

Luke eventually realised that Jess was talking to him and couldn't find the words he wanted to say. He didn't *know* what he wanted to say.

'Luke, do you like it?' Jess asked again, and he heard her insecure laugh. 'I kind of need an answer or else we go back to square one.'

'I think it's wonderful,' Kelly said with a quaver in her voice.

'Superb, Jess,' Owen agreed.

Luke licked his lips and looked from Jess to the TV screen and back again. 'I'll think about it. I've got to go.'

Luke hurried out of the room and pounded up the stairs to his room. Dragging off his damp jersey—he hadn't had time to change between Jess's arrival and getting Kelly sorted out with dry clothes—he shucked his wet boots and jeans and changed into a pair of track pants and a sweatshirt.

Warmer, he sat down on his bed and looked at his hands. He had to decide what he was going to do about Jess. The campaign was complete and she needed to get back to Sandton—to her business, her family, her life. Leaving him alone at St Sylve.

He didn't think he could bear it. He didn't want to be alone, but how could he ask her to stay? He wanted her at St Sylve, wanted to see her face first thing in the morning and last thing at night. But he had no right to ask her to give up her life, her business, her home, when he wasn't prepared to take their relationship any further.

He was terrified of marriage. It felt as if a noose was tightening around his neck every time he even considered the concept. Jess couldn't—shouldn't—give up her life for anything less than a solid, watertight commitment.

Six weeks ago he'd had a peaceful life: a mutually satisfying sexual relationship with a nice woman, good friends for company, work to keep him busy. A normal, busy life without a complicated woman in his bed—in his head. He'd come to terms with his childhood, made peace with his failed marriage, put his relationship with his father into perspective.

Then Jess had skidded back into his life and spun it upside down.

Sex was no longer just about sex. He'd lost his family but he'd been slapped in the face with hers. He was about to have his longest dream aired on national TV. And she was in love with him. He hadn't asked for this—any of it. Why did he have to deal with all this? It was...overwhelming, distracting, too damn much!

He felt as if he'd fallen into a vortex of information and was being sucked down...sucked dry.

'Luke?'

Luke looked up and saw Jess in the doorway, her hand resting on the doorframe. *God, what now?* Could he not just have five damned minutes on his own?

'Can I come in?'

It irritated him that she felt the need to ask. This had been as much her room as his over the past week. He nodded and she walked over to him, that yellow envelope still in her hand. She sat down next to him and he could see the shimmer of raindrops in her hair.

'I'm sorry you didn't like the advert.'

Honesty forced him to answer truthfully. 'I loved the advert. It was just a...surprise.'

Jess shoved a shaky hand into her hair and tapped the envelope on her knee. 'I brought you a present. I hope you like it.'

Luke took the envelope off her lap, lifted the flap and pulled out a wad of papers. Placing them on the bed next to him, he flipped through the documents and quickly realised that the papers related to his mother and his childhood. His past... Jess had been delving into it. A core-deep slow burn started in his stomach and an icy hand clutched his heart. She had no right to interfere.

*That's not true.* He heard the small voice in the back of his head. *You're angry and miserable and maybe looking for a fight. Looking for an excuse to push her out of your head. In the space of an hour she's pushed every button you have...*

'Your mother didn't leave you. She was coming back for you—'

*'Shut up!'*

Luke jumped to his feet and looked down at her with furious eyes. Forget maybe—he *definitely* wanted a fight. *He knew what buttons to push too.* 'You really do have a habit of thinking that you know it all, Jess.'

The colour leached from Jess's face and she stared back at him, her eyes enormous in her face. She looked at the papers on the bed, sucked in a breath and tried for a normal voice. 'You don't understand! Luke, it's not what you think. It's *good* news!'

'I don't care! What did I say when you suggested that I contact my aunt?'

'That you didn't want to do it,' Jess replied in a small voice.

'What part of that sentence didn't you understand? How *dare* you take the decision to investigate my past out of my hands? If I wanted to know I am quite capable of finding out myself!'

'I'm sorry. I thought I was doing a nice thing!' Jess protested. 'I thought you needed to know—that I was helping.'

'You know, the first time I met you I thought you were an arrogant, snotty witch. Essentially, nothing has changed.'

When shocked hurt ran across her face he knew he had scored a direct hit, but she recovered quickly.

'That wasn't what you were thinking every time you took me to bed.'

'Hey, your body was on offer. I'm a man. I just took what was available.'

'That's an awful thing to say.'

It was, but he didn't care. Somewhere in a place that was beyond his temper and his anger and his fear, Luke realised that he was hurting her—that every word that dropped from his lips was like acid hitting her soul. He didn't mean it, but he was bone-deep terrified of the implications contained in that envelope—knew that they would change his perceptions about the past, change *him*. He didn't want to deal with any of it. Not with Jess's love, with the anger he felt that his mother had died, leaving him with his monster father, with knowing how much he'd needed her in his life. He just wanted to lash out...to put all this turbulent emotion somewhere else... on someone else.

Jess had a massive target on her forehead. It wasn't noble, and it wasn't nice, but *she* was somewhere to put this burning, churning rage that had his heart, stomach and throat in an unbreakable grip.

Jess wrapped her arms around her middle. Fine tremors passed through her body—a combination of cold and emotion. She felt annihilated and utterly lost... Who *was* this man who was doing his best to hurt her? This wasn't the Luke she'd thought she knew, the man she'd come to love. He was cold, hard, ugly.

'Why are you doing this?'

'Doing what? Being honest?'

Jess took a step forward and slapped her hand on his chest. 'Don't you dare! Don't you *dare* call this being honest! This is you being a chicken-crap coward! This is you being scared of being close to someone, of exploring your feelings, of admitting that I mean more to you than a quick fling.'

Luke scowled at her. 'Get real. This is about you making decisions on my behalf, insinuating yourself into my bed and my life—'

*'Insinuating myself into your bed and your life?'* The words roared out of Jess with the force of a freight train. 'Who was the one who kept saying that this was a bad idea, that we shouldn't sleep together because it would get complicated? That was *me*!'

'Well, we did, and I knew that I'd regret it!'

Luke's eyes were a deep green and as hard as granite. He was slipping further and further away from her to a place where she wouldn't be able to reach him.

'Luke, please don't do this…' Jess's anger faded and she put her hand out to him. She winced when Luke jerked away from her touch. He was gone, slipped over. She'd lost him…

Jess felt her heart crack. 'Why are you deliberately mis-construing my actions?' she demanded. 'I tried to give you a heads-up eight years ago about St Sylve and you tore me apart. I believe that you need to know that your mum loved you—adored you—but I'm being told that I'm an overbear-ing, interfering, controlling witch.'

Jess heard her voice grow stronger and she squared her shoulders and looked Luke in the eye.

'And the icing on the cake? You slept with me because I was *handy*? Nice, Luke.' Jess scrubbed her hands over her face. This day had gone to hell in a handbag… Her voice vi-brated with emotion when she spoke again. 'I thought you were *it*, Luke.'

'It?'

'The person I wanted to be with for the rest of my life. It just goes to show how utterly stupid I can be on occasion.' Jess's voice broke. 'But you know what? I deserve more and I definitely deserve better. There were kinder ways to get rid of me, Luke.'

She took her keys out of her back pocket and played with them, fighting back tears. She looked around the room.

'Please ask Angel to pack up my stuff. I'll pay her to do it. I'll send a courier company to pick it up. I can't be here another second. Consider me history, Luke.'

When she was at the door she thought she heard him say her name, softly and laced with pain. But when she turned around Luke was still sitting on the edge of his bed, staring down at the carpet between his legs. It was just her active imagination, conjuring up scenes and possibilities that were impossible.

Walking away from him, from the place—the person—she considered her home took more courage than she'd known she had.

It was two-forty a.m. and Luke couldn't sleep. Instead he lay on the leather couch in front of his flat-screen, watching the final advert for St Sylve for the... He'd forgotten how many times he'd watched it. He watched Jess jump into his arms, felt his heart clench each time she did it.

The rain hammered down outside, as it had done for the past week. He'd spent the day placing sandbags next to the stream that ran past the eastern vineyard. The stream was pumping, and more rain upstream would cause it to break its banks and flood the vineyard. He recalled his grandfather talking about that same stream bursting its banks in fifty-eight and washing away a good portion of the vines.

He had no problem learning from his forefathers' mistakes.

It was learning from his own that he was having problems with.

Earlier tonight, unable to sleep, he'd reopened the envelope Jess had left behind and properly read the papers inside. The contents of which he was still trying to process...

According to the notes Jess had jotted down, his aunt had died shortly after his father passed away, but her daughter, who now lived in the cottage, had kept her mother's papers and knew about Katelyn.

Long story short: his mum hadn't left him. According to the daughter, his mother had left him at St Sylve for a couple of days while she sorted out a house to rent close to her sister. She'd already moved the bulk of his toys and clothes and his father had known that she was leaving.

He'd been an *oops*—a very welcome mistake for his mother, a way to be trapped into marriage for his father. They'd married, and the relationship had always been stormy.

His father's affairs and his inability to share his time, his money and St Sylve with her had led to her decision to leave.

She'd been on her way to collect him when she'd died. Subsequently his father had refused his aunt permission to see him or to have anything to do with him. She'd sent letters and birthday presents every year. When Luke had left school his aunt's health had been failing and she'd decided to let fate run its course. If he chose to seek her out then so be it.

He might have decided to track her down...if he'd known about her. Naturally he'd never seen the letters or the presents. How typical of his father, he thought. He hadn't wanted his mother, but her leaving St Sylve should have been on *his* terms, not hers, and he'd been left with a reminder that she'd left without permission: Luke himself.

Luke tucked a pillow behind his head. He now realised—could finally accept—that Jess had done this for *him*. She knew that there was a festering ulcer buried deep in his heart. She'd lanced it by tracking down his cousin—had started the process of healing by bringing him these papers. She knew it was necessary for him and also knew that he probably wouldn't have done it without her pushing.

The folder of papers she'd left signified a particular type of freedom: the knowledge that he'd been wanted—loved. If he'd left with his mother he wouldn't have had the material benefits his father had given him...but he would have been happier. Settled, not so neurotic about relationships.

*Thanks, Dad.*

Some time earlier, while reading the papers, he'd finally admitted that he was utterly in love with Jess.

Quickly following that thought had come acceptance that he *was* a 'chicken-crap coward'—that he'd been scared of loving Jess in case he lost her, terrified of facing and dealing with the pain...and guess what? He *had* lost her. She was gone.

He missed her...and he felt sick every time he remembered

that she wasn't part of his life any more. Life together. It was what he wanted. She was the other chamber of his heart—the reason the sun came up in the morning. He could see her ripe with life, carrying his child. She would be the most fantastic mother—the glue that would hold his family together. He felt settled with her—calm, in control. Nothing much was wrong with his world if he could see her smile first thing in the morning.

He finally understood what love felt like...*Jess*.

Just Jess.

They were meant to be together; they would be together. He just had to find a way to make that happen.

Logistically, it was a nightmare. Her home, her life, was in Sandton. His was here at St Sylve. How much could he give up for her and, more importantly, would she even have him?

If he had to he would leave St Sylve. It would be a wrench, but if there was a choice between St Sylve and Jess, being with Jess would win. St Sylve was his heritage but Jess was his soul.

Luke rolled over, pointed the remote and switched the TV off. As soon as it was light he'd head for the airport, catch the first plane he could find and go to Jess.

He'd go to her because wherever she was, simply, was where he wanted—needed—to be.

Jess paced her mother's kitchen, a glass of red wine in her hand, her thoughts a million miles away. Her father sat at the kitchen table, sketching, and her mother was making an apple crumble that Jess knew, from thirty-odd years of eating her mother's food, would taste like cardboard.

When she refused to eat some she would only be telling the truth when she explained that along with destroying her heart Luke had also taken her appetite.

Clem stood at the stove, and Nick was somewhere in the

house fixing something. He and Clem were in town for a couple of days to give Clem her 'city fix'. It amused Jess that Clem's need for a city fix always seemed to coincide with something that needed to be done at her parents' house. It was, Jess knew, Clem's very clever way of re-establishing and cementing Nick's relationship with his parents after years of little or no communication.

Clem walked over to her and put her hand on her shoulder. 'Oh, Jess, I *do* know what you're going through. The month I spent without Nick was the loneliest, hardest of my life.'

Jess rested her head on Clem's shoulder, dry-eyed but exhausted. 'It's been a week and my heart is shutting down...I never knew it could hurt this much.'

'I have to tell you that your brothers are making plans to go down there and beat the snot out of him,' Clem informed her. 'There have been mutters about broken knees and cracked heads.'

Jess looked horrified. 'They can't! Honestly, why can't they mind their own business?'

'Because you *are* our business, Jessica Claire,' her father said, his eyes focused on his sketch. 'But I have faith in that young man. He just needs to get his head around the fact that he's loved and in love.'

'You don't know Luke, Dad. He's stubborn...'

'But I know young men. I raised four and I was young myself once. Every one of your brothers took some time to shake off their...*ahem*...attachment to their bachelor lifestyle, to their freedom. I did the same.'

'David cried and squealed like a girl when I told him I wouldn't put up with him seeing other girls and that getting stoned regularly was not an option,' Liza informed them crisply.

Her comment made Clem laugh, and Jess just managed a smile. She pulled out a chair and slumped into it. She wished she could tell them Luke's reluctance to get involved wasn't a normal man's fear of commitment, that it was rooted in his childhood, in his mother's death, his father's lack of love.

Jess looked up at Clem. 'You were right, Clem. Heck, *he* was right... I shouldn't have interfered.'

Clem shrugged. 'He'll come to realise that you did it out of love and he'll forgive you.'

'I doubt it,' Jess replied.

David looked up from his sketch of Clem. 'Did his cousin say anything about Katelyn's paintings?'

'Apparently they are all in the attic at her cottage. Janet didn't realise that Katelyn was such an important artist.'

'Is she going to sell them?' Liza asked.

'No, she said they are Luke's, and she'll leave them where they are until he decides what to do with them. If he decides to do anything with them,' Jess muttered darkly. 'The list of paintings was in the envelope with the rest of the documents.'

'I'd love to see them,' David said reverentially.

Jess picked up a fork and traced patterns in the bright tablecloth with its tines. 'You and me both. But there is no chance of that, Dad.'

'Keep the faith, darling.' David patted her hand. 'And if nothing happens with Luke, just remember that your mother has the numbers of at least three young men who'd like to meet you.'

Jess couldn't smile at his joke. She doubted she'd ever date again. That was the trouble with meeting your soul mate— it was difficult to imagine, comprehend being with another man. Even if said soul mate wanted nothing to do with her.

Liza saw something in her face that made her step forward and run a hand over her head. 'Forget your brothers. I have a good mind to beat him up myself.'

Jess looked up into her mum's sympathetic face. 'It just hurts so much, Mum.'

Liza wrapped her arms around Jess's neck and Jess rested her cheek on her stomach. 'I know, baby girl. I know it does.'

Later on that afternoon, not knowing that he'd missed Jess by a couple of minutes, Luke stood at her parents' front door and met Nick's cold grey eyes. He thought that the possibility of Nick's fist rocketing into his jaw was quite high. Jess's brother scowled at him, and the muscles in his forearms bulged when he folded his arms and widened his stance. Luke thought he could take him, if he had to, but if Nick punched him he wouldn't retaliate. He deserved the punch and more.

'You have five seconds to state your case before I rip your head off,' Nick snarled, his grey eyes thunderous.

Luke thought fast and decided to keep it simple. 'I love her and I want to marry her.'

Nick stared at him and Luke braced himself. Nobody was more surprised when Nick's face cleared, his arms dropped and a huge smile split his face. 'Cool. C'mon in. Jess isn't here, though.'

Luke stayed where he was. 'You're not going to hit me?'

Nick looked amused. 'Do you want me to?'

'No, I'll pass. But…why not?'

Nick swung the front door open. 'You took nearly a week to realise that you are an idiot. I took a month. The point is you got there, and you are doing something about it. You *are* doing something about it?' he asked.

'Of course I am,' Luke replied irritably.

'Then why are you here and not at her place, grovelling?'

'I'm not quite ready to see Jess yet. Well, I am—but there's something I have to do first and I need help.'

Nick clapped a hand on his shoulder. 'I'm your man. I can't wait to watch the merry dance my sister leads you for the rest of your life, mate.'

*As long as she's dancing with me, I don't give a damn,*

Luke thought. 'I need you and at least one other of your brothers to help me transport something...'

Jess was at home and wishing she could stop waiting for Luke to call. She propped her feet up on the coffee table and sighed. She had a huge, Luke-sized hole in her life and a smaller St Sylve hole next to it. She kept telling herself that life had a funny way of sorting itself out, but the words weren't sinking in. She had loved and lost. Millions had, and it wasn't the end of the world...it just felt like it.

Jess sat up, hearing a key in her front door lock, and turned around to see the door opening. 'For crying in a bucket, Patrick! Hold it up!'

She heard another couple of muffled swear words from... *Nick*? Looking towards the front door, she saw three pairs of feet: trainers, loafers and—oh, God—scuffed work boots. And three pairs of legs behind a massive brown-paper-wrapped frame.

Jess stood up, her hand to her heart as the frame wobbled and Luke cursed. 'Damn! Be careful. Okay, lower it against the couch. Slowly... This was not the greatest idea I've ever had.'

Jess had no words so she just stared at them, watching as Nick glared at Luke across the top of the painting. 'I said that, Sherlock.'

Patrick straightened and theatrically placed his hand on his back. 'Gee, I thought I mentioned it too. But, no, you had to make the grand gesture.'

Luke grinned at them. 'You sound like a bunch of groaning grannies. For two sports freaks, you two could moan for Africa.'

Nick glared at him. 'Bite me.'

Luke was here—finally here. His back was to her and she sucked him in. His hair was almost ludicrously long, curling over his collar and falling into his eyes. The long sleeves of his T-shirt were pushed up over his elbows and he wore his oldest, most faded and frayed jeans. Three-day-old stubble completed his surfer-boy look.

Jess's mouth watered.

Then her heart hardened as she remembered that he thought she was an overbearing control freak, an interfering witch. And how dared her brothers use the key she'd given them for emergencies to saunter into her house without so much as a hello or any type of greeting?

She was sick of arrogant, egotistical, selfish men!

'You have thirty seconds to leave my house before I start going bananas,' Jess told them, her voice hard and cold. She waved at the brown parcel—obviously a painting. 'And take that with you. I have nothing to say to you, Savage.'

'Well, I've got a couple of things to say to you,' Luke replied in a mild voice as his eyes flicked over hers, softened and bounced back to her brothers. 'Okay, you two can leave now.'

Nick and Patrick exchanged a long, considering look and Patrick shook his head. 'Forget it… I want to know why you chartered a plane to deliver that painting and why we had to babysit it like our firstborn in a truck over here. Are *you* going anywhere, Nick?'

Nick folded his arms. 'Heck, no! Clem would kill me if I didn't get every romantic moment. Get on with it, Luke, you're wasting time.'

'Like I'm *really* going to have this conversation in front of you two,' Luke scoffed.

'Nobody is having a conversation with anybody!' Jess stormed to the door and gestured for them to get out. 'You're all leaving—now!'

Luke looked at her brothers. 'C'mon, guys, give me a

break. I need to talk to Jess and you're not helping. Just go! Please?'

Nick placed his hands together in an attitude of prayer and bowed low. Patrick followed suit. 'May the force be with you,' Nick intoned.

The brothers bowed again before backing out through the front door and slamming it behind them.

Luke said something uncomplimentary about them under his breath before he raised his head to look at Jess. 'Hi.'

Jess shoved her shaking hands into the front pockets of her jeans. 'What are you doing here, Luke? I thought you said everything of importance a week ago.'

'Not quite.' Luke looked around her small house. 'Nice place.'

Jess shrugged and sent a curious look towards the painting—it could *only* be a painting—then gestured to the kitchen. She had no idea why Luke was delivering a painting to her house after a week of silence and her pride refused to allow her to ask. 'Do you want something to drink?' she asked in a polite, cool voice.

Luke nodded and followed her into the sunny kitchen. Jess handed him a bottle of beer and they took up their customary positions of leaning against opposite counters. They spent a couple of minutes just looking at each other.

Luke eventually broke their hungry silence. 'You look good.'

Jess lifted her eyebrows. He was either using flattery or her looks hadn't gone to pot yet. 'You look tired.'

Luke picked at the label on his beer bottle. 'Listening to those two bitch for hours will do that to a man.' Rolling a tiny ball of paper between his fingers, he flicked it towards the dustbin.

'I'm surprised to see you and my brothers on such good terms,' Jess said, annoyed. Where was her siblings' outrage on her behalf? The desire to beat him up—metaphorically, of course. She didn't want him actually hurt—because he'd broken her heart? Traitors, every last one of them.

'Well, I practised my grovelling on them before coming here.'

'Is that what you've come to do? Grovel?'

'If I have to.' Luke placed his untouched bottle of beer on the counter and rubbed his hand over his jaw. 'I hope it won't come to that. I have a great deal to say to you and I hope you'll hear me out.'

'You're here, in my kitchen, and I can't kick you out or gag you, so I don't have much of a choice, do I?' Jess retorted.

It was so unfair that he could look so good and she couldn't touch him. That he was so close and yet still so inaccessible. She couldn't read his eyes, couldn't find a clue to what he wanted to say in his inscrutable face, his tense body.

'Thank you for finding out what happened to my mother.'

'Even though I interfered and took the decision out of your hands?' Jess asked, sceptical.

Luke shoved his hands into the back pockets of his jeans and rocked on his heels. 'I was scared to do it—scared of what I'd find out. I had finally come to terms with my mother's death and I didn't want to have to live with something else. When you handed me that envelope I felt like you were pushing me somewhere I didn't want to go.'

Jess grimaced at the reluctant note she heard in his voice. 'You're still not happy I did it.'

'I've been on my own for so long that I find it difficult to accept help—to feel comfortable with someone...'

'Meddling? Interfering? Snooping?'

'Concerned about me,' Luke said firmly. 'It'll take some getting used to.'

Jess felt her heart roll over in her chest but dismissed the spurt of hope as her imagination. 'That implies that there will be a tomorrow for us?'

'I'm hoping that there will be a lifetime of tomorrows.'

Jess licked her lips. 'You called me a control freak and overbearing, said you understood why my exes kicked me into touch. Snotty and interfering…'

'I know, I know…I'm sorry. But I'd been slapped with a whole lot of things that day that I didn't know how to deal with and I was reeling. You were in the splash zone.'

'Like what?' Jess demanded.

'When you—briefly I'll admit—thought that I'd slept with Kelly, I was hurt. I wanted you to trust me implicitly, but you hesitated.'

'I did trust you—when I started thinking and not reacting.'

'Then I saw the ad, saw all my dreams captured on screen, and I felt at sea. And then I realised that you loved me…'

'Not any more,' Jess stated, her colour heightened.

'Liar,' Luke countered. 'I realised that you loved me but I didn't know what to do about it. How could I ask you to leave your family, your business, your life to live with me? Someone who has no idea how to be part of a family, who doesn't know how to give you what you need? Then you hit me with my past and it was too much…it was all too much. I miss you, Jess. I need you in my life.'

'You hurt me,' Jess said in a small voice. 'You took my heart out and stomped on it. And now you're back, asking me to risk it again?'

'I want to be with you, Jess. I want you to be my family.'

Luke rubbed his shoulder with his hand. Jess heard his expulsion of air.

'After my anger subsided and I looked at the folder I needed some time to think it all through: my mum, my father, you.'

'And?'

'And I'm glad to know that my mum loved me. I realise

that my childhood is over and, most important, that I want to be with you—make a commitment to you. I don't do that lightly or easily, because when I do, I do it with everything I have.' Luke stepped forward and placed his hands on either side of Jess's hips, effectively blocking her in. 'I'm so in love with you.'

Jess gnawed on her bottom lip and looked up at Luke with wide, scared eyes. 'So what are you suggesting, Luke, exactly?'

'I realise that you can't leave your business, so can we find a compromise? You spend a week with me at St Sylve, then I spend the next week with you here?'

When Jess didn't answer, Luke sped up. 'If that doesn't work for you I'll leave St Sylve, let Owen run it. Hire a vintner...go back to venture capital full-time.'

'You'd hate it,' Jess pointed out.

'But I'd be with you, which is the most important thing to me.' Luke raised an enquiring eyebrow at her still-troubled face. 'What's the problem, Jess?'

As Luke turned those amazing eyes to hers she stepped away and paced to the fridge and back, wringing her hands. 'Look, Luke, you say you love me now, but I don't know if you are going to change your mind again. I don't know if I can run that risk. I don't know if my...' She stuttered to a stop and then forced the words out. 'If my heart can stand it.'

Luke looked at her, his face expressionless. Then, taking her hand, he yanked her towards the lounge and made her stand in front of the wrapped painting. He looked at her, a small smile on his face. 'Somehow I knew that I would need a grand gesture.'

Jess was utterly bemused as Luke went to stand at the side of the package. Bunching the paper at the corner edge with his fist, he looked at Jess, his heart in his eyes. 'This is my most prized possession—possibly the only material thing I'd try to rescue from a fire. And you fell in love with it a couple of weeks ago.'

Luke ripped the paper and revealed the enormous painting that graced the large space above his bed at St Sylve. The mountains jumped out at her and the mist glistened. Jess wanted to climb into the painting with Luke and make love between the vines.

Ignoring her galloping heart, she forced a shrug. 'I don't understand.'

Luke patted the frame. 'This is, apart from you, my greatest treasure. If there was one thing I'd risk my life to save it would be this. I just want to know if I can share it with you.'

'But why? Are you giving it to me? You can't give it to me!' Jess squeaked. 'It's one of only two paintings you have of your mother's.'

Luke half smiled. 'I can, because the same thing that calls to me in this painting calls to me in you. Your strength, your generosity, your utter courage and your bloody stubbornness. And because I love you. You've got to know how much I love you.'

Jess couldn't help her knees buckling. She sat down on the edge of the couch and stared up at Luke, absolutely baffled. She felt Luke's arm around her shoulder and instinctively dropped her face into his neck, winding her arms around his head in case he disappeared as quickly as he'd appeared.

Luke ran his hand over her hair. 'Sweetheart, are you crying? Because if you are Nick will beat me to a pulp. Not that I don't deserve it, but I'd rather avoid it if I can.'

Jess lifted her head and her eyes were clear, bright and happy. She hiccupped a laugh. 'Do you mean it?'

'Which part? The loving you or the Nick beating me to a pulp?' Luke teased.

Jess slapped his chest and placed her thumb between her teeth. 'Luke?'

Luke kissed her hair. 'I love you, Jess, with everything in me. I think I probably fell in love with you eight years ago and never really stopped. I'm sorry I hurt you. Let me share your life, Jess. In Sandton, if you want to stay here, or at St Sylve.'

Biting her bottom lip, Jess stared at the painting and back at Luke, who suddenly didn't look as confident as he usually did. Maybe she hadn't loved and lost as she'd first thought.

Forcing her bubbling laughter away, Jess pursed her lips. 'My decision rests on a couple of assurances from you.'

'As much wine as you can drink, I'll replace any thong I rip with two more, and my house and land and my heart are in your hands.'

'Shut up,' Jess ordered, her mouth twitching. 'I want a child. Or two. Maybe three.'

'Sold,' Luke responded quickly, joy flooding his face. 'What else?'

'I want to go home—back to St Sylve—and I want the painting to go back into our bedroom. And I want you to marry me. So if you don't think that might happen some time in the future maybe you should walk away now.'

Taking her chin, he lifted her face to look up into his. 'I was made to love you, to look after you, to protect you, to make beautiful, beautiful babies with you. Will you marry me?'

Jess's mouth fell open. 'You're proposing? Right now?'

'That's what "will you marry me?" means. Feel free to say yes any time.'

His eyes held an element of doubt and she reached up to touch his jaw with her fingertips. 'I'll marry you because my sun rises with you, because I want to carry your beautiful, beautiful babies, because I want to tell you every day that nobody will ever love you as much I do and will.'

Luke rested his forehead against hers. 'Oh, Jess, you take my breath away. I don't have a ring for you yet. I was focused on getting you back and hadn't dared hope that you might consider marrying me. Maybe we could have one designed?'

Jess sent him a look long of adoration. 'Just knowing that I'm going to spend the rest of my life with you is enough.'

Luke cupped her face in his hands. 'I love you so much.'

He kissed her thoroughly, reverentially, and Jess fell into his embrace, happiness seeping out of every pore. Her hands were undoing his shirt buttons when his mobile rang.

Luke cursed, yanked it out of his pocket and looked down at the screen. He turned the screen to show Jess. 'Nick, your nosy brother.'

Jess pressed a kiss to his chest. 'Ignore him.'

Luke dropped the phone, but it had barely hit the cushions when it rang again. Two seconds later Jess's mobile started to chirp in the kitchen.

Jess dropped her head back and hissed her frustration. 'They'll keep calling until they know what's going on.' Jess reached for Luke's phone and put it to her ear.

'Can I not just be amazingly happy for five minutes without you guys wanting in on the action?' Jess demanded, her hand on Luke's cheek. She smiled as Nick spoke, said goodbye and then sent Luke a bemused look.

'Nick says that you're not to forget about the silky bantams. Um…why do you need to buy some chickens?'

Luke just laughed and kissed her.

# EPILOGUE

SIX WEEKS LATER Jess's family swept in *en masse* to an exhibition of Katelyn Kirby's paintings. They were surrounded by an amazing collection that had the art world buzzing— but what was the first thing her mother said on seeing her?

'He still hasn't put a ring on your finger!'

Jess rolled her eyes and pulled her left hand out from her mother's grasp. 'Mum! Luke and I are getting married in six months' time. An engagement ring is not going to change that.'

'Every girl should have a ring!' Liza stated.

'And I'll get one...when Luke finds exactly what he is looking for,' Jess told her, and turned to greet the rest of her extensive family. 'You're late. Luke is about to do his speech.' Jess snagged her father's jacket and pulled him back. 'Dad, you can view the art later...come here.'

Clem made her way to stand next to her and slipped an arm around her waist. 'It's good to see you so happy, Jess. You *are* happy?'

'Absolutely.'

'And how are you coping with your business?' Clem asked, taking a glass of champagne from a hovering waiter.

'Ally has picked up the reins and is not letting go. I have very little to do with the Sandton office except for designing the initial concepts.'

'And the Cape Town office?' Nick asked from his position behind Clem.

Jess looked rueful. 'I haven't set it up yet, and I don't know if I'm going to. I've been doing a bit of consulting here and there, looking after clients in the city.'

Clem lowered her voice. 'And St Sylve? Is it on a bit more of an even keel?'

Jess looked past Clem's shoulder at Luke. 'There's been a pick-up in sales and that's encouraging. I'm also renovating the manor house to turn it into a venue suitable for small weddings, functions…family weekends away, so I'm swamped. Happily, crazily busy. We're designing a house that we want to build on the other side of the farm, and…'

'And Luke keeps you busy…?' Nick added dryly.

Jess fluffed her hair and grinned. 'He most certainly does—and in the most delightful ways possible.'

Nick scowled. *'Blergh.'*

Jess laughed and stood in the middle of the half-circle her family made. She watched Luke, looking tall and strong and amazingly attractive in his black tuxedo, step up to the podium. She felt the glow in her stomach when he looked for her, and his eyes were warm and loving when they connected with hers. They were wildly in love and amazingly happy. Jess, ring or not, considered herself a very lucky woman.

Luke looked around the room and smiled. 'Welcome to this exhibition of Katelyn Kirby's art—my mother's art. As most of you know, she died when I was really young, but this huge collection of her work has recently come to light and I wanted to share her talent with the world. Some of the paintings here are not for sale—my fiancée, Jess, and I have decided to keep some—but the rest of her art, including her sketches for jewellery designs and sculptures, are being sold to raise money for a foundation we've established in her name to fund the training of talented, disadvantaged young artists.'

A few minutes later Jess watched as Luke walked towards her, with that slow, sexy smile on his face. He greeted her family before dropping a sexy kiss on her mouth. His green eyes sparkled as he looked down at her.

'I have a present for you,' he said.

Jess did a little dance in her ice-pick heels. 'You do? Will I like it?'

'I hope so. It has the added benefit of getting your mum to stop nagging you—and me.' Luke sent Liza a full, teasing look and grinned widely when she wrinkled her nose at him. Turning back to Jess, he pulled out a box from his pocket and flipped open the lid.

Jess stared down at the soft, romantic, deeply unusual ring. It was unique—swirls of gold and platinum, with a deep sapphire winking up at her.

Luke's voice was laced with emotion when he slipped it on to her finger. 'My mum designed it, and when I saw her sketch I thought of you—thought that she'd drawn it with you in mind. I snuck it out of her portfolio before you could see it so that it would be a surprise. What do you think?'

Jess bit her lip in an effort to hold back her tears. 'I love it. I love *you*.'

Luke cupped her face with his big hands. 'Love you more.'

Nick broke the emotionally charged moment. 'Jeez, Savage, if you're going to get soppy you'll end up being our least-favourite brother-in-law,' he drawled. 'It puts far too much pressure on the rest of us to be romantic.'

Luke grinned at Nick, Jess plastered to his side. 'I'll be your *only* brother-in-law,' he pointed out.

Nick pulled a face, laughter in his eyes. '*You're it?* Then I definitely need another large drink!'

\* \* \* \* \*

# FALLING FOR HER FRENCH TYCOON

**REBECCA WINTERS**

Once again I turn to my oldest son, whom I often call Guillaume, because he's a Francophile like his *maman* and fluent in their beautiful language. Turning to him for information about my favourite place on earth is better than any book. His knowledge continues to stun me. We have the most marvellous conversations and I learn so much. How I love him!

# PROLOGUE

*July 31*

NATHALIE FOURNIER RANG Claire Rolon, the best friend of Nathalie's deceased stepsister, Antoinette. The friendship between the three of them went back to childhood.

"Claire?"

"Nathalie! I'm so glad you called! It's been ages."

"Way too long. I'm thrilled you answered. Do you have a minute?"

"Yes. Robert is upstairs playing with the baby while I finish the dishes. Go ahead."

She took a deep breath. "I know Antoinette would have confided in you before she got pregnant two and a half years ago. Is there anything you can tell me about her lover who disappeared on her without explanation? Our family didn't know she'd even been involved with someone until the doctor said she was pregnant. By then she'd sunk into a deep depression."

"Your stepsister was very secretive."

"So secretive she never spoke his name to us and

as she died from infection ten days after her baby was born, we still don't know who his father is," Nathalie lamented. "Now little Alain is fifteen months old and I'm taking the steps to legally adopt him. Before I do, though, I need to try to find his father."

"You're kidding! How could you possibly do that?"

"Hopefully with a little information you could provide." Nathalie gripped the phone tighter. "You probably think I'm crazy."

"Of course I don't."

"You were the closest person to her, Claire. If she said anything, it would have been to you. Any clue you could give me would help. Did she let it slip where or how she met him?"

"She did say he worked at the Fontesquieu vineyard."

Her heart raced. "You're certain of that?"

The Fontesquieu vineyards near Vence, France, were one of the largest and most prestigious, producing the legendary rosé wines of Provence. The land had been deeded to them by royalty centuries ago, and the most coveted vineyard in all Provence was currently run by a titled billionaire. She'd heard stories about the vineyard all her life.

"Yes. Apparently they met at a bistro in Vence where a lot of the vineyard workers from the Fontesquieu estate hang out during the harvest."

"Do you remember the name of it?" Nathalie cried, encouraged by what she'd just learned.

"It was unusual. The Guingot, or some such name, but I don't imagine he would be at that vineyard after all this time. I wish there was something more concrete to tell you. It's not much to go on. I'm so sorry. I think you'll need a miracle."

"Don't be sorry, Claire! The vineyard is the place where I'm going to start looking. One more thing. Did she say what he looked like?"

"Unfortunately not. Only that he was a Provencal and the only man she would ever love."

That meant he'd been a local Frenchman, probably dark haired and eyed.

"You've given me more information than I could have hoped for. Thank you with all my heart."

"Good luck. Let me know if you learn anything."

"I will. You're such a good friend. Thank you for being so honest with me. I know she swore you to secrecy."

"She did, but it's been a long time since then. For Alain's sake it would be wonderful if you're successful."

"Wouldn't it? Talk to you soon."

Nathalie hung up, deep in thought.

At the beginning of the summer, Nathalie had broken up with the man she'd thought she might marry. Guy couldn't handle her bringing Alain into their marriage—he wanted his own child with her.

That's when she'd told him she probably couldn't have children. When she'd explained about having primary ovarian insufficiency, he couldn't handle that news. Guy had said he'd wanted to marry her, but he'd refused to consider adopting Alain. Because she wanted her nephew more than anything, it became clear that marriage was out of the question.

Alain meant everything to her.

# CHAPTER ONE

*August 31*

ADRENALINE GUSHED THROUGH Nathalie as she sped toward the Fontesquieu vineyards of Vence—queen of
the cities of the French Riviera, in her opinion. They
stretched eye to eye above the blue Mediterranean, row
after row of immaculately tended *terroirs* with their
healthy grape vines dotting the undulating green hills
and summits.

The August afternoon sun had ripened the luscious
grapes, filling the air with a sweet, fruity smell as she
neared the Fontesquieu estate with its enormous seventeenth-century chateau, rumored to contain twenty-
two bedrooms. It reminded her of the book *My Mother's
Castle*, made famous by the French author and film-
maker Marcel Pagnol. He'd been born in Provence too
and had written some of her favorite books about his
childhood memories.

But the Pagnol family's quaint little vacation home in
Provence couldn't compare to the one she could see out
the window of her trusty old Peugeot. The magnificent

chateau had always been closed to the public, but the estate drew artists and tourists from all over the world.

Nathalie couldn't imagine the wealth of a family like the Fontesquieux. She'd been born in Provence and had passed by the vineyard many times, but she'd never enjoyed its scenery more than this afternoon.

With pounding heart, she followed the signs posted to find the tent set up for people seeking temporary work grape picking. After planning this since her talk with Claire a month ago, the day had come for her to get a job that would last only the three weeks of the grape harvest. In that amount of time, she hoped to find the man who had fathered her nephew, Alain, if he was still there. But as Claire had said, it would take a miracle.

When she reached the nearby mobile home park she'd visited earlier in the week, she parked and walked down the road toward a line of people waiting outside the tent in the distance.

Before entering, a man—probably early twenties—with dark blond hair handed everyone an application to fill out. He also gave them a list of items they would need if they were eventually hired. She put that list in her purse and sat down at a small table to fill out the form before getting in line. He eyed her with obvious male interest before it was her turn to enter the tent.

The line moved slowly until there was only one person in front of her being interviewed. That's when she saw the man vetting everyone and stifled a gasp. She wished she had a better description of Alain's father. All she had to go on was that he was a Provencal, which meant dark haired and dark eyed. The man sitting there certainly filled that description, but it could be a coincidence. Was it possible she'd found him?

The breathtaking, late-twenties-looking male could easily be the heartthrob Antoinette had fallen for! Her darling stepsister's now sixteen-month-old child possessed this man's square chin and black hair. He had the same type of build and olive skin.

Thousands of Frenchmen claimed those same qualifications, but this one's piercing black eyes had a distinct look that reminded her so much of her little nephew, Nathalie was astonished. To think, it might be Alain's father sitting there not ten feet away interviewing would-be grape pickers. By applying for this job, she could have found him!

According to one of the people in line, hundreds of workers had already been hired during the week. Today represented the last group seeking temporary employment.

*"Prochain?"* he said in a deep voice that reached her insides.

Nathalie's heartbeat sped up as she realized she was next in line and needed to follow through. She moved forward to sit opposite him on a chair beneath the tent. The heat of the sun had made the interior uncomfortably warm.

Though he was seated, she could tell he was a tall man, lean in that appealing masculine way. He wore a white shirt with the sleeves pushed to the elbows and as he took the application from her, she noticed a small, pale, café-au-lait birthmark on his underarm beneath the elbow. She had to stifle another gasp because the back of Alain's right calf had the same birthmark.

Maybe it was a coincidence. Millions of people had them, but this was just one more bit of evidence to convince her he could be Alain's father.

Nathalie noticed that he wore a watch and no rings, but that didn't mean he wasn't married. His nails were immaculate. When he looked up, their eyes met and her breath caught.

Heat crept into her cheeks as she got lost in his intense gaze. They were both taking measure of each other while she waited for him to say something. He couldn't have recognized her as Antoinette's stepsister. Nathalie was a blonde. Her stepsister had been a brunette. They came from different sets of parents with different last names.

His virile male beauty stunned her. Her stepsister, who'd been two years older than Nathalie, would have taken one look at him and that would have been it! How well Nathalie understood the instant attraction. She couldn't look away.

He continued to study her features. "Mademoiselle Fournier? I see here you've had no experience as a *vendangeuse*."

"That's right. I didn't know that was a prerequisite."

"It's not, but it's hard labor, seasonal, and the pay isn't that great. Why would a pharmacist from La Gaude apply to do entry-level work like this?" La Gaude, France, was a town a fifteen-minute drive from Vence along the Côte d'Azur, the playground of the world's rich and famous.

She felt those black all-seeing eyes travel over her with a thoroughness that caused her to tremble, and she looked down. He was so gorgeous she was in danger of forgetting why she'd come. For her little nephew's sake, it was vital Nathalie pull this off. She needed to think fast.

"I've lived in Provence all my life and thought that for once I'd use my vacation time to find out what it's like to work in a vineyard as world renowned as this one."

On their website she'd seen one photo of the Duc Armand de Fontesquieu, the gray-haired, eighty-year-old patriarch and CEO. She'd seen no other pictures and realized they had to be a very private family.

Though many vineyards used machinery, some vintners—like the vastly wealthy Fontesquieu family with their many *terroirs*—also hired pickers called *coupeurs*, plus collectors and sorters for the grape harvest vendange. It lasted for the first three weeks of September. She'd done her homework.

After a slight pause, he spoke. "You do realize that we have no accommodations for you here."

She raised her eyes to him again. With that comment, she sensed he didn't believe her reason for wanting the temporary work.

Though it was this man's job to vet would-be workers, she sensed he had reservations about her. Obviously the "no previous vineyard work" written on the form bothered him. Naturally anyone could apply for grape picking, but their vineyard would welcome those with experience.

"Yes. That's why I've rented a mobile home at the park down the road from here." Actually she'd come two days ago to put a hold on one until she knew the outcome of this interview.

He gave her a level stare. "Keep in mind you'll have an hour for lunch and quit at four thirty. If you're still interested in working here by Monday morning, report to the tent at six o'clock and the assistant vineyard manager will let you know if you've been hired."

It was all up to this man who would have the weekend to check out her references. He spoke with authority. There was an aura of sophistication about him that let her know he had a position of importance at Fontesquieux and had likely worked here long enough to have met Antoinette at the bistro.

"*Merci*, monsieur." She got up, aware of him watching her as she walked past the people standing in line, and left the tent. The younger man outside giving out applications flashed her a smile, but she looked away and headed for her car, not wanting to encourage him.

When she got behind the wheel, she was still feeling shaky from all the sensations bombarding her. It might be a long shot, but now that she suspected she'd met the man who could be Alain's father, she'd do everything possible to get to know him. When she sensed it was the right moment, she'd show him photos of Antoinette and Alain, including the birthmark. If he was the father, she couldn't imagine him not wanting to see his child.

Of course, if she didn't get hired, then she needed to find innovative ways to cross paths with him, starting tonight. She planned to seek out dinner at the bistro Claire had told her about. Maybe *he'd* be there... Just imagining his handsome features left her breathless.

Having finished the interviews, Dominic Laurent Fontesquieu stopped in the midst of fastening his briefcase full of applications. He couldn't resist taking another look at the Fournier application.

The woman with translucent green eyes and natural silvery blond hair had robbed him of breath. Her deportment and stunning beauty had captivated him. As Dominic studied the particulars on her application, her image swam before him again.

*Age: twenty-seven.*
*Home address: La Gaude.*
*Cell phone...*
*Email address...*
*Employed full time at La Metropole Pharmacy.*
*Driver's license.*
*Own car.*
*Bank account.*
*Covered by social insurance.*
*Degree in pharmacology from Sophie Antipolis University in Nice.*
*No experience picking grapes.*

He tapped the paper against his jaw. What was missing here? Only everything else about her life that might answer the question of what prompted her to apply for this temporary work.

This mysterious, gorgeous, educated woman suddenly appears at the vineyard out of nowhere, wanting to know what it's like to help with the harvest for a few weeks?

Dominic didn't buy it for a second. He put the application in the briefcase with the others before leaving the tent, unable to get her off his mind. He was so attracted to her, it shocked him.

Vetting would-be workers was one of his brother Etienne's jobs as director of the vineyard so he usually oversaw the vendange hiring. But he'd been struck down by a nasty flu bug for the better part of a week and their grandfather Armand had rung Dominic's apartment in the south wing of the chateau and demanded that he fill in for his brother.

Little had Dominic known that the most beautiful woman he'd ever laid eyes on in his life would be among the applicants. He'd wanted to catch up with her after she'd left and take her to dinner to get to know her better. But that had been impossible when other people needed to be interviewed.

Frustrated, he headed for his office in a building on the estate behind the chateau. He left the applications for his assistant, Theo, to deal with until Etienne recovered and drove the short distance to the chateau. Once he reached his apartment, he took a quick shower to cool off.

Until today he'd never found a woman whose looks turned him inside out in just one short meeting. In fact he'd doubted if such a woman even existed. But this afternoon, a pair of translucent green eyes had caught him completely off guard.

Throughout the eleven years he'd been away from home in Paris, he'd enjoyed several intimate relationships with beautiful women. But he'd never experienced this instant, intense, earthy kind of attraction to a woman, not even when he'd been a teenager. And he sure as hell hadn't seen a woman like her show up for work at the vineyard before.

After putting on a robe, he went to the kitchen to make himself a sandwich. While he ate, he phoned Etienne with an update and told him not to worry, Dominic would continue to cover for him and told him to get better. After hanging up, he needed a distraction. He turned on the TV to watch the news, but nothing helped get his mind off Nathalie Fournier.

She was on some kind of mission. He was certain of it. Though a pharmacist, maybe she had an ambitious streak and did freelancing undercover for a newspaper or a wine industry magazine to make extra money.

He wished his cousin Raoul was home so they could talk. They were closer than brothers and always confided in each other. But Raoul and his father, Matthieu, the comptroller of the company, were in Saint Tropez at a vintners' conference and they wouldn't be back until Sunday night.

Any conversation would have to wait until Monday. *And then what, Dominic?*

Maybe some politician was paying a lot of money for her to get an exclusive on the vineyard. Was it hoped that her digging would turn up something she could expose concerning the migrants who worked at the Fontesquieu vineyard? No one would suspect her under the guise of a pharmacist, of all things.

He supposed anything was possible and didn't like what he was thinking. Half a dozen ideas of what she might be up to percolated in his mind, as his domineering grandfather was always guarding against trespassers.

Dominic's thoughts turned to his autocratic grandfather who'd been born with a *divine right of kings* syndrome. He felt a bleak expression cross over his features. The austere man's dictatorial personality had forced the whole family to live under his thumb. He'd forced arranged marriages for all his six sons and daughters, and insisted they all live and work together at the massive chateau, determined to keep it all in the family.

Armand had screwed up more lives than Dominic dared count. Under his tutelage, Dominic's own father and mother, Gaston and Vivienne, had put unbearable pressure on him and his siblings to marry certain moneyed, elite people they'd picked out for them. At eighteen, Dominic had refused to be told what to do.

No one in the family—including his parents—had had a good or happy marriage, souring Dominic's taste for the institution. Early on he'd made up his mind to study business and carve out his own future. It had been imperative he get away from the family dynamics to survive. His dreams had gone far beyond being a vintner and he'd left home for Paris under the threat of being disinherited, but he hadn't cared.

He'd begged his brother to go with him, but Etienne

had held back, too unsure to challenge their father and grandfather. Their older sister, Quinette, had already been married off.

Ultimately, Etienne stayed and Dominic had left alone, putting himself through college. After graduation he'd studied investment banking in Paris and, in time, he'd worked for a firm there where he'd made a considerable fortune in investments, coming home only for vacations and various events.

He would have stayed there permanently, but four months ago he'd received a frantic call from his mother that his father was seriously ill with pneumonia and might die. Dominic had intended to return to Vence only temporarily but his grandfather immediately insisted Dominic take over his father's position as funds manager while the older man was ill.

Still hesitant to remain in Vence, it was Raoul, now vice president in charge of marketing and sales for the Fontesquieu Corporation, who'd been the one to beg Dominic to take the job and not go back to Paris.

The two of them had been best friends growing up, always watching out for one another. Over the years they'd always stayed in touch, Raoul visiting Paris when he could. In the end, Dominic hadn't been able to refuse Raoul and so had stayed on while his father was recovering.

He was no fool though. Ever since his return, he'd known his grandfather had an ulterior motive in wanting Dominic to take over the management of funds. Because of a bad year of frost and rain two years ago, the vineyards in France had suffered severe financial losses and even their family had been impacted despite their assets in other businesses.

Dominic knew his father and grandfather were plotting for him to marry Corinne Herlot, who'd bring the fabulous Herlot industrial fortune with her. She'd been at several family parties, but he could never be interested and had planned to leave for Paris by the time the harvest was over.

At least that was what he'd intended *until* today when Nathalie Fournier had appeared. Now there was no way in this world could he leave yet…

Nathalie could hear the sound of jazz outside the swinging doors of what turned out to be the Guinguet bistro. There were people going in and out, enjoying the balmy Friday night air with its hint of fruit from the vineyards. She could well understand the lure this atmosphere had held for her stepsister.

Easing past couples, Nathalie walked inside the crowded establishment filled with small round tables and people slow dancing to the music. In the romantic atmosphere, she realized she hadn't had a date since breaking up with Guy three months ago.

It had hurt that he wouldn't want to take on anyone else's child, whether it was Alain or a child they might adopt after marriage. She couldn't imagine a childless union, but knew that adoption wasn't an option for everyone. She'd hoped Guy would be open to it but he couldn't have made his feelings against it clearer.

She'd learned of her condition at the age of twenty. Nathalie had ovulated only once by then. That was seven years ago. Since that time, she'd ovulated only twice. After what had happened with Guy, her natural worry was that any man she would meet in the future might have reservations about adoption, but she couldn't think about that now. Nathalie knew it had been the right decision to stop seeing Guy and didn't regret it.

Her mind kept going over what had happened to Antoinette. Her stepsister had fallen madly in love with a man she'd met in this very bistro. She'd loved him so much she'd had his baby.

Today Nathalie felt certain she'd met her stepsister's lover inside that tent. One look at him and she'd understood the chemistry. Love at first sight, sweeping Antoinette away. But clearly the fire had been only on her stepsister's part because he'd disappeared on her.

He couldn't have known he'd left her pregnant, could he? After meeting him, Nathalie knew he was the kind of man who could have any woman he wanted. Antoinette had likely been a dalliance for a month, then nothing more.

Now that Nathalie had met him, she feared that if he was Alain's father, he wouldn't want anything to do with a baby he hadn't intended to sire. Nathalie was beginning to think this had been a terrible idea and she should leave this whole thing alone. Alain had a surfeit of love from her and his grandmother. That would have to be enough.

"Mademoiselle?"

A man's voice caused Nathalie to turn around. She'd been admiring some of the paintings of the Fontesquieu chateau and gardens adorning the walls.

"Perhaps you remember me?"

She blinked. "Yes. You were the man handing out applications earlier today."

"That's right. When I saw you walk in alone just now, I thought I'd say hello and offer to buy you a drink. My table is right here."

This was probably how it had happened for Antoinette. Her lover had approached her in exactly the same way. Nathalie had to do some fast thinking. If she accepted the invite, she could at least learn the name of the man who had interviewed her. But she wasn't attracted to this man and didn't want him to misunderstand.

"Thank you, but I only came in to look around."

"You can do that right here." He pulled out a bistro chair for her so she would sit down. Then he took the other seat. "Have you been in here before?"

"Never."

"My name is Paul Cortier, by the way."

"I'm Nathalie Fournier."

"*Eh, bien*, Nathalie, please allow me to order you the specialty of the house, although you may not like it. Guinguet is an acquired taste."

"Guinguet? Like the name of the bistro?"

"*C'est exacte.*" He signaled for a waiter who took their order. "The word comes from the *guinguettes* that were popular drinking places on the outskirts of Paris years ago. They served local sour white wine, a tradition this bistro keeps up."

"Who makes the sour white wine here?"

"The Fontesquieu Vineyards."

"Of course. Your employer."

"That's right. They make enough of it to keep the owner here in business."

"Even though their grapes are red?"

Paul chuckled. "There are lots of secrets about red grapes I'd be happy to explain to you on another occasion. Perhaps on a tour of the winery itself? I'd be happy to arrange to show you personally."

She shook her head. "Thank you, but just so you know, I'm not interested in a relationship with anyone, Paul." It was the truth.

He squinted at her. "At least you're honest."

The waiter brought them each a small goblet of pale white wine. After he walked away, Paul lifted his glass. "Try it and let me know what you think."

Nathalie, who didn't actually like wine, took a sip, then struggled not to make a face.

Paul laughed. "Somehow I knew that would be your reaction. It's not for everyone. But since you'll be helping with the harvest, I thought you'd like a sample. Sort of a christening for you."

She took another sip to please him. "I may not be hired."

"Unless you have a police record, I don't see any problem. Please tell me you don't." He was a charming flirt who never gave up.

She chuckled. "Not as far as I know."

"That's the best news I've had since I handed you an application."

"I guess I'll find out Monday morning if I made the cut. My interview didn't last long since the man saw on the application that I knew nothing about grape picking."

He cocked his head. "Is that true?"

"Yes, but I think it would be interesting to learn."

"It's hard work."

"Ooh. I'm sure there's a great deal to learn and endure." She took one more sip, but knew she could never acquire a taste for it. "Now I hope you don't mind, but I have to get going. When you spoke to me, I had only come in here to take a look around because one of the people in line told me about this place. It was very nice of you to buy me a drink." There was no sign of the striking French god who'd interviewed her earlier.

"I'm sorry you have to go. Let me walk you out."

"That won't be necessary."

"No problem. I'm leaving too." He cleared their way through the crowds and walked her to her car, where she got in.

She spoke to him through the open window. "If I'm hired, we'll probably see each other again."

"I'm planning on it. Otherwise I'll ask my boss why you didn't get the job. He'll go to Dominic for an explanation."

"Dominic?"

"Dominic Fontesquieu. He's one of the family heads who interviewed you earlier today."

*What?*

"He rarely does any interviewing, but his brother, Etienne Fontesquieu, director of the vineyard, has been ill. If there was a problem with you, Gregoire will get it straightened out with Etienne so you will be hired. You can trust me on that."

"Thank you very much, Paul. *Bonne nuit.*"

# CHAPTER TWO

NATHALIE DROVE AWAY with her heart in her throat. Could Alain be the son of Dominic Fontesquieu? A man who came from one of the most prominent, titled families in France?

Had it been an illicit affair on his part that he didn't want getting back to his family? Had he sworn Antoinette to silence because of his name?

Maybe he'd been married and couldn't afford a scandal that would make the news. If he were divorced now, it could explain the lack of a wedding ring. Or maybe he didn't like to wear rings. She wondered if he'd kept his name a secret from Antoinette.

Suffused with more questions than before, Nathalie drove faster than usual, needing answers. Fifteen minutes later, she entered the house and found her mother in the family room watching TV while she worked on some embroidered blocks for a quilt. All was quiet, which meant Alain was asleep.

Nathalie sat down on the couch. "I'm glad you're still up, Maman, because I've got something of vital importance to tell you."

Her mother took one look at her and turned off the TV.

"Please don't be upset with me if I tell you something that might make you angry."

"Why would you say that?"

For the next ten minutes, Nathalie told her about her talk with Claire a month ago and her plan to look for Alain's father. She explained about her visit to the Fontesquieu vineyard to apply for work, and ended by telling her about today's discovery.

"This afternoon I found a man I believe could be Alain's father and learned his name."

Her mother leaned forward. "Good heavens, Nathalie. What do you mean you think you've found him?"

When Nathalie told her what had happened today, her mother jumped to her feet looking startled. "Alain could be a Fontesquieu?"

"Yes. If the man who interviewed me is the one, I can see why Antoinette fell for him. He's...so incredibly attractive, I can't believe it." Nathalie had been mesmerized by him.

"I've never heard you talk this way about a man before."

She drew in a breath. "That's because I've never met one like him in my whole life. It would explain what happened to Antoinette." She cleared her throat. "On the drive back just now, I decided that if I'm hired on Monday, I'll work there long enough to find out his marital status. If he's divorced or single, then I'll approach him. But if he's married and has children, then for the sake of his wife and family, I'm not sure how I'll inform him."

"Oh, Nathalie." Her voice shook. "Darling... You're going to have to be careful without positive proof."

"There *is* proof if you compare the two of them, even without a DNA test. The resemblance is uncanny. And there's something else. Dominic Fontesquieu has the same small birthmark as Alain."

"I'm afraid that still doesn't prove paternity."

"You're right."

Her mother seemed anxious.

"Don't worry, Maman. I promise to talk everything over with you before I make any kind of a move."

"You honestly believe this Dominic could be the one?"

"In my opinion, yes. Just think—if he knew he had a son and wanted him—how wonderful it would be for Alain to get to know at least one of his parents. He's such a treasure, I would think any father worth his salt would give anything to claim him."

"I agree, but I'm afraid to credit any of this because—"

Nathalie got up and hugged her. "Because it would be a dream come true if Alain's father wanted him and they could be united."

Her mother nodded. "But darling, it could be a nightmare if there isn't a good ending to this story."

"I know, Maman. Not every man would welcome that kind of news. I won't do anything until we're in total agreement."

Dominic was already awake at five Monday morning when his phone rang. He checked the caller ID. Something had to be wrong for his brother to call this early.

"Etienne? Have you taken a turn for the worse?"

"*Non, non,* but the doctor won't let me go to work for a few more days. *Desolé*, Dom." His voice still sounded an octave lower than normal.

"I'll be happy to fill in until you're better and will help Gregoire."

"Thanks, brother."

Nothing could have made Dominic happier since he wanted to get to know Mademoiselle Fournier. "Stay in bed and relax. Theo did all the background checks on Friday's applicants and informed Gregoire. No red flags on anyone."

Which meant none on Mademoiselle Fournier, whose image refused to leave his mind. She'd never been in trouble. No parking infractions or car accidents, no warrants out for her arrest. He hadn't really expected anything negative to come up on her but relief had swept through him when he learned she was squeaky clean, even though he still had the feeling she'd come to the vineyard for a hidden reason. He planned to get to the bottom of it.

"That's good considering we need workers," Etienne murmured. "This is a bigger harvest than last year, *Dieu merci.* Such news will make Grand-père happy."

"I'll drive to the tent now."

"Paul will be there to help. Thanks, Dom."

*"Au revoir."*

After hanging up, Dominic quickly showered and shaved. On his way out the door dressed in jeans and a fresh white shirt, he grabbed a plum and a baguette to hold him over until lunch.

Hurrying to the main garage on the property, he picked one of the trucks rigged with gear to help the workers and headed for the tent at the base of the western *terroirs*. Judging by the temperature outside, it was going to be another hot day, which meant the bulging grapes needed picking now.

Mademoiselle Fournier was in for some hard, menial work. By the end of the harvest he'd discover why she'd really come to the vineyard. With more excitement than he should be feeling, he parked near the tent where Gregoire and Paul were addressing the latest crop of new workers.

Though dressed like the others in rainproof layered clothing and gum shoes to protect themselves from the morning dew, she stood out from everyone else. Her height plus the feminine mold of her body made it impossible for him to look anywhere else.

This morning she'd tied her shimmering hair back at the nape of her neck with a band, revealing high cheekbones and a softly rounded chin. He'd studied the enticing shape of her mouth on Friday and the image had stayed with him all weekend, making him wonder how he'd last until he'd be close to her again.

He parked next to the other two trucks and waited until Gregoire gave final instructions to the workers. One by one they climbed into the truck beds with the aid of ladders. From here they'd be driven to the vineyard needing attention.

At that point Dominic got out of his own truck. He lowered the tailgate and attached his ladder so the last ten workers being ushered by Paul could climb in.

He was happy to see the pharmacist among them and watched as Paul said something to her that produced a smile before she climbed in. Paul was a gossip, the last person Dominic wanted around their new worker. He would make sure that ended fast, he thought as he shut the tailgate.

Gregoire waved to Dominic before driving into the vines. Paul followed and Dominic brought up the rear. When they reached the designated *terroir*, he shut off the motor and walked around to open the tailgate.

After the workers used the ladder to get down, he climbed up and opened the locker. "Before you follow the others, I'm handing out scissors, gloves and knee pads for all of you to use while you work here. For those of you who have done this before, you know the gloves help prevent stains, but it's your choice whether to wear them or not. I presume you've brought water bottles and sunscreen." Everyone nodded and waited their turn.

"At the end of the day, more trucks will be here to take you back to the tent area."

In a few minutes they were ready and followed Gregoire and Paul's groups, lining up and down the rows of grapes to get started. Dominic took a walk along another row, satisfied to see that the trailer had arrived for the collectors who gathered the picked grapes to transport to the winery.

When Paul had to leave to help some of the other workers, Dominic took advantage of the moment to catch Mademoiselle Fournier alone. She was kneeling on the pad and had started cutting grapes. He noticed her gloves stuck in one of the back pockets of her jeans.

"*Bonjour*, mademoiselle."

She looked up in surprise, giving him the full view of her light green eyes. The woman's beauty took his breath away.

"*Bonjour*, monsieur."

"You prefer not to use gloves?"

"Maybe I'll put them on later, but I need to practice without them first to get a feel for the work."

He was surprised as that's what he would have advised. Paul had obviously shown her what to do and already she'd put some grapes in the bucket provided.

"Did you apply sunscreen already?"

"I did at the last minute."

"That's good. The heat is already building. You don't want to get a sunburn before the end of your first day. You'll also likely find you need an over-the-counter painkiller to deal with aches and pains tonight."

An enticing smile broke out on her lovely face. "I brought some just in case. That's very kind of you to be concerned."

"*He*, Dominic."

"*Salut*, Paul." The other man had come back. Dominic still held her green gaze. "Just remember not to kill yourself off today. You'll need your strength for tomorrow."

She smiled. "I appreciate the warning. *Merci*, monsieur."

Dominic nodded to Paul, then walked toward the truck in the distance. On his way back to the office, he ate his snacks, but he'd need coffee. To his relief Theo had already made it for both of them.

No sooner had Dominic poured himself a cup and walked into his private office to get busy than Raoul arrived. All the family offices were in the same building.

"You're a sight for sore eyes, *mon vieux*. Come on in and shut the door."

"I was hoping you'd be here." He'd brought a cup of coffee with him and planted himself on a leather chair opposite Dominic's desk.

"Anything new at the conference in Saint Tropez?"

Raoul shook his head. "The Provencal vineyards seem to be doing marginally better, but it's going to take years before every vintner in France recoups losses from two years ago. *Dieu merci* for the personal investments you've helped me make."

"You're not worried about money, are you?"

"I might be."

"That sounded cryptic."

"Let's just say I'd like you to go over my accounts and let me know what I'm worth. I might need some of it before long."

Dominic sat forward. "I'll look into it before the day is out. But promise me you're not thinking of doing something drastic."

"Like what?"

"I don't know. Like leaving the way *I* did, maybe?"

He knew his cousin's marriage had been in shambles from the start, and that both Raoul and his wife carried a deep sorrow from losing their little girl, Celine, who had died at one month from a bad heart. Dominic wondered how much longer the two could keep up pretensions.

"My greatest regret is that I didn't go to Paris with you years ago. Let's face it, Dom. You were the only one in the family with the guts to get out before being swallowed alive."

"But I'm back now." For how long he didn't know. It depended on Nathalie Fournier, who'd swept into his life on Friday, bringing a beauty and charm that had put some kind of a spell on him. His desire to get to know her had stoked an unprecedented hunger in him, though his cousin didn't know that.

Raoul stared hard at him. "Yes, but you're still free to make your own decisions. Nobody owns you and your life is intact."

"No one owns you, Raoul."

"You're right. I take ownership for my guilt and mistakes with Sabine."

Dom let out a troubled sigh. "As you can see, the tentacles brought me back temporarily."

"The day you came home was my salvation."

"You're mine, Raoul. Whatever you're planning, don't leave."

"Not yet anyway. I need to know where I stand financially before I do anything."

"I'll get busy on it." Something serious was going on with Raoul.

"Thanks. Now enough about me. I hear Etienne is still sick."

"He's finally getting better. I'm filling in for him a while longer, but something odd has come up I want to talk to you about."

"Go ahead."

Dominic told him everything, but didn't reveal the strength of his attraction to the pharmacist. "Am I being paranoid that she's up to something questionable?"

Raoul studied him for a minute. "Being an undercover freelance reporter is a big stretch from being a pharmacist. But I'd trust your instincts as they're rarely wrong. If you feel something isn't right, then it isn't. What's your plan?"

"I'm going to get to know her."

"After a few days you'll know if she's out for a scoop on the business. It has happened before. Grand-père forced the perpetrators to pay stiff fines and do jail time."

"That's our grandfather." Dominic didn't want her to have to face that type of punishment for trespassing. If that was what she was doing.

Just then, Raoul received a text. After reading it, he looked up. "I've got to get over to my office."

"I'll call you tonight."

"What would I do without you in my corner?"

On that note, he dashed off.

Dominic sat back, pondering his cousin's counsel to follow his instincts about Miss Fournier. He planned to find out what made her tick.

After pulling all the information on Raoul's investments, he did some figures and prepared a form to give his cousin. By afternoon he'd finished his work, so he drove his car back out to the *terroir*. Dominic made sure he'd shown up early enough to catch sight of the woman who was constantly on his mind.

Paul and Gregoire kept moving up and down the

rows to help the workers. At 4:30 p.m. he saw her and several others leave the vineyard, though she walked down the road rather than climb into one of the trucks.

Dominic called to her as he pulled his car alongside her on the road. "Mademoiselle Fournier?"

She swung toward him, her eyes lighting up when she saw him behind the wheel. "*Bonsoir*, monsieur."

"Since I'm on my way back to the chateau, allow me to drive you to your mobile home."

"Oh—thank you very much." It surprised him that without hesitation she climbed in the other side with her backpack.

He started driving at a slow pace. "How was your first day?"

A fetching smile broke out on her flushed face. "You don't want to hear about it."

Her comment made him laugh. "It had to be a change from preparing prescriptions for people."

"Working here with the vines is another existence. No matter how sore I am, it makes you part of this world of living greenery." She had a unique way of putting things that seemed to confirm his suspicions that she could be a writer. She darted him a smile. "How was *your* day?"

Was she trying to get information from him? "You'd be bored to tears." In truth he'd accomplished less than usual and it was all because of the beautiful woman sitting next to him.

"I'm sure that's not true. For my part, I already feel a camaraderie with some of the other workers. The Lopez family next to me is so cheerful."

Dominic remembered interviewing them after she'd left the tent. "It doesn't sound like you're ready to quit yet."

"Oh, no. I'm in for the count."

"Why?" More than ever he wanted an answer to that question.

"I learned as a child that way back when one of your ancestors was titled and given this land. Not very many people can claim a heritage like yours. It made fascinating reading."

All her answers sounded truthful. "Why fascinating?"

"When I was a little girl, I grew up on fairy tales. Your chateau is the embodiment of those painted on the covers of the books I loved. The thought of working in your vineyard sounded intriguing. Is it true your grandfather holds the title of Duc?"

"It's a defunct title." Maybe she was writing an historical account for a publisher and wanted information from the CEO himself. Did she hope for permission from Dominic?

"Even so, it adds a certain mystique from the past that makes you and your family seem out of the ordinary. When I was at the Guinguet, I noticed several paintings of the chateau and sculptured gardens hanging on the walls. It's very cool."

Minute by minute she was enamoring him. Eventually they reached the park. "Where is your mobile home?"

"It's the third one in the second row."

He kept driving and pulled up behind a blue car. Now

that he knew where to find her, he didn't want to let her go. She had a vitality that intrigued him. Much as he wanted to take her to dinner this evening, he knew she was exhausted after her first day.

"Voilà, mademoiselle. Home in one piece."

"Bed is going to feel good tonight."

He could imagine. "I'll see you tomorrow."

"Thank you more than you know."

She got out of the car and he watched her until she waved to him and let herself inside the mobile home. When he was convinced she was safely inside, he backed up and left the park. Tomorrow he had plans for the two of them.

# CHAPTER THREE

TUESDAY MORNING NATHALIE woke up at 5:00 a.m. with new aches and pains. Picking grapes was a killer, but she was determined to see this through. Whether he was Alain's father or not, the hope of seeing Dominic again was all she could think about. The man had already captivated her. He had a polish that attracted her to him like mad.

After showering, she hurriedly dressed and tied her hair back, covering herself in sunscreen. After eating breakfast, she packed a sandwich, fruit and water in her backpack, where she'd left the knee pads and scissors. Then she stole from the house.

Right now Alain was still sound asleep. So was her mom, who wouldn't open the pharmacy until eight. She'd hired Denis Volant, another pharmacist from Nice, to help run things while she was undercover at the vineyard. Minerve, the woman who tended Alain, was scheduled to arrive at the house at 7:30 a.m.

Already the air was warm and once again it seemed that it would prove to be a hot day. Nathalie drove along the road to the mobile home and parked her car around the side. After freshening up inside, she left and started walking toward the workers' tent at the vineyard to wait for the truck.

But that meant Paul would be there. Having no desire to encourage him, she changed her mind. As she started out for the *terroir* on foot, she was surprised when a familiar sleek black Renault sedan drove past her.

She glanced at the driver. The sight of Dominic Fontesquieu caused her heart to leap. Everything about him spoke of sophistication and a privileged life most people would never know anything about. It was there in his manner and speech.

He pulled to the side ahead of her on the roadway and got out of the car. In jeans and a pale gray crew neck, his male charisma was devastating. Those black eyes played over her.

"You're still alive," he murmured in that deep voice she loved.

She smiled. "Barely."

"That's honest at least."

"You did warn me."

His hands went to his hips in a totally male stance. "Then I suggest you get in my car now to reserve your strength."

"That's very nice of you, but I don't want to put you out."

"Not at all. I can't allow word to get around that one of our new pickers has been worked to exhaustion after her first day."

She laughed gently. After hoping she'd see him

today, she didn't dare let this precious opportunity get away. "You're a lifesaver. Thank you, monsieur."

"My name is Dominic." He opened the passenger door for her so she could get in carrying her backpack. He'd just thrown her a lifeline to get to know him better.

The interior smelled of the soap he used, teasing her senses. In a minute he'd climbed behind the wheel and they were off to the *terroir* in the distance. "I pass by here several times a day checking on the carriers. If ever you need a ride, just let me know."

Encouraged by the offer, she said, "I might take you up on that since by the end of the day I'm quite sure I won't have enough strength to climb in one of the trucks. You weren't kidding when you said I'd need painkiller."

"The pain will pass."

"I hope so. I've never appreciated the kind of hard work involved. While I was cutting grapes, I marveled to think of all the care needed to keep the vineyard healthy and thriving. No one should complain about the price of wine. Ninety-nine percent of the world has no clue what goes into making it."

He darted her an amused glance. "That's quite a testimonial. What's your favorite kind?"

"I don't have one. I dislike the taste of wine and much prefer to eat the grapes."

A burst of deep male laughter came out of him.

"I know that sounds crazy, especially when you work for a vineyard, but I just don't care for it, and I really despise the sour white wine they serve at the Guinguet."

"You mentioned that yesterday."

Did it bring back memories of being there with Antoinette?

"That's right. One of the workers suggested I go there to relax, so Friday evening I drove there and looked around before driving home. Monsieur Cortier saw me and asked if I'd like to try their famous sour wine." She shook her head. "It was awful. He said it comes from the Fontesquieu winery, but I can't imagine anyone wanting to drink it."

"I don't like it either."

"You're not offended by my frank speaking?"

"Not at all."

Too soon they'd arrived at the *terroir*. Afraid he would realize how much she was enjoying their conversation, she got out of the car. "You saved my life giving me this ride."

"It was my pleasure. I'd like to get to know you better—why don't I come by at noon to take you to the winery for lunch? Since you don't like wine, it ought to be an interesting experience for you to see how the other half lives."

His smile thrilled her. "You'd do that?"

"A man has to eat. I'd rather have company."

"So would I."

Dominic Fontesquieu had a sense of humor and was incredibly easy to talk to. When she'd been hired on here, she'd been intent on finding Alain's father. She'd never expected that she'd meet a man who swept her away with every look and smile. The fact that he could have been Antoinette's lover made this whole situation more complicated. "*A bientôt*, Dominic."

He leaned across the seat. "I'm sorry, I don't recall your name."

Her heart thumped. "It's Nathalie."

"*A bientôt*, Nathalie."

He'd just said he'd see her soon. Once again the sound of that low male voice wound its way to her insides.

A tremor of excitement raced through her as she shut the door and hurried toward the row where she'd been working. Without looking back, she could hear the engine as he drove away. Her hope to spend time with him was coming to fruition much sooner than she'd anticipated.

He'd said he wanted to get to know her better. He wasn't the only one. It shocked her how much she longed to be with him again. For someone of his status, there wasn't an atom of arrogance in him, which made him so appealing she couldn't get enough of him.

Before long the trucks came with the workers and she plunged into her day. But knowing Dominic would be picking her up at noon carried her through the rest of her morning. His irresistible charm had seeped its way beneath her skin and she found herself thinking constantly about him. That was a side effect she hadn't anticipated when she'd considered trying to look for Alain's father.

But therein lay a problem. She needed to learn a bit more about him before she revealed why she'd come to the vineyard in the first place. That meant she had to close off her personal feelings about him because this was all about Alain. She couldn't let it be about her desire for the man himself. She just couldn't!

"Did you know you're talking to yourself?"

She snipped another bunch of grapes in frustration before glancing at Paul. *"Bonjour."*

"How about going out with me after work tonight? I know you don't want a relationship, but can't we be friends at least?"

"Of course, but I'm afraid I have plans."

"Is there a night when you'll be free?"

Nathalie wasn't interested, but didn't want to be rude since he was one of the supervisors here. "Maybe Thursday evening right after work? Get a pizza? I saw a pizzeria near the Guinguet."

He nodded. "Thursday it is. I'll pick you up."

"No, no. I'll meet you there in my car."

She heard him sigh. "Have it your way."

"Thanks for understanding. *Ciao*, Paul."

When he moved on, she got back to work. As for Dominic, Nathalie realized she couldn't allow the situation about Alain to go on much longer before telling him why she'd come.

Nathalie kept checking her watch. When it was noon, she grabbed her backpack and hurried out to the road. Dominic sat in his car waiting for her. She couldn't believe how excited she was to see and talk to him.

He reached across the seat and opened the door for her. When she climbed in, he put her pack in the back, then flashed her a smile that melted her bones.

"You came!" The white crew neck shirt brought out

his olive skin. He was such a striking man with that black hair and all-seeing black eyes, she could hardly breathe.

"As if I wouldn't," his voice grated and they took off down the road.

"I'm so lucky to be whisked away in the middle of the day."

"It's a treat for me too."

Something was going on here. She knew how she was feeling about him, about how she'd felt the moment she'd met him. It was like an explosion going off inside her. If she wasn't mistaken, he was just as attracted and couldn't stay away from her.

Was he the man Antoinette had met? Her conflict was growing. How ironic that Nathalie had hoped to find Alain's father, yet now that she thought Dominic could be the one, a part of her didn't want him to be the man her stepsister had loved.

Before long they approached a chateau that looked older and smaller than the main chateau. There were clusters of cars parked outside. Dominic drove around the back of it. "We'll eat lunch first, then I'll take you on a tour before you have to return to work."

After he'd helped her out of the car, Dominic took her inside a vaulted room with some interesting framed documents and pictures to do with wine. The place was filled with tourists seated at tables drinking wine and enjoying lunch.

Once he'd found them a table in the corner, he deserted her long enough to talk to the aproned man behind the ancient-looking bar. Armed with two bottles of Perrier water and two *croques monsieurs*, he returned.

She took a bite of the melted ham and cheese sandwich. "Mmm. I haven't had one of these in ages. It's delicious. Does every winery offer food like this?"

"Not many."

"The sales must skyrocket after someone has been here."

He finished his food. "That's the idea." His eyes gleamed as he looked at her. "I can get you coffee if you'd prefer it."

"Thank you, but water is much better while I'm working."

"I couldn't agree more. When you're ready, I'll show you around the winery."

"Let's go now. I'd love to see everything possible before I have to get back. I don't want Gregoire to think I'm taking advantage."

"We can't have that." That slow smile made her pulse race.

She held on to her half-full bottle of water and followed him through a door that led to the heart of the building. The huge vaulted rooms filled with machinery and barrels overwhelmed her. The place reminded her of a scientist's laboratory all devoted to producing sumptuous wines that kept the Fontesquieu Corporation one of the top winemakers in the world.

Dominic smiled at her while they walked from room to room. "You're not saying anything."

That was because his native intelligence pretty much staggered her. "I'm too busy marveling over this amazing world. I'm afraid I feel guilty that I don't like wine."

A chuckle escaped him. "Your liver is much healthier leaving it alone."

"I don't think I dare quote you," she quipped, loving this hour spent with him while he explained the winemaking process, overwhelming her with knowledge he'd been learning since birth. He knew so much about everything that it seemed he could go on forever, but it was past time to leave. "I should get back to work."

"I was afraid you'd say that," he whispered. "I'll explain to Gregoire it was my fault that you're late. Come this way."

Dominic led her to another exit not used by the public and they walked around the building to his car. As he cupped her elbow, his touch sent a dart of electricity through her body, making her come alive.

He helped her in before driving her back to the *terroir*. After he stopped, he said, "Since I don't want this day to end, why don't I pick you up after work?"

She sensed he wanted to be with her as much as she wanted to be with him. It was hard to believe this was really happening. "Only if you have time."

"I'll make it," he declared in a firm tone of voice that sent an unmistakable message of his desire to be with her.

"Thank you for lunch and the tour, Dominic. To be shown around by an expert has been a highlight for me I'll never forget." She meant what she'd said and knew she sounded breathless.

"That makes two of us."

He handed her the backpack before she got out of the car. Their hands touched, once again making her feel weak with longing. Nathalie walked to the row where she'd been snipping grapes. When she reached her spot, she finished the bottled water and got busy, counting the minutes until she could be with Dominic again.

When the heat reached its zenith, Nathalie checked her watch. It was four thirty. Quitting time. She gathered up her things, so eager to see Dominic, it was ridiculous. But after reaching the road, there was no sign of his car. Undoubtedly something had held him up because she knew he'd had every intention of coming for her.

Disappointed, she avoided the trucks and started to walk toward the mobile home, anxious to get out of the hot sun. Three-quarters of the way back, she saw the black Renault coming toward her. It shouldn't thrill her to see him, but it did. She was in so much trouble. When she'd followed through on her plan, she hadn't considered being enthralled by the man she'd been searching for.

He stopped and got out. "I'm sorry to be late, but it couldn't be helped."

"Please don't apologize. I know you're a busy man."

In seconds he'd opened the passenger door. This time their arms brushed as she climbed inside, making her acutely aware of him. The AC felt wonderful and she was relieved she didn't have to walk. He made a U-turn and drove them back toward the mobile park.

He pulled up behind her blue Peugeot. "Why don't you go in and freshen up, then we'll drive somewhere for a bite to eat before I bring you back here. Lunch didn't fill me and I'm starving."

"I'm hungry too. Thanks. I'll be out soon."

His invitation opened up a whole evening where she could learn more about his personal life. Totally intoxicated by him, Nathalie slid out of the car and unlocked the door of the mobile home. She hurried inside and took a quick shower. After putting on jeans and a blouse, she brushed her hair.

Her body trembled on the way out to his car because her feelings for him were growing to the point he was all she could think about. She hurried back to the car and got in. "Where are we going?"

"I've ordered us some takeout so you can stay in the car and rest while we eat."

A soft laugh escaped her lips. "Only someone who has picked grapes before would understand how I feel."

He started the car and drove them out to the main road into Vence. "It was my first job. I think I was about four when my *papa* walked me and my five-year-old brother, Etienne, to the vineyard and showed us what to do."

She turned to him. "Did you live near this one when you were little?"

In the next breath, he said, "Are you going to tell me that after Paul plied you with sour wine, he didn't tell you who I am?"

Oh, boy. She'd walked right into that one. "No. I was only trying to be discreet. Paul *did* say you were a Fontesquieu, but the last thing I've wanted to do is presume anything and he didn't go into detail."

Dominic didn't respond. Within seconds he turned a corner and pulled up in front of a café. "I'll be right out.

After I get back, you can tell me why you really came to the vineyard for work you don't need."

She groaned inwardly. Nathalie wasn't wrong about his being strongly attracted to her, but it was clear he hadn't believed her reason for being here.

He soon returned with their food and headed toward the Fontesquieu estate once more. After he pulled to a stop and shut off the engine, he handed her cannelloni, salad and an espresso.

"Thank you, Dominic. This smells and looks delicious." But her heart was pounding so hard, she feared he could hear it.

He tucked into his meal before turning to her. "Now, how about telling me what newspaper or wine magazine you're working for undercover?"

Her heart plummeted. "Is that why you showed me around the winery?"

"I took you there because I wanted to be with you, and because I was hungry. But in case you were after a story, I thought I'd show you the inner workings, something not everyone is allowed to see. If you've been hired by a newspaper to find out how the migrant workers are treated at the vineyard, I wanted to give you a favorable impression."

She ate her food, trying to find the right words. Obviously their family had been bothered by infiltrators before. Nathalie couldn't blame him for being suspicious since she didn't meet the profile of the normal picker.

"I'm not a spy, Dominic. Your assumptions are understandable, but they would be wrong about me," she said in a quiet voice. "Is it impossible for you to imagine that I simply want to work here for a few weeks to enjoy a new experience?"

His black eyes bored into hers, reminding her of Alain. "Yes. Our background check proves you're a full-time pharmacist. If you're truly not here undercover, why don't you tell me the truth about why you chose to work at this specific vineyard for a few weeks?"

She finished her espresso. "This is embarrassing."

"I'm listening." He'd never taken his eyes off her.

"Three months ago I broke up with a pharmaceutical distributor. We met in graduate school in Nice several years ago and continued to see each other off and on. After Christmas I thought maybe he could be the one. But in time I realized we were wrong for each other." Guy's reaction to her being unable to have children had worried her that another man would probably feel the same way. She couldn't help wondering if the man sitting next to her would reject her for the same reason. "Since I'd already arranged my vacation time for a trip we obviously did not end up taking, I decided to do something different that would bring me a little money, not cost me."

"Vintners are noted for paying lower wages," he murmured.

"Nevertheless, I need to save all I can for the future." Now came the lie. "After passing your vineyard, I saw that you were hiring workers for the three-week harvest and thought it would be a fascinating way for me to spend my vacation from the pharmacy.

"I also believed that working with the soil would be so different, it would be cathartic for me. There's nothing like a new challenge." Considering she was doing this for Alain's sake, she hoped lightning wouldn't strike her. "But you would have every right to tell me to walk away now."

"Is that what I'm doing?" he asked in a silky tone.

"No. I'm offering to go." She didn't have enough proof he could be Alain's father to confront him. "If you'll wait long enough for me to get my backpack, I'll return the equipment handed to me. The man running the mobile home park will be glad if I give up mine since there's always a demand for one." She started to get out.

"Wait—" he said, reaching for her arm. She felt his touch to her toes. "You're doing an excellent job, according to Gregoire's nightly reports. Forgive me for jumping to the wrong conclusion about you. It's just that there's nothing my grandfather dislikes more than someone who trespasses on the property for ulterior motives."

"Of course, and you had every right to be suspicious of me when it's clear I'm not desperate for a job."

*I'm only desperate for answers.*

"That's very generous of you," he murmured. "Maybe you won't believe me, but I'm sorry if I've offended you. Let's hope working with the vines might work its magic for you, even if you dislike the taste of wine." The sudden smile he flashed was enough to reduce her to jelly. "You're not fired, Nathalie."

His ability to admit he'd been wrong made her admire him more than he'd ever know, but she was also filled with raw guilt because she hadn't told him the real reason she'd come. All she needed was a little more information.

"Thank you for a second chance, and for buying me dinner."

"To prove I'm telling you the truth, I'd like to take you on a walk through the vineyard tomorrow evening after you've eaten. You mentioned you'd like to see more of it while we were at the winery. Will your aching joints be able to handle it?"

She turned to him. "There's nothing I'd love more," she whispered.

*"Jusqu'à demain soir,"* he whispered back.

Arriving back home, she climbed out of his car and rushed inside the mobile home, where he couldn't see her breakdown. Nathalie had to face the truth. It had been only a few days, but she'd already fallen hard for him. Love at first sight was no joke. Nothing like this had ever happened to her before.

It wasn't just his dashing dark looks or the background he'd come from. He was a man of extraordinary substance. There was a kind of nobility about him. That's what made it so difficult for her to understand his behavior if he'd had an affair with Antoinette.

If he was the one who'd fathered her child, how could he have disappeared on her stepsister with no explanation? Nathalie needed to learn the truth about him soon and not get carried away by her growing feelings for him.

He'd shaken her with his ability to see inside her and question her motives. She should have told him the truth, but had held back because of too little proof. One thing she knew by now. You didn't play games with a man like him.

Dominic's mind reeled as he drove home.

He'd wanted to believe Nathalie's explanation even though he felt she was still hiding something from him. Why it bothered him so much was a mystery to him. A virtual stranger couldn't possibly be this important to him no matter how beautiful or intriguing.

But the closer he got to the chateau, he knew that wasn't true. He'd been intimate with some attractive women over the years, yet nothing remotely like this had ever happened to him before.

Even if Nathalie was to disappear suddenly and he never saw her again, the fact that he could be swept away by her this fast had changed him in a fundamental way. Nathalie had lit a fire that wasn't going to go out.

It seemed there *was* a woman out there for him, one he wanted to get to know and would do whatever it took to do so. She was an original with a verve and freshness that was a constant delight to him. Her thoughts about everything fascinated him. If he believed in witches, he'd think she'd put him under a magical spell.

Dominic didn't know he could feel this way about a woman. Meeting her had revealed the real reason why he'd reached the age of twenty-nine and still hadn't married. Was it possible he'd unknowingly been waiting for her to come into his life?

He entered his apartment a different man. Needing more coffee, he went in the kitchen to fix it, then called his cousin and gave him the figures he wanted. Silence followed. "Raoul? Why aren't you saying anything?"

"I'm surprised that much money has accrued. It's all because of your expertise. But I'm afraid I may need more than that."

He took a deep breath. "Talk to me."

"When I got home from Saint Tropez Monday night, I told Sabine I was filing for divorce."

Dominic let out a sound, overjoyed for him. "That's the best news I've ever heard."

"Except that you don't know the bottom line."

He frowned. "What do you mean?"

"I can't go into it now. Can you meet me at our usual place Thursday evening to talk?"

"Of course."

"Suffice it to say all hell has broken loose. The family has already heard about it, and it's getting ugly."

"I've got your back all the way. You know what I mean."

"I do. Before we hang up, tell me about you."

"I wish I knew."

"Why do I have a feeling this is about Mademoiselle Fournier?"

He paced. "I was with her this morning, at lunch and after work."

"All in one day? You've got to be kidding me!"

"I know I sound like I've lost my mind. She's not who I thought she was, but I still don't know why she came here."

"And I can tell you're not going to give up until you get answers. I take it she's a knockout."

"You have no idea. I didn't know I could have feelings this fast for another woman."

"That's how it happened with me. One evening while I was checking on the inventory at the Guinguet I met Toinette. As you know, my world changed that night when I called and told you about her. But circumstances forced me to break off with her in order to marry Sabine. I've never been the same since. Thank heaven you're back home and not in Paris because I need to reveal a truth you don't know about yet. I'll tell you on Thursday. For now, I've got to go."

Raoul rang off before a puzzled Dominic could say goodbye. No matter how bad it got, he was thrilled Raoul had decided to get out of his marriage. He'd do whatever he could to help his cousin.

As for his own situation, before any more time passed, Dominic needed to talk to Corinne. He didn't want to put this off any longer. It wasn't fair to her to let her go on expecting an imminent marriage proposal. She was attractive. Dominic knew she'd meet another man, hopefully one who would love her for who she was, whether she came from money or not. She deserved to find true happiness. So did he.

Once he told her the truth and ended any thoughts her parents had put in her mind about marrying him, her pride might be hurt, but it was the only way to handle what their two families had tried to set up.

He had his own life to live. And now that he'd met Nathalie Fournier, he couldn't imagine her not being in his life.

# CHAPTER FOUR

"Maman?"

Wednesday evening had come. Dominic would be arriving shortly to show her around the vineyard. It was a beautiful evening and she was going crazy waiting for him so had called her mother to check in.

"Yes. What is it, darling?"

Nathalie had left work to eat dinner and was freshening up in the mobile home. She'd brushed her hair, leaving it loose, and wore a fresh pair of jeans and a yellow pullover. "I'll be home a little later than usual and don't want you to worry."

"That's all I've done since our talk. I don't think it's wise to keep this up. Either walk away now, or tell Dominic Fontesquieu why you're there."

"I will. I just need a little more information and to think everything through. If worse comes to worst and he demands an explanation, I'll tell him the truth. Depending on the outcome, I'll bring him to the house so he can see Alain for himself."

Her mother's sigh was telling. "You could be wrong and it could cause trouble."

"It won't come to that, Maman. When I get home, we'll talk."

After they hung up, her mother's concern ate away at her. Was Nathalie wrong about Dominic having been Antoinette's lover? Of course, the only way to find out was to ask him and hope he'd be honest with her.

But to approach him about such a sensitive matter was daunting. "Did you have a brief affair with a woman you met at the Guinguet during the harvest two and half years ago? If so, then I believe you could be the father of my deceased stepsister's son."

Deep in thought, she was startled by noise outside. He was here. A burst of adrenaline shot through her. She reached for her purse and hurried out the door. Dominic had parked his car behind hers and Nathalie climbed in the passenger side before he could get out.

"Hi," she said, knowing that once again she was out of breath. It happened every time she saw him. He smelled so good and had dressed in a blue sport shirt and khaki trousers. There could be no other man like him in existence.

His black eyes ranged over her, taking in every inch. "You look too beautiful for a woman who's been picking grapes all day."

"That isn't true, but I like hearing it."

"If you'd glance in a mirror, it would remove all doubt."

His words brought heat flooding to her cheeks. "Where are we going to go?"

"I thought we'd take a walk in one of the *terroirs* at

the upper elevation. It overlooks the land down to the sea for a spectacular view."

The male sight before her eyes was so spectacular, she was at a loss for words.

He backed around and drove down the road past the place where she picked grapes. When they came to a crossroads, he turned right and followed another road. It paralleled more rows of healthy vines for a long time, then rose until he pulled over to the side and parked.

"The grapes have all been picked here," she observed.

"That's right. They've turned a few days sooner because of the elevation. The *terroir* you're working on is one of the last that has to be denuded."

She shook her head. "There's so much to learn. Tonight the vines seem to be lined up like soldiers to the horizon. It's an amazing sight. If I were an artist, I'd like to paint the vineyard the way it looks right now. I love it."

"I love your descriptions of everything." The tone in his deep voice filled her with warmth. "This is my favorite spot in the whole vineyard."

After getting out of the car, she let out a soft cry. "I can see why, Dominic. This landscape is like a little part of heaven."

He grasped her hand as if claiming her. They started walking between two rows of vines. A gentle breeze bathed their bodies. "You know what Louis Pasteur once said. A bottle of wine contains more philosophy than all the books in the world."

"Fontesquieu wine," she corrected him. He squeezed

her hand a little harder. "I feel horribly guilty that I don't like the taste of wine."

"But you like the grapes." He gave her a meaningful look. "All is forgiven because you appreciate the vineyard housing the limestone and shale soil that feeds the roots."

A gentle laugh escaped. "Thank you for trying to make me feel better."

"You mean I didn't succeed?" he teased.

"You *know* you did." He had a captivating way about him.

They kept walking beneath a sky full of stars. As their bodies brushed against each other, she'd never known such rapture in her life. At the end of the row, he moved behind her and put his hands on her shoulders.

"Did you know your hair is the color of starlight?"

She could feel his breath on her temple. "Dominic—" His name came out sounding ragged.

A kiss against her neck opened the portals, releasing her longing for him. She turned in his arms and began to kiss his jaw, relishing the feel of his hard, male body. Their mouths slowly came together, seeking and finding what she'd wanted from the moment she'd sat across from him. This was ecstasy. Never in her life had she known this kind of passion.

When he finally relinquished her mouth with reluctance, he said, "Don't you know how dangerous it was to come out here with me tonight?"

His question penetrated deep inside to that spot reminding her they wouldn't be together like this if she weren't trying to find out if he'd been Antoinette's lover. For a little while tonight she'd forgotten.

Shocked by how carried away she'd been, she looked up at him. "Thank you for reminding me. Maybe we'd better go back." Nathalie eased out of his arms and started walking fast, reaching the car first.

He didn't try to catch up with her. While she was a trembling mass of need, Dominic seemed in perfect control driving them down to the mobile home park. He stopped behind her car and turned to her.

"I won't be able to see you tomorrow, but I'd like to see you after work Friday evening if you're free. We'll go to dinner."

Friday evening… That would have to be the night she asked him about Antoinette. "I'll make sure I am." She got out of the car. "I won't ever forget tonight's experience."

With her heart palpitating out of her chest, she rushed inside. The kiss they'd shared had turned her world upside down. To love a man like him, and have to tell him she couldn't have his baby…

After work on Thursday, Nathalie drove to the pizzeria in town and met Paul outside the entrance. They made their way inside and had to wait before being shown a table with menus propped on the red-and-white-checked cloth. She could tell it was a popular place, especially at dinnertime.

After studying the menu, Paul flicked Nathalie a glance. "How do you like your pizza?"

"A little bit of everything except for anchovies."

"Sounds good to me. Anything else?"

"Coffee."

A waitress came over for their order and hurried off.

Nathalie eyed Paul. "Wouldn't it be nice if the Fontesquieu family hired a food catering service that pulled into the vineyard every noon and evening? Think how happy it would make all the workers!"

He smiled. "That's a thought I'll pass on to Gregoire." But not to Dominic or Etienne, either of whom could make it happen.

"I saw clouds gathering this afternoon."

"It'll rain tomorrow."

"I can feel the extra humidity. It ought to make grape picking more interesting."

He grinned. "You mean messy, dirty and wet."

"I guess I'm going to find out."

"Want to go to a film after we eat?"

She shook her head. "I have to get back to the pharmacy where I work and do inventory. That's why I brought my car."

"You're a pharmacist?" Surprise was written all over him.

"By profession."

"But I thought you were on vacation." He looked stunned. "You have to go tonight?"

She nodded. "They need help so I promised to come in."

"Even when you've got a full day's work tomorrow?"

"I can't turn down a promise."

"You're one amazing woman."

Thankfully their food arrived at that moment.

"This pizza is good."

"It's all right," he muttered. "I'd rather we went out for a real dinner."

"Honestly, I'm too exhausted working seven days a week to do anything but fall asleep watching TV. Monsieur Fontesquieu warned me to take it easy so I don't burn out and collapse. Actually, he saw me walking and gave me a lift home the other day. It was very kind of him. If he has a wife who knows about it, I hope she'll understand he was only helping a lowly, exhausted grape picker make her way along the road."

Paul shook his head. "He's never been married."

The unexpected news filled her with joy for several reasons. "I see."

"Not yet, at least. According to Gregoire, who's on close terms with Etienne, Dominic Fontesquieu is on the verge of getting married to a woman with the kind of money most people only dream about."

After hearing he wasn't married, the revelation of impending marriage to a wealthy woman came as a shock. If that was true, how could he have kissed Nathalie like he did last night? Or made plans to be with her tomorrow evening?

Distressed, she wiped the corner of her mouth with a napkin. "Paul, I'm afraid I have to leave." Nathalie pulled some euros out of her purse and put them on the table before standing up. "Stay and finish the pizza."

"Don't forget to wear extra rain gear in the morning."

"I will. See you in the morning. *Merci* for the friendly chat."

Nathalie was tormented as she sped home. After the

kiss they'd shared, she didn't know what to think about Dominic. At least he didn't have a wife or children to consider if he were to learn he'd fathered Antoinette's baby. But if he were getting married soon, he shouldn't have been with Nathalie. Following that thought, the news that he had a son could turn his world upside down.

What was she doing? This couldn't go on any longer.

On Thursday, Dominic had been summoned to the salon of his parents' apartment at the chateau. He knew why.

His father, clearly recovered from his pneumonia, sat on one of the damask couches with his mother, whose stylish black hair showed a few streaks of silver. Dominic's older sister, Quinette, and her husband, Philippe, both serving on the board, had settled on the love seat. Etienne wasn't there because he hadn't shaken his flu completely.

He kissed his parents and sister and nodded to his brother-in-law, but he didn't sit down. "I came as soon as I could. It's obvious you've heard news before I could tell you myself."

"Corinne's mother called me this afternoon to tell me you won't be seeing her anymore."

"That's right, Maman. We've been thrown together at various family parties you arranged, but I never was *seeing* her."

"I simply don't believe it." Her voice shook. "She sounded hysterical. We've all been planning on your marriage."

"I can't help that. I'm not in love with Corinne, and

she doesn't want to be married to a man who can't give her the kind of love she needs."

She turned to his father. "Talk to him, Gaston."

"I tried talking to him when he left home at eighteen. My foolish son has cavorted with Parisian women with no class for too long. His judgment disgusts me."

His chilling pronouncement couldn't disturb Dominic. His father was lamenting all the money Corinne would have brought to the marriage. "I'm aware of that, Papa, but I have to please myself."

His mother's dark eyes filled with tears. "What's wrong with you, Dominic?"

"Maman," his sister remarked. Having been stuck in a bad marriage, she'd begun to see the light and had taken his side.

He smiled at Quinette before he said, "If I ever find the right woman, you'll be the first to know, *ma mere*. In the meantime, if you'll excuse me, I have plans. *Bonne nuit*."

Now that his parents had let him know they were devastated, he left to meet Raoul at Chez Gaspard, a café on the outskirts of Vence where they could enjoy privacy.

They met there when they needed to talk away from the estate. Tonight there were two households in chaos at the chateau.

Raoul was already waiting for him when he entered and walked to the back table in the corner. The waiter brought coffee Raoul had already ordered for them. Once he'd left, Dominic handed Raoul the financial report.

"Thanks for this." He lifted his dark head and sat forward. "I promised you some new information. As you know, I'd been dating Sabine and made the mistake of sleeping with her once, a mistake I regretted because as time went on I knew my feelings for a permanent relationship with her weren't there. I had to tell her the truth even though it hurt her and I broke it off with her.

"Right after that I happened to meet Toinette Gilbert and found myself in love for the first time in my life. She'd become my heart's desire. We saw each other for a month and I wanted to marry her.

"But out of the blue I got a phone call from Sabine. She told me she was expecting our baby and we had to get married immediately. Her doctor verified it with me.

"I was horrified. Of course, I had to tell Toinette the truth, the most painful thing I'd ever had to do in my life. She said goodbye to me and refused all my phone calls. I never saw her after that. My world had crashed around me."

Dominic could attest to that fact. "You did the honorable thing, Raoul. When I heard you two were expecting, I knew that was the only reason you would have married her, especially after telling me you were in love with Toinette. But what is it I still don't know?"

"I'm getting to that. Only the birth of little Celine helped me to go on. I loved our daughter and was devastated after she died. While I was at the hospital, I talked to the doctor and asked if her heart was the reason why she'd been born a month early. The doctor told me no. Celine had been a full-term baby."

A gasp came out of Dominic. "So the baby wasn't yours."

Raoul stared straight at him. "No. If I hadn't asked the doctor that question, Sabine would have kept that a secret for the rest of our lives. After coming home from Saint Tropez the other night, I decided it was time to tell her I was divorcing her, and I confronted her about the baby that wasn't mine."

"How did that go?"

"She admitted it. Her explanation was that she'd always wanted me, but turned to another man because I'd never proposed."

"*Incroyable.* Did the other man ever know?"

"No," he said in a solemn voice.

"So you've been living with the pain of that lie ever since the funeral."

His cousin nodded. "Because you were in Paris, I didn't want to burden you. Instead I got some professional advice and was warned to put off a divorce until Sabine had recovered enough from Celine's death to deal with it."

A groan came out of Dominic. "How bad are things at this point?"

"Bad. I've been served papers from Sabine's attorney and have been talking with our attorney, Horace Millet."

"He's the best. What is she demanding?"

"Fifty million dollars in damages for lack of affection since she knew from the start I hadn't been in love with her. That was her excuse for being with another man while she waited for a proposal from me. She

claimed she'd wanted marriage to me all her adult life."
He sat back in the chair. "Well, she got it."

Dominic looked across at him. "You could counter-sue because of her lie."

"I could, but we've both been suffering over Ce-line's death. There's been too much grief as it is. I just want this period of my life over. Horace has drawn up papers declaring a legal separation. Since her attorney has indicated that Sabine is refusing to move out of the chateau until the divorce is final, I'm moving out. I've liquidated a few assets to keep functioning before Papa freezes my accounts. Both sets of parents are refusing to accept the divorce and are fighting it."

"Of course they are." And Raoul was too full of in-tegrity to expose Sabine's lie to the family.

"For now I'm planning to live at the Aurora Hotel in Vence until this is over. I'm checking in there after I leave you."

"No, you're not. You're staying with me. I have two extra bedrooms. Both families are trying to take ev-erything away from you. That means I'm not letting you spend money on a hotel. You need to be close to the office."

"I can't do that to you."

"Raoul, if I were in your shoes, I know you'd tell me to move in with you, so let's not waste any more time talking about it. Come on. Follow me back to the cha-teau and let's get you moved in. While we do that, I'll fill you in on what's happening with me. It'll be fun. I've got more space in the apartment than I know what to do with."

"Dom—"

"We share a special bond, right?"

*"Oui,"* his voice grated.

Dominic put some Euros on the table and they left for the chateau. Under the circumstances, he couldn't be happier to have his best friend close.

Within the hour, they'd set Raoul up in one of the bedrooms. His cousin eyed him as they both went to the kitchen for more coffee. "The family will have a collective heart attack when they find out the two bad boys have joined forces, but I could not care less. Have you ended it with Corinne yet?"

"I took care of that last night. When you texted me a little while ago, I was on my way to the parents to be castigated."

"How did that go?"

"According to Maman, Corinne's mother is in hysterics. I know I hurt Corinne for expectations never met, but there were no outward histrionics."

His cousin's dark brow lifted. "Let's change the subject. What's going on with Mademoiselle Fournier?"

"I haven't fired her yet if that tells you anything." Dominic was still shaken by the taste and feel of Nathalie, who'd welcomed his kiss last night with the same urgency he'd been feeling from the beginning.

"Do you still suspect her of something?"

"I don't know," he ground out. "Maybe I'm wrong and she's exactly who she says she is. After hearing about Sabine's lie of omission, I pray to God Nathalie has told me her whole truth by now."

His cousin eyed him with concern. "You sound like a man in love."

Dominic's head reared. "It may have finally happened, Raoul." But he would be in pain until he knew all of her and her heart.

"Does she feel the same way?"

"She hasn't said the words yet, but I know it in my gut." The way she'd kissed him had been proof of that.

Rain fell on Friday. Nathalie's work was wet and messy. She needed to shower and wash her hair after finishing work, as Dominic would be coming by to take her out for the evening.

Learning that he planned to be married soon had shaken her. If he were Alain's father and wanted a relationship with his boy, then how would Nathalie handle it? She was Alain's aunt and they would be sharing him. How was she going to shut off her feelings?

This evening she put on a pale blue short-sleeved blouse and a white skirt with a small blue print. She hadn't worn anything dressy around him. Her hair had natural curl. She brushed it until it swished against her shoulders from a side part, then she put on her leather sandals. Nathalie wore no makeup other than lipstick.

When he knocked on the door, she opened it and sucked in her breath. He stood there wearing a silky black shirt and gray trousers. No man had ever looked so devastatingly gorgeous to her. "Dominic—"

Tonight was her chance to ask him questions about Antoinette. She'd started down this path for Alain's sake and needed to see it through. "Thanks for being on time. I'm hungry again."

He chuckled and backed around. "And here I thought I'd have to wait. You're a constant surprise."

"So are you."

Dominic darted her an amused glance with those gleaming black eyes before they got in the car and headed for Vence. He drove through the town and up into the hills. They wound around to a restaurant with date palms and cypress trees overlooking the breathtaking landscape.

He escorted her inside and they were shown to a table out on the veranda with a sweeping view. The waiter handed them menus.

"Everything's good here."

Nathalie looked over the options. "What's your favorite?"

*"Suprême de veau rôti, crème provençale."*

"That sounds delicious." She loved veal. "I'll try it."

The waiter came back with coffee and a wine list.

Dominic's gaze held hers as he told the waiter, "We'll pass on the wine." After giving him their order, the waiter walked off.

"I would imagine wine from the Fontesquieu vineyards makes up a good portion of every restaurant's list in Provence and elsewhere."

"My cousin Raoul could tell you all about it. He's in charge of marketing and sales."

"That has to be an enormous responsibility."

"But nothing like the responsibility you have as a

pharmacist. When you make a mistake, it could be life threatening."

She nodded. "That's true."

"What made you choose that for your career?"

Now would be the perfect time to tell him about the family Alain had been born into.

"My parents were both pharmacists. That's how they met and got married. I was born soon after their marriage, then my *papa* died. I never knew him, only my stepfather, also a druggist who was a widower with a daughter. He married my mother. I grew up wanting to be a pharmacist too. After I graduated, they took me on at the pharmacy they owned."

"Sounds like my family."

"In a way." Their eyes held. "My stepfather ran everything until he died several years ago."

"I'm sorry."

"So am I," she whispered. "Since then my mother has hired another pharmacist to help us."

"Do you live with your mother?"

"Yes." And one precious boy.

Their dinner came, interrupting their conversation. She started eating. "This veal is superb. I'm glad you suggested it."

"It never disappoints. Tell me, are you an only child?"

Her heart thudded. Stick to the truth as much as you dare. "No. I just had my stepsister, but she died sixteen months ago of an infection."

"Your family has known a lot of grief," he commiserated. "My parents lost a daughter right after she was born."

"They must have suffered."

"So have you after breaking up with the man you thought to marry."

She sipped her coffee. Since meeting Dominic, she hadn't given Guy a thought. "That has turned out to be a good thing. I can't imagine anything worse than getting married, only to discover you made a mistake. To settle when you already have questions about that person makes no sense to me."

"I couldn't agree more," he said with almost savage conviction. It sent a shiver down her spine.

Taking her courage in her hands, Nathalie said, "Rumor has it you will be getting married soon." She had to find out.

"Paul needs to be careful what he passes on, though it's not his fault what he hears. Marriage was never on my agenda. Otherwise I wouldn't have asked you to come to dinner with me this evening."

Heaven forgive her, but that news meant more to her than he would ever know. If she dared tell him about Alain, and he agreed to take a DNA test to prove paternity, he could be with his son without the complications of a new wife. But only if that was what Dominic wanted more than anything in his life. Alain deserved a father who would cherish him.

Knowing he wasn't getting married prompted her next question. "Why *did* you invite me out this evening, Dominic?"

His eyes narrowed on her mouth, making her whole body go limp. "You can ask me that after our walk in the vineyard?" She averted her eyes. "Because I wanted to." Somehow she felt he'd spoken the truth just now. "Why did you accept, Nathalie?"

Her heart thundered in her chest. "If I tell you the real reason, will you believe me?" They were both circling each other.

"I deserved that."

She was able to tell him one honest truth, though she was riddled with guilt. "Because *I* wanted to be with you too."

Dominic's chest rose and fell visibly, communicating an emotion that appeared to match hers. There was a growing sensual tension between them that couldn't be denied, haunting her more and more.

The waiter came over to suggest dessert. She declined. So did Dominic, who asked for the check. When it was paid, they left and went out to his car.

Nathalie looked up at the sky. "It's still overcast, but I don't think it will rain again tomorrow."

"It won't," he assured her and helped her into the car before walking around.

Once he was behind the wheel, she sent him a covert glance. "If you ever decide to give up being a vintner, you'll make a better weatherman than any meteorologist."

"I wouldn't want the job. They make too many mistakes. Technically I'm no longer a vintner. Not since I left for Paris eleven years ago and went into investment banking."

Eleven years? She blinked. When had there been time for him to meet Antoinette? Had she been wrong about him this whole time? "So you weren't born with grape juice running in your veins?" she teased.

He chuckled. "Maybe, but I was much more interested in what made the world go round. Big business intrigued me."

Nathalie knew there was much more he hadn't told her, but this was a beginning. Before the night was out she might even learn enough to broach the subject of Alain.

# CHAPTER FIVE

TWILIGHT HAD FALLEN over the town, giving it a magical look. Nathalie felt like they were the only two people who existed. Instead of driving her straight back to the mobile home, Dominic took her on a long drive around the other side of the vineyard, letting her see the vast property.

"The air smells so sweet, I feel like I'm in a dream. There's a peace here in the vineyard impossible to describe, yet it's alive. Glorious! I read an article on the Fontesquieu website that said there is something special about the manner in which vines in France attach themselves to the landscape. The author suggested that France is where the vines are *supposed* to be."

Dominic nodded. "My family believes as much."

"So do I."

He glanced at her. "When I took you to the winery, I wondered if you'd seen the plaque on the wall right by us."

"I did. It said, 'God planted the best vines on earth here in Provence.' I loved it." She drew in a deep breath. "Seeing all this with you, I believe it."

If the man sitting next to her had been Antoinette's heart's desire, it was understandable that she'd succumbed to him. But more and more Nathalie was beginning to feel that he wasn't Alain's father, and she didn't want this evening to end.

Maybe he was reading her thoughts because he said, "Do you mind if we make a detour to Saint Jeannet before I take you back home? My brother asked me to check on a special shipment of red wine my grandfather has been waiting for, and until Etienne gets better I'm trying to help him. It'll only be ten minutes out of our way."

The question filled her with exhilaration. This would give her more time to be with him. "Tell me about the shipment of red wine, Dominic. I thought you only produced rosé wine."

"We produce everything."

"Even sour wine."

He smiled. "That too."

"Will you tell me what you know about the emperor Charlemagne? I hear there's a story to do with him and red wine."

Dominic chuckled. "One of those stories is purported to have to do with his fourth or fifth wife. She was a beautiful German princess with many gifts and he adored her. When she died, he never remarried. But getting to the point, being a tall proud man with a prominent white beard, he wanted to look his best for her when they were married. Yet there was one problem."

Everything the brilliant man sitting next to her said or did enamored her. "What was that?"

"According to history, he was a big meat eater and red wine drinker. But she didn't like the red stains on his beard."

Nathalie studied the red stains on her own fingers and could well understand.

"Word has it that she demanded he drink only white wine. From then on only white grapes were commanded to be planted on a certain section of the hill. That's when Corton-Charlemagne in Burgundy was born and still continues."

"I had no idea. How fascinating."

"Except that it's partly myth. Other sources say it was Charlemagne's mother who didn't like her royal son looking terrible with those dreadful red stains."

She laughed. "That sounds more realistic."

"Are you ready for this? Some sources say he didn't have a beard. According to scholars, it was customary in the Middle Ages for artists to put facial hair on the rulers, symbolic of their virility."

"Oh, dear—don't tell me that and ruin this picture I have of Charlemagne with his *barbe fleurie*."

It was Dominic's turn to laugh that deep laugh she loved. "Too much authentic research destroys most of our beliefs."

"You're right. It's much more fun to enjoy our own version of life. Since I'm with an expert and we're talking about red wine, please explain about red grapes having many secrets. I cherish the memory of you taking me on a tour of the winery."

His hand reached over to clasp hers, sending waves of longing through her body. Both their emotions were spilling over. "To keep it simple, all grape juice is white. Only the red skins contain a dark pigment. If the juice is separated from the skins shortly after being crushed, it remains white."

"I see."

"If the juice is left in contact with the red skins during fermentation, it becomes that delightful pink color. Left longer, it becomes red wine."

"I'm embarrassed to know so little about it."

He turned to her. "That's because you're not a wine drinker. Those who are show surprise to learn that eighty-eight percent of the wine produced in Provence is rosé. It has a delicious fruity flavor. Some people refer to it as summer water."

Another chuckle came out of her.

"Other drinkers prefer white wine, which is sweeter. Red wine is heavier. But as I explained, our winery produces everything."

During their conversation, she hadn't realized they'd reached the town of Saint Jeannet. He pulled up to a big warehouse before letting her go. He flicked his gaze to her. "I'll only be a minute."

The whole time they'd been talking, she realized she hadn't asked him any personal questions. But after hearing he'd been away from Vence for so many years, she was beginning to think he couldn't have been Antoinette's lover.

It was a lovely night to be out, and being with him was so stimulating to her, there weren't enough hours with him to satisfy everything she was desperate to know. Her whole body tingled from his touch.

He'd returned to the car while she'd been deep in thought. "Let's go."

"Was the shipment there?"

"Not yet. I need to inform Etienne." He pulled out his phone to text him, then started the car and they left for Vence.

"Will your grandfather be upset?"

"I'm afraid he was born in that condition, but he'll live to see another day."

"What's your grandmother like?"

"She's afraid of him and allows him to rule her life."

"Are you afraid of him?"

"Let's put it this way. I learned not to like him or my father." She winced from so much honest emotion. "They have a hard streak that dominates their existence. As soon as I turned eighteen, I left to go to school in Paris."

"Didn't they try to prevent you from leaving?"

"Yes. They told me that if I deserted the family, there'd be no money, no inheritance. That suited me fine. From my bank account I withdrew the pitiful amount of money I'd earned and bought a third-class train ticket for Paris. I slept all the way. When I arrived, I found a job at a warehouse the next day and bunked with some of the workers until I could pay for a semester of college."

"You're amazing!"

"No—only desperate to get on with the life I wanted to lead. At that point, I took out a school loan and got another job as an eighteen-wheeler truck driver. It paid more and I could sleep behind the cab while I had to make deliveries between classes and on weekends."

"Where did you drive?"

"All over Paris and the outskirts. In the process, I made lots of contacts. After a month, I found a rooming house so I could bathe and eat breakfast daily. That's how I lived while I pursued an education in money management. After college I worked for an investment firm."

Dominic was getting to her in ways she didn't think possible. Nathalie knew he had to be a remarkable man, but hearing some of his history told her she would never meet a more extraordinary human being.

"Did your family know where you were?"

"My cousin Raoul knew. That was all that mattered to me. Do you know the sad part of this is that I wanted to have a close relationship with family, but it never happened. My father is made in my grandfather's image, which explains why we don't get along. Both men are driven and cold."

"What about your mother?"

"She's not as cold, but is in lockstep with him over aspirations for their children. You have to do it their way. There is no other."

Her heart pained for him. "I'm so sorry, Dominic."

"It's life, but I don't want to talk about them. I'd much rather focus on you."

He drove swiftly to the vineyard and pulled up behind her car outside her rental. After shutting off the engine, he turned to her. "We'll only need pickers for another ten days at the most. Since the *vendange* is so short a season, I'd like to spend as much time with you in the evenings as possible before you go back to work at the pharmacy. How would you feel about that?"

The question sounded like heaven. Nathalie's mind was spinning with possibilities now that she thought he might not be Alain's father after all. "Maybe one evening I'll provide groceries and cook. Another night you could do the same." During one of their conversations she would ask him straight out if he'd known an Antoinette. After that, anything could happen.

"I'll bring the food for tomorrow's meal."

"Um. That sounds perfect."

She undid her seat belt. "Thank you for a lovely dinner and drive. Learning about red grapes has made me feel more legitimate as a grape picker. Good night."

To her surprise, he got out and walked her to the door. "I wish you didn't have to go in." The next thing she knew he'd cupped her face in his hands and lowered his dark head to kiss her. She'd been wanting this all evening.

The feel of his mouth on hers sent rivers of warmth through her body, but his kiss didn't last long enough. She moaned when he stepped away far too soon for her liking.

"*A demain*, Nathalie." His voice sounded husky.

After letting her go, he walked to his car and drove off. She waited until he'd disappeared before getting in her car to drive home. Her legs had turned to mush. Tomorrow evening couldn't come soon enough.

On Saturday Dominic drove into town for groceries, then went to his office to do work until it was time to drive to Nathalie's. The sun had shone all day and warmed everything. On the drive over, he talked to Raoul.

"Just giving you a heads-up that I'm spending the evening with Nathalie."

"If you want to bring her here, I'll go to the hotel."

"Thanks, but it's not necessary. To be honest, I wouldn't take her to the chateau. Too many eyes. For the rest of the harvest we're having dinner at her place and taking turns cooking meals."

"Cooking."

"That and other things." Dominic chuckled. "You'll have my kitchen to yourself. Nathalie's no longer in a relationship with the man she thought she would marry. Within another week, I'm going to know a lot more about her."

"Do you still feel she's not being completely honest?"

"Unfortunately, yes. But I have to believe it's something I'll be able to handle."

Raoul sobered. "I hope so for your sake."

So did Dominic, who could see her coming up the path. "Talk to you later." He hung up and got out of the car. Whether she wore her silvery-gold hair tied back or loose, she was a vision.

"Imagine meeting you here," Nathalie teased with a smile.

"I've been imagining it since I left you last night."

She blushed and opened the door to her rental. He followed her inside with the groceries. "I'll be out in a minute," she said before disappearing into the back.

"Take your time while I put things away and get our

meal started." He'd bought items for his own version of *salade niçoise* with fresh fish and rolls.

By the time she'd emerged in a sleeveless pink blouse and khaki pants looking enticing, he'd prepared café au lait and handed her a cup from the kitchen counter.

"Um…" She took a sip. "Fabulous. You're going to make someone a wonderful wife one day." She always said something unexpected that amused him.

"Our dinner is waiting."

"I know. I can smell the tuna aroma from here." She walked over to the table in the little dining area and sat down on one of the chairs. "This salad is a work of art. You're spoiling me rotten!"

He wanted to do more than that.

They both ate with relish. Being with her made him feel like a light had been turned on, illuminating a world he was seeing only for the first time. "I detect red stains on your fingers."

"Me and Charlemagne," she teased. "They're unsightly, but I don't like wearing gloves. I can't do as effective a job with them on."

"You and a lot of workers."

A laugh escaped her lips.

"Wouldn't you know one of the sons in the Spanish family working by me told me there's a place called the Guinguet that has a live band on Sunday night. Everyone goes there. I pretended I didn't know."

He smiled into her eyes. "I went there a few times in the past myself." *Was that true?* Had he met Antoinette there? When? "I presume this Casanova intends to take you."

"He knows I'm not interested."

Dominic finished his roll. "That's two down in a week. How come I'm still standing?" The desire to make love to her was going to consume him before long.

A glint entered her gorgeous eyes. "Because *you* didn't ask me to go to a place where they serve sour wine." With that clever remark, she started to clear the table. "While I clean up, you're welcome to watch TV."

"I'd rather help you." He was determined to find out what she was hiding and handed her more dishes as she loaded the dishwasher.

She darted him a glance. "Do you mind if I ask you a personal question?"

"Not at all."

"Paul said you were filling in for your brother, Etienne, because he'd been sick. What is *your* official position in your family's business?"

Why did she want to know that? He felt he was getting closer to her secret. "As I told you earlier, I went to Paris and studied investment banking. After graduation I worked for a firm there before I came home four months ago because my father was ill. As it turns out, I've been deciding on the investments the company makes. In other words, I took over my father's job as funds manager."

"I see. Another huge responsibility that takes brilliance," she murmured. "You have to be an accountant whiz too."

"That's part of it. You wouldn't be looking for a career change, would you? Are you after an administrative job and need an in?"

She flushed. "No. I enjoy my work. But I do a lot of thinking while I'm out picking grapes. So much goes into running a family business like yours. It's overwhelming to me. You have to know everything about soil, grapes, weather conditions, and that's just for starters. There's hiring and payroll. I think about the equipment you need.

"Someone has to have the incredible expertise to make wine. Another person has to know how to distribute and advertise. A man like you has to make life-and-death decisions about money. When and where to invest. It all blows my mind."

Dominic stared into her eyes. "Where has all this come from?"

"I didn't realize until my stepfather died how much went into his buying the pharmacy and making it thrive. He had to learn so much to go into business after having worked for someone else. There were nights when he was up until late working on everything. I never understood what he went through." Her eyes glistened with unshed tears. "Now my mother has the load."

"One you share."

"I'm trying. Working on the vineyard has opened my eyes to so many things. We've only had to consider hiring one pharmacist to help out. But we have to provide insurance and make sure we can afford to pay another wage."

"It's a fine line at times."

"It certainly is. Your family has to hire hundreds of workers at harvest time, not to mention your regular employees. Every application has to be vetted. You carry a huge burden in order to pay your employees and deal with all the ups and downs. I can't tell you how much I admire a family like yours that has kept their business solvent for hundreds of years. You have an unmatchable work ethic."

While she'd been talking with such heartfelt emotion, he heard her cell phone ring. "Excuse me a minute, Dominic." She pulled it out of her pocket and checked the caller ID. "It's my mother. She probably wants to know how soon I'll be home tonight."

"You're leaving?"

"I always go home at night." That piece of information came as a surprise. "I'll call her back."

If that was true and she never stayed here alone at night, the news pleased him. "In that case I'm going to leave now so I don't prevent you from driving home too late."

She looked up at him. "You'll come tomorrow evening?" she asked in a throbbing voice. Those light green eyes beseeched him. "I'll make the dinner."

His breath caught. "Try to keep me away. *Bonne nuit*, Nathalie." This time he gave her a long, hard kiss, then bolted for the door, not daring to stay any longer.

The more she'd talked to him tonight, the more he'd been ensnared. No other woman he'd known had shown her kind of sensitivity and understanding of his family's unique work. The well-heeled type of women in his family's world weren't interested in much more than his overall financial worth.

But his fear that it could be a front was ripping him apart. Was it possible she'd seen Dominic somewhere and planned to work at the vineyard to get close to him? The thought pained him when he wanted to pull her down on the couch and start kissing the daylights out of her. Hell and hell.

# CHAPTER SIX

SUNDAY MORNING, NATHALIE left home earlier than usual to buy groceries. She drove to Vence and put everything in the fridge before reporting to the vineyard.

Dominic must have wondered what was wrong with her to go on about his family. She hadn't been able to help it. If Alain truly was his son, then he belonged to a remarkable man with an amazing history.

Her mother wanted her to give up on this. It was wrong to date Dominic when she was holding back this huge secret that could backfire. Nathalie knew her mother was right, but since he'd admitted he'd been to the Guinguet in the past, that placed him where Antoinette could have met him.

Here she'd been thinking Dominic hadn't been the one involved with her stepsister, but this new information threw her. The one thing she had to do now was find out *when* he'd been to the bistro. Had he gone there after returning from Paris during one of his visits home? Once she knew if the timing fit, then she'd break her silence.

As soon as four thirty rolled around, she left the vineyard under a semicloudy sky and hurried to her temporary home. She wanted to get there first and make herself presentable.

Relieved that she didn't see his car outside, she rushed in and took a quick shower. After she'd put on a green skirt with a lighter green blouse, she brushed her hair and caught it back with a light green scarf.

He still hadn't come when she started the chicken crepes and prepared a strawberry and cream dessert. By five thirty she started to worry. The thought of him not coming caused her more misery than she should be feeling for this man.

While she was making coffee, she heard a knock on the door. She hadn't heard him drive up. With her adrenaline gushing, she rushed to open it. "Dominic?" she cried.

"I'm afraid not."

*Oh!*

She'd just come face-to-face with a man who bore such a strong family resemblance to Dominic in looks and coloring it was unbelievable. She reeled and clung to the door.

"Mademoiselle Fournier?"

"Yes?"

"I'm Etienne Fontesquieu."

She'd already guessed as much and was stunned. He had Alain's eyes too!

"My brother asked me to stop by in person since he couldn't reach you on the phone."

That's right. She'd turned it off so it wouldn't wake Alain this morning. Her body was shaking. "Please, come in."

"I'd better not. I'm getting over a cold." She could hear it. "Dominic wants you to know he's been unaccountably detained and is aware you've gone to a lot of trouble to make dinner." She'd been living for tonight. "He asks your forgiveness and will get in touch with you."

*Dominic*...

"That's very considerate of you, especially since you're not well."

"I sound worse than I am."

"Please let your brother know I understand. Thank you."

"Thank *you* for doing such a good job for us. Gregoire tells me you've caught on fast. I'm impressed. Have a good evening."

He turned and walked back to his silver Mercedes. From a distance, his tall, lean silhouette reminded her of Dominic. She let out a troubled sound. Good heavens—had she gotten it wrong and *Etienne* had been Antoinette's lover?

Nathalie shut the door and sank down on the couch in shock. If she'd met Etienne first, she would have thought *he* could be Alain's father. At this point she was convinced she'd lost her mind.

After this experience she'd lost her appetite too.

What if Dominic's distrust of her had prompted him to send his brother here to check on her and find out what she was up to? Maybe Etienne didn't trust her either. Once she'd gathered her wits, she put the food in the fridge.

After driving back to La Gaude, she flew into the house. "Maman?"

When there was no answer, she tiptoed to Alain's room. Her mother was looking down at him in the crib. When she saw Nathalie, she put a finger to her lips. Nathalie went back to the living room to wait.

In a minute her mother walked in. "What's wrong? You sounded upset when you called out."

"I am. I met Dominic's brother, Etienne, today." Nathalie launched into the reason why he'd stopped in to see her. "They share an amazing family resemblance. Alain could be Etienne's son."

A small cry came from her mother. "That does it, Nathalie. You've got to give this up. I think you should quit your job at the vineyard before you do something that will cause irreversible damage. You're tampering with other people's lives. It's something that is out of your hands. Don't you see what is happening?"

"Yes." Meeting Etienne had thrown her completely. Worse, she'd fallen for his brother, a man who was still a mystery to her and could have been Nathalie's lover. "But as I told you last night, I learned Dominic had been to the Guinguet several times in the past. I need to find out when. Tomorrow night I'll ask him if he ever met a girl at the bistro named Antoinette."

"He'll demand to know why you want that information."

"At that point I'll tell him that she was my stepsister and died before she told me the name of the man she loved. She'd kept it a secret, and I wanted to know why. Then I'll add that I decided to follow a few clues that led me to the Fontesquieu vineyard."

Her mother's worried expression didn't change.

"Maman, if Dominic continues to deny all knowledge, I'll believe him and ask him if his brother might have known Antoinette. I promise I won't say anything about the baby."

"Nathalie? He's too intelligent not to figure that out."

She folded her arms to her waist. "For Alain's sake I have to find the truth if I can. Do you really wish I would give this up?"

"Yes, but I know you won't and suspect you're more than attracted to Dominic. Am I right?"

She lowered her head. "I'd give anything if I weren't."

"It's going to get worse the longer you keep seeing him."

"I know. But it's a risk I'm still willing to take for Alain's sake. Thanks for supporting me. I love you."

She kissed her mother and went to her bedroom. After putting in a wash, she packed some more clothes and finally went to bed exhausted. The next morning, she left for Vence after having packed her lunch. She also turned on her phone.

Dominic filled her mind to the exclusion of all else. The knowledge that he'd be coming over tonight made it difficult to breathe. Nathalie stopped there first to get her backpack. The walk to the vineyard didn't take long.

She'd just reached the next row to start cutting grapes when her cell phone rang. Her heart leaped when she saw Dominic's name on the caller ID.

She put down the scissors. "*Bonjour*, monsieur."

"*Bonjour*, mademoiselle."

His distinctive voice melted her insides.

"Would you please let Nathalie Fournier know I'll be arriving tonight with our dinner? I owe her one after not showing up last evening." He hung up before she could respond.

His call brightened the already beautiful day. She hardly noticed the work she had to do. When she left the vineyard at four thirty, she came close to a run in her excitement to see Dominic again. She'd brought a summery dress in a small floral print on white to wear this evening. Even if he didn't believe her reasons for coming to the vineyard and all this was about to come to an end, she wanted to look her best.

Nathalie had been listening for his distinctive knock that came as she was brushing out her hair. She hurried to open the door. Tonight he wore a silky claret-colored shirt and tan chinos. He carried a grocery bag.

"Well, if it isn't the mysterious monsieur!"

His black eyes were alive. "I hope mademoiselle is ready for coq au vin straight from the chateau kitchen."

"Hmm. After Guinguet Fontesquieu, do I dare try it?"

His deep laugh rang out to delight her. "I don't know. I'll eat first. If I don't expire, you'll know it's safe. But I need to be invited in."

"You don't need an invitation."

"I'll remember that." He walked through to the kitchen while she shut the door and followed him. His gaze traveled over her. "You look lovely tonight."

*You look incredible.* "Thank you. I've set the table and the coffee is ready. We can eat whenever you want."

"You know me. I'm hungry now. Let's dig in while

it's hot." He pulled the ingredients from the bag and they sat down to enjoy what turned out to be a fabulous meal. "How went another day in the life of our latest *coupeuse*?"

She laughed. "Backbreaking, as if you didn't know. I'd much rather talk about your day." Hopefully she could ply him with enough questions to learn the truth.

Once again Dominic had to ask himself why Nathalie seemed so interested in *his* day. "In truth I've been counting the hours to be with you. I'm sorry about yesterday."

"It doesn't matter."

"Of course it does. That's why I asked Etienne to come in my place and make my apologies in person. He texted me around six and told me all was well, adding, 'She took my breath. How did you manage that, Dom?'"

Heat crept into those beautiful cheeks. "I realized something important had held you up."

"Yesterday I had a phone call from my cousin Raoul. After living in a tumultuous marriage, he's decided it has to end and has asked his wife for a divorce, *grâce à Dieu*. He should never have married her."

"How sad."

"I had to help him with some important business. You have no idea of the turmoil he's been through."

She breathed deeply. "More and more I'm relieved I ended it with Guy. Your cousin's situation reminds me of what I avoided by not marrying him."

Dominic wanted to believe her. He put down his coffee cup. "Raoul is my best friend and always has been. Over the last couple of years I've seen him so unhappy. His wife is making demands. I'm trying to help him. We didn't get back from Nice until ten."

"He's lucky to have you."

"One of these days his nightmare will be over. In the meantime he's rooming with me in my apartment at the chateau."

"Where does your cousin usually live?"

"In the other wing of the chateau."

She blinked. "I know it's massive, but you *all* live there together?"

His brows lifted. "A horrifying thought, isn't it?"

"Only if you want to be private."

Dominic smiled at her. "That's why I lived in Paris for as long as I did."

"But you came home once in a while."

"Yes, for visits and vacations. If I decide to stay in Vence, then the day is coming when I'll buy my own home. Raoul is planning to do the same thing. It's just as well they're separated until they go to court and a settlement is made."

"I feel terrible for him. Did they love each other before they got married?"

"He'd been seeing her, but hadn't proposed marriage though both their families wanted it desperately. One night he met a girl and overnight fell deeply in love with her, wanting marriage. But then came the news that Sabine was pregnant.

"Raoul had only slept with her once and regretted it before breaking it off with her. But hearing the news

about Sabine's pregnancy, he had to end his relationship with the woman he loved. At that point he did the
noble thing and married Sabine. Sadly their baby died
a month after she was born. He buried his heart with
his little girl. Since the funeral there's been an emptiness in him that worries me."

"I can't imagine so much pain."

Their eyes held.

"You're not a Fontesquieu," Dominique murmured.
He noticed her shudder.

"Would you believe Etienne was pressured into his
marriage at around the same time? He should have married a girl he was crazy about, but the family didn't
consider her good enough to marry and wouldn't hear
of it."

She shook her head. "Does that mean he's also on
the verge of divorce?"

"It could happen, but they have a little girl, Sophie,
to think of."

She pushed herself away from the table to retrieve
dessert from the counter.

"I shouldn't have unburdened myself to you. You're
far too easy to talk to."

"Please don't say that. Your worries help me forget
my own." She brought the two *tartes aux pommes* to the
table and sat down. "I'm curious about something. Since
you all live at the chateau, are your offices there too?"

Was it natural curiosity on her part? Even if she had
a hidden reason for asking the question, it made him
chuckle. "No. Maybe you haven't seen the big modern

office building behind the chateau. We each have our own suites."

Her eyes smiled. "But you never really get away from each other. Togetherness has to be the reason your family's business has risen to such heights."

Something was going on in her beautiful head. Nathalie had a charm about her that was tying him in knots. He needed to put distance between them this evening. Whether he discovered her reason for coming to the vineyard or not, he couldn't be around her much longer before he took her in his arms and made endless love to her.

"I've enjoyed tonight more than you know, but I have some business to take care of and need to get going. Let me clear the table first."

"No, no, Dominic. You brought this wonderful food and I've loved it. I'll take care of everything else. Tomorrow evening I'll provide the dinner."

"I'd like that, but I have an even better idea. As your employer, I'm giving you the day off tomorrow to spend it with me. How would you like to cook in the galley on my cruiser? It's docked in Nice. We'll leave in the morning and enjoy a full day and evening on the water together. It's a beautiful sight watching the sun go down over the Mediterranean while we swim and eat." Tomorrow he'd break her down.

His suggestion lit up her whole expression. "That would be incredible."

"Then we'll do it. Don't bother to get groceries. We'll buy them in Nice."

She walked him to the door. "I won't be able to

sleep." He'd had close to none since he'd met her. Dominic was besotted by her. "Thank you for everything."

"Pick you up here at eight in the morning. Bring your swimming suit."

"I'll be ready."

He gave her a swift kiss before striding to his car. It took all the self-control he possessed not to crush her against him. Tomorrow everything was going to change.

Nathalie had trouble getting to sleep that night. Dominic's story about what had happened to his cousin had sounded so much like what had happened to Antoinette, it had shaken her. Maybe she was losing it and tried to put it out of her mind.

The next morning her heart pounded out of rhythm when Dominic arrived at eight. He'd dressed in a blue pullover and white cargo pants. It should be a sin for a man to be so devastatingly handsome and marvelous. For today she didn't want to think about anything but being with him, and wished she could thrust her guilt aside. Of course, that wasn't possible.

She'd showered and changed into white shorts and a short-sleeved lavender top. After catching her hair back with a clip, she was ready and walked out the door with her overnight bag. He helped her into the car and they reached Nice in a half hour under a sunny sky. What perfect weather!

She turned to him. "Shall we have steaks tonight?" He'd stopped at a grocery store and they hurried inside to find what they wanted. "The rest we can get in the deli."

He nodded and reached for several baguettes to go with their meals. Before long they left for the pier where he kept his white thirty-foot cruiser with a black stripe. Everything was state of the art. This was a world most people could only dream of. Yet she couldn't forget he'd left it for a decade or longer to pursue the life he'd wanted. As far as she was concerned, he was a Renaissance man.

They both carried a bag along the dock. He got in the cruiser first with the groceries, then helped her in, but didn't let her go. "I've been waiting to do this all the way here. I need to kiss you. Really kiss you."

"Dominic—" Unable to help herself, she threw her arms around his neck hungrily and met that male mouth she'd been longing to taste again. Swept away by rapture, she lost track of time and never wanted to let him go.

Someone let out a loud whistle from another boat that reminded her they weren't alone. She eased herself away from Dominic, whose black eyes were glazed with desire. "I'm taking you to a place where we can be strictly alone." He handed her a life preserver and helped her put it on. "Let's go below and put away the groceries. After I show you around, we'll get going."

He pointed out the bedroom and bathroom on the lower deck. They wanted for nothing. Nathalie hadn't known joy like this in her whole life. To think she'd ever thought of marrying Guy. Being with Dominic had transported her to another dimension of living.

Yet the chateau, the cruiser, all the trappings of a privileged life had nothing to do with how she felt when she was with him. He'd brought her alive. They could be stranded on a desert island with nothing but each other and she would have felt she'd found paradise. That was when she knew for certain she was in love with him.

They went back up on deck, where he undid the ropes and they cast off. "I'd like to take you to a place I love to go when I have time. Have you ever been to Les Calanques de Cassis?"

She shook her head. "Even though I've lived on the French Riviera all my life and went to the university in Nice, I've only heard of them. My friends didn't have boats." The Fontesquieu family lived a different life than 99 percent of the world.

"Then you're in for a fabulous treat. They're magical coastal inlets," he spoke with excitement. "Great cliffs of limestone that form mini fjords with sandy beaches. We'll find one for ourselves."

"I can't wait."

"We'll head there now."

When they'd reached the buoy, he opened the throttle and they sped toward the open sea. She'd had some good times in her life, but nothing like the experience she was having now with a man who was perfect to her.

She walked over to the side to take in the incredible sights along the coast. Soon they were passing Antibes. She wheeled around. "I've been there to see the Picasso museum, but I never saw the town from the water. It's all so breathtaking."

"To be honest, I prefer the sight standing a few feet away from me on those fabulous legs. You're rather breathtaking yourself."

She laughed in delight. "Keep it up, Dominic. Every woman loves to hear flattery like that."

"You're not every woman and it's not flattery."

Nathalie turned away and clung to the side of the boat. No. She was one of the small percent who couldn't have children. The pain of that knowledge had run marrow deep since meeting him.

Before long they passed Cannes with its profusion of glittering yachts and a Mediterranean beach that drew film stars and sheiks from all over.

"I miss you, Nathalie. Come and sit by me."

In an instant she moved to sit across from him and studied his chiseled male features through her sunglasses. There was never a more beautiful man born. "This is heaven for me."

He looked back at her through his own sunglasses. "I'm trying not to think about my life without you in it. The day you applied for work, my world changed."

"So did mine," she answered honestly. "I've been so happy." It frightened her that in coming to the vineyard, she'd met the man who'd changed her life for all time.

Today she selfishly wanted to put every thought out of her head except to enjoy every single second of this precious time with him. Depending on where the conversation led this evening, it might never come again.

"Do you miss the pharmacy?"

What pharmacy? Her mind was so far away from any thoughts except for him, she was a total mass of unassuaged longings only he could satisfy. She smiled. "What do *you* think?"

He grasped her hand, threading his fingers through hers. "I think I'd like to sail away with you and never come back."

*Don't say things like that, Dominic.*

It wasn't possible. She couldn't allow herself to imagine a life with him. "That's a tempting thought, but not realistic." She stood up. "I'm going to get us some sodas. I'll be right back."

He watched her leave. Whatever she was keeping from him had made her squirm, but he wasn't worried. Dominic wouldn't let things alone until he'd gotten the truth out of her. There was no way he'd be taking her back until all was exposed.

Two hours later they'd come in sight of Les Calanques. He headed for his favorite channel.

"Oh, Dominic—I've never seen anything so fabulous in my life! It's like entering a canyon of sheer cliffs with a fairy-tale backdrop. The white of the limestone with the blue sky above is out of this world."

He knew she would love it as he drove his boat in and headed for the sandy little beach at the end. It wasn't quite noon yet. Any boaters would probably come out later when it was warmer. For now they had this piece of paradise all to themselves.

After cutting the motor, he laid anchor and looked over at her. She'd already removed her life jacket. "How soon can you be ready for a swim?"

"Right now." She flashed him a smile to die for and took off her clothes to reveal a jade-colored bikini beneath. He came close to having a heart attack before peeling off his own clothes down to his black swimsuit. She beat him to the transom and jumped in the water.

He heard a shriek and laughed. "It'll warm up."

"Now you tell me!"

Dominic dived off the boat and swam under the water, catching her around those fabulous legs. They played for a while until he couldn't take it any longer and dragged her to the warm sand. Pulling her down next to him, he said, "You thought you would get away from me, but I'm telling you right now I'll never let go."

She lay there breathing hard with the sun bringing out the gold threads of her silvery-gold hair. "With those light green eyes, you look like a goddess who has enchanted me."

"This whole day has been one of enchantment."

He plunged his hand into her hair, which had come undone. "I want you, Nathalie. More than any woman I've ever wanted in my life."

"I want you too," she confessed, running her hands over his shoulders. He began to kiss her, starting with her throat, then every feature of her face until he found her mouth. Desire consumed him as she responded with an abandon he could only dream about. They were on fire for each other.

"I can't believe I had to live this long to meet you."

"I know. I feel the same way," she murmured against his lips. "You're too good to be true. I—" She paused because they could both hear voices and laughter. "Oh, no. Someone has found our spot."

Damn. She'd been about to say something that could

have been important for his peace of mind. "Come on. Let's swim back to the boat and fix a meal. Hopefully they'll go away after a while."

He helped her to her feet and they ran into the aqua-colored water, anxious to get away from the encroaching world. By the time they'd climbed on board the transom with their bodies free of sand, the other boat had reached the small beach.

"You shower first, Nathalie. I'll get lunch."

"Tonight I'll make dinner." She grabbed her clothes, but he didn't let her go until he'd given her another kiss that made him crave a thousand more. He would need a lifetime and beyond to be with her and still never have enough.

Soon they were at the galley table away from prying eyes, eating a deli salad and rolls. She'd put her shorts and top back on.

"How long have you had this cruiser?"

"I bought it five years ago. It provided me a safe place when I came home for visits."

She cocked her head. "Safe?"

"I needed my space."

"Away from the chateau. Of course."

Nathalie's pulse started to race. This was it. "Was there a special woman in your life, Dominic? Either here or in Paris? You know what I mean."

*Tell me the truth,* her heart cried. She needed answers now.

His eyes narrowed on her face. "Not enough to get married. No blondes with shimmering hair like yours.

The Fontesquieu men haven't had the best luck when it comes to marriage, but I live in hope."

It sounded less and less like he was Alain's father. Her mind shifted to Etienne. What if Alain was *his* son? The damage that knowledge would do to his already unhappy marriage would be disastrous considering he already had a child.

Whoever had gotten Antoinette pregnant had been the love of her life. But no matter how tragically hers had ended, Nathalie was beginning to realize she didn't have the right to interfere. Her mother had been right. She'd been so obsessed with finding Alain's father, she hadn't considered what new nightmares she could be creating.

Her eyelids smarted. She couldn't keep this up anymore. After she'd finished eating, she got up from the table and took her dishes to the sink.

"Dominic? It's getting busy. Since we no longer have this place to ourselves, why don't we head back to Nice. Somewhere along the way I'll fix dinner and we can watch the sunset. What do you think?"

For an answer, he finished clearing the table. "What's bothering you? Up until a minute ago, we were communicating. Don't tell me it's nothing." He put his hands on her shoulders.

At his touch, she trembled. "This is all moving too fast."

"Fast or not, it's happened," he whispered into her hair. "I don't want what we have to be over. Not ever." He slid his hands down her silky arms before turning her around. "I need you, Nathalie. You're all I can think about."

"Please let me go," she begged, but he didn't listen and found her mouth. *"Dominic—"*

"You want me too. I know it."

In the next breath, she surrendered to a force she couldn't control. She couldn't get close enough to him. For a few minutes, the world disappeared while they tried to satisfy their hunger. All she knew was ecstasy with this unforgettable man who filled her arms and heart.

But when he started to move her toward his cabin, she found the strength to break free of him and braced herself against the counter. "We can't do this, Dominic." After the passion that had enthralled her, she was in literal pain trying to avoid his touch.

He struggled for breath. "What do you mean?"

"I—I never meant for this to happen," she stammered. "It's all wrong."

"How could it possibly be wrong? We both felt an attraction during the interview. It's been building every second since and you know it. I've never felt this way about another woman in my life! Nathalie? Look at me."

"I can't."

"All along you've been hiding something from me. Tell me what it is."

"I don't dare."

"I knew it!" he bit out, and raked his hands through his hair in frustration. "Why are you so terrified? Help me understand."

"I shouldn't have applied for work at the vineyard. It was a mistake, and now I'm paying for it. Forgive me for the trouble I've caused you. I never meant to hurt you when you've been so wonderful to me."

"What in the hell are you talking about? Have you run away from a husband I don't know about and you're hiding at the vineyard, afraid he'll find you?"

"No!" she cried, shaking her head.

"Are you working for some editor to get information about the family business? You can tell me the truth."

"No! No one is involved but me."

"Involved how?"

"I can't answer that. Would you please let me go, Dominic? I'm begging you."

"Whatever this is, we can fix it."

She backed away from him. "The only solution out of this is for us to stop seeing each other. Let me honor my contract to pick grapes until the harvest is over."

He drew in a harsh breath. "How could I possibly stay away from you now? Deny it all you want, but our feelings for each other aren't going to fade. Before you came into my life, I'd decided this experience would never happen to me. Then you showed up in that tent. I could no more walk away from you for good than stop breathing!"

"Don't say that!" Tears trickled down her cheeks. "You mustn't."

"Why? Let's hear the truth. Are you dying of a disease and don't want to tell me?"

*Not a disease, but I can't give a man children.*

"I promise it's nothing like that," she cried.

"*Bon.* I'll drive us back to Nice. But this isn't over."

After cupping her wet face in his hands and kissing her breathless, he left the galley. She heard him race up on deck. Then he was back with her life jacket. He tossed it on a chair, then took off again. In another minute he'd started the motor.

The long journey back was pure agony for her. She cleaned up the galley before going up on deck. He said he didn't want dinner. What she'd done to him was tearing both of them apart.

By evening he'd deposited her at the door of the rental. He didn't try to kiss her again before she went inside. When she heard him drive away, she wanted to die, but there was a reason she hadn't told him the truth tonight.

She still didn't have proof that either brother was Alain's father and didn't dare probe further since she could be wrong and hurt everyone. It didn't matter that she'd had the best reason in the world for doing what she'd done. She'd gone way too far and her feelings for him needed to be cut off for good.

She'd ventured where she shouldn't have and would suffer for having given in to her guilty longing for him. It had to end now before she did damage to two men who had no comprehension of why she'd come to the vineyard to work.

Knowing that she was doing the right thing, she drove back to La Gaude at full speed. When she entered the house still in tears, she found her mom on the phone with Nathalie's *tante* Patrice, her mother's sister, who lived in Nice with her husband and family. Alain had already been put to bed. Her mother took one look at her and ended the conversation.

"You're so pale, it alarms me. I'm almost afraid to ask what's happened."

Nathalie sank down on the chair. "I spent the whole day with Dominic and had a chance to confront him. But I couldn't do it because I have no proof that either brother was involved with Antoinette. He knows I've been holding back." She wiped more tears off her cheeks.

"I was afraid of this," her mother murmured.

"I'm too involved with him, but it's not too late. If I give up the job in the morning and never see him again, no one but you and I will know anything."

"Does Dominic know you're quitting?"

"No. He'll find out after the fact."

Her mother got to her feet. "I can tell how much he means to you. If he feels the same way—and I suspect he does—he's not going to stay away from you."

"I know him. He'll come to the vineyard tomorrow to get the truth out of me. But I won't be employed there or living in the mobile home."

"Which means he'll come here."

"I hope not, but I'll have to face that moment if it happens. I'm going to go to bed now and get up extra early to take care of what I have to do. Get a good sleep, Maman." She kissed her and hurried to the bedroom, but there'd be little sleep for Nathalie.

She got up at the crack of dawn after a restless night and drove straight to the vineyard, praying there'd be no sign of Dominic. She waited in her car until she saw Gregoire. No one else was there yet. He'd just arrived in his truck. She got out with the equipment she'd been given and ran up to him.

"Gregoire? Forgive me, but an emergency has happened at my home and I can't work here any longer."

He frowned. "I'm sorry."

"So am I. Here are the things I was given to start work." He took the items from her. "You've all been so nice to me. I can't thank you enough for taking me on. I hope you find a replacement without too much trouble. Say goodbye to Paul. He was a great help."

Gregoire gave her a perplexed nod before she ran back to her car and headed for the mobile home. She'd never cleaned things so fast in her life, hoping against hope that Dominic wasn't around and wouldn't see her car. When she'd finished, she drove over to the manager's office and turned in her key.

Once back in her car, she left the vineyard. She'd cried so many tears last night in bed, she didn't know she had any more in her. But she was wrong and could barely see her way home to La Gaude.

# CHAPTER SEVEN

DOMINIC HAD BEEN struggling to get some work done in his office when Etienne unexpectedly walked in at lunchtime. He looked up. "Hey, bro. You're looking better."

Etienne frowned. "I wish I could say the same thing about you. From where I'm standing, I'd say you've come down with that wretched flu."

"I'm afraid I've got something much worse." He hadn't slept all night trying to work out what was going on with Nathalie.

"Then you're not going to like my news."

"What do you mean?"

"I just received a message from Gregoire at the office and came over on the double to see you."

"What's wrong?"

"Mademoiselle Fournier showed up at the vineyard early this morning and told him there was an emergency at home. She said she couldn't continue to work at the vineyard. After thanking him for everything and handing over her supplies, she drove off. I just called the manager of the mobile home park. He said she cleaned her home and dropped off the keys early. That was it."

Dominic jumped to his feet, feeling as if he'd just received the final blow to the gut. He rubbed the back of his neck, incredulous that she would actually quit. But last night her panic had been real. He should have foreseen her flight.

"Thanks for telling me, Etienne."

"I'm sorry to bring you this kind of news. It's obvious this woman is important to you."

"More than you know."

"Is there anything I can do?"

"Thanks, but no. I appreciate everything you've done. I've got a decision to make."

He nodded. "Call me if you need to talk."

His brother walked out, leaving Dominic standing there stunned. He'd felt her fear on the cruiser and realized he couldn't get anything out of her. It had propelled her to take flight this morning. Needing to channel his energy, he reached for his phone to call her, but all he got was her voice mail. No surprise there. He asked her to call him back, but knew she wouldn't.

After telling Theo he'd be gone from the office for the rest of the day, he drove to the chateau to change into casual clothes, then left for La Gaude.

When he reached the town, he turned on the GPS to find the La Metropole Pharmacy and parked near the front. He didn't know if she'd be working there today, but this was a place to start.

After parking the car, he entered the pharmacy that had a number of customers. One man stood behind a counter waiting on people. Dominic looked around until he spotted a striking older blonde with a slender figure who had to be Nathalie's mother. She was talking to a customer in the back. There was no sign of her daughter. That meant Nathalie was probably home.

Dominic walked back out and drove to the address on Olivier. She lived in a very modest, soft-yellow Provencal *bastide*. A red car had been parked in front. Around the side he caught sight of her blue car. His heart skipped a beat. He walked to the front door and knocked.

There was no response so he knocked again. Maybe she'd seen him from one of the front windows and intended to ignore him. After another minute he turned and headed for his car, defeated for the moment.

"Dominic? Wait!"

He wheeled around in time to see her hurry toward him wearing a colorful top and jeans. Her hair flounced around her shoulders. "I didn't realize you were out here." Her normally beautiful skin looked mottled from crying.

"I received alarming news today to hear you'd quit your job and given up the rental. Gregoire told Etienne it was because of an emergency at home. I tried to reach you on the phone. When I didn't hear from you, I came to see if you were all right."

"I'm fine, and I'm so sorry about everything. Now they have to find a replacement for me." She sounded full of remorse.

"They already have, but you and I need to talk. I'm not going to take no for an answer."

She nodded. "Just a minute while I grab my purse. I'll be right out."

His world had just gotten a little better while he waited to help her in the car. She returned and he drove them into the hills. He parked on an overlook shaded by more olive trees and turned off the engine.

"I planned to phone you later today because I owe you an explanation, Dominic."

"How about starting with the truth. Why did you quit?"

"I had a good reason."

"Convince me."

She moistened her lips in a nervous gesture. "After your brother left the other evening, I didn't like what was happening to me."

"What do you mean?"

"The news that you wouldn't be coming for dinner disappointed me much more than it should have."

"That's a bad thing?" he asked in a husky tone.

"It is for me. I never dreamed that working at the vineyard would mean I could be attracted to another man. I felt it was best to leave and still do."

Dominic had been listening. "Nathalie... You and I have experienced *coup de foudre*. It makes no sense that you're trying to put distance between us when we know we're both on fire for each other. That kind of attraction is so rare I still haven't recovered and know you haven't either. Which means there's something else you can't or won't tell me. I'm not going to leave you alone until you do."

She'd been looking out the window, then turned to him with a sober expression. "I came to the vineyard because...because I'm looking for someone."

That's what all this was about? He took a deep breath. "A man or a woman?"

"A man."

He didn't like the sound of that. "Obviously it's someone who's important to you."

"Yes."

*Ciel.* "How important?"

"So important I've gone overboard looking for him and am regretting it."

"You mean you wish we hadn't met."

"I didn't say that," her voice trembled. "But I've been guilt-ridden over applying to work at your vineyard in order to look for him."

"Why did you think to come to our vineyard of all places?"

"Because at the beginning of the summer I learned he worked at the Fontesquieu vineyard. I planned to take my vacation around the harvest so I could apply for work. By some miracle, you hired me."

The revelation racked him with pain. He studied her profile. "Did this man disappear?"

"Yes, as if he'd been wiped off the face of the earth."

Dominic's brows furrowed. "What does he look like?"

She let out a troubled sigh. "All I can tell you is that he's a Provencal."

That meant he was probably dark haired and dark eyed. At this point Dominic was shattered. "If you were in a relationship at the time he disappeared, did you contact the police?"

"No. He wouldn't have gone off like that if he'd wanted to be found."

*Nathalie...* "Yet you're still looking for him."

"Yes. I—I just wanted to know why he disappeared." Her voice had faltered again.

She'd been in love with him! *That* was why she hadn't married the guy she'd met in pharmacy college. "If you find him, what will you do?"

"The question is no longer relevant. I've given up trying to find him. That's why I quit my job at your vineyard. There's no place else to look and I've decided to let it go."

He slid his arm along the back of the seat, refusing to let this alone. "I take it your guilt over what has been happening between us is the reason you don't want to go on seeing me."

She nodded without looking at him. "I can't have a relationship with you."

"Why? Deep down do you still hope to find him one day?"

"If only to have closure."

There were degrees of pain. "If you'll tell me his name, I can run a search by my vintner sources and possibly find him."

"I would never ask you to do that, and couldn't anyway because he never would use his name. He was so secretive I'm convinced he was hiding who he really was. I wish I knew the reason. He was around for a month, then he was gone for good."

Dominic rubbed his jaw, tortured by everything she'd revealed. "But in that time he made a lasting impression."

"Yes."

"Nathalie... How long ago did he disappear?"

"It's been two and a half years."

"That long?" He was incredulous.

She nodded. "That's why it's absurd for me to keep looking. For all I know he's been in another part of the world all this time."

But at this point Dominic was frozen in place.

Two and a half years ago, Raoul had been forced to break off with Toinette.

Was it possible? Raoul was a Fontesquieu... All the men in their family were tall and dark. Provencal. That's how Nathalie had described him.

No...

Dominic didn't even want to think it. But what if by a stroke of fate, Nathalie *had* been the woman Raoul had adored, and she had used a different name with him?

Why would she be looking for him now? She knew he'd had to marry another woman. Did she come to the vineyard to find out about his life because she'd never been able to let him go in her heart?

If it was true, Dominic was haunted by the thought that Nathalie had loved his cousin and had been looking for him. He knew Raoul had never forgotten his love for her.

Dominic's eyes closed tightly for a minute when he considered yesterday when he'd started kissing her again in the galley. If she hadn't stopped him, they might have ended up making love all night long. *Bon Dieu.*

Until he'd had a certain conversation with his cousin

tonight and ascertained the truth, he needed to take her home *now*.

"Dominic? I know that what I've revealed has shocked you."

*You mean* crucified me. "That's one way of putting it, but I'm glad I have the truth at last and will drive you back to your house."

"Thank you. I hope you can forgive me."

"There's nothing to forgive. The vineyard is grateful for the excellent work you've put in. Pretty soon those red stains will be gone." He started the car and took her home.

She opened the door and jumped out the second he pulled up in front of her house. "Whether you believe me or not, I've loved every moment we've spent together." There were tears in her voice. "I'll never forget you, Dominic."

Those throbbing words would stay with him all the way to Vence. "*A bientôt*, Nathalie."

He'd rebelled against saying goodbye to her. But if she and Raoul had been lovers… His cousin would soon be free of Sabine. He and Nathalie could finally be together.

Raw pain clawed his insides as he drove to the estate and hurried inside his apartment. He and his cousin were going to have the talk of their lives. For the first time in his, he felt like death.

But Raoul texted him later and told him a problem had come up at work and he'd had to drive to their warehouse in Saint Jeannet. He wouldn't be back until the next evening.

It was just as well since Dominic needed to calm down before he talked to his cousin. He didn't want them to have been lovers.

Dominic couldn't bear it.

Nathalie had been staying home for the rest of the week to take care of Alain while her mother ran the pharmacy with Denis. It gave Minerve some time off. Next week Nathalie would go back to her routine at the pharmacy.

She adored her nephew and played with him to her heart's content. He would be her baby one day, the only one she would ever have. She would spend the rest of her life giving him all the love she could while she loved Dominic in silence. There was no man in the world like him.

If he was the one Antoinette had fallen for, Nathalie understood why she'd told Claire he was the only man she would ever love. Nathalie couldn't imagine loving another man either.

On Saturday morning she took Alain to the local park as usual and walked around with him, holding his hand. His little giggles while they fed the ducks in the pond delighted her. When she could tell he was tired, she took him home for lunch and a nap.

While it was quiet, she phoned Claire to tell her everything that had happened. "I quit my job." She'd also said goodbye to Dominic, but she didn't confess her feelings for him to Claire. That would have to remain her secret.

"I know you had hopes, but I can't say I blame you."

"You and Mom were right. I have no proof. But I want to thank you with all my heart for your help."

"Oh, Nathalie. I was happy to give you any information I could. What are you going to do now?"

"Start adoption proceedings for Alain."

"How wonderful!"

"I'm his doting, would-be mother. After it's official, I want him to start calling me Maman and we'll all live together with my mother. He loves his *grand-mere*."

"Antoinette was lucky you're there for her son. I miss her."

"So do I. One day I'll bring Alain by to meet you. Thanks again for everything. Talk to you soon."

"I'd love that. Au revoir, Nathalie."

They clicked off, but she was restless and went to her room to take a shower. As she was getting dressed in a skirt and blouse, she received a text. Maybe it was her mother. She reached for her phone on the dresser.

*Dominic.*

The blood pounded in her ears as she read it.

I have some information you've been wanting. If you're interested come to my office between five thirty and six today. You can pick up your paycheck at the same time. If you don't come I'll have it deposited in your bank. Dominic—

She let out an agonized groan. To hear from him now when the separation had been so excruciating for her... What information did he think he'd found for her when she believed either he or his brother could have been the man involved with Antoinette? Or not. Did she dare break down and walk through fire in order to be with him again?

While she stood there in utter turmoil, that fluttering organ she called her heart gave her the answer. Fool that she was, she answered back. I'll come.

Having done that, she rushed around to get ready and left the house after her mother got home at three.

She battled fear and excitement all the way and felt feverish by the time she drove onto the estate. The road led around the magnificent seventeenth-century chateau. Seeing his home in all its glory up close brought back the conversation she'd had with Dominic about his family.

The big modern business building beyond the chateau and sculptured topiary trees looked out of place. She studied the cars parked in the lot on the side. The black Renault and silver Mercedes caught her eye immediately.

On trembling legs she got out of her car and entered the door of the main entrance.

A well-dressed, attractive receptionist seated at a desk smiled at her. "*Bonjour.* Can I help you?"

"Yes." She could see Dominic's name on the door to the right. "I'm Mademoiselle Fournier. I was told to pick up my paycheck in Monsieur Dominic Fontesquieu's office."

"*Très bien.* I'll let him know you're here."

A few seconds later the door opened. The tall, dark Frenchman she loved with all her heart and soul stood there dressed casually in jeans and a tan sport shirt. Every inch of him was so arresting, she felt inundated with longings, but lines marred his handsome face and she noticed a certain pallor. Maybe he'd caught his brother's flu.

"I'm glad you could make it. *Entrez*, Mademoiselle Fournier."

He'd never been this formal with her. "Thank you."

Nathalie stepped inside, but came to a sudden halt. She'd thought Dominic would be alone. Out of the corner of her eye, she saw another tall, dark-haired man standing near the desk wearing a blue business suit. He was on his phone.

After he hung up, he turned in her direction. She let out a tiny gasp, unable to trust the sight before her eyes. This man reminded her of Dominic and Etienne. With his coloring and those familiar features, he had to be *another* Fontesquieu! Incredibly he had a look of Alain, as well. Now she really knew she was losing it.

His smiling black eyes looked over her with male interest. "Dom? Aren't you going to introduce us?"

Dominic didn't answer. What was going on?

"I'm Nathalie Fournier." She spoke up to ease the sudden tension. "And you?"

"Raoul Fontesquieu."

Dominic's cousin! The one going through the painful divorce. "It's very nice to meet you, Monsieur Fontesquieu."

"I hear you did an excellent job of picking grapes while you were here. Not everyone has a knack for it."

"I don't know about that, but thank you."

He walked over to Dominic and patted his shoulder. "We'll talk later at home."

That's right. She remembered his cousin had moved in with Dominic while getting his divorce.

Raoul flashed Nathalie another glance. "It's a pleasure to meet you."

Dominic walked him to the door. After his cousin left, he turned to her, but he looked like a different person. The lines around his compelling mouth had disappeared, but he didn't say a word to her, making her uncomfortable.

"Dominic, I wouldn't have come if I'd known you were busy."

"I asked you to come. My cousin only dropped by for a minute."

"Why are you staring at me like that?" She didn't understand.

"Because you're even more breathtaking than when we swam in the lagoon."

So was he. She swallowed hard. "You said in your text that you had some information for me I've been wanting."

Nathalie heard his sharp intake of breath. "You don't have to believe me, but until just a little while ago I thought I might have found the man you've been looking for. But my source was mistaken."

"I believe you because I know you wouldn't make that up."

"Thank you for that," he said in a thick-toned voice. In the next breath, he walked over to his desk and handed her the envelope with her paycheck. She put it in her purse.

"How are things going with your cousin?"

"It's a waiting game until his court date. His wife is fighting to stop the divorce."

"That's awful."

He grimaced. "Other things are worse, like not being able to see you anymore. Are you really planning to go through your whole life putting your personal life on hold while you wait to find the man who disappeared without a trace?"

*Don't.*

"I—I shouldn't have come and need to get home." Her voice faltered. "Thank you for the check." She started for the door.

"Just know that when you leave, there's a man here who's aching for you. That ache isn't going to go away."

She knew all about the pain he was describing. Nathalie hurried out of the building to her car. The situation had become impossible.

To add to her turmoil, there was the shocking realization that Raoul Fontesquieu could have been Antoinette's lover. The thought wouldn't leave her alone.

On the way home, she went over the conversation with Dominic when he'd told her about Raoul's unhappy marriage.

*"I'm so sorry. Did they love each other before they got married?"*

*"He'd been seeing her, but hadn't proposed marriage. Both their families wanted it desperately. One night he met a girl and overnight fell deeply in love with her, wanting marriage. But by then Sabine was pregnant.*

*"Raoul only slept with her once, but he did the noble*

*thing and married her. Sadly he had to cut everything off with the girl he loved. Then their baby died. He buried his heart with his little girl. Since the funeral there's been an emptiness in him that worries me."*

*"I can't imagine so much pain."*

*"You're not a Fontesquieu."*

The same looks ran in some families. Sometimes it was astounding. The Fontesquieu men were incredibly handsome in a similar way that made them unique. But she had to be realistic. Although Alain had many of their traits, he might not belong to any of them and probably didn't.

It was imperative she put all this behind her for good.

What her family needed was a vacation. They hadn't been anywhere since her stepfather died, and ought to go someplace far away with Alain.

When she arrived at the house to discuss it with her mother, she discovered Tante Patrice and Oncle Tommaso had dropped in for a visit. They were playing with Alain. He laughed so hard he got the hiccups.

Nathalie loved their extended family and got into the mix, spending a wonderful evening with them. She caught up on their news about her two cousins who were married and had children. One of the little girls named Angelique had just had her second birthday. She and Alain could play together.

After a while they talked about Nathalie's plans to adopt Alain. He would be her life from now on.

# CHAPTER EIGHT

SUNDAY MORNING, AFTER being awake most of the night, Dominic got showered and dressed. He and Raoul went out for breakfast and talked. Very soon now his trial date would be set with the judge.

Afterward they went house hunting for Raoul, who had no desire to return to his apartment at the chateau once he was divorced. They found several possibilities. As they drove on, Raoul said, "Let's find one for you too, Dominic."

He frowned. "If I were getting married, I'd do it in a shot."

"Since I know you're head over heels in love with Nathalie Fournier, I don't understand why there's an *if*. Dom—I've poured out my soul to you. Now it's my turn to listen while you tell me what has you gutted."

"I finally learned the truth. She's in love with a man who told her he worked in our vineyard, but he disappeared on her two and half years ago. They were only together a month. Nathalie came to our vineyard trying to find him. She didn't know his name, but she described him as Provencal." He flashed his cousin a glance. "Because certain pieces of information fit, I thought it might be *you*."

Raoul let out a strange sound. "So *that's* why you called me into your office just minutes before she showed up? You thought she was the woman I'd loved?"

"I thought it could be a possibility and she'd used another name with you."

"Well, now that you know I'm not the one, why aren't you with her right now?"

He shook his head. "Until she finds this man and has closure, she refuses to be with me."

"Closure is different from being in love. It's been over two and a half years since she last saw him!"

"Then how do you explain why she quit work at the vineyard?"

"Because she has fallen in love with you, but you've been her employer. She's probably nervous about getting involved. I saw the way she looked at you. After the vibes I got from you two yesterday, I can promise you she couldn't still be in love with that other guy.

"Come on. Take me back to your apartment so you can go after her and break her down. Don't lose the woman who makes your life worth living. She'll most likely be home."

Raoul had been talking to a desperate man. His advice made so much sense, Dominic dropped his cousin off and left for La Gaude under a warm noon sun. Before long he turned the corner onto her street.

The red car he'd seen in front of her house the other day was gone. He saw Nathalie get out of the blue car parked at the side of the house. Her long shapely legs emerged first. She wore navy shorts and a sailor top.

He pulled to a stop, not wanting her to see him yet.

Next, she opened the rear door and reached for a little boy maybe the same age as Etienne's daughter, buckled in a car seat. She kissed his black curls several times before putting him down so he could walk. The child reached for her hand.

That trusting gesture caused Dominic's throat to swell with emotion.

*Her son?* He was staggered by the fact that Nathalie was a single mother and hadn't been able to admit it to him.

Dominic wondered how she'd been able to handle being away from her little boy during the harvest. She said she lived with her mother, who was also a pharmacist. No doubt Nathalie had hired someone to take care of him while she'd been working at the vineyard.

As for her picking grapes, it explained why she came home every night instead of staying in the mobile home. No wonder she'd come looking for the man who'd made her pregnant. With her stepfather deceased, she and her mother were her son's only support.

All of these thoughts ran through his mind. Yet he wondered why she'd waited until this summer to look for the man who'd changed her life.

Not about to give up, Dominic pulled out his phone and texted her.

Nathalie? I'm out in front of your house. When I came to see you just now, I watched you take a little boy inside with you. Is it his father you're looking for? I would like to talk to you and see what I can do to help. When will you be free?

A minute later she responded.

I'm putting him down now. It may take a half hour.

At least she hadn't said no.

Then I'll grab lunch for both of us and come back.

He drove to a bistro and picked up some food for them. When he returned, she came out of the house having changed into jeans and a blouse. She looked good enough to eat.

"Do you have to stay out in front?" he asked after she'd climbed in the car.

"No. My mother is home today."

Good. "In that case I'll drive us to that overlook we went to before."

He felt her cast him a covert glance. "I can't believe you came." There was a tremor in her voice.

"As you can see, I'm unable to stay away from you." Dominic drove up into the hills and parked the car under the same olive tree. "I bought us some meat pies and coffee." He reached in back for their lunch and they both started to eat.

"Thank you. I don't deserve how good you are to me."

"I'd like to do a lot more for you if you'd let me."

"Dominic—I never planned to be with you again, but

now that you've seen Alain, I can't keep the truth from you. Over sixteen months ago my stepsister had a baby."

"Your *stepsister*..."

He groaned as unmitigated joy streamed through him. Her stepsister had been the one in love with this mystery man. Everything was finally starting to make sense.

"Yes. She adored him and named him Alain. But ten days after he was born she died of a staph infection."

"I'm so sorry that happened to her." He studied her profile. "How hard that had to have been for you and your family."

"You have no idea."

"I'm sure I don't." He leaned closer. "You've been such a good listener I want to hear whatever you're willing to tell me."

Nathalie smoothed a strand of hair behind her ear. "She was an elementary school teacher. One evening she and some other teachers from her school went to the Guinguet, a place I'd never heard of. I was working in Nice at the time and learned all this from her best friend, Claire, who lived across the street from us."

At the mention of the Guinguet, Dominic's heart began pounding like a jackhammer.

"Apparently it was love at first sight for her, but she kept him a complete secret from our family. According to Claire, her affair lasted a month, then he suddenly stopped meeting her. Two months later she went to the doctor and found out she was pregnant. I remember that she was in a terrible depression throughout her pregnancy and refused to talk about the man she'd loved."

*"Incroyable,"* Dominic murmured.

"She refused to give our family any information about the man and insisted we never talk about him again. She begged us to leave the whole subject of Alain alone."

"But you couldn't do that." How he loved this woman!

Nathalie looked at him with tear-filled eyes. "I honored her wishes until the beginning of this summer after I broke it off with Guy. When I told him I was going to adopt Alain, it changed our relationship. He didn't want to bring her son into our marriage. For that and other reasons, I said goodbye to him."

*Grâce à Dieu.*

"Oh, Dominic, Alain is so adorable and it seemed so terrible he didn't have a mother or a father, I couldn't bear it. So I thought that before I started adoption proceedings, I'd at least try to find my stepsister's lover, as he has a right to his child.

"That's when I called Claire to gather any information she could give me. All she said was that he was a Provencal, had worked on your family's vineyard and Antoinette met him at Le Guinguet. At that point I started wondering about the man she'd loved. Knowing her, he had to have been someone exceptional. Maybe something serious had happened to him and he couldn't let her know why he'd stopped seeing her. He left before she learned she was pregnant so he never knew he was a father."

All the time she was talking, Dominic was fitting

two and two together so fast, his thoughts were running away with him.

"I'm pretty sure she'd met a married man who'd wanted an affair and forced her to keep quiet about it. Since none of us knew the truth and never would, she asked our family to put the questions away and simply love Alain. I know now it was wise advice. I'm through looking."

"Nathalie—" He was trying to control his emotions. "Now that I know the truth, then there's no reason we can't go on seeing each other."

She averted her eyes. "I couldn't. Please don't ask. If you wouldn't mind driving me back home now, I promised my mother I wouldn't be long."

Beyond frustrated, he started the car and they left for her house. "Is it because of the man you'd planned to marry, your feelings for him prevent you from wanting to be with me?"

"You know I don't have feelings for him any longer or I wouldn't be this involved with you, but I'd rather not talk about it." He could feel her separating herself emotionally from him.

In a minute he turned the corner and pulled up in front. "What will it take for you to agree for us to be together? I didn't make up what happened when you melted in my arms on the sand. I need an answer I can understand."

"I'm…frightened to tell you."

*What?*

"Am I some kind of monster to you?"

"Of course not!" she cried.

"Nathalie—" He'd reached his limit.

She turned a pained face to him. "How would you feel if I told you I thought my stepsister had either had an affair with you, or Etienne."

"Say that again?" Surely he hadn't heard her correctly.

"My nephew looks so much like all of you, it's uncanny."

"Do you have a picture of him?"

She nodded and pulled one out of her wallet. His heart almost failed him when he examined the black-haired cherub up close. She'd spoken the truth. "I can't believe it," he murmured. "Alain is a double for some of the baby pictures of me and Etienne. Talk about look-alikes." He handed it back to her. "It's remarkable."

"I couldn't believe I'd met two men in one family who could possibly be his father. Then came another shock when I met your cousin in your office. He shares the same looks with you and your brother. I never saw anything like it. After you told me his marital history, I—I've wondered if Raoul could be the one," she stammered.

This was unbelievable! "You're right. Your stepsister's son has a remarkably strong resemblance to all three of us."

Her eyes beseeched him for answers. "Who would have thought?"

He swallowed hard, trying to digest everything. "I only saw Alain from a distance earlier."

"He has that same lustrous black Fontesquieu hair. You should see his piercing dark eyes in person. All three of you could claim him. When I first met you, *you* fit the description my stepsister had given Claire. You worked on the vineyard and I couldn't help but think you could have been with her."

Dominic was dumbfounded. "All this time we've been together you've thought *I* could have been her lover...?"

"At first it seemed more than plausible, but I never expected to become involved with you. That first day you took my application, I could see you written all over Alain. He has a birthmark on his leg. I saw the same one on the underside of your forearm and thought you could be the one. It's the only reason I returned on Monday to see if I'd been hired."

"You noticed that?"

"Yes. But then on the cruiser you told me about the women in your life you enjoyed, but didn't marry. I deduced you probably hadn't been with her. But you can't imagine my guilt over being attracted to you when I thought she could have been with you and had your baby."

"I'm still trying to take this in." He was incredulous.

Nathalie stirred restlessly. "You did admit you'd been to the Guinguet several times."

"So you thought that's where it all started with me."

She nodded. "I lived in hopes of getting closer to you and learning all I could first. But then my world was turned upside down because your brother, Etienne, stopped by the mobile home. You have no idea what meeting him did to me. After you told me your brother had loved another woman before his marriage, but the family thought she wasn't good enough for him,

I thought… Well, you know what I thought. Couple that with my meeting your cousin, and I couldn't go on with my plan."

A man could take only so much. "Do you have a picture of her?"

"Yes."

"May I see it?"

She hesitated before opening her purse. After pulling out her wallet, she handed him a photo.

He took a look at it. "She's very attractive, but I've never seen this woman in my life."

A hand went to her throat. "This whole situation is hopeless."

Dominic's heart almost failed him. Exasperated, he said, "Nathalie? Why didn't you just come out and ask me the first time we were alone?"

She shook her head. "How could I have dared do that when you were a perfect stranger? After Paul told me that you and Etienne were both members of the Fontesquieu family, not mere employees, that made my fear worse. Then I met Raoul. In my own way I *did* infiltrate, and you knew something was off."

"True, but you could have handed me this picture. I could have asked them if they'd seen her or knew her without telling them my reasons."

"You're right. But to tell you the whole truth would have seemed like an accusation, especially if you and the others were innocent of being with her. You could have lied to protect yourselves. I wouldn't have blamed you."

Her reasoning made a bizarre kind of sense.

"I thought… Oh, what does it matter? All this time

I've been functioning under a premise that's way off. I'm so sorry."

"Nathalie—" he said, but she interrupted him because she was beyond listening.

"My mother wanted me to leave everything alone, but I was so certain I was right. You must think I'm a fool." She opened the car door.

"Wait—"

"It's no good. We still don't have answers and I'm not going to ask Etienne or Raoul anything. That's why I stopped picking grapes. This has to be goodbye, Dominic."

Before he could credit it, she slid out while he was still holding the photo, and ran toward the house. Dominic didn't try to stop her. Tonight it was more important he get answers. Whatever the outcome, his whole life and hers were going to change.

He left for Vence and drove straight to his office. Theo had already gone home. Dominic phoned Etienne.

"We need to talk. Can you come to the office now?" Dominic had decided to question his brother first.

"Give me a half hour."

"You've got it."

They clicked off. If by any chance Etienne had been with the woman in this picture, then his brother needed to know. Dominic had been in Paris and wouldn't have known if his brother had gotten involved with Nathalie's stepsister.

While he waited, he took care of some business Theo had left for him. Before long Etienne walked in. "What's going on? You sounded ultraserious."

"That's because it could be. I have something to show you. Maybe you should sit down."

"That bad?" Etienne remained standing with his hands on his hips.

"Have you ever seen or known this woman?" Dominic handed him the two-by-three colored photo.

Etienne's dark brows furrowed before he studied it, then shook his head. "She's a beauty, but I never saw her in my life. Who is she?" He handed the photo back to him.

For his brother's sake and his own, relief swamped Dominic. "You're not going to believe what I have to tell you." For the next little while he related everything Nathalie had said, right down to the birthmarks.

His brother whistled. "Mademoiselle Fournier believes her stepsister got pregnant by a Fontesquieu?"

Dominic nodded. "She swears the boy could belong to any one of the three of us."

"You've seen him?"

"She showed me a picture. It could have been one of us when we were that age."

They stared at each other. "Well, it isn't you, and isn't me. When was this supposed to have happened?"

"According to Nathalie, their affair took place two and a half years ago."

Etienne's eyes narrowed. "That's when Raoul got married. Are you thinking what I'm thinking? People have often said they think we're all brothers."

"I know," Dominic murmured. "As late as yesterday evening I thought it was possible Nathalie had been involved with Raoul because I didn't know about her stepsister. Naturally, when I introduced them, they didn't know each other. There's only one thing to do. Show Raoul this photo."

"Agreed."

"If this is the woman Raoul fell in love with, then his life is going to get a thousand times more complicated."

"When are you going to talk to him?"

# CHAPTER NINE

MONDAYS WERE ALWAYS busy at the pharmacy. Nathalie went in at nine and waited on customers with a quick break for lunch. Her mom stayed home to take a breather from work. Nathalie told Denis to go home early and she would close up at seven, her one late night during the week. It was time she did her part.

The last customer left the pharmacy a few minutes after seven. Nathalie locked the door and was walking to the rear of the store when someone knocked on the front door.

She turned and walked back, thinking it was the customer who'd just left. But it was Dominic! Her heart plummeted to her feet.

"Will you let me in for a minute, Nathalie? I have something important to tell you."

*Help.* "No, Dominic. I've already said goodbye to you."

"It can't be goodbye. I've found your nephew's father. We need to talk."

*What?*

She knew Dominic was honesty personified. That

meant he'd shown Antoinette's picture to his brother and cousin. Which one had recognized her? Nathalie pressed a hand to her heart, unable to believe this was happening.

"Where can we go now that you've closed for the night? I'll follow you."

She didn't dare go anywhere alone with him. Better to stay right here with the lights on. She unlocked the door. "Come in."

"Thank you."

There was no one more appealing to Nathalie than Dominic. Tonight he'd dressed in a business suit and tie. No doubt he'd come from some kind of meeting. She looked uninspiring in a white lab coat over a dress, no makeup and her hair pulled back to the nape. But right now that wasn't important.

"Which one of them recognized her?"

He studied her features. "Raoul."

"So *he* was the one?"

Dominic nodded. "I asked him to tell me if he'd seen or knew this woman, then I handed him the photo. He took one look at it and paled before asking me how I came by it. That's when I told him you'd been looking for the man your stepsister had loved, but I didn't tell him there was a baby."

"Oh, Dominic—" She hugged her arms to her waist, hardly able to contain her emotions.

"He remembers her telling him she had a stepsister and can't believe it's *you*! He wants desperately to talk to you anywhere, anytime you say."

Her eyes met the burning blackness of his. "I want that too," her voice trembled.

"You have no idea how eager he is and will do whatever you suggest."

She shook her head. "That's wonderful!"

"*He's* wonderful. You've only met Raoul for a moment, but you don't know him yet. There's no better man in this world."

Nathalie had difficulty swallowing. "Obviously my stepsister felt the same way or she would never have gotten involved with him. Where would he prefer to meet?"

"That's up to you. You could come to my apartment since he's living there with me."

She moistened her lips nervously. "When would be a good time?"

"As soon as you can make it. Since I told him, he's been so anxious to talk to you about your stepsister, he hasn't been able to settle down."

"I've been in that state since I learned she was pregnant." She drew in a breath. "Is he free this evening?"

"Yes. I could drive you there and bring you back."

"That wouldn't be a good idea. Give me a minute to freshen up, then I'll follow you to the chateau. After my talk with your cousin, I'll drive home because I have to help with Alain."

He nodded. "So be it."

"I'll see you out and lock the door, then let myself out the back door."

Dominic left the pharmacy while she rushed to take off her lab coat and run a brush through her hair. After texting her mother that she wouldn't be home for a while, she put on lipstick.

Her mom wouldn't believe it when she heard the news that Alain's father had been found. Nathalie could hardly believe it either. Finally Nathalie locked up and followed the black Renault to Vence.

It gave her a strange feeling to park outside one of the entrances to the chateau, knowing she would be entering the home of the man she loved with all her heart and soul.

He unlocked the door that led upstairs to his private suite of rooms. The elegance of the sumptuous chateau wasn't lost on her as they walked down a hall lined with paintings.

When he opened the door at the end, his cousin stood there in the salon waiting for them in a sport shirt and trousers. Raoul was the tall, striking Fontesquieu her stepsister had given her heart to. Naturally, Dominic had alerted his cousin that they were on their way.

Raoul stared at her for a full minute after she walked inside. "You and Toinette might be stepsisters, but you share one similarity. She is a raving beauty too."

Nathalie was so overwhelmed to have found him, her eyes filled with tears. "You called her Toinette. That was my stepfather's nickname for her too."

His handsome features softened. "When I met her, she introduced herself as Antoinette Gilbert. I shortened it." Raoul held the photo in his hand. "This is the only remembrance I have of her. May I keep it?"

"Of course. We have hundreds at home."

"If you two will excuse me, I'll go in the other room."

Raoul turned to Dominic. "Are you kidding me? Stay! You're the reason any of this is happening. Please sit down, Nathalie."

She sank down on one of the leather couches. Nathalie could tell a man had been living here. All the masculine touches proclaimed Dominic's more modern abode. He sat next to her.

Raoul found a chair and cleared his throat. "Whether you believe me or not, I want you to know that your stepsister is the only woman I've ever loved in my life. We knew how we felt about each other by the end of that first night we met at the Guinguet."

The same thing had happened to Nathalie by the time she'd left the tent that first morning. Meeting Dominic had changed her life forever. She could fully relate.

"Before I'd met her, I'd been seeing a woman named Sabine Murat. We slept together once, but I knew deep down I didn't love her the way I should, and I ended things. Soon after, Toinette came into my life. I felt I'd been reborn and wanted to marry her on the spot. Then came the nightmare when Sabine phoned and said she was carrying my child."

Nathalie nodded. "Dominic told me."

"The worst moment in my life came when I had to tell Toinette the truth."

"She'd been so deeply in love with you, no wonder she went into depression."

Pain was written all over Raoul's face. "Toinette heard me out, then said goodbye to me and I never saw her again. I tried phoning her many times so we could talk, but she didn't answer. Of course, I couldn't blame her. No one could overcome such a cruel reality."

Tears trickled down Nathalie's cheeks. "Since then Dominic told me you've lost a baby."

"Yes. I loved our little Celine, but I found out recently she wasn't my daughter."

"Oh, no—" Nathalie cried.

"It's in the past and I'm getting a divorce."

Nathalie shared a worried glance with Dominic. "Raoul—there's something vital you need to know. It's the only reason I've been looking for you."

"What is it?"

"Antoinette died of a staph infection over sixteen months ago."

Raoul went white as a sheet. Dominic rushed over to him, but he shot to his feet. "She's gone?"

"Yes."

He rubbed the back of his neck, looking totally shattered.

"She's buried in La Gaude. But what's more important right now is the fact that she had *your* baby before she died."

Raoul staggered backward. "*My* baby?" The man had received too many shocks.

"Yes."

"I—I can't believe it," his voice faltered.

Nathalie smiled. "He looks like you, but he also resembles your two cousins."

"*He?*" Raoul cried.

"Yes. Alain is almost seventeen months old now. My stepsister named him that before she died. My mother and I have been raising him since my stepfather died."

"Toinette called our son Alain?" Suddenly the pain on his face gave way to joy, answering the most vital question for her. "That's a name in my family's line. We talked about having children."

Nathalie stood up with a smile. "Well, you got your wish. I have no proof he's yours, not without a DNA test. But here's a picture of him."

When she handed it to him, he took one look and sank back down on the couch with a low sob before studying it.

"I'm going to leave now, Raoul, and give you a chance to think about everything." She needed to get away before she broke down in tears too.

"Please don't leave yet, Nathalie."

"I have responsibilities at home. Dominic knows how to get in touch with me when you're ready. I'll see myself out."

She might have known Dominic would follow her to the car. After she climbed inside, she started the engine before looking up at him through the open window. "I pray I've done the right thing. A man has the right to know he's a father."

He reached in to brush the tears off her cheek. His touch sent a quiver through her body. "Equally true, a son has the right to know his father. Because of you, that's going to happen."

Dominic's words sank deep into her soul.

"You've done something so courageous and honorable, my cousin will be down on his knees to you when he sees the boy he and your stepsister created out of love." She felt his breath on her mouth before he gave her a brief kiss.

She lowered her eyes. "You should go back in. He needs you."

*"Nathalie—"*

She heard his cry, but couldn't remain there. After putting the car in gear, she headed for the entrance to the estate. The touch of his mouth remained with her all the way home. How wonderful it would feel to be able to give him a son or daughter...

Twenty minutes later she reached the house. Her mother had already put Alain down for the night. Nathalie found her cleaning the high chair and putting things away.

"Maman?"

She lifted her head. "Where have you been?"

"At Dominic's apartment in the Fontesquieu Chateau. It's a long story. He came to the pharmacy at closing time, and now I have news."

"What is it?"

"I gave Dominic a picture of Antoinette from my wallet. Neither he nor Etienne had ever met or known her. Then he showed it to Raoul Fontesquieu, his first cousin who's vice president of sales and marketing. I met him at the vineyard a few days ago. Raoul also resembles his cousins."

"You mean all three men look alike?"

"To an incredible degree. Right now he lives with Dominic while he's going through a bitter divorce. He took one look at the photo and confessed he'd been in love with Antoinette and would have married her but for impossible circumstances. I'll tell you about them later."

Silence surrounded them. "Is this the truth?"

Nathalie nodded. "Then I told him he had a son named Alain and showed him a photo. Though a DNA test would be needed for proof, he sounded and looked so overjoyed, his reaction thrilled my heart. But I left to give him time to absorb the news.

"He's had a shock, especially to hear that Antoinette had died. I have no doubt we'll be hearing from him before long, unless another impossible circumstance happens that prevents him."

A light entered her mother's gray-blue eyes. "He really loved her?"

"With every fiber of his being."

Her eyes filmed over and the two of them embraced. "Darling, this means you don't have to feel guilt over how much you care for Dominic."

Nathalie grasped the back of the nearest kitchen chair. "But I do."

"What do you mean?"

"Maman—I fell for Dominic when I believed he and Antoinette had been lovers. Knowing she was my step-sister didn't stop me from kissing him and wanting to be with him all night. That was wrong."

Her mother shook her head. "But look what has happened because you were so anxious to find Alain's father. I believe you were guided."

"Maybe. But there's something else. You know what it is. I can't have children. The doctor told me it would take a miracle. I love Dominic with every fiber of my being. He says he loves me, but I can't give him a son or daughter. After what happened with Guy, I—I don't know if I could handle it if it changed Dominic's feelings for me. I'm frightened, Maman."

"But, darling—"

"I don't want to talk about it. *Bonne nuit*."

"Can you believe I have a son?" Raoul stood in the apartment a different man since hearing the revelation.

Dominic eyed his cousin. The news had made new men out of both of them. Nathalie no longer had to feel guilty now that she knew he and her stepsister had never been involved. As for Raoul, he had a whole new reason to live. "It's the greatest news you could have been given."

"I'll have to keep this quiet until my divorce is final."

"I agree."

"Would you talk to Nathalie and ask her how soon I could see Alain in private?"

His pulse raced. "I'll call her right now and find out what can be arranged. Even if she's in bed, she'll understand the urgency."

"What would I do without you, Dom?"

Feeling euphoric, he patted his cousin's shoulder before pulling out his cell phone. With the whole truth revealed, nothing could keep him and Nathalie apart now. His pulse raced when she picked up on the third ring.

"Dominic?"

"*Dieu merci* you're home safely. I needed to hear your voice and am calling for my cousin. How soon can he see his little boy? Considering Raoul is in the middle of a divorce, it should probably be someplace away from your home where he won't be seen."

"I can understand that. How soon could he come?"

"Tomorrow. You set the time and the spot."

"There's a park I take him to not far from the house. It's at the Place des Canards. We could meet tomorrow around noon by the pond with the ducks. Afterward I'll take him home and leave for the pharmacy."

"Does your mother know what has happened?"

"Yes. I've told her everything. She believes this was meant to be."

His eyes closed tightly for a minute. "You're an angel, Nathalie."

"I'm anything but."

She was still struggling with her guilt. He had plans to help her with that. "Raoul agrees with me. *A toute à l'heure.*"

Tuesday morning they both cleared their schedules to be gone from the estate at noon and left for La Gaude in Dominic's car. En route, Raoul asked him to stop at a store where he could buy a toy. He soon came out with a bag that contained a little blue-and-white sailboat like the one Raoul owned.

Using the GPS, they found the Place des Canards and parked along the side of the road near the pond. He couldn't miss Nathalie's gleaming hair, which she'd left loose today. In those jeans and frilly blouse, her feminine figure took his breath away.

Alain formed a contrast with his black curls. Today

she'd dressed him in a navy short-sleeved romper with small red-and-white horizontal stripes.

They got out of the car and approached slowly so they wouldn't startle him. She saw them first and smiled. *"Bonjour."*

That brought Alain's head around. Up close Dominic could see why Nathalie had believed her nephew looked like their family. In person the resemblance to the Fontesquieux was absolutely uncanny. One day he'd grow to be a tall, dark-haired duplicate of his father.

"Alain?" She picked him up so Raoul could get a good look at him.

Raoul eyed him in wonder. "He has Toinette's cheeks and mouth." The moment he spoke in an awe-filled voice, Alain squirmed. His eyes, black as poppy throats, darted toward the pond.

"I've brought something for him, Nathalie." He pulled the little sailboat out of the bag.

She smiled. "Oh, look, Alain."

When the toddler switched directions again, Raoul handed him the toy. "Here's a *bateau* for you."

"Can you say *bateau*, sweetheart?" He started turning it around in his hands. "You'll have to play with it when you're taking your bath."

Between the way she loved her nephew, and the incredible sight of seeing father and son meet each other for the first time, Dominic's heart was melting on the spot.

"Look, Alain. *Canards!*"

As she pointed to some that had come close to the edge, Alain pointed too. *"Cans."*

"Yes. Lots and lots of them. And now you've got this *bateau*."

*"Bat!"* he burst out, causing all three of them to chuckle.

Her eyes met Raoul's. "He knows about eight words. So far all of them are one syllable."

Raoul grinned. "What does he call you?"

"Nat."

"And your mother?"

"Gran."

"I'm anxious to meet her."

"She feels exactly the same way." Nathalie lowered Alain to the grass. "Let's walk over to the bench where we left our bag and feed the *canards*."

Alain toddled alongside her in his sandals, clutching his toy. He had a lean build like his father all right. Anyone at the park would think father and son were enjoying the sunshine with Nathalie. Once more Dominic thanked providence that she'd never been with his cousin.

She pulled out a bag of wheat grains provided by the park. Raoul took some and threw them near one of the ducks. It was eaten immediately. That prompted Alain to do the same thing.

While the two were happily occupied, Dominic walked over to Nathalie and put his arm around her shoulders. "This is a moment my cousin will remember all his life, and you're the reason for it."

She lifted those light green eyes that were filled with

unshed tears. "They look wonderful together, don't they? If only my stepsister could see them."

He pulled her closer. "Maybe she can," he murmured against her neck. "After all, you were given divine inspiration to find him. Thank heaven for a woman like you who was willing to pick grapes on enemy territory to achieve a result like this. My heart almost stopped beating when this exquisite woman handed me her application. I haven't been the same since."

"Mine almost stopped too," she admitted. "I couldn't believe I was looking at the man I thought could be Alain's father."

Dominic sucked in his breath. "Raoul lost his raison d'être when he had to give up Antoinette and then lose his child, even if he found out Celine wasn't his. You don't know it yet, but learning he has a son has made him feel reborn. He'll praise you forever for what you've done."

They could hear Raoul's chuckle before Alain came running back to Nathalie and wrapped his arms around her legs. She smiled down at him. "Did you have fun?"

Raoul followed with a smile that filled his handsome features with happiness. "I want to see him every day."

"I *want* you to," Nathalie cried with excitement.

"I could come every lunch hour."

"That would be perfect! Minerve, the nanny who takes care of him while my mother and I are at the pharmacy, could plan to meet you here. She drives a red car. We'll tell her about you. If you come here tomorrow at noon, I'll take off work so you can meet her.

He's already seen you today, so it won't be a surprise for him tomorrow."

Raoul tousled Alain's curls. "I don't know how to begin to thank you for what you've done, but I'll find a way."

"After close to seventeen long months it's been my joy to unite you at last. Now if you'll forgive me, I can tell he's hungry. I need to take him home."

"Understood."

Dominic watched his cousin hunker down to look at Alain close up. The love in his black eyes was alive. "I'll see you tomorrow, *mon fils*."

Nathalie put the sailboat in her bag, then picked up Alain and waved to them. Alain copied her. Raoul walked with her and helped put Alain in his car seat. After Nathalie drove off, Raoul strode to Dominic's car with an illuminated expression of joy.

When he climbed inside, he turned to him. "Tell me I didn't dream this up. It's like having a part of Toinette back. Tomorrow I'll talk to Nathalie about a DNA test. I already love him in a way I didn't know was possible."

That was the way Dominic felt about Nathalie.

"I'm beyond happy for you, Raoul. That rose-colored villa with the swimming pool we saw is looking better and better. I can see a little boy and his father having fun out there with a bunch of colored *bats*." They both laughed. "Why don't we stop by the Realtor on our way home?"

"You're reading my mind, Dom. I want to put in an offer before anyone else takes it off the market. Sabine plans to wipe me out, but no matter what, I have a son to love and raise. Because of circumstances, I've missed out on Toinette's pregnancy and seventeen months of Alain's life. Never again. There's no way I'm letting the divorce rob me of another second to be the father my son needs."

While Dominic waited for him outside the realty office, he texted Nathalie.

I have to see you tonight. Will you be at the pharmacy?

Her answer wasn't long in coming.

No. I'll be home.

That was good news.

I'll come by your house and pick you up at seven. No excuses, Nathalie. Alain's existence changes things for all of us. One way or another we're family now.

This was only the beginning.
She texted back.

You're right. Let your cousin know that tomorrow Maman will come to the park too so she can meet him.

Raoul would be thrilled.
He texted her again.

Parfait! A demain, ma belle.

* * *

*Ma belle...*

Dominic had never used that endearment with her before.

Nathalie looked down at Alain, who'd just fallen asleep in his crib holding the *bateau*. Too much was happening too fast, but it was the result she'd wanted, even if she hadn't realized it until now.

Today the world had shifted. There'd be no adoption. Alain belonged to Raoul. At the pond, his rightful *papa* had claimed him. In a millisecond, he had become a true Fontesquieu. Nathalie knew in her heart her step-sister would be overjoyed to see her son and the man she'd loved together forever.

But now Nathalie had to make a drastic decision about what to do with the rest of her life. Her mother had done the heavy lifting after Alain had come into their lives. She would always want to live near her grandson and Raoul.

The question for Nathalie was how to get through the rest of her life when she would be Alain's *tante* from now on rather than his adoptive *maman*. She and her mother would have to help Raoul with the transition once Alain went to live with him. But Dominic and Raoul were closer than brothers. Dominic would always be around. Nathalie couldn't imagine how that would work.

She couldn't bear the pain of living this close to Dominic's orbit. Though they hadn't made love, it was what had been in her mind and heart that counted. She'd pushed thoughts of Antoinette away when she'd been in Dominic's arms. If he had thoughts of marriage, she feared his reaction when he learned she couldn't give him a child.

That meant she needed to leave La Gaude and start a new life in a place where there was no danger of running into him. Nathalie owned her car and had saved enough money to rent an apartment. She *should* be living on her own now anyway. It would have to be close enough to still be able to visit her mother without difficulty. They could plan times together when Alain would be there with her.

For the rest of Tuesday afternoon, Nathalie got on the computer to look for jobs available for pharmacists in the greater Provence area. Before her mother returned from work, she'd found an opening at a privately owned pharmacy in Menton, a city of twenty-five thousand on the French Riviera. The hour's drive from La Gaude would be perfect. They needed a pharmacist full time and the pay sounded good.

Nathalie applied for it online. She believed her mother and Denis would get along just fine without her, and they could always hire another pharmacist to help out.

Knowing she'd done this much to plan out a new future for herself helped Nathalie to find the courage she'd need to face Dominic with the truth about her condition when he came by for her this evening. It was time to get ready. She'd watch for his car and hurry outside. One day her mother would meet Dominic, but not tonight.

# CHAPTER TEN

DOMINIC PULLED UP in front of the Gilbert home. Today the stakes had changed. Their lives were about to be transformed forever.

Even before he shut off the engine, Nathalie came walking out to his car wearing a stunning gold-on-green print dress. His breath caught at the shape of her gorgeous figure. Her hair caught the fire of the setting sun. No other woman matched her beauty inside or out.

He leaned across the seat and opened the door for her. She climbed inside, bringing her delicious floral scent with her. "Thank you, Dominic." She wouldn't look at him.

Without telling her his plans, he drove down the street.

"Where are we going?"

"I'm taking you to Vence. There's something I want you to see. It won't take long."

"I'd rather we didn't. Can't we stay here? All I want to know is if your cousin is truly happy."

He darted her a glance. "You already know the answer to that question. But tonight I don't want to talk about Raoul. You and I have other business that's only important to us."

"No, we don't!" she cried, turning to look out the passenger window.

"That's what you think."

"I only agreed to see you in order to work out arrangements for Raoul."

"Tonight I want to talk about us." Since he could tell she was attempting to shut him out, he turned on the radio to a soft rock music station. It didn't take long to reach Vence.

He wound around to a street on the heights of the city with a panoramic view of the sea. The modern white villa peeking out from the cypress trees had appealed to him while he'd been house hunting with Raoul. Five bedrooms, three thousand square feet and a swimming pool. Everything that had been missing while he'd lived in a massive old chateau most of his life apart from those years in Paris.

Dominic pulled up in front and shut off the engine.

"Why did you stop here?" He heard that panic in her voice again.

"This villa is for sale. I'd like to know what you think of it."

"It's lovely, but it has nothing to do with me."

"It could have everything to do with you once we're married. I've been inside and think it would be the perfect home for us and the children we're going to have."

She suddenly buried her face in her hands. "I could never marry you, Dominic."

He reached across to caress her shoulder. "I could never marry anyone else. I'm madly in love with you."

"A marriage between us isn't possible."

"Give me one good reason why."

Her head lifted abruptly. She turned to him. "Because I can't give you children, and just now I heard in your voice that it's what you want most."

Pain rocked his body. "On the cruiser you said you weren't dying of a disease or anything like it."

"I'm not, but I do have a condition. It's called primary ovarian insufficiency. By twenty years of age, I'd only had one period. Amenorrhea is the name for it. The doctor put me through a series of tests. Since that time I've only ovulated twice and I'm twenty-seven. I'm one of the five to ten percent of cases that happens to younger women. It means pregnancy will pretty well require a miracle. You don't want to marry me."

"Nathalie—"

"There's nothing you can say to make me change my mind. Right now I'm in so much pain, I can't be around you. Please take me home."

Devastated that she could be this tortured, he had no choice but to drive her back to La Gaude. There had to be a way to reach her, but it wouldn't be right now. He needed to come up with a plan. Silence filled the interior all the way back to her house.

When he drove up in front, she turned to him. "What I wanted to tell you when I came out to the car earlier was to please ask Raoul to deal with me and my mother from now on. There's no reason for you to act as the go-between any longer. You've had more to deal with than any man should have to."

"Doesn't it matter to you that I fell in love with you and wanted to do whatever I could to be with you?"

"That's because you're the most decent and honorable man I've ever known." Her voice trembled. "You were always wonderful to me even when you suspected I'd applied for work with ulterior motives. Just look what I did, Dominic. I suspected three men of being Alain's father and tried to prove it. Who does something like that?" she blurted in pain.

Dominic grasped her hand in exasperation. "How can you say that when you brought about the miracle that restored your stepsister's boy to his birth father?"

She shook her head. "It doesn't matter. I'm so honored you would want to marry me, but you deserve a woman who can give you children." She eased her hand away, then opened the door.

Talk about agony.

"I'm sure we'll see each other accidentally from time to time over the years. I have no doubt Alain will get to know you and love you. Between his father and you, he'll have the greatest role models in the world to learn from. It's so much more than I could have hoped for when I started down this slippery slope."

Dominic watched her get out and disappear inside the house. If another miracle didn't happen fast...

He drove back to the chateau needing help before he drowned.

# CHAPTER ELEVEN

THE MEETING AT the park on Wednesday was an emotional one for Nathalie. Her mother had been bowled over by Raoul, who'd come alone to meet her and Minerve. They planned to go to the hospital on Thursday at noon for the DNA tests. It wouldn't be long before Alain became the newest official member of the Fontesquieu family.

Nathalie was thankful Dominic had gotten the message and didn't accompany his cousin. She couldn't have handled seeing him today.

This time Raoul had brought a little toy car for Alain, bringing a smile to his adorable face. The two of them proceeded to throw more food to the ducks. Already Nathalie could tell a bonding was taking place between father and son.

When her mother and Minerve started walking Alain to her mother's car, he didn't want to go. He'd been having too much fun with his *papa*.

Raoul helped him in the car seat, then asked Nathalie to stay for a minute after they'd driven off. "Before you go, there's something else we have to talk about."

Nathalie knew what it was. Her heart sank. "I'm sorry, but I've got to get to the pharmacy. Denis is alone right now."

"Can you give me five minutes? This is an emergency."

"If you mean Dominic—"

"You know I do," he interrupted her. "He came home last night a shattered man. You can't do this to him. Your fear about being unable to have children is unwarranted when it comes to Dominic."

"You don't know that. The man I thought I would marry couldn't handle it."

"You don't know Dom. He loves you, and your rejection of him without giving him a chance to tell you how he feels about your condition is crucifying him. In time it's going to crucify you. I know what I'm talking about. If you shut him out, you're making the worst mistake of your life."

She switched her gaze to him. "What do you mean?"

"I had to tell your stepsister the truth when I found out Sabine was pregnant. There was no altering the outcome. I felt like a monster who didn't deserve happiness. But your situation is entirely different. Let Dom tell you what's in his heart. More than anyone in the world, I want him to be happy. He adores you, Nathalie."

Raoul's words rang so true, the tears coursed down her cheeks.

"I couldn't fix my situation, but you have every chance to find happiness with Dom. Just let him in. I'm begging you. I also believe in my soul Toinette was urging you on to find me."

"You can honestly say that?"

"As God is my witness. Dominic was the conduit. Don't you think she's been in heaven suffering because she refused to tell your family about me?"

Her heart leaped. Was that true?

"You've been an answer to prayer and I'll spend the rest of my days being the best father I can be to our child. I've been given a second chance to redeem myself, all because of you. I love you for what you've done for me and Alain, Nathalie. You were there for him all that time. His wonderful aunt."

By now she was sobbing.

"Before you leave, remember there's another man out there who loves you body and soul. Don't be afraid. Have faith in his love for you. If you don't, that would be the real tragedy. Dom told me it was love at first sight for the two of you. That good old *coup de foudre*. It caught me and Antoinette too. The four of us are a lot alike."

She nodded. They definitely were.

"Don't you think it's time you let Dom out of his prison? He's the reason my miracle happened to me. I'm pleading with you not to let him spend another night in hell. That's where he was last night. I know because I was with him and felt utterly helpless to comfort him. He's waited twenty-nine years for a woman like you to love him."

Nathalie kept wiping her eyes. She wanted to believe him.

"I have one more piece of good news. My court date is in ten days. When it's over, then I'm taking a needed

vacation so my son and I can be together twenty-four/
seven. I've put money down on a house for us."

He and Dom had both been house hunting. The
knowledge sent another thrill of excitement through
her body.

Raoul gave her a hug and left for his car on a run.

Nathalie drove to the pharmacy in a daze. Last night
she'd filled out an application to be a pharmacist in
Menton in order to put distance between her and Dominic. But Raoul had said so many things she couldn't
dismiss, she had difficulty concentrating at work. When
it was time to close the pharmacy, she went out to her
car and headed home at top speed.

As soon as she walked in the house, she saw her
mother and Alain sitting on the living room floor playing with his building blocks. Nathalie got down with
them.

Her mother smiled at her. "Today Raoul called you
an angel. I agree. Your desire to find him means our
Alain is going to have a wonderful life with his *papa*.
He told me everything about his heartbreaking choice
back then. I have real compassion for him considering
the kind of family he's come from."

"I can't blame him either, Maman." She put another
block on Alain's.

"Antoinette could have looked all over and never
found a man more exceptional. He's so crazy about
Alain already, it's extraordinary. I can only think of one
other besides your father who's his equal."

They stared at each other. "You mean Dominic."

"You know that's who I mean. You never gave up

and he never let you. If that isn't love, then I don't know anything."

"You know a lot."

"Then stop worrying you can't have children. We've been through a lot of sadness and grief over the last two and a half years. It's time we filled this house with real happiness. Finding Raoul is just the beginning."

Nathalie got to her feet. "Do you have Raoul's phone number?"

"Yes. He gave me his business card with his cell phone number. It's in the kitchen on the counter."

"Thanks." She tousled Alain's curls before walking in the other room. Once she'd put the number in her own phone, she texted him.

Do you know where Dominic is tonight?

Raoul answered back so fast it took her by surprise.

Dom and I have a meeting with Etienne at the Tour de l'Est. There's been a problem with the latest batch of wine. We'll be on our way in a minute. I'll keep you posted.

In her mind's eye she knew the location of the Tour de l'Est. It was a massive round tower on the property. In her readings she'd learned that the land deeded to the Fontesquieux contained some battlements from the fifteenth century. Since they'd cleared out the old weapons and munitions from the east tower, its eight-foot-thick walls with rooms on four floors had been used to store their wine.

Now that she'd found the courage to talk to Dominic, she groaned to think he wasn't available.

She sent another text.

Thanks. Please don't tell him I asked about him.

In came his response.

Your secret is safe with me.

The blood hammered in her ears as she made the decision to drive to Vence tonight and take a look at the tour. Maybe she'd be able to catch him. After putting on one of her favorite dresses, she hurried into the living room.

"Maman? I'm leaving for the vineyard. I might be late."

Her mother smiled at her. "I hope you are. That man has brought a light to your eyes that has never been there before."

She took a quick breath. "I love you, Maman." Nathalie leaned over to kiss them both and raced out the front door.

Dominic had just left the office for the Tour de l'Est with Raoul in his Jaguar when he received a call from their grandfather.

Raoul darted him a glance. "Aren't you going to get it?"

"No. The old man's furious because I ended it with Corinne. All that money could have come to the Fontesquieu treasury. I don't live in the same universe as our *grand-père*."

"Does anyone?"

Nathalie had shown Dominic what life had to offer if you were lucky enough to meet your soul mate. He hadn't believed such a thing existed until she'd entered his world. In the short time he'd known her, she'd taught him what it was to lay down your life for someone you love. In her case, her stepsister's son. She'd risked the unknown with nothing to go on but a hope and a prayer of uniting a father and son.

Tears stung his eyelids. She might not want to be with Dominic right now, but he had to have faith that in time she would change her mind. They were meant to be together whether she could have his baby or not. He felt it to the very depths of his being. Otherwise there was little sense to life.

Raoul drove them past the winery where they could smell the fermentation before reaching the tour. A dozen cars and trucks filled the parking area. They got out and walked inside the double doors of the old battlement.

"Hey, bro." The two of them entered the vaulted conference room on the ground floor. Etienne was already there talking with a group of storage workers and managers. "Where's the fire?"

Etienne handed them each a bottle of wine. "It's always a fire with Grand-père. He insisted the three of us meet. Sorry you had to come. These bottles have undergone six rackings over thirty-day intervals and still have a problem. Take a look."

Dominic examined his. "You're right. The wine has failed to clear."

"As I indicated on the phone, it's definitely nonspecific. I don't think any bacterial contamination is at work. In my opinion it will probably clear, but it may take up to a year or so."

"Unfortunately Grand-père doesn't want to wait that long." Raoul had checked his bottle. "He's always in such a damn hurry. There's one thing we can do right now."

Dominic nodded. "Arrange for the wine to be moved. Store it in a cooler place for several weeks. All that's required is a drop in temperature of ten degrees. If nothing changes, we'll come up with plan B."

"That's the route I'd go."

"Then we're all in agreement." Etienne gave the group instructions and they left. He walked back to Dominic and Raoul. "I'll let the old man know what we decided as soon as I get home so he won't have a fit. Sophie's come down with a cold. I need to spend some time with her before bed. Thanks for coming. See you later."

After he left, Dominic stared at his cousin. "Pretty soon you'll be able to tell everyone about your son and you'll be putting him to bed in your new house. Just think. When Alain grows up, he might become a wine expert like you."

"He might hate the wine business."

"Maybe he'll become a pharmacist like his grandfather Gilbert."

"True. I can promise you one thing. I'll allow Alain to find his own way in life, whatever it is."

"You think I don't know that?"

Raoul nodded. "The divorce can't come soon enough for me. How about we go to the Guinguet before we go home? That's where I met Toinette and want a night to reminisce."

Just the mention of it reminded Dominic of his conversation about red wine with Nathalie. Everything reminded him of her. He couldn't deal with any more pain. "I don't know, Raoul. I'm lousy company."

"I'll take your lousy company over anyone else's. Come on. We could use some noise and music." They walked out to the car in the cooler night air. The beginning of the harvest had brought Nathalie with it. Now the grapey fragrance meant the harvest was almost at an end and the fruit was being turned into wine. The thought of it being over with her was untenable. He wanted her so badly, he was in agony.

Soon they arrived at the bistro where many of the Fontesquieu employees hung out. Unfortunately, Nathalie dominated his thoughts. His cousin had the right idea to keep him occupied until he went to bed. But nothing could be done about the empty nights.

"Tonight calls for a celebration." Raoul called the waiter over. He ordered some tapas and their best rosé wine. Dominic had never seen him so jubilant. After such a tragic marriage, he understood his cousin's euphoria. But he hoped the family wouldn't get wind of anything until after the divorce was final. One word about Alain could bring new pain to Sabine and make things uglier.

In a few minutes their waiter came to the table with their order, but he also placed a small goblet of white wine in front of both of them.

Raoul shook his head. "I didn't order this."

"It's compliments of *la blonde exquise*. She's over at the bar."

They both turned around. Dominic almost went into cardiac arrest to see Nathalie walk toward them in a filmy violet dress, holding a similar goblet. His gaze collided with the jewel green of hers.

"Welcome to the Guinguet, messieurs. I thought you might enjoy the special Guinguet wine made by the famous Fontesquieu family. I'm buying this evening. It's an acquired taste to be enjoyed for a very important occasion. You two fine-looking specimens appear to be able to handle its unique flavor."

She leaned over to click each of their goblets with hers. "Here's to a harvest with unexpected bumper crops. Our family historians will be forced to add two new names to our family trees. *Salut*."

"Nathalie!" Dominic cried as her words sank in.

She smiled into his eyes. "Drink up, *mon amour*."

He watched her put the goblet to her lips before he had the presence of mind to drink his. For the first time in his life, the sour wine tasted like ambrosia.

With a secret glance, Nathalie wordlessly acknowledged Raoul's departure from the bistro. Then she slid into the chair he'd just vacated. After she fed Dominic a tapa, she ate one. Suddenly Dominic reached across the small round table for her hands, grasping them for dear life.

"What happened since the last time you claimed you couldn't be with me?"

"Your cousin spoke to my heart. He said there was a man out there who loved me body and soul. To quote him, 'Don't be afraid. Have faith in his love for you. If you don't, that would be the real tragedy.' I knew it was true and came as fast as I could to find you."

Dominic's black eyes burned with love for her. "Let's get out of here. I need to hold you so I can believe this is really happening."

He got up and pulled her to her feet. Still gripping her hand, he drew her through the crowd to the outside of the bistro. "Where's your car?"

"Around the corner."

"How did you know I was at the Guinguet?"

"I followed you and Raoul from the tour after I'd texted him earlier. He told me you would be there."

A painful squeeze of her hand told her how happy that had made him. They were both out of breath when they reached the Peugeot. "Mind if I drive?"

"I want you to. I'm shaking too hard to get behind the wheel."

Dominic helped her in, then hurried around and got in the driver's seat. He had to adjust it to accommodate his long, powerful legs. She handed him the keys. Within seconds he'd started the engine and drove out to the street.

Nathalie didn't care where they were going. She

clung to his hand, dying to get in his arms and stay there. As he drove them to the heights of the city, she knew where they were going. The moon shone down on the beautiful site of the white villa surrounded by the dark cypress trees.

"I've bought the place, so it means we're private here."

"You already did?"

"Yes. No matter how long it took for you to come back to me, I wanted it for us."

"Darling—"

He pulled into the driveway and drove up to the side of the villa. In the next breath, he turned off the car and reached for her. "Do you have any idea how long I've been waiting for this? I'm only going to say this once. We'll adopt as many babies as we want when we decide it's right. What matters is that we'll be man and wife. Do you hear me?"

"Yes, darling."

He lowered his mouth to hers in an explosion of needs they'd had to repress.

She moaned aloud. "Dominic… I love you so much you can't imagine," she cried, giving him kiss for kiss until they were devouring each other.

Time became meaningless as they attempted to appease their hunger, but the fire kept building. Over and over again their passion engulfed them. He was such a gorgeous man in every way, no amount of love she could shower on him would ever be enough. Every touch of his hands and mouth ignited her senses.

From the first moment she'd looked into his eyes at

the interview, he'd brought her alive. Until then she'd been in a deep sleep, but no longer. He was the answer to her existence.

"You're the most beautiful thing to come into my life, *mon tresor*," he murmured, kissing her with abandon. "I'm so crazy in love with you, I don't know how long I can wait for our marriage."

"I feel the same way and never want to be apart from you again."

He cupped her face in his hands. "Let's have a wedding as soon as possible with your mother as witness."

She fingered his luxuriant black hair. "What about your family?"

"I'm afraid we'll have to leave them out of it. Tell me you understand."

"Of course I do," she cried without hesitation. Eleven years away from his family was explanation enough.

"You're incredible," he cried, kissing her with increasing hunger.

"Tomorrow I'll tell Maman we're getting married right away."

"How about Sunday, four days from now?"

"If only we could."

He kissed the base of her throat, then her mouth. "I know a justice of the peace whose funds I've managed on the side since my return from Paris. Andre Godin is now a wealthy man. When I ask him to marry us at your house, bypassing the usual waiting time, he'll do it."

She hugged him harder. "I'm convinced you can do anything you wonderful, wonderful man." Nathalie could cry for joy over what was happening.

He gave her another long, hard kiss. "I'm thinking that while we furnish the villa, we'll stay at a hotel in La Gaude so you're close to Alain during the transition and can go on working at the pharmacy."

"Maman will love that."

"When Raoul's divorce is final, we'll have a big party for all our families and friends. Whether my family shows up or not will be up to them. After that we'll take a honeymoon. For now it will be enough to be your husband."

It sounded like heaven on earth. Beyond words, Nathalie covered his mouth with her own. Again they were lost in the thrill of knowing they would become one in just a few days. Nothing else mattered.

"I know you need to get home," he eventually whispered against her lips. "I'll drive us to the chateau for my car and follow you home."

"I'll be fine."

"Let me be the judge of that. You're the most precious thing in my life. If anything were to go wrong now, I wouldn't survive. Do you hear what I'm saying?"

"Yes. Oh, yes!"

# CHAPTER TWELVE

ON THE RIDE home from La Gaude, Dominic made a few important phone calls and constructed a list of all the other things he had to do before Sunday. Near midnight, he let himself in the apartment so euphoric over the miraculous outcome at the Guinguet, it took him time to realize Raoul wasn't there.

Eager to share the news of his impending marriage with his cousin, he texted him. Within a minute his phone rang. He clicked on. "Raoul? I just got home. Where are you?"

"I've been in Nice, but I'm back on the estate. See you shortly." He clicked off fast.

His cousin didn't sound at all like himself. Raoul's jubilance of earlier had vanished. Worried about the change in him, Dominic went to the kitchen to make them coffee. They had a lot to talk about.

"Dom?"

"In the kitchen."

His cousin walked in. "I can't tell you how happy I am for you, Dom. I knew Nathalie would come around."

"You had a lot more faith in her than I did." He put

their coffee on the table, but when he glanced at Raoul, he saw a man in pain. "Sit down and tell me what's wrong."

"Horace contacted me after I left the bistro and told me I'd better come to his office in Nice because there was a problem."

"Has Sabine demanded more money?"

"She's demanding that the two of us go to counseling to try to save our marriage, claiming she still loves me. Her reason is that with professional help we could start over again."

Dominic sat back in the chair. "Counseling? That doesn't sound like Sabine."

"No. It sounds like both sets of parents have gotten together to try to stop the divorce. Hell, Dom!" He shot to his feet, raking a hand through his hair. "No amount of counseling can make me love Sabine. That's what I told Horace."

"Does he know about Alain?"

"Not yet."

"What's he going to do?"

"Respond with my answer to the judge. But Horace imagines she'll come back with possibly a hundred million dollars in damages since our family has billions. Horace said he'll hammer out the best settlement he can."

"Whatever the judge decrees, you know I'll help."

"You're the best, Dom, but it's my problem and I'll have to solve it. One good thing did come out of tonight's meeting. He's still asking for the same court date that was set."

"Good. For Alain's sake you need to be divorced ASAP."

A glimmer of a smile broke out on his face. "So when are you two getting married?"

"This Sunday."

He shook his head. "When you make up your mind about something, there's no stopping you. How can I help?"

"You already have. Nathalie told me your talk with her reached her heart. None of this would be happening without you. We're going to have a ceremony at her house with her mom and Minerve. That's it. Andre Godin will officiate. And within less than two weeks your divorce will be final."

"God willing, Dom."

"Nathalie Durand Fournier, do you take Dominic Laurent Fontesquieu to be your husband in sickness and in health? Do you vow to love and cherish him for all the days of your life?"

She couldn't believe this moment had come. Her heart was so full of love for Dominic she really did have trouble breathing. With those dark eyes and hair, and wearing an elegant dove-gray suit, he was so gorgeous it didn't seem possible she'd won the love of this man.

"I do," she cried softly.

With a smile, the judge turned to Dominic. "Dominic Laurent Fontesquieu, do you take Nathalie Durand Fournier to be your wife, in sickness and in health, always watching over her, loving her and protecting her for as long as you both shall live?"

"I do," he answered in a thick voice.

"Then by the power invested in me, I now pronounce you man and wife. What God has brought together, let no man put asunder. You may now kiss your bride, Dominic."

Her new husband pulled her into his arms and kissed her with such hunger her legs started to tremble.

When he finally let her go, the judge said, "You may now present each other with rings."

Dominic drew a diamond ring out of his jacket pocket and slid it home on her ring finger. It had a dazzling sparkle as she took the gold band from her little finger and put it on his ring finger. The engraving said *Mon Bien Amie*.

He kissed her deeply again before relinquishing her once more.

The judge beamed at them. "It has been my pleasure to marry a man I've highly esteemed for years." He gazed at Nathalie. "How I envy him."

She felt the heat rise into her face. "Thank you, Your Honor."

He shook Dominic's hand, then said a few words to her mother before leaving the house.

"Oh, darling." Her mother ran to her and they hugged. "It was a beautiful ceremony and you look so lovely."

"So do you, Arlette," Dominic murmured. "Now I know where Nathalie gets her fabulous looks." He gave her a hug.

Alain made some noises that caused them to turn around. He was getting restless. Minerve had been holding him during the short ceremony. Nathalie's mother reached for him so Nathalie could hug Minerve. She'd been a part of their family for a long time.

"I'm so happy for you, Nathalie." On a whisper, she said, "If he were my husband, I don't think I'd ever be able to let him out of my sight."

"I won't if I can help it."

Dominic hugged Minerve. "Thank you for supporting us and for being so good to Raoul. You've made all the difference while he's been bonding with Alain."

The older woman's eyes filled. "This has been a happy time for all of us. I hope his divorce is final soon. I know he wants to show off his son to everyone."

"It'll happen before long," Nathalie chimed in. She looked at her mother. "Now we're going to leave, but I'll be at the pharmacy in the morning as planned."

"It doesn't seem right that you can't go off on a honeymoon, but I understand what's at risk here."

After knowing how difficult Raoul's life had been when he'd met Antoinette, her mother knew it was vital everything stay secret for a while longer. None of them wanted anything to go wrong at this point.

Nathalie gave Alain a kiss and hug, then hurried out the door with Dominic carrying an overnight bag.

The Soleil Hotel was only two minutes away from Nathalie's house. That was good because Dominic couldn't last any longer before he got his bride all to himself. She looked a vision in a white silk and lace wedding dress that came to the knees of her shapely legs.

He parked the car and walked her inside to their room

down the left hall. Each room had a balcony that overlooked La Gaude. Earlier that morning he'd procured the card key and had arranged for flowers to be put on the dresser and table.

Once inside their room, he lowered their overnight bags to the floor and caught her around the waist from behind. "You're trapped now, *ma belle*. There's no escape."

She whirled around, her green eyes burning with love for him. "I have news for you, *mon amour*. I told Minerve I'd never let you out of my sight and I meant it."

Slowly he unpinned the gardenia corsage he'd given her. After he'd unfastened the buttons of her wedding dress, she slipped out of it while he removed his suit jacket and tie.

"I love you, Dominic. You'll never know how much."

He studied her exquisite features, taking his time. "We have all day and night to show each other. I can't wait any longer."

"I don't want to wait," she cried.

He picked her up in his arms and carried her through the sitting room to the bedroom. Once he'd followed her down on the bed, he lifted a lock of hair to his lips. "Do you know you have strands of gold and silver? You're like a princess come to life with your hair splayed around you. And you have a perfect mouth. When we met in the tent, I couldn't take my eyes off you. You beguiled me."

"You enchanted me." She kissed his jaw. "When I left the tent, I wasn't the same woman who'd gone in. I didn't know a man like you existed."

"By some miracle we've found each other. I swear I'll love you forever, *mon coeur*." Burning with desire for her, he lowered his head to kiss her seductive mouth. At the first touch he was gone. Her response enraptured him, sending him to a different world where all that mattered was to love and be loved.

The sun was going down by the time Nathalie became aware she was lying against her husband's rock-hard body. Dominic's legs had trapped hers and his arm lay across her hip possessively. No woman on earth would ever know this kind of joy because there was only one Dominic. Being loved by him made her feel immortal.

Nathalie wanted to know his possession again and started kissing him. They'd married a lot sooner than many couples, but that was part of the fascination of loving him and learning new things about him.

"Nathalie," he murmured. Suddenly he'd come awake and pulled her on top of him. "No man ever had a lover like you. To think you're my wife!" He started to kiss her again, filling her with rapture.

The room had grown dark by the time they came awake again. She eased reluctantly out of his arms. "It's almost ten o'clock, Dominic. We haven't eaten all day. You must be starving. I'll call for room service."

While she reached for the house phone and put in an order for meat crêpes, crème brûlée and coffee, he'd gone in the other room for their bags. When he returned, he was wearing a striped robe, and he answered the door to bring in their food.

They ate in bed. She faced him. "I've never been this happy in my life. If my stepsister hadn't loved Raoul the way she did, we would never have met. The thought of that…" She couldn't finish.

"I don't like to think about it either, so we won't." He moved the tray to the floor, then pulled her into him. "I've been so impatient to make you my wife we haven't talked about the practicalities of being married."

She raised up on her elbow. "You sound worried."

"In a way I am. Your mother lost your stepdaughter, then your stepsister. Soon Alain will be living with his father. Today I took you away from her. I want both of you to be happy."

Tears stung her eyes. She was married to the most remarkable man in the world. Nathalie flung her arms around him. "I love you for thinking of her and caring about her. There's no one like you, but La Gaude isn't that far away from Vence. We'll work things out."

"What if she moved to Vence? I'd help her get into a house near our villa. She wouldn't have to work anymore and could have time for friends as well as being a grandmother. Raoul's house is only two streets away from us. I'd like to be there for her and offer support if the idea appealed to her."

She shook her head in disbelief. "You're so generous and amazing. What did I ever do to deserve you?"

"I keep asking that question about you. The women who've been in my life have been so different from you. There's nothing shallow about you. You're an exceptional woman in every way, Nathalie. It means you've had exceptional parents. I see the way you are with Alain. The love you've shown him is a revelation."

"He's easy to love," she said in a broken voice.

"The day I saw you get him out of your car, he reached for your hand. I thought he was your son. There was a tenderness in the way you treated him. It was a defining moment for me where you're concerned and brought tears to my heart. I knew at that moment I loved you desperately."

"Oh, Dominic." She half sobbed and clung to him. "Do you know when I knew I loved you forever? I was telling you about the man I was trying to find. And even after you thought I loved him, you offered to help look for him because that's the kind of unselfish person you are. You even said you'd talk to your vintner friends. You don't know what that did to me. That day, like all the others with you, will live in my memory."

"Nathalie—"

He caught her to him and started making love to her again. Far into the night he swept her away. She couldn't believe it when morning came. He was already awake, kissing her so she'd wake up.

"It couldn't be time to go to work!"

"I'm afraid it is."

"I can't leave you."

"You think I want to let you go? But we'll have tonight. I'll pick you up at five."

"I can't bear to leave you, but I have to. I'd better hurry and shower."

"Go right ahead. Of course, I'd be happy to help

you." His grin turned her heart over. "But it might make you late for work by six or seven hours."

Blushing from head to toe, she grabbed the robe he'd taken off and ran to the bathroom to get ready. Within ten minutes they were both dressed and walking out to his car.

En route to the pharmacy, she clung to his hand. "If this is the way it's going to be from now on, I can't do it. Leaving your arms this morning has been agony."

"How do you think I feel? I'll be in my office all day watching the clock until it's time to come and get you. My assistant, Theo, will tell me to go home because I'm worthless. This is why we're going to need a honeymoon soon."

"Where will we go? I don't know if I want it to be far away. Traveling to get someplace will take time away from lying in your arms."

"Then we won't go anywhere. We'll just stay home and go out on the cruiser for weeks on end. We'll explore the other sites of Les Calanques to our hearts' content." He'd pulled up in front of the pharmacy.

"Do you promise?"

He caught her to him and kissed her long and sensuously. "Anything you want."

She kissed his jaw before getting out of the car. "There's nothing else in life I want but you."

"In that case, be ready to leave Vence right after work. I'll pack for you."

Her eyes lit up. "What have you got planned?"

"You'll find out."

"Dominic—"

"I've cleared it with your mother."

He drove off, taking her heart with him.

When Dominic drove up to the pharmacy at five, his brand-new wife came running out. His heart leaped at the sight of her. Once in the car, he reached for her and kissed her with abandon. But too many onlookers caused him to relinquish her mouth.

"Let's get out of here." He started the car and merged with the traffic. "Where are you taking me?"

"To the airport. We're flying to Paris on my private jet."

*Paris?*

"For how long?"

"Two days. We'll eat dinner en route. I own an apartment there where we can be private and make plans for our future."

She let out a squeal of joy. "I feel like I'm in a dream."

"Before I met you, I didn't believe in dreams and planned to go back to Paris."

Nathalie gazed at him in alarm. "When?"

"Once the harvest was over. My father has recovered and I had no desire to remain on the estate any longer. In fact, the morning I had to help do Etienne's job at the tent, I was already making plans to leave for good. And then you sat down in front of me, and every coherent thought left my mind but one. *Who was this gorgeous creature who'd come out of nowhere?* Suddenly the idea of leaving Vence held no appeal. That was longest weekend of my life waiting for Monday to roll around so I could talk to you. Until I saw you, I'd been holding my breath for fear you'd changed your mind and wouldn't come."

She leaned closer and put her hand on the back of his neck. "There was no chance of that, *mon amour*, not after meeting the most exciting man to ever come into my life. Whether you were Antoinette's lover or not, I knew I had to see you again and get to know you no matter how brazen I was. I had no willpower where you were concerned."

He reached for her hand and kissed the palm. "We were meant to be, Nathalie. Whatever life has in store for us, we'll face it together." They'd reached the Nice airport and he drove to the private jet section where his jet stood on the tarmac.

Dominic looked into her eyes. "Are you ready?"

"I was ready the moment our gazes collided beneath the tent," her voice trembled. "It was like falling into space, and you were there to catch me. Don't ever let me go."

"As if I could. You're my heart."

"And you are mine. Forever."

\* \* \* \* \*

# MILLS & BOON MODERN IS
# HAVING A MAKEOVER!

The same great stories you love,
a stylish new look!

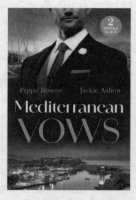

## Look out for our brand new look
# COMING JUNE 2024

### MILLS & BOON